# WindChance

By Charlotte Boyett-Compo

Twilight Times Books
Kingsport Tennessee

WindChance

This is a work of fiction. All concepts, characters and events portrayed in this book are used fictitiously and any resemblance to real people or events is purely coincidental.



Paladin Timeless Books, an imprint of
Twilight Times Books
POB 3340
Kingsport TN 37664
http://twilighttimesbooks.com/

First paperback printing, May 2005

Library of Congress Cataloging-in-Publication Data

Boyett-Compo, Charlotte.
Windchance / by Charlotte Boyett-Compo.
p. cm.
ISBN 1-933353-19-8 (pbk. : alk. paper)
I. Title.
PS3552.O8958W557 2005
813'.54--dc22
2005007040

Cover art by Ardy M. Scott

Printed in the United States of America.

# PART ONE

## Chapter One

"SAIL HO!"

The strident cry broke the morning air like a blast of the arctic air that had been at their heels since dawn.

"Where away?" The Captain raised his spyglass and swept the rolling vista before him.

"To the starboard, Cap'n. Thirty yards off the bow. She's lying dead in the water."

"Making repairs?" the First Mate asked as he joined his captain at the rail.

Catching sight of the unknown vessel lying off their weather beam, the captain shook his head. "Don't see anyone on her decks." He raised his eyes to the crow's nest. "What do you see, Haggerty?"

"Nary a soul moving on her, Sir. Looks deserted," was the boyish reply.

"Ghost ship," the First Mate mumbled, crossing himself.

"Stow that talk, Mister!" the captain snarled, shoving his First Mate aside as he strode away. "Mister Tarnes!" he called out to the Second Mate, who was at the helm, "bring her about. Let's see what we've got over there!"

"Aye, aye, Cap'n!" the sailor replied and swung the brass-rimmed teak wheel in a lazy arc to starboard.

Genevieve Saur pushed away from the taffrail of her brother's brigantine, The Wind Lass, and strolled on legs well accustomed to the rolling dip of the seas, to the quarterdeck where her brother and his First Mate were arguing. A smile dimpled her small face and she thrust her hands into the pockets of the cords she wore when on board her brother's ship.

"You going to board her, ain't you?" Mr. Neevens, the First Mate, was growling.

"Aye, we're going to board her!" Genevieve's brother growled back.

Neevens shook his shaggy gray head. "Not this old tar! I ain't going aboard no ghost ship." He screwed up his weathered face and stuck out a pugnacious jaw to emphasize his point. "I ain't boarding no ghost ship!"

Genevieve grinned when her brother cast her a furious glance. She shrugged in answer to his silent plea for help. She watched his gray eyes hardened with pique.

"We're going aboard her, Neevens, and that's the end of that!" Weir Saur shouted at his First Mate. He fixed his winter gray eyes on his sister. "You coming?"

"Naturally," Genevieve replied, eyeing Neevens with a pretend look of admonishment. "I don't believe in ghosts."

"And what about beasties?" Neevens snapped. "You afraid of them, missy?" The old man held her gaze, his whiskered chin thrust out, his watery eyes steady.

"There are no beasties on that ship!" Weir shouted. "Ghost, either!"

"You'll see," the First Mate shot back. "You'll see!" He spat a thick stream of tobacco juice over the rail and squinted his fading eyes at his employer. "You come back without a head attached to them smug shoulders, Cap'n, we'll see who was right about beasties and such! You ever heard the tales of the NightWind?"

A vicious crosswind, aided by a troubled sea which was beginning to show signs of a coming blow, heeled the Wind Lass over on the starboard tack and cold waves broke over the knightheads, shot high in the air and dropped with a roar onto the forecastle as the brigantine made for the unknown vessel.

"See?" Neevens grumbled. "NightWinds don't like to be bothered!"

Looking windward, the Captain frowned and his voice was a curt bellow as he looked up into the shrouds. "I want those topsails close reefed." He turned his eyes down to his sister. "I don't like the looks of that sky."

Genevieve turned her head and saw what had her brother concerned. The sky was a mottled gray; darker streaks of yellow were shot through the lower section of sky, making the flesh of the horizon appear bruised and sickly.

"Gale?"

Weir nodded, his mind on the nimble-footed sailors scurrying up the rigging. "Take in the topgallants while you're at it!"

The Wind Lass slipped effortlessly over the heaving waves, a steady hand at her helm. She slid in beside the unknown vessel and dropped anchor, riding the sea with a rolling pitch that left no doubt as to the turn of the weather.

"You going with us or not?" Weir asked his First Mate as the old man peered cautiously over the distance between the two ships as though something would lurch across the spans to take hold of his scrawny body.

Mr. Neevens snorted, spat, and looked at his Captain. "Might as well," he grumbled.

Genevieve hid a smile as she turned to study the other ship. There was no name on her bow, no identification markings. Her hull had been painted black but here and there along the wood, great gouges of paint had flaked away leaving gray streaks where the weathered wood shown through. Her rails were tarnished, the wood chipped in places, some of her rigging flapping loose in the freshening wind. Her sails had been furled, lashed down to the yards and masts, and the creaking timbers and the rub of the shrouds were the only sounds that greeted the boarding party as they boarded her at a quarter to nine on that Friday morn.

"Where the hell is the crew?" Weir asked as he studied the decks, which looked as though they hadn't been sluiced in a good many days. Salt was caked in the cracks of the decking, splashed up the masts. The hatchway stood open, the darkness from below decks a sinister gash of silence.

There was a smell about the ship, an alien, somewhat malevolent aroma which seemed to make the eerie quiet all the more prevailing.

"You ever smelled anything like that?" Mr. Tarnes, the Second Mate, asked his captain.

Weir shook his head. "Smells almost like burnt flesh, doesn't it?"

"Do you suppose the beasties had a barbecue last eve?" Genevieve quipped, elbowing Mr. Neevens in his scrawny ribs.

"That'll do, Genny," her brother cautioned, giving her a stern look from beneath his chestnut brows.

"Well, let's go on below and see what we can find," the girl quipped, unconcerned by her brother's fierce scowl. "There's nothing up here."

"You afraid of anything?" Mr. Tarnes snorted. He looked at the young girl with the look of a man long-accustomed to dealing with precocious females.

"I'm not particularly fond of snakes," Genny admitted.

"Well, I'll venture to say there are no snakes on board," Weir growled as he walked to the hatchway. He looked down into the darkness, and then with a deep breath, stepped gingerly down the companionway.

The cabins were empty, the galley devoid of provisions, and the captain's stateroom almost denuded of both furniture and nautical charts and equipment.

"Pirates," Mr. Tarnes said, nodding. "They was hit by pirates." He looked around the great cabin. "Took everything that wasn't nailed down and then some."

"Shanghaied the crew?" Weir asked, trusting Tarnes' knowledge of the subject.

"That'd be my guess, Cap'n." He poked among a pile of scattered papers on the captain's desk and lifted a single sheet of parchment. Squinting his eyes, he read the paper, drew in a quick, troubled breath and then handed it to Weir as though it were poisonous. "Sailing order, Sir."

Weir scanned the parchment. His brows drew together and he looked up at Tarnes. "A prison ship?"

"Ain't marked as such," Tarnes told him, "but that there order says she was carrying prisoners bound for Ghurn Colony." A wry grin settled over the man's rugged features. "Looks like the pirates got them some additional workers if this here lady was carrying prisoners."

Genny shivered. It wasn't that she was bothered by the mention of pirates; after all, wasn't that what she and Weir had decided to take up now that they had lost their family holdings? Wasn't that why they were out here in the middle of the South Boreal Sea learning the ropes from Tarnes and Neevens? What bothered Genny Saur was the mention of the penal colony at Ghurn. If things didn't go right for her and Weir, that was where he was bound to wind up. As for her, she'd swing from the nearest yardarm since there were no prisons for women, only nunneries, and she knew gods-be-damned well she wouldn't let them place her in one of those hell-holes.

"Did you hear that?" the First Mate suddenly squawked as he pushed up hard against Nathaniel Tarnes. He grabbed the other man's arm in a punishing grip and plastered himself to Tarnes.

"Hear what, you old fool?" Tarnes snarled, pushing the First Mate away from him. "All I hear is your teeth chattering!"

"No," Genny replied, looking at her brother. "I heard something, too."

"Like what?"

"A thump. There! Did you hear it?"

Weir cocked his head to one side, listening. His eyes narrowed. "Aye, I heard that."

"Sounds like it's coming from the hold." Tarnes shoved Neevens out of his way and ducked out of the Captain's cabin and walked to the forward companionway which led the lower deck. He stopped, listened. "Aye. It's coming from the hold."

"Could they have locked the crew down there?" Genny asked.

"We've been on this ship nearly an hour. Don't you think they'd have heard us board and have made some noise before now?" Neevens inquired, his eyes jerking about for the beasties he expected to see at any moment.

"Could have thought the pirates had come back," Tarnes told him.

"I ain't going down there," Neevens informed them. He pushed himself against the cabin wall. "I just ain't, that's all there is to it."

"Fool!" Tarnes called him.

The hatchway down into the hold was battened down, locked with a heavy padlock that appeared to be newer than the hasp into which it had been fitted. It took both Weir and Tarnes' combined strengths to pry the padlock open with a crowbar Genny found above decks. Once the padlock was off and the hatch opened, an overbearing stench assaulted the boarding party's nostrils, making eyes water and stomachs roll.

"By the holy ghost!" Tarnes gasped, covering his mouth and nose with a hastily-drawn kerchief. "What the hell is that smell?" He gagged, swallowing a rapidly-rising clump of bile which was threatening to erupt from his watering mouth.

"If that's the crew, they've been down there awhile," Genny murmured, holding her nose and breathing heavily through her parted lips.

"I've never smelled such foulness," Tarnes mumbled, his eyes watering from the stench.

"Ho, there!" Weir called into the blackness of the hold. "We're from the Wind Lass. Is anyone there?"

There was silence from the ebony depths.

"It could have been rats we heard," Weir said.

"Mighty damned big rats to have made a thump like we heard." Tarnes squinted his eyes, leaned over the hatchway and peered into the darkness.

"I can't see a bloody thing."

"Genny, go find us a lantern or something. I'm not going down there without a light of some kind." Weir Saur was a brave man, but darkness was not something he was comfortable with.

Genny nodded at her brother's request, well understanding his one weakness, and left to do his bidding.

"Ho, there!" Weir called out again. "Is anyone there?" Only more silence and a horrible waft of the stomach-churning stench greeted his hail.

"God, but that's a right offensive odor!" Tarnes said. "What the hell could cause such a smell?"

Weir didn't know and he wasn't so sure he really wanted to find out. The smell had an evil about it that bespoke the very bubbling pits of hell. "Whatever it is, there sure can't be anything human living in it. I can hardly breathe up here."

A flicker of light washed over the men and they looked over their shoulder to see Genny striding forward with two lanterns swinging in her hands. The light from the amber-tinted shades cast her small oval face in an ivory glow, lighting her forehead while the area below her nose was lost in deep shadow. If Mr. Neevens had seen her coming at him like that, he would have bolted for sure.

"When I was in the galley, I found something very interesting, Weir," she told her brother.

"What?" Weir Saur accepted one of the lanterns from his sister.

Genny handed the other lantern to Tarnes. "There were a lot of herbs and roots lying scattered about the cook table and there was a crucible of quinine on one of the shelves."

"Sounds like they had fever on board," Tarnes said.

Genny nodded. "There's a lot of that at the penal colonies, I hear. Looked as though they were brewing a remedy for malaria."

A sound from behind them made the three turn in surprise, but upon seeing who had joined them, they relaxed.

"Find anything?" the newcomer asked.

"We're about to go down into the hold. We heard a sound earlier, but there wasn't any answer to my call," Weir said.

Genny looked at the newcomer and smiled, as she smiled every time she was within eyesight of Patrick Kasella. Her gray eyes twinkled, her ivory complexion ran a peach blush and her heart skipped a beat or two every time her brother's best friend and partner looked her way.

"What is that godawful smell? Is that coming from the hold?" Patrick asked, smiling briefly, brotherly, at Genny before turning his attention to Weir. "Surely that can't just be bilge water."

"I don't think so neither, and it's getting worse the longer we stand here," Tarnes quipped. He stepped gingerly over the hatch and put his booted foot on the top rung of the ladder leading into the hold. "I'm either going to see what's causing it or faint from the smell of it."

The men didn't see the hurt look fall over Genny's face at Patrick's easy dismissal of her; not that the Ionarian had ever looked at her with anything other than easy dismissal. In his charming, North Boreal way, Patrick, or Paddy as his friends called him, treated Genny no differently than he did the rest of Weir's crew. That he didn't seem to see her as a budding young woman bothered no one but Genny; certainly not Weir who didn't want any man looking at his sister in any way other than brotherly.

Weir stepped down the ladder behind Tarnes and Patrick followed. The men didn't think of Genny until she bumped into Paddy's back as she stepped off the ladder.

"Damn it, Genevieve!" Weir cursed, eyeing her with displeasure. "We don't know what we're going to find down here!"

Her pert nose in the air, Genny glared at him, her lips pursed tightly together, still stung by Patrick's unknowing disregard. "So?" she challenged.

"You've got no business being down here until we find out what's causing that godawful smell!" Weir snarled. "There could be plague or the likes down here!"

"Hush!" Tarnes cautioned. He squinted. "There it is again." He hefted his lantern and peered about the hold. The stench was worse where they stood, enveloping the four of them in an atmosphere that was almost palpable.

"I'll look to the aft," Weir said as he took Genny's arm. "You come with me."

Paddy followed behind Tarnes as the Second Mate made his way amidships and then, finding nothing but splintered wood from broken open cargo, ventured further into the deeper darkness of the stinking hold.

Weir stumbled over a coil of hemp and bumped hard into the bulkhead, banging his shoulder painfully against the wood. He almost dropped the lantern in the process, but Genny reached out to steady him.

"Did you hear that?" she asked.

"I didn't hear anything," Weir grumbled as he wiped his hand down his pant leg. There was thick, slimy moisture on the wall of the ship's hold. "What did it sound like?"

The young woman listened hard, shushing her brother as he repeated his question. She inched forward, searching the planking beneath her feet.

"Look at this, Weir," she said as she pointed.

Weir came forward and lowered the lantern. "There's nothing but bulkhead back there."

Genny wasn't so sure. "Do you see anything odd about the wood?" she asked, stepping over another coil of rope as her vision followed the planking.

"No," he told her. He held the lantern a bit higher. "I don't see anything odd. It's flat. What else should it be?"

"We didn't find anything but unsalvageable cargo," Patrick told them as he and Mr. Tarnes joined them. "Nothing that could have made the sounds you heard."

"We may have found something, Paddy," Genny said.

Weir rolled his eyes, looked at Patrick. "Little miss know-it-all thinks there's something odd about the bulkhead."

Genny stooped down, touched her hand to the horizontal planking covering of the bulkhead, tapped on the wood. There was a hollow sound. She looked over her shoulder at her brother. "There's something behind this wall."

Patrick eased around Tarnes and hunkered down beside Genny. He rapped on the planking and gagged. "Mother of Alel!" he gasped. "Whatever that smell is, it's coming from behind here." He turned his head away and gathered a mouthful of saliva and then spat, hoping to exorcise the bile riding up his gullet.

"Is there a latch of some sort on this wall, Paddy?" Genny asked, running her hands over the wood.

Reluctant to even touch the wood concealing such a foul odor, Patrick nevertheless put his hands on the planking and felt, wincing at the feel of the slick wood beneath his flesh. His fingers touched something cold, stopped, went back, and fumbled until the smooth expanse of metal ran under his fingertips.

"Here! Weir, hold that lantern closer!"

Bending forward, Weir Saur thrust his lantern close to his friend's shoulder and caught sight of the iron bolt set into the wood. He watched keenly as Patrick threw the bolt back.

"Where's the handle?" Genny asked, seeing none.

"Inside spring lock," Patrick told them as he pushed on the door to release it.

"Holy ghost!" Tarnes gasped, reeling from the stench, which shot out from behind the moving panel.

Genny thought she would vomit as the smell assailed her. She crabwalked back from the door as Patrick pulled it further open.

A hollow sound, a rusty sound that moved from behind the panel and the four froze.

"There's something there," Tarnes warned.

A pitiful sound, a human sound, seeped from behind the panel. It was a groan, a cry for help.

"There's a man in there!" Weir whispered as the lantern light from Tarnes' hand fell partially into the hidden area behind the planking.

Patrick looked up. "No, there are two."

## Chapter Two

HE WAS THE MOST PITIFUL SIGHT WEIR SAUR HAD EVER SEEN IN HIS LIFE.

Long, dirty blond hair, matted with filth, alive with crawling, breeding vermin, hung in thick clumps down a pathetically thin back that was covered with age-old lash marks. A ragged beard, covering much of the man's lower face and hanging well down his chest, was slick with grease, mottled with dried vomitus and the gods alone knew what else. Some fingernails were broken into the quick while others were long and chipped, dirt-caked. That part of his flesh, that wasn't marred with thick white scar tissue, was gray from years without benefit of bathing. Weir could count every rib along the man's sides, measure the frail shoulder blades, as well as the thrusting hipbones. Unconscious, barely breathing, the man nevertheless had a steady, if weak, heartbeat. It appeared as though he was surviving the horror of his situation by a mere thread of stubborn resistance to give in to his fate.

The other man found in the hidden section of the hold had not fared any better.

Somewhere close to sixty, that man was semi-conscious, babbling to himself, shivering from fever, riddled with uncontrollable spasms that bent and twisted his body as he lay on a makeshift bed in the Captain's cabin of the unknown ship. Not as thin as the other man, the older of the two also looked malnourished, desperately in need of food. His sunken cheeks, heavily whiskered face, and dark-rimmed eyes were gaunt, fever-bright. His gnarled hands clutched at the bedcovers one moment then thrust straight out in front of him the next as though warding off some sort of physical threat.

"No!" the toothless mouth would gasp. "Don't hurt us no more, Sir! Don't hurt us no more!" Saliva dribbled from the slack mouth sprayed the air as another burst of pleading shot from the man's cracked parched lips. "The lad is sick. He is sick!"

"How could anyone treat a human being like this?" Genny asked, her eyes instantly filling with tears as Weir and Patrick had pulled the first man from the place in that they had obviously been kept.

"Don't hurt us!" the older man cried out, clutching twisted fingers together as he stared wild-eyed at Weir. "Please don't hurt us!"

"You're safe," Patrick told him, reaching out to grip the man's thin shoulder. "We're friends. You're in good hands, now."

The old man swung his haunted gaze to Patrick, took instant measure of the man, and nodded. "Get him out, Sir, would you please? The boy is bad off."

Weir and Patrick helped the old man up, steadying him as Tarnes took hold of him, helping him to unbend his obviously arthritic limbs from the confines of the narrow place in that he had spent time.

"Hurry, Sirs!" the old man pleaded. "He's awful sick."

"I can see," Patrick said, spying the blood-streaked vomitus splattered inside the hideyhole."

"Is he alive?" Tarnes asked as Weir pulled the second man, limp, and red-hot to the touch, from the cage.

"Not by much," Weir answered. He laid the man down on the planking and bent over him, putting his ear to the thin chest. "He's breathing, but that's about it."

Patrick surprised Genny when he had easily hefted the man in his arms and strode purposefully toward the hatchway with him.

"Damn it, Patrick!" Weir growled. "Aren't you afraid of catching his fever?"

"If he doesn't get help, he'll die for sure," Paddy snarled. "Besides, this fever isn't contagious."

"How do you know that?" Weir demanded, but Paddy ignored him.

Paddy carried the unconscious man to the captain's cabin, with Tarnes close behind supporting the staggering weight of the older man. Weir yelled across to the Wind Lass for the Healer who had accompanied them on their journey. Once in the cabin, Patrick gently lowered the unconscious man to the captain's bare bunk and ordered a pallet set up for the older man. No sooner had a spread of canvas been laid on the cabin floor, than the old man fell hard into a deep, disturbed sleep, mumbling over and over again: "See to the lad, mate; please see to the lad."

As they waited for the Healer to come aboard, Patrick stood beside the bunk and stared down at the man with a look no one could quite fathom. When a sailor from the Wind Lass brought a blanket or two to cover the unconscious man, Patrick took the woolen material and laid it gently over the still body, tucking in the corners around a barely-moving chest.

"Why would they have hid them down there, do you suppose?" Weir asked.

"I don't think they were hiding them," Patrick growled. "They were punishing them."

"For what?" Genny asked in a thin voice. "What could they have done to warrant such treatment."

Patrick swung his eyes to her. "Just for the hell of it, that's what." He returned his gaze to the man. He nodded. "You know what that is?"

Weir looked at his friend.

"That tattoo on his wrist," Patrick clarified. "The old gent doesn't have one. I checked."

Weir glanced at the odd marking on the man's upturned wrist and shook his head. "I've never seen anything like it."

"It's a Serenian penal colony identification mark," Tarnes informed his Captain. He looked over at Patrick. "Ain't it?"

Patrick nodded, never taking his eyes off the man lying so still in the bunk. "It's the Maze." He folded his arms across his chest. "It's the tattoo they give a prisoner whose been incarcerated in the Labyrinth."

Weir flinched, looked sharply at the man in the bunk, and took a step back. He turned his eyes to Patrick. "They must have been taking him back. He probably escaped."

"That would be my guess," Paddy snarled.

The Healer shooed them all from the cabin when he boarded. It was an hour before he came above decks to appraise his Captain of the man's condition.

"He's got the fever from the looks of him, barely alive. If he makes it through the afternoon it would surprise the hell out of me."

"Isn't there anything you can do?" Genny's eyes leapt to the hatchway leading below decks. "There was quinine in the galley..."

"He's got Labyrinthine fever, missy," the Healer snapped. "There isn't any cure for that. Quinine might help with malaria, but it won't do anything for this kind of fever."

"What will?" Patrick asked, a hard edge to his voice.

"You might try praying," the Healer shot back.

"What about cleaning him up?" Genny prodded. "Maybe some broth? Will bathing him make him sicker?"

Looking at her as though he thought her daft, the Healer's chin rose in the air. "It is my opinion you'll be wasting your time, but if you can find someone willing to bathe that..." He looked back at the hatchway and shuddered delicately, "...person, then by all means try."

"I'll bathe him," Patrick growled, rudely shoving the Healer out of the way. The angry Ionarian warrior headed for the hatchway.

"And I'll help!" Genny echoed.

"The hell you will!" Weir shouted, making a grab for his sister's arm. "You'll keep your ass on deck here, Genevieve Saur. I'll help Paddy!"

"I'll get water and the like for you!" Tarnes called out as his Captain disappeared down the hatchway. He turned a jaundiced eye to Genny. "You heard your brother. You stay put. We'll handle this."

"Bring a razor, too, Tarnes," Weir advised.

Genny turned her fierce scowl to the Healer. "Is this fever contagious?"

Shaking his head, the man seemed to be bored by the whole conversation. "No."

"Then I don't see any reason why I can't..."

"Because your brother said so!" Tarnes snapped. He took hold of her arm and shook her.

"You do what he says for a change!"

## Chapter Three

THE ILL MAN HOVERED OVER THE FINE LINE BETWEEN LIFE AND DEATH FOR over a week, and not once in the entire time did he so much as bat an eyelid or move a muscle. His flesh, now bathed and kept dry, was so hot it burned the hands that tended him. His face, now shaved, was a deep, dull red color, badly sunburned. His hair now cut and deloused, was lusterless, with the feel of straw about it. Through cracked and bleeding lips, his breathing grew labored at times, harsh, rattling in his chest, but would often subside into shallow normalcy with a hitching gasp and long pause that drew the immediate attention of those at his bedside.

His back had been seen to, the lash marks salved. His wrists and ankles, as well, for he alone of the two men, had been heavily weighted down with irons about both wrists and ankles. A thick dog collar of iron had been removed from his neck where the shackles had been soldered in place.

The old man had lain in a near-stupor for two days, babbling, rambling on and on about people and places, events; but when he at last came to himself, his first words were for news of his fellow survivor.

"Is he all right? Is the boy alive?" He tried to get up, but Tarnes eased him back down.

"He's as well as can be expected," Tarnes assured the old man, and watched as still-feverish pale green eyes had closed in thanksgiving. "He's over there."

Turning his head, the old man looked at the still figure on the bunk across from his for a long time and then finally closed his eyes again.

"They tried to do him in, they did," the old man mumbled, his lips quivering as though he were in great pain. "They didn't want him to make it back alive."

"Back to the Labyrinth, you mean?" Tarnes questioned, wiping a cool rag down the old man's weathered cheek.

"Aye," the soft word came. "They wanted him to die."

"Why?" Tarnes removed the rag and dipped it into the basin of water that sat on the floor at his feet, rung it out, and then placed it across the old man's wrinkled brow.

"He'd caused the Captain a heap of trouble."

"How?"

There was a long pause and then the green eyes opened and stared into Tarnes' very soul.

"By living." The cracked lips trembled. "Simply by living, son."

Tarnes felt a great pity well up inside him for the man lying on the bunk across the cabin. The scars on the young man's back, Tarnes reckoned the count to be about sixty, had caused the Second Mate many a restless moment. One didn't have to experience a lashing to imagine how bad it could be. He glanced over at the unconscious man and then looked back down at the older one.

"You weren't a prisoner, were you?"

The old man shook his head. "I was one of the crew of the Vortex."

"The Vortex? Is that the name of the ship?"

"No," was the reply. "The ship you found us on was the Tamarind. She was a privately owned bark. The Vortex was in dock at Ghurn for repairs when they brought him back, so they commandeered Captain Janssen's bark, the Tamarind."

"Brought who back?"

"Him," the old man, jutting his chin toward the unconscious man. "They caught him down near Hellstrom Point and was bringing him back to the Labyrinth. Only two ships sail to that godawful place; the Vortex is one of 'em. The other ship was already on her way back to Boreas."

"I take it this Captain Janssen wasn't too pleased at having his ship taken over," Tarnes remarked as he lifted the old man's head and placed a cup of cool water to the chapped lips.

After taking a few sips of the quenching coolness, the old man nodded, putting his head back down to the soft pillow. "Was downright pissed, he was. He didn't like sailing down to Tyber's Isle." He looked into Tarnes' eyes. "That's where the Labyrinth is."

"I know," Tarnes replied. He narrowed his eyes. "I thought the charts to that place are only in the hands of a very few men. How'd this Captain Janssen know where to find Tyber's Isle?"

"Oh, he didn't take his ship out, Sir," the old man told him. "Captain Linstrom did; he was the Captain of the Vortex. The entire crew on board the Tamarind when we left Ghurn Harbor was from the Vortex; but Captain Janssen was made to go along because he'd put up such a fuss about his ship being commandeered and all. Captain Linstrom was going to blindfold him once we got to the sea lanes that lead into Tyber's Isle."

"What happened to your crew?" Tarnes asked. "Pirates?"

The old man nodded. "That and the fever what took hold of a third of us before we'd cleared land good. Captain Linstrom was the first to die of it, but that was after we was well out to sea." He turned his head and gazed at the man on the other bunk. "That's when Janssen tried to kill him, you see. He figured if the boy was dead, there'd be no reason to go to Tyber's Isle." He looked back at Tarnes. "There were sea charts that had belonged to Captain Linstrom for

Janssen to use. Janssen didn't know that until I told him where to find them; they was in the Captain's sea chest. When Janssen found out he could still make it to Tyber's Isle, he was pissed even more."

"So he tried to kill your friend to keep from having to make the trip."

"We ain't rightly friends, Sir," the old man informed him. "I don't even know the boy's name, but I tried to help him all I could." The lips trembled again. "He escaped that gods-be-damned prison; he shouldn't have ever been caught. No man should ever be caught what escapes that hellhole. If you'd have seen what they did to him when they caught him, you'd have thought so, too."

"I agree," Tarnes confirmed. "Most of the men sent there don't have any right being there."

The old man looked hard at Tarnes. "You seen his hands?"

Tarnes nodded.

"I saw them do that to him." The rheumy green eyes shifted. "I've seen it done a number of times, but won't ever get use to it. When they brought him on board the Vortex, they did it. They spread-eagle him to a yardarm and nailed his hands to the wood, and then left him hanging there the rest of the morning."

Tarnes nodded. He had once seen a man punished in the same way the unconscious man had been. The unfortunate prisoner had suffocated due to the strain of hanging in such a position. The constriction had finally halted the air going into his lungs. It had not been a pleasant sight and had greatly effected a much younger Norbert Tarnes. "I've heard crucifixion is the usual punishment for running away from the Labyrinth. I guess he knew what could happen to him if he got caught."

"Aye, he knew," the old man agreed, "but he wasn't expecting what else Janssen done to him, though. He sure as hell didn't deserve it, either!"

"What was that?"

A low groan from the other bunk made both men turn. Tarnes shot up from his place beside the old man and bent over the other man, peering closely into his flushed face.

"Can you hear me?" Tarnes asked, gently shaking his charge. The question was answered by another low groan, dry and wispy, heavy with pain. He looked around at the old man. "What's your name?"

"Me? Stevens, Sir. Jarl Stevens." He struggled weakly to sit up in the bunk, but his head swam unmercifully and he laid back down, closing his eyes to the wave of nausea that washed over him.

"Does he know who you are?"

Swallowing against the bile riding up his parched throat, the old man waved a dismissing hand. "I don't think I ever got the chance to tell him."

Tarnes soothed a fall of limp blond hair over the young man's brow and was relieved to find his flesh cooler to the touch. He watched closely as the closed eyes tried to open, the parched lips part as another groan was forced out.

"You're safe, lad," Tarnes assured him. "You're aboard the Wind Lass bound for Montyne Cay." He stroked the damp cheeks, wiping away the dotting of sweat. "You're safe. Just rest easy." He tugged the covers up closer and sat back on his haunches, closely observing the flicker of movement now beginning to stir on the man's face.

"He waking up?" Stevens called out.

"Appears so."

"Wish I knowed his name for sure. I know he's from Virago, was a Lord or some such rank."

Tarnes glanced around. "How do you know that?"

Stevens opened his eyes and looked at the Second Mate. "They wouldn't have taken so much trouble to go looking for him and bring him back if he wasn't. Only them what the Tribunal wants to keep get tracked down so."

Norbert Tarnes thought about that for a moment and then nodded. There was a man he knew who had been sent to the Labyrinth. That man had made good his escape. No one had bothered to go looking for him; he hadn't been anyone of importance, just a common criminal. Such men were considered expendable and when the penal colony officials and the Tribunal spoke of "no man ever having escaped the Labyrinth"; they meant men of consequence, men who mattered.

"I wonder what the poor bastard did to warrant being sent there, then," Tarnes remarked.

"Made a mighty powerful enemy of somebody," Stevens told him.

"Tarnes?"

The Second Mate looked up, grinned at Patrick Kasella. "He's coming around, Paddy."

"How's his fever?"

"He's cooling down a mite." Tarnes stood, moved out of Patrick's way as Kasella hunkered down beside the bunk. "Ain't opened his eyes yet, though, but he's trying."

Patrick reached out a hand and gently touched the man's flushed face. "You're going to be all right," he whispered. "You're with friends, now."

"I told him he's safe." Norbert Tarnes stretched, his hands going to the small of his back as he popped his spine. "I reckon I'll go get some sleep if you're going to be here awhile."

"Go on. I'll watch him."

"This other gent's name is Stevens. He was one of the crew. He doesn't know this lad's name."

Paddy flashed the old man a quick look. "Is that so?" he growled, then settled his blue gaze on the man trying to swim up out of the depths of unconsciousness.

"That wasn't a prison ship you were manning, Mr. Stevens," Paddy stated. "What were you doing transporting prisoner's to the Labyrinth?"

"They were hauling just the one," Tarnes told him, concerned with the harsh tone of voice Paddy used in questioning the old man. "Stevens says the lad is from Virago. He thinks he's a Lord or something."

"He would have to be," Paddy snapped. He looked up at Tarnes. "You going to hit the rack or not?"

The Second Mate blushed, his face a dull red, and he stared down at Paddy with a look of hurt on his weathered face. "Don't be taking your spite out on me, boy. I had nothing to do with what was done to the fellow, and neither did Stevens." Tarnes' sniffed. "He says he tried to help the man."

Patrick Kasella snorted and it was a burst of both disgust and disbelief. He didn't bother to answer Tarnes, instead keeping attention on the man whose eyelids were beginning to flicker.

"That's it, my friend" Paddy said in a soft, encouraging voice. "You can wake up. You're with friends, people who're going to protect you now, and you don't have anything to worry about." He laid his hand on the man's fevered brow. "You'll be just fine from now on. I promise."

Tarnes was about to turn away, to leave, when he saw the man's eyelids open slowly, hesitantly. He stopped and took a step closer to the bunk, watching intently as the eyes opened, closed, opened again, tried desperately to focus, flickered and then held. The Second Mate could see the effort it was taking for the man to focus, but when he did, his fever-bright gaze settled on Patrick Kasella's smiling face.

"J'Nal," Paddy said quietly. It was a Viragonian greeting that meant: peace. "We're glad to see you awake." His tone of voice was gentle, reassuring, and friendly. There was a soft smile on his handsome face.

There was no word to adequately describe the color of the eyes that stared out of the man's pale face. They were neither blue nor black, but a color in between. The irises were speckled with pale yellow striations. Long, tawny lashes slipped slowly closed and when the lids opened again, the color seemed to have shifted to another shade.

"I've never seen eyes that color before," Tarnes remarked.

The man's attention wavered; he seemed to be trying to understand the friendly words.

"You don't have anything to worry about, my friend." Paddy held up his right arm, unbuttoned the cuff of his shirt with his left hand, pushed back the cambric sleeve, and turned his arm so his wrist was facing out. He waited until the midnight blue stare slid downward from his face to look at the offered wrist. When the man flinched, then jerked his stare back to his face, Paddy nodded. "I wouldn't lie to you. You're safe and you're with friends. The Captain's name is Weir Saur and he's a good man; he'll not let the Transporters take you from us. I swear it."

Norbert Tarnes turned away. It wasn't often that Patrick Sean Kasella let anyone know he carried the tattoo of the Labyrinth on his wrist.

## Chapter Four

THE PATIENT'S GAZE FOLLOWED HER ABOUT THE CABIN, AS SHE FUSSED with this and that, but when she turned toward him, he would quickly look away and pretend he was asleep. He didn't answer her soft, girlish questions; seemed to be ignoring her constant conversation as she worked. Her voice was sweet, cultured, pleasant to his ears, but he couldn't have answered her even if he had wanted to.

Genny watched him covertly as she dusted the shelves in Weir's cabin. She laid her brother's treasured books—the only things the taxman had allowed him to take from the estate when they had been summarily evicted from their ancestral home—on the desk, and began to hum softly to herself. It was an old tune: The Prince's Lost Lady. The song was a sad ballad and it swept the smile from her face and she stopped humming, swinging her head around to see him watching her again.

"I know you've been watching me," she told him. She stopped her dusting, folded her arms over her chest, and turned to face the bunk. "You might as well stop trying to pretend you're asleep."

A flicker of a smile touched the still lips and the blue-black eyes opened slowly, lifted, and merged with Genny's.

"Good morn!" the impish girl grumbled, nodding once quickly at her companion, and then unfolded her arms, turned back to her dusting. "Don't feel as though you have to answer!"

He would have if he could, if only to take the anger from her soft voice, but he couldn't make himself speak. When the man called Patrick had come to question him, he could do no more than shake his head at the gentle interrogation.

"When you're ready," Patrick had said. "We won't rush you."

And no one had; but this young woman, this beautiful, sensuous young woman, had been trying her best to wear him down with her teasing smile and easy banter. Now, her tactics were beginning to change: she was adding a touch of hurt feelings to her repertoire. He saw her glance around at him and frown.

"You can talk, can't you?"

He nodded.

A light of triumph lit her pretty face. "But you just don't want to, is that it?"

He looked down at the covers. He shook his head.

Genny threw her hands into the air. "I give up with you!" she said with a hard sigh.

She couldn't read his expression, she was not all that accustomed to the many ways in that men looked at women, but she thought she detected a hint of hurt in his sunburned face. "Or is it just that you still don't trust us?"

"Leave the man alone, Genevieve."

Genny turned to see her brother standing in the doorway, a cup of steaming brew in his hand.

"I was only trying to..." Genny started to say, but her brother waved away her explanation.

"My sister," Weir announced as he came into the cabin and hooked a foot under the low stool beside the bunk, "is an expert at annoying people." He pulled the stool toward him and then sat down, extended the cup toward the silent man on the bunk. "Just ignore her and she'll eventually go away." He glanced at his sister, smiled at her look of pique. "Go bother Paddy, Genevieve," he ordered as he settled the china cup in the man's hand.

"Well, at least he wants my company!" she sniffed, flouncing for the door.

"Don't be so sure," Weir warned, winking at the convalescing man. He thought he detected just a hint of an answering grin deep in the wounded eyes looking up at him.

"Women," he whispered as Genny slammed the cabin door shut behind her departure. He leaned toward the other man and grinned. "You can't live with them; you can't live without them; you can't sell them to the highest bidder, eh?" He laughed. "Unless you're a Hasdu!"

The man on the cot looked down at the steaming cup.

Weir understood. He and Paddy thought somewhere along the line someone close to this man had hurt him very badly; it was evident in the lack of trust he was exhibiting despite everyone's effort at putting him at ease, at assuring him he was safe.

"She hurt you pretty bad, didn't she?"

The remarkable blue stare shifted in surprise to Weir.

Weir smiled gently. "It's a man's curse, sometimes: trusting a woman. Were you lovers?"

There was a slow nod.

"And she betrayed you?"

Another slow nod for reply.

"I'm sorry."

There was a slight shrug.

Weir didn't know what else to say. So far, this was the most they'd gotten out of him. No words as yet, but at least some questions had been answered. He reached out and touched the man's thin arm. "Drink that," he ordered, nodding at the cup. "You've probably never had anything like it and I promise you will enjoy it."

The weak man lifted the cup, put the rim to his lips and seemed to sigh as though he would do as he was told simply because he'd been told to.

"The old man we found with you is finally up and about. He was anxious to get to work. Not a bad sort, is he?"

Weir's companion shook his head.

"Helped you, did he?"

A brief, thoughtful nod.

"That's good." Weir yawned, stretched, and then stood up, arching his back to relieve the tension in his shoulders. He looked about the cabin, pleased to see his sister had at least started to clean the bookshelves. He jerked his head toward the stack of books on his desk. "Do you read Serenian?"

Another nod: hesitant, unsure.

"Then, help yourself." Weir leaned over and picked up three books at random. He read the titles, cocked a brow at his companion, and then handed a thick volume of short stories to him. He was more pleased than he could admit when a hesitant hand took the thick tome from him. "Enjoy it."

The patient followed Weir's departure from the cabin, stared a long time at the closed door before finally looking down at the book cradled lovingly against his thin chest. He pulled the book away from him, read the title, closed his eyes, and hugged the volume of short stories to him once more.

## Chapter Five

"HE STILL HASN'T SPOKEN?" JARL STEVENS ASKED. HE STOPPED IN HIS TASK of sluicing the deck and leaned on his mop, looked hard at Patrick Kasella.

"He will," Paddy said, stepping briskly past the old man. The sight of the ex-prison ship guard never failed to anger him.

"You want me to try talking to the lad?"

Patrick spun around, his hand came up, and he pointed a rigid finger at the old man. "You keep the hell away from him! Do you hear me? He doesn't need anyone reminding him of what was done to him!"

"And I suppose you know what was done to him?" Stevens shot back, his craggy brows drawing together.

"Aye, I sure as hell do!" Patrick shouted.

"All of it?" was the sly rejoinder.

"What do you mean by 'all'?" Norbert Tarnes, the Second Mate, inquired from his position on the main deck.

"Keep out of this, Norb!" Patrick growled. He walked back to the old man and glared down into a face weathered from many years at sea. "I know what they do to escaped prisoners, Stevens. He'll get over it; his hands are almost healed now." He leaned forward, intending to intimidate the smaller, shorter man. "If you want to stay on this ship until we make landfall, you'd best stay the hell out of my way. That man is no longer your problem. We'll make sure he gets all the help he needs."

"And will he get over what Janssen did to him, too?" Jarl Stevens snapped, throwing the mop down to the deck. He put his gnarled hands on his hips and stood toe to toe with Paddy. "You think he'll just forget about being keelhauled under the Tamarind and nearly drowned?"

Patrick's face blanched. His mouth dropped open and he turned to look into Norbert Tarnes' shocked face.

"That's what they did." Stevens eyed the man looming over him with contempt. "They tied him up and drug him under the ship. The lad was barely alive when they brought him up. He was terrified of the water even before he went under. You could hear him screaming all the way to Necroman and back when they pushed him over the side. Of course, that was after he'd been screaming and pleading and begging them for over an hour not to do it."

"Maybe he's strained his throat and all, Paddy," Norbert Tarnes remarked. "Maybe that's why he ain't said nothing to us."

"He was hoarse by the time that son-of-a-whoring-slut had him heaved over the rail," Stevens told them. "He ain't said a single word since they pulled him out."

"Why didn't you tell us this before?" Paddy shouted. "We should have been told!"

"You didn't ask me nothing!" Stevens reminded the warrior. "You ain't said bidey-bye to me since I was able to be up and about! I figured you'd come looking for answers when the lad didn't give you none, but no: you think you know so damned much!"

Norbert Tarnes could see the explosion coming, looked down at Paddy's balled fists and hurried forward to avoid the confrontation he knew the young Ionarian would later regret. He wedged himself between the two men, not an easy feat, since they were practically nose to nose despite the difference in heights.

"Maybe you ought to tell us everything you know, Stevens." He turned his back to Paddy and pleaded with Stevens to co-operate. "Anything we can learn that might help the lad, will be greatly appreciated."

Stevens snorted, turned his head, and spat a thick glob of phlegm over the rail. He craned his neck and peered around Tarnes to study Patrick.

"I'll say my piece if I ain't interrupted by the likes of this fool."

Paddy nudged Tarnes with his body, was surprised when the older man didn't, and wouldn't, move out of the way for him to get to Stevens.

"Steady as she goes, Paddy," Tarnes mumbled, pushing Kasella back with his skinny rump. "Let the man have his say."

"Maybe you should get the Captain so this don't have to be repeated twice," Stevens advised. He hawked another clump of mucous from his toothless mouth and leaned down to pick up his mop.

"Weir!" Patrick shouted at the top of his lungs. He didn't look away from the old man as he yelled.

Seating himself on a coil of rope, Jarl Stevens propped himself up with the mop handle, his arthritic fingers curled around the wooden spindle, and began his tale as soon as Weir and Mr. Neevens, the First Mate, arrived.

"We was just off the coast of Virago when the storm struck. We took on nearly three feet of water in the lee scuppers and down in the hold in less than thirty minutes; that's how bad the blow was. They was manning them pumps faster than a sailor drilling his first whore after a six-month sea voyage. It wasn't one of my jobs, manning them pumps, 'cause the smell of that bilge water sloshing about in there never failed to make me violently ill and I weren't no good to nobody; but that day, we needed every spare hand to man them pumps. When

I finally came topside, the storm was ripening. We'd already doubled-reefed the topsail and furled the foresail. The Captain was looking worried like and he ordered us aloft to take in every square inch of canvas. We clewed her down as tight as a virgin's thighs, we did, but she was beginning to lie over almost to her beam-ends. One of the topsail halyards was snapping about the masts like the cracks of a boson's cat and pretty soon, the Captain had me up there on them son-of-a-bitching yards. I looked down and that was when I saw the lad in that cage."

"What cage?" Weir asked, not remembering anything on board the Tamarind that could be described as such.

"When they took him down from the yardarms, after he was crucified, they put him in this cage that they'd brought over from the Vortex. It was nothing more than a glorified chicken coop, it was, and they stowed it up on the deck so everyone could see him."

Tarnes rubbed his whiskered chin. "Aye, I saw that thing." His gaze went to Paddy.

"Thought it was for the livestock."

Stevens snorted with contempt. "That's about how the lad was considered."

"Get on with it!" Paddy growled. "I know all about those damned pens!"

Stevens ignored him. "Anyways, water was rushing in through the bow ports and over the knightsheads like one of them geysers you find up in Chale. The lad was soaked through already and every time another wave broke over him, he'd cry out." Stevens shook his head. "I knew then the lad was afraid of the water. Afraid of drowning, you see."

"And the Captain realized that," Patrick snarled through clenched teeth.

Stevens nodded. "The screaming was a dead give away, I reckon," he said with irony.

"What happened then?" Weir asked, not liking the image of a terrified man caged in a death trap with water surging in all around him.

"Well, we fought that storm for over three hours before she began to lessen any. By then, some of the canvas had shredded on the topgallants and I was sent aloft to reef 'em. It was while I was up in the rigging doing repairs that the blow came back harder than ever. I laid myself out on them yards like it was my dead wife's dear bosom and hung on for my life.

"Them waves shot over us all of a sudden and through the rain, I saw the helmsman let go of the ship's wheel. One minute he was lashed to that wheel, the next he was over the side, his yelling lost in the wind. The ship ran head on over a coral reef and I heard this grinding sound all the way up to where I was a holding on for dear life. The topgallant let go with a snap, the sheets ripping all the way down, one half blowing out to sea, the other flinging itself around the mast where I was praying like I'd never prayed before.

"Water surged up through the aft hatchway and I knew the hold was rapidly filling with water. The Captain yelled to man the jolly boats and even as he was shouting, the storm stopped."

"Just like that?" Tarnes asked, disbelief in his voice.

Stevens snapped his fingers. "Just like that! One minute we was all goners, the next we was heeling leeward, turning slowly like we was on a pivot and we dropped off that coral so quick it clicked our teeth together."

Patrick Kasella, having been raised on the rolling waves of the sea, lifted one eyebrow in contempt and shot Stevens a look that said he didn't believe a word the old man was saying.

"Believe it or not, as you will, but that was the way of it!"

"They must have been in the eye of the storm," Mr. Neevens commented.

"And then?" Weir injected, quickly.

Stevens drew himself up and directed his remarks to the Captain. "There wasn't that much damage done to the hull, you see. We got her patched up quick enough, but we'd still shipped a lot of water in the hold and we knowed she was going to have to be dry docked for a true repair. That was when the Captain had this notion about the lad."

"He put him down in that hidden section behind the bulkhead," Tarnes said. There was true grief in the old man's voice.

Stevens nodded. "It seemed to me Captain Janssen was of a mind to let the lad drown down there. When I finally got down to him, he was already waist deep in bilge and screaming for all he was worth." The old man's eyes filled with tears. "I should have left the lad where he was. He really weren't in that much danger of drowning, you see; we'd patched the hole up pretty tight. But it was that mindless screaming, you see; it ate at my vitals. I couldn't stand it no more so I drug him out." The old sailor wiped a hasty gnarled hand over his face. "He was clinging to me like a vine."

"And then somebody found out you'd let him out?"

There was a haunted look on the leathery face of Jarl Stevens. "Aye. That was the way of it."

"And that's when they keelhauled him?"

Stevens shook his head and turned his eyes out to sea. "No. Not then."

"There was more?" Patrick asked, a finger of dread scraping down his back.

Stevens nodded. "Mr. Kullen, the First Mate, he'd come down to check on the lad, to see why he'd stopped screaming. He saw me standing there holding the lad and all hell broke loose. He shouted for some men and they came skipping down that companionway like ghosts on the wind and they was all over me and the lad before you could say a word. They drug him topside at Mr. Kullen's orders, the lad begging them all the while not to put him back in the cage, thinking that was what they was up to."

"But they had something else in mind," Weir said quietly.

"Aye. Kullen had 'em seize the lad's wrists to the shrouds and then they laid the cat-'o-nine on him. It was the fear of the storm they'd been through, I reckon, that made 'em so violent and all. The need to go at something to calm themselves down. The lad was..." Stevens searched for the right word.

"Expendable," Patrick furnished.

"Aye. Handy, too. Who cares about a prisoner? I felt sorry for the lad 'cause all the while they was whipping him, he was mumbling something about wanting to die, you see. That was when the Captain took it in his mind to kill him, I guess."

"How many lashes did they give him?" Patrick had turned away, speaking over his shoulder to the old man.

"I don't know. Thirty, Forty. What difference did it make? He'd been beat before. But I know this much: by the time they was through with him, the lad was a gibbering fool. That cat-'o-nine was slick with his blood 'cause Kullen, himself, wielded the whip and he liked the sound of them metal barbs hitting flesh, he did; he put his back into that evil business that day, running that steel-tipped thong as hard as he could down the lad's back."

"There are men like that," Patrick mumbled, vicariously feeling the pull of a cat down his own back.

"Aye, and Kullen was one of the worse. Then Janssen ordered him keel-hauled." Stevens shuddered for he could still hear the young man's screaming, pleading as Janssen had ordered him tied and dropped over the side.

"He was already afraid of the water and that must have seemed like a true hell to him," Weir said.

"He was like a wild man, he was," Stevens agreed. "He was thrashing about, spraying blood from his torn back everywhere, but they seized his wrists and ankles and threw him overboard, him screaming like a Chalean banshee all the way to the water."

"But he survived that, too," Paddy said, admiration filling his voice.

"Aye!" Stevens said emphatically. "Aye, he did! They brought him up and he was still breathing."

"That must not have set well with Janssen," Tarnes remarked.

"It might not have, but we got a code we live by on the seas, Tarnes, and I know you know it well: if a man survives what they did to that lad, he's charmed! There weren't a man on board that would have allowed Janssen to try keelhauling him again although he was about to."

Patrick turned around. "He was going to throw him back overboard?"

"Aye, he was! But we all voiced our opinion about that foolishness. So Janssen made them take him back below." The old man shrugged. "He'd lost interest anyway, 'cause the lad had come to and was just staring straight ahead of him like he was in another world. Janssen thought the lad's mind was gone, and who'd have blamed him?"

"How did you get locked in the bulkhead with him?" Tarnes wanted to know.

"It was right after the watch yelled: 'sail ho!' and we saw this clipper bearing down on us. She had poured on all her canvas and was streaking across that water like an avenging angel or the like. We knowed her to be a pirate ship 'cause she was flying the skull and crossbones. Pretty soon she was steering sidewise our hawse and I knowed we was in trouble. Janssen had sent men aloft to spread all the canvas, to wet down the sails, but I knowed it weren't no use. She was going to catch us, and you know what pirates do to a penal colony crew." He ran one gnarled finger across his neck.

"So, I snuck down there and crawled in with the lad. I knew they wouldn't do no more than take the cargo and split the crew. We'd repaired that hole in the hull, but we was still shipping some water. She weren't all that seaworthy, you see, so I knowed they wouldn't want her."

"And just what the hell were you going to do: sail her yourself?" Mr. Neevens snarled.

Stevens glared at Neevens. "I was going to get him in one of the jolly boats and make for the nearest land, but once I got in that damned cage, I couldn't get myself back out again. The latch caught!"

"When we called down to you, you didn't answer," Paddy accused. "Why?"

"I didn't know if you was friend or foe!" Stevens defended. "I'd had to keep my hand over the lad's mouth while the pirates was on board. He was moaning, you see, the fever having set in on him from the beating and the drenching. You'd have probably never heard us if his irons hadn't rattled."

"It's a damned good thing they did," Tarnes told him.

Stevens looked at the Second Mate. "Aye, I suppose it is."

"And you don't have any idea who he is," Weir probed.

"I didn't say that."

Patrick stared hard at the man. "You said you didn't know his name!"

Stevens' eyes narrowed. "I said I didn't know it for sure, but you never asked if I had a notion as to who he might be."

Weir sighed, putting up a hand to forestall Patrick's bellow. "Who do you think he is, Mr. Stevens?"

The old salt looked at the Captain and grinned; liking the title of respect he hadn't heard in a long, long time. "I believe he might be the Duke's son."

"That Duke's son?" Paddy snapped, despite Weir's cautioning look. "Virago has a piss pot full of Dukes!"

"The old man everybody was afraid of, the one that died in that mishap on board the Lady Tasha."

There was a sudden silence that seemed to still everything on board the Wind Lass. Three men faced Jarl Stevens with faces blank and set.

"Duke Sorn? Giles Sorn?" Weir asked.

"That's the one. If I'm right, that there's his oldest boy, Syn-Jern."

Weir jerked, looked away from the probing stare of his best friend, Patrick Kasella. He walked to the rail, braced his hands on the shining teak railing, and stared out to sea. He felt cold all the way to the tips of his toes.

"You knew him? Duke Sorn?" Stevens asked.

Weir nodded though he didn't turn around. When he spoke, his voice was tight. "Aye, I knew the bastard."

Stevens looked to Patrick. "Is there something I ought to be told?"

Paddy swung his attention from Weir's rigid back to the concerned face of the old man. "Maybe. If your friend in there is who you think he is, then you just might have something to worry about."

"The sins of the father," Weir whispered. His concentration was steady on the rolling green of the ocean span.

Not liking the silence, the looks Paddy and Tarnes were giving him, Stevens drew himself up. "That boy couldn't have done nothing to you. I know for a fact he's been in the Maze for nigh on ten year!"

Weir pushed away from the railing and turned to face Stevens. "But he might be Giles Sorn's son."

"What's that got to do with the price of tea in Chrystallus?" Stevens growled.

Saur squinted. "It was Giles Sorn who turned my father in to the Tribunal." He left the rail and came forward, his shoulders hunched with fury. "It was Giles Sorn who paid the back taxes on my father's lands and then took them for his own." He reached Stevens.

"And it was Giles Sorn who put my sister and me off that land after our father was murdered trying to keep those same lands!" He snarled down into Steven's face. "My sister Genevieve was sent to the Galrath nunnery to be raised. I was luckier; I was sent to the orphanage in Fealst. That was nearly twenty years ago! It wasn't until two years ago that we found one another again. We've got Giles Sorn to thank for that. The son-of-a-bitch died before I was old enough to avenge my father's death and being taken away from the only family I had left!"

"But that was the father," Stevens protested. "That boy in your cabin can't be no older than you. He couldn't have been a part of that evil. He'd have been a boy himself!"

Weir Saur shook his head. "It doesn't matter!" he mumbled, thrusting his hands into the pockets of his cords.

"It sure as hell does!" The old man reached out to take hold of Weir's arm, but the younger man stepped away, twisting his shoulder from the man's approach. "You can't blame the boy for what his father did! You can't make him pay for another man's debt."

"I paid for my father's debt!" Weir snapped. "I lost my home; I lost my belongings; I lost my father! I was blamed for what my father did! If that man is Giles Sorn's son, he has a debt to me!"

Stevens didn't like the sound of that. "What kind of debt?"

"I swore on my father's grave that I would make the Sorns pay for taking our land, for killing him, for separating Genny and me." A muscle in his jaw bunched. "You ask what debt?" Weir's voice went low and deadly. "He owes me his life!"

## Chapter Six

PATRICK KASELLA ENTERED THE CABIN AND FELT SOMETHING AKIN TO true remorse well up inside him as he took in the scene before him.

Lying asleep on the Captain's bunk, their unknown guest was hunched over the volume of short stories Weir had loaned him. The book was clutched tightly to him; his head was tucked down, off the pillow, his right cheek resting on the book's title. He had drawn his knees up to his chest, the edge of the book pressed tightly between his legs as though he were guarding it even in sleep. Now and again, the man would twitch, begin to straighten his legs and then stop as though he had encountered an invisible barrier, and Paddy knew that was the legacy of the cage in that this man had no doubt spent countless, uncomfortable hours.

Sitting down on the stool beside the bunk, Patrick watched the man sleeping, feeling to the roots of his being the same unbearable loneliness he knew this man had experienced. He drew in a deep breath, letting it out slowly, wishing to put off indefinitely what he must find out. As he exhaled, he saw his companion awake and look at him with trusting, inquisitive eyes.

"You're Syn-Jern Sorn, aren't you?" Paddy asked before he could lose his nerve.

If there was surprise, it didn't show. The only emotion that seemed to pass over the man's face was one of relief. The chiseled lips parted, trembled as though he was about to speak, then closed.

"Do you know who Weir is? The Captain of this ship?" Patrick felt as though he'd been kicked in the gut when the man nodded. Patrick ran his hand through the thick ebony of his hair, stood up, and paced the room.

It was difficult to speak, painful even, but Syn knew he had to try. It took him several attempts before any intelligible sound came out. His voice was rusty with disuse, croaking, and grating. He wasn't surprised that the man standing at the far end of the cabin waited patiently for him to speak, to get the words out, to piece them together in a way that made sense.

"He's going to kill me isn't he?" came the hoarse, halting words.

Patrick shook his head. "I hope not." He looked away. "I honestly don't know."

Again the effort was horrendous, excruciating. "But he's taken an oath to do so."

Patrick flinched. He was looking into a face that had resigned itself to death, whether quick and painless, or lingering and hard, and it tore at his heartstrings, hurt him deep in his soul. He watched as Syn-Jern Sorn, his best friend's sworn enemy, eased his legs out, and picked up the volume of short stories. He seemed to be caressing the book as though it were a cherished lover, running the palm of his hand over the pebbly texture of the leather binding before he extended it carefully to Patrick.

"Thank him for loaning this to me. It was always one of my favorites."

Paddy took the book and laid it on the desk where a dozen or more other novels were scattered. He heard a soft sigh and looked back to see Sorn watching him, gauging his concern.

"Don't worry about me. No one ever has before."

The tone, the words, the look, cut Paddy to the quick. He felt his temper soaring, felt the fury at an unjust world welling up inside him and his words were harsher than he intended, his own tone cruel and snappish.

"How old were you when your father cheated Trevor Saur out of his lands?"

"It doesn't matter how old he was."

Paddy spun around and his face hardened with anger. "Weir promised me he'd let me handle this, Genevieve," he warned.

For a moment she didn't speak. Even from where he stood, Paddy could feel the anger directed Sorn's way, feel the implied threat in the way Genny was standing, her hand on the hilt of the dagger at her thigh.

"You owe us, Sorn," she said, her words tightly clipped, lethal as she glared at Syn-Jern Sorn. "You can pay with your life!"

"Genny!" Patrick scolded, taking a step toward the young woman, intent on getting her out of the cabin.

She backed away from Paddy's advance, yanked the door open behind her, and then swung around the heavy portal, banging it shut behind her.

Paddy looked quickly to the bunk. "I'm sorry," he began, but he could see a faint smile on Sorn's face. He was puzzled by it until the thick, emotionless words came.

"I have that effect on women."

"Genny's young. She sees things in black and white. Galrath was hard on her."

"The convent?" Syn-Jern asked with shock.

"Aye. She was there from the time she was three until just a few years ago. She's twenty-five, now."

"And Saur?"

"Fealst," Paddy answered. "He had it real good compared to his sister."

Syn-Jern sighed heavily. "Tell him I'm sorry about his lands. Tell him if it's any consolation, they were taken away from me, too."

"You couldn't have been more than eleven when Weir's lands were taken. How old were you when you were sent to the Labyrinth?" He didn't wait for a reply. His agile mind remembered Stevens saying the young man had been in the Maze ten years. He looked around. "Twenty-one, twenty-two."

"Twenty-one." There was softness, hopelessness in the voice.

"You're thirty-one now?" He saw Syn-Jern nod. "So you must have been sent to the colony right after your father died on board the Lady Tasha."

"Aye," came the soft reply.

"What happened to the lands? Who took control of them when Giles Sorn died?"

The first real emotion showed on the sad face. "Me."

"Did you know they had been stolen from Trevor Saur?"

"I knew they had been his lands."

"How did you think your father had come by them?" He had to find out and he hoped against hope Sorn would give him something to work with, something to take to Weir that would prevent a tragic ending to all this.

Sorn took a long breath, seemed to gather his thoughts. "I was told he was awarded the land for payment of back taxes."

"Who has control of them, now?"

At first Paddy didn't think Sorn was going to answer. He was silent for so long, he began to wonder if the man was trying to think of some plausible lie; if he was fabricating some excuse that would clear him of any of his father's wrong doing. But the words he spoke at last, the look on his features, gave evidence that his words were true, if painful.

"As far as I know, the Tribunal has all the lands." There was bitterness in the words, hatred in the tone. "They took everything when I was sent to Tyber's Isle. I have nothing to give him, Master Kasella. There's nothing left." He lowered his eyes.

"But..."

"But, what?" came a sharp question from the doorway. Weir stood there, his mouth tight.

"If you want my life, I will gladly let you take it. I have no further use for it."

## Chapter Seven

WEIR SAUR HAD GROWN UP IN AN ATMOSPHERE OF LOVE IN THE orphanage at Fealst. The Charitable Sisters of Compassion who ran the home for abandoned, orphaned and abused children, had done a marvelous job of raising the rambunctious boy. They had afforded him every opportunity to grow in wisdom, tolerance, truthfulness, honor, and compassion; and they had taught him the basic rule of humanity: treat others as you would like to be treated. Although blessed with a mischievous nature that oftentimes made the Sisters grit their teeth in exasperation, he had garnered their love and respect because of his innate sense of fairness and leniency toward those less fortunate than himself.

Having his mother die while giving birth to his sister, Genevieve, and his father murdered, having known terrible loneliness and pain at an early age, it was understandable the boy would look to the Sisters for the affection he craved. Although he had tried to hide his need when first sent to the orphanage, the Sisters had recognized the little boy's silent cry for help. The one thing that the Sisters had not taught him, had not even tried to teach him, was the ability to recognize that hidden pain in another human being. That was a talent, an ability, with that Weir had been born, and an ability that had been finely honed from his own years of heartbreak.

Despite the elation he felt at having Giles Sorn's son in his grasp, Weir saw deep pain in Syn-Jern Sorn. He felt it to the bottom of his soul.

And it made him furious.

"Was your crime so terrible that you wish death over life?" Weir snarled, stalking to the bunk. "Do you think you will be redeemed if I kill you, Sorn?"

Patrick moved closer to the bunk, wanting to put himself between the two men.

"I don't blame you for hating me," Syn-Jern whispered, his voice getting stronger, less halting. "Do what you need to."

"Don't tell me what to do!" Weir yelled. His eyes blazed, his body quivered with fury. "I'll decide what should be done to you!"

"Weir." Paddy's voice was soft, a quiet warning, and a gentle plea for sanity.

Saur's head snapped around and he fixed his friend with a sharp, penetrating stare. "If I want to kill him, Kasella, you can't stop me!"

"I can try."

Syn-Jern looked over at the Ionarian and saw the set face filled with challenge. He knew if it came right down to it, Patrick would intervene if Saur tried to do him harm.

"You know what his family has done to mine! You know! I have every right to avenge my father!" Weir exploded.

"Even if this man did nothing to warrant your hatred?"

"He's a Sorn!"

"Aye. He hasn't denied that, but why don't you ask yourself why, if he has the protection of that family, he wound up in the Labyrinth."

Weir turned back to Syn-Jern. "Who did you cheat out of their lands? Somebody who could fight back? Somebody important, who had the Tribunal on their side?"

"I..." Syn-Jern began.

"Did you have your men kill for that land, too?"

"No, I..."

"Or did you just have them thrown off the land, have the children sent to orphanages and hell-hole nunneries?"

Syn-Jern shook his head, wanting to explain, but Saur's violent outburst made him cringe back against the pillow as Weir drew back his fist.

"Or did you do the deed yourself? Huh? Did you?" He shot his arm forward only to have his hand caught in a fierce grip.

Paddy's hand was strong, immobile as he clutched Weir's fist in the wide palm. His chin was set, his body poised to do more than just keep Weir from hitting a defenseless man. His words were soft, but there was underlying steel bracing them.

"Give the man a chance to answer you, Weir."

Syn-Jern's voice was low, gruff as he answered. "It doesn't matter why I was sent to Tyber's Isle, Lord Saur. I was innocent of the crime, but..."

"I don't care about any of that!" Weir glared at Sorn. "What happened to my family's lands? The lands your father stole from us?" Weir spat.

"He said the lands are now in Tribunal hands," Patrick informed Weir. "Taken as punishment for his crime."

Saur snorted. "From one thieving bunch to another! What difference does it make? I'll never get them back until I have enough money to bury the Sorn family and any other bastards who try to stand in my way!"

"If the lands still belonged to me, I would gladly give them back to you," Syn-Jern told him, flinching at the hiss of disbelief that issued from Saur's twisted mouth. "I would, Lord Saur; I swear to you I would. If I had known there were members of your family still alive, I would have tried to return them to you long ago; but they told me Trevor Saur's children were dead."

"Aye!" Weir snarled. "It wasn't because of a lack of diligence on your father's part that we weren't!"

Paddy put a calming hand on his friend's shoulder. "Chances are the Tribunal wouldn't have allowed him to return the lands if he'd been able to find you or Genevieve." He looked hard at Weir. "You know that. Your father had been declared a vagrant when he couldn't pay the taxes; the land would have reverted to the Tribunal if Giles Sorn hadn't paid the levy."

"None of that matters now, does it?" Weir shouted. "The lands that were in my family for hundreds of years, land on which Genny and I were born, are gone from us forever because of that man there!" He pointed his finger at Syn-Jern. "You give me one good reason why I shouldn't slit your thieving throat!"

Syn-Jern shrugged. "I can't." He leaned back against the pillow. "As a matter of fact, if you did slit my throat, you'd be doing me a favor."

## Chapter Eight

PADDY LEANED OVER THE RAILING NEXT TO HIS FRIEND AND LOOKED down into the water rushing past the Wind Lass' hull. He glanced at Weir's set face and decided to let him open the conversation if there was to be one. It had been well over two hours since Saur had walked silently from his cabin, away from the resignation that had settled over Syn-Jern Sorn's calm face.

"What am I going to do with him, Patrick?" Weir said.

Patrick let a full minute pass before he pushed away from the railing, put his back to the teak, and braced his hands behind him. He watched Weir's men scurrying about the rigging. "He's as innocent of what his father did as you are of what yours did, Weir."

Weir knew that, but he really didn't want to hear it. He turned his head and looked at Patrick. "You're on his side, aren't you?"

Paddy shrugged. "There is no side, my friend." He looked over at Weir.

"You think I should forget about making him pay, is that it?"

Patrick smiled sadly. "I think he's suffered enough, don't you? Do you think there's anything you can do to him that will hurt him as much as what the Tribunal has already done?" He looked across the ship. "Their cruelty can be far more exacting than a normal man's."

"And do you think you'd be so set on me pardoning him if you hadn't spent time where he did?" Weir challenged.

"You've never been there, Weir, and pray to Alel you never do. That godawful hell-hole takes more out of a man than I hope you'll ever experience."

## Chapter Nine

GENEVIEVE SAUR'S LOOK WAS AS HOT AS THE EMBERS OF HELL'S FIRE AND as hard as flint. She watched Norbert Tarnes and Jarl Stevens helping Syn-Jern Sorn up the companionway to the main deck. Her mouth twisted as they eased him down on a coil of rope and then stood talking to him, smiles of encouragement on their faces. She flicked her stare away, found Patrick Kasella watching her from his place at the helm. She snorted and looked away as though the sight of him had offended her, as well. Her gaze went back to where Sorn was sitting; his thin body slumped in weariness after the climb up from the cabin. She hated the sight of him, but the way he looked at that moment infuriated her.

His face was pale, paler than the other men who trod about the decks of the Wind Lass were. If his pasty complexion was due to long weeks lying in bed, it didn't matter to Genny. She compared his pallor to the robust, sun-kissed flesh of her brother's crew.

He was thin, thinner than any man on board; and his shoulders were bowed. He had the look of defeat about him.

She snorted again. This time it was an ugly sound filled with her emotions, and she saw him lift his head and look her way. She stiffened as she stared back at him with coldness.

It was his eyes that bothered her the most, she decided. They were blank, lifeless, filled with misery. He looked at her much as a lost puppy would have and it made her furious.

"She'll come around," Tarnes said in a quiet voice, seeing where the young man was looking.

Syn-Jern shook his head. "To her, I'm the enemy."

"Give her time, lad," Jarl Stevens told him. "Her brother's giving you the benefit of the doubt; she just might, too."

He saw her toss her head, turn her back, and he felt her rejection to the bottom of his soul.

"It ain't been easy for you, has it, son?" Norbert Tarnes asked, laying his hand on Syn-Jern's slumped shoulder.

Syn-Jern shook his head. "Once you've been labeled a convict, women will always look at you in a wholly different light."

"I reckon they tend to be afraid of you," Tarnes acknowledged.

"That little missy don't look to me as if she's a'feared of any manjack on board this here ship!" Stevens sniffed. "A might uppity, I'm thinking."

With his penetrating gaze still locked on the back of the lovely woman standing on the aft deck, Syn-Jern drew in a long breath. "She has reason to fear me," he said, surprising both older men; but when they asked why, he didn't reply.

ꕥ

There was no word for how sore he was.

There was no word for how tired he was.

They'd been working on him for over two months now. He'd started out just strolling partway around the deck, Stevens close at hand in case he stumbled. His legs had been weak, threatening to topple him to the deck, but soon they were strong enough to do one lap. Then two. Then three. Sit-ups were next, his legs held by whoever happened to be nearby. He couldn't do many of them at first, but it wasn't too long before he could do ten. Then twenty. Then forty.

And the food!

He hadn't eaten so much food in his entire life. At first, he couldn't force down more than a few spoonfuls, but within a few days; he was eating everything they set before him. It started out then to be two meals per day. Then it became three. Now, it was four.

"We gotta put meat on your bones, boy!" the cook had scolded him when he had tried to refuse the extra helpings. "If'n you want to pull your weight on the Lass."

A week later, he was doing pull-ups on one of the yards. He hadn't even blushed when on his first try he couldn't put his chin to the teak once. The men laughed, taunting him, but he knew they were laughing with him, not at him, and it made the next day's effort easier.

Then he'd been told to run around the deck instead of walking.

"Want me to show you how's it done, boy?" Neevens had snorted down to him one day as he lay gasping for breath on the deck. The old man's rubbery lips had pursed in a smile. "Faith, boy! My old granny can run faster than you!"

"And her petticoats down around her ankles, too, eh, Tarnes?" Stevens had joked, dancing a jig away from Neevens as the First Mate had set out after him.

Now, at the beginning of his third month, with the ship only days away from her home port, he could do two hundred sit ups, a hundred pull ups. He had filled out to the point that he was looked at by the other men with admiration and just a tad more than envy, and could lap the ship at a fast enough clip that bets were often laid on his time.

He was learning the life of a sea-going man to the delight and satisfaction of the crew. When he'd conquered the intricacies of scrambling about the rigging as well as the other men, he became one of them. Only one incident marred the occasion and that was when Neevens informed him he was going to have to learn to swim if he planned on sailing with them.

"No, I don't want to learn," Syn-Jern answered.

"Well, you got to!" Neevens began, but Stevens stood up and jabbed him painfully in the ribs. "Hey! What'd you do that for, you old bastard?"

Stevens nodded his head toward Syn-Jern. "The lad says he don't want to learn right now." He jerked his head in Syn-Jern's direction. "He knows what's best for him."

"Most cowards do."

The men groaned, even Neevens, who had realized his error too late. They looked around to see Genny leaning against the topmast, her glower steady on Syn-Jern's bent head. They watched as her face lit with contempt when the young man raised his head and looked at her.

"Ain't you got something you need to be doing, Genevieve Grace?" Tarnes snapped, frowning at her.

"All that training for nothing," she said, ignoring the looks aimed her way. "You know the old saying, don't you?" Her eyes were on Syn-Jern, boring into him, but she wasn't speaking to him, hadn't spoken to him since that last day in Weir's cabin. "You can drag a horse to the water, but you can't make him drink?" Her face turned vicious. "Well, you can show a coward how to be a man, but you can't make him one!"

"That's enough!"

Patrick Kasella trod heavily toward his best friend's sister. He reached out an unforgiving hand and clasped Genny's upper arm in a cruel grip.

"Damn you, that hurts!" she spat, trying to pry his fingers from her arm.

"Aye, well, now you know what hurt feels like, don't you?" Paddy growled down into her angry face. "Would you like to feel the cat-'o-nine on your pretty little back, Genevieve? Would you like to be dragged under the keel of this ship?"

"Don't," Syn-Jern said in a soft voice. No one but Stevens, who was standing near him, heard.

"Or how'd you like to be turned over to the Tribunal's torturers, Genevieve? Be stripped down and examined like a piece of meat? Have some sadistic bastard torment you day and night and not be able to do a gods-be-damned thing about it?"

"Paddy, leave her alone." Syn-Jern got to his feet.

"You're hurting me, Kasella!" Genny spat through clenched teeth. "Let go!"

"Want to feel what it's like to be put in irons, Genevieve? Huh? Feel the iron locked around your wrists and ankles? They're heavy, you know. So heavy you can't walk and you can't hardly lift your arms."

"She doesn't understand," Syn-Jern said a bit louder. He took a step forward.

"Or what about being locked up in a cage? How'd you like that, Genny?"

Syn-Jern reached out and put a hand on Patrick's arm, but the man was so angry, he didn't bother to turn around to see who was trying to interfere. Kasella shook off the hand and gripped both of Genevieve Saur's arms in his strong hands.

"How'd you like to be hurt like he's been hurt, Genny? Have the flesh stripped off your body inch by bloody inch and then have some snooty, arrogant little bitch rub salt in the wounds?"

"That's enough!"

Paddy felt himself being pushed none-too-gently away from Genny. He staggered, was kept from falling by Tarnes' quick thinking, and looked around to see Syn-Jern looking at Genny.

"He didn't mean what he was saying," Syn-Jern told the girl. "He doesn't understand how you feel toward me, but I do." He was looking at her so intently, his thoughts on her well being, that he didn't really see her face turning ugly with disdain. He made the mistake of putting his hand on her shoulder, to comfort her.

"Don't you dare touch me, you bastard!" she shouted at him, jerking away from his hand. "Don't you dare put your filthy hand on me!" She backed away from him, her body rigid with hate. "I'll castrate you if you do!"

Every man on deck winced, seeing the pain and humiliation driven deep in Syn-Jern's already-tormented soul. They watched as he took a deep breath, nodded acceptance of her threat.

"You thoughtless bitch!" Patrick shamed her, reaching out to take hold of Genny's arm, but she moved back, well away from him.

"He might have all of you fooled," she defended, "but I see him for what he is!"

"And what exactly is that, missy?" Tarnes growled.

"You don't get sent to the Labyrinth for no good reason!" she shouted.

"Aye, but you can!" Patrick argued. "I should know that better than anyone!" He jabbed his finger at his own chest. "I made an enemy of the wrong man; he had me sent to Tyber's Isle for it!"

"Aye, well, you weren't a Duke, though, were you, Patrick Kasella?" Genny shot back.

"Dukes have enemies, too," Neevens put in, then turned to look at Syn-Jern. "Don't they?"

A strange look passed over the younger man's face. "Very powerful ones," he answered. He shifted his gaze to Genny. "You want to know what I was in prison for, Lady Saur?" He didn't wait for her to answer. "It was for killing a man."

There were mumbles from the men gathered.

"Then why didn't they hang you?" Genny sneered.

"Oh, they wanted to," Syn-Jern told her. "And probably would have if my grandmother hadn't intervened. But Monique Hesar is a very powerful woman in Virago."

"Hesar?" Tarnes questioned. "You be kin to the royal family? To Prince Innis?"

"Third cousins," Syn-Jern answered, his gaze still locked on Genny. "But it didn't prevent His Highness from having me flogged and deported. He didn't like me any better than Genevieve Saur does."

"Land ho!"

Heads turned, loud whistles of excitement exploded from the crew's lips and, the group scrambled across the deck, forgetting the man and woman who still stood where they were, facing one another. As preparations began for docking, the two seemed oblivious to what was going on around them.

"You should have been hung," Genny finally said, breaking the silence between them.

"Aye," he answered. "I agree."

"Perhaps we can grant your death wish, Duke Sorn," she grated, then spun on her heel, and left him staring after her.

# PART TWO

## Chapter One

THE SOUTHERN COAST OF IONARY WAS A WONDER TO BEHOLD. BUFF-colored dunes rose high along vast stretches of sea-carved stone, pocked with ragged holes and soaring nature-made arches under the swirling waters of the South Boreal Sea's rise and ebb. White caps surged inland along the clean sand beaches and broke amongst the spindly sea oats growing at the foot of the dunes. High along the upper reaches of the cliffs, gnarled and wind-bent pines and scrubs stood sentinel, looking out to sea, ever watchful of the Ionarian coastline. The straggling section of Ionary, the southern-most tip of the country seeping down between Serenia to the East and Virago to the West, held a certain splendor to behold.

Grass huts dotted the peaceful beach, some found inland. Some made this wild and beautiful coast their home, manning the ships that plied the seas and plundered the vessels sailing upon her.

This ragged coast hosted the home base of at least eight pirate ships. The Wind Lass being one of the ships sailing from this isolated port.

Not actually part of the kingdom of Ionary, the peninsula nevertheless Ionarian soil, bore the name of its royal rulers: Montyne Cay. The village, itself, was governed by a council of five men, pirates all. They made the decisions for the populace, settled disputes, carried out their verdicts, and, most importantly of all, and saw that the village was protected from outsiders and citizens, alike. Those who do not abide by the laws and codes of Montyne Cay were asked to leave and were not allowed to return. The five men of the council judged those who refused to leave on their merits. If they were found to be undesirable, they were transported. If they returned, they were imprisoned.

Patrick Kasella sat on the Council of Five.

The populations of Montyne Cay ranged from seventy-five to ninety, depending on how many ships were in port during the count. Very few of the residents were native to the region, most having ventured on the seas, either willingly or pressed into service elsewhere, before finally finding their way to the majestic horseshoe-shaped cove where the ships of the trade docked. Most of the women, with the exception of two Necromanian warrioresses and one Chrystallusian lady of questionable lineage were native-born Ionarians. The men sitting on the Council of Five represented the five nations sailing under the Privateer Brotherhood of Montyne Cay: Ionary, Chale, Serenia, Necroman, and Oceania. Virago and Chrystallus were not part of that representation.

"We don't trust that damned navy of theirs," Neevens had explained to Syn-Jern one evening when Sorn asked why no Viragonian flags flew from any of the ships in port.

"You let one of their so-called pirate ships in here and the next thing you know, you just gods-be-damned well might have their whole bleeding armada breathing down your neck. That godawful Tribunal of theirs has been threatening for years to dig us out of Montyne Cay. They would if they could find us, I reckon."

"What about Chrystallus?" Syn-Jern inquired. "They don't have much of a navy, do they?"

"No navy at all!" Neevens scoffed. "Have you ever heard the like? What kind of kingdom don't have a navy?" He had shown his contempt of the Chrystallusian rulers.

"Little men, they are; about so high. Weird eyes, funny way of walking and talking. You ever see that girl of Brod's? She's from there."

Syn-Jern smiled. "She's lovely."

"Hell fire, boy! You been cooped up too long!" Neevens snorted, "if you think Lin See's 'lovely'!"

"How do you think she views us?" Syn-Jern laughed. "To her, our eyes must look funny; we must sound strange to her ears; seem out of proportion because of our height."

"Ain't the same!" Neevens blustered, striding away. "Ain't the same, at all!"

Sitting on one of the tallest cliffs, his eyes out to sea, Syn-Jern thought back to his conversation that night on board the Wind Lass and sighed. Things had been a helluva lot simpler then. Now, they were as complicated as they could get.

"Want some company?"

"You're a glutton for punishment, Saur," Syn-Jern remarked, craning his head to look up at his visitor. The sun was behind Weir Saur and all he could see was the height of the man and a white halo of light around his head. "I'd have thought you'd had your fill of me for one day."

Weir chuckled and sat down, crossed his ankles and braced his forearms on his raised knees. "I have these feelings, sometimes," he said. "They say my mother had the 'sight'." He glanced at his companion. "She was from Oceania."

Syn-Jern nodded. "I've heard it said Oceanian women have such power."

Saur's voice was hesitant when he spoke. "As I've heard, there are some Viragonian men who wield those same powers.

"It's happened once or twice before," Syn-Jern said softly.

"And you've never told anyone."

"Who should I have told?" Syn-Jern asked. His tone was sharper than he intended. He tore his gaze away and returned his vision to the heaving seas.

Weir laid his hand on Syn-Jern's arm. "Was your life really all that bad, Syn-Jern, or is that just the way you remember it being?"

Swinging his head around, Syn-Jern stared at Weir. "You saw what happened today? If I'd done that when I was a child, my own mother would have had me burned at the stake as a warlock! She was a very religious woman. You have to remember: before the Burning War, Holy Dale, where she was born, was the motherhouse for a group of nuns. She would have lit the faggots beneath my feet had I been accused of witchery."

"Syn-Jern, you can't believe that. A mother..."

"Maybe not your mother, Saur. Maybe not any woman you've ever known. But my mother would have." He pushed himself away from the ground and stood, glaring out to sea, imagining his mother's face as though it were before him that very moment. "She was terrified of the Tribunal, even more so of that sect of sorcerers that run the Tribunal."

"The Domination?" Weir had heard tales of the priests of the Brotherhood of the Domination; tales that had made the hair on his arms stir.

"Aye, them," Syn-Jern hissed. He narrowed his gaze. "The High Priest who had me condemned to the Labyrinth is one of them." He looked down at Weir. "The bastard's name is Demonicus."

Weir flinched. "He was Chief Taxman when my father's estate was sold."

"The one and the same."

"He's on my list," Weir stated, speaking of the list he had made of men he meant to see ruined for being a part of his father's murder.

"He should be at the very top!"

"If your mother feared the Tribunal, why did she marry your father? Wasn't your grandfather sitting on the Judiciary Panel when they married?"

Syn-Jern nodded. "Lexus Sorn, aye. I never knew him, never even saw him, but I was told he was one of the men behind all the important decisions at the palace."

"He wielded that much power?" Weir asked, astonished that Syn-Jern had been so highly connected to the royal family.

"He was the power when Nyles Hesar, Innis's father, was Prince. They say Prince Nyles and my grandfather were lovers. Nyles, I was told, worshipped the ground Lexus Sorn walked; he gave him carte blanche to do whatever he wished in Virago."

"Until Innis came to power." Weir grinned nastily. "I've heard his rod is bent the same as his father's."

Syn-Jern laughed and it was an ugly sound. "Aye, I've heard the same."

"What happened then? Didn't I hear somewhere that Lexus Sorn vanished after Prince Nyles' death?"

He looked down at Weir. "No one knows where he went. Both men had taken wives to squelch the gossip about their real relationship else Lexus would never have consented to touch a female; he had been ordained at the Abbey of the Domination. My father was an 'accident' just like me: a moment's drunken stupor that led to calamity."

"Lexus was part of the Domination?" Weir asked, stunned.

Syn-Jern nodded. "Oh, aye. I was told he was one of the higher ranking members of that evil bunch and had been since his eighteenth birthday."

Weir shivered, drew his legs into the circle of his arms. No wonder Syn-Jern had so shocked everyone that morning: he was related to the magical powers of the Domination.

"I won't let it happen again, Weir," Syn-Jern told his companion as though he'd read his mind. "I've spent most of my life trying to keep that very same thing from happening."

"But why? Can't you control it?"

He shook his head. "No." His hands curled into fists at his side. "If Patrick hadn't pushed so damned hard this morning, it wouldn't have happened then."

Weir looked out across the bay, his thoughts on what had happened earlier in the day.

What had started out as a teasing game of one-upsmanship had escalated into a full-scale battle between the two men who had become very close over the months on board the Wind Lass. Patrick hadn't been hurt in the fracas, but he had been severely trounced in a way no one could have suspected or anticipated. After it was all over, no one who knew Syn-Jern Sorn would ever look at the man again in the same way.

"I could have killed him, Weir," Syn-Jern admitted, his fists clenching and unclenching. "I've done it before."

Weir stood, concerned for the man standing beside him. "But you didn't."

"I wanted to!" Syn-Jern spat. He turned to Weir. "I wanted him hurt! I wanted him beaten! If I'd turned the full power of that vengeance on him, you'd be burying him right about now!"

"I don't understand how you could have kept such an ability quiet. Didn't anyone ever suspect you were capable of doing what you did this morning?" Weir, himself, had been shocked, shaken to the core at the morning's events, but he had wondered all day why Syn-Jern had never used his power to save himself over the years.

"Listen to me, Weir," Syn-Jern snarled, taking Saur's arm and shaking him,

"You don't know what my childhood was like. You have no conception of how evil people can really be. I was a mistake, Weir, a slip-up. I wasn't supposed to have ever been born, and my mother never, ever, let me forget that. Because of me, she was forced to leave her beloved Holy Dale. She never forgave me for that, either."

He held up his free hand, the fist balled tightly closed. "You see this? This is the only touch I ever felt from my mother. She never held me; she never hugged me; she never kissed me or sang to me or comforted me. My god! She didn't even suckle me! I had a wet nurse for that. If she could have let me die, she would have. She tried to kill me before I was even born, but it didn't take. She tried twice, twice, and both times it failed. By the time she found someone else to try, she was too far along in her pregnancy and the old woman refused to do it."

There was horror spreading across Saur's face. "What about your father? Where was he when..."

"Did you ever see him?" Syn-Jern shuddered, seeing his father's face flash across his vision. "The man was hideous! He was grossly fat, obscenely so, and he reeked of body odor. I don't think he ever bathed. He had a bulbous nose, most of his teeth were missing, and what little hair he had was as orange as a carrot. He was as uncouth as he was foul.

"To my knowledge, he only slept with my mother the one time. He was visiting Prince Doron McGregor at Norus Keep. My mother's father, Ruan McGregor, a second cousin to Prince Doron, knew Giles Sorn would be there. He had tried to foist his daughter Anne off on Sorn once before, but my father would have no part of it. Angry and with every intention of joining the two houses, my grandfather had Giles drugged, then 'found' his daughter and Giles together in bed. The old man threatened to go to the Prince for recompense for his daughter's loss of her maidenhood if Giles didn't marry her. My mother once yelled at me that Giles had raped her while he was drunk, that he had forced her into his bed. I don't suppose I'll ever know the truth of it. All I do know for a fact is I was conceived that night at Norus Keep."

"So according to your father, he was blackmailed into the marriage?"

"Aye, and was infuriated by it. Theirs was a marriage neither wanted, but my father couldn't afford a reprimand from King Drude McGregor, Doron's father, and my mother's great uncle, so he wed her, but he never stayed with her. When he found out she was pregnant, he packed her off to Tern Keep, his manor house near Ciona, because he said he didn't want to see how ugly she would become while she was carrying his heir. He never came to visit."

"Was there no one to champion her, then? What of her mother?"

"My maternal grandmother, Monique McGregor, had no idea how things stood. She did not hear of it until years later when I was brought to Holy Dale to live. Had she known, perhaps things would have been better for me; but she was estranged from her daughter and had no great love for her."

"I take it your mother took her anger out on you," Weir said quietly.

Syn-Jern smiled sadly. "Never did I feel a loving touch, Weir. Not once. The women who watched me were as cruel as they came. They seemed to enjoy hearing me cry. The least little thing I did wrong warranted a beating. If I spilled something at the table, I went without food for a day. If I soiled my clothes, I was locked in my armoire for hours on end. If I dared to talk back to them, and believe me that was a mistake I made only once or twice, I had my mouth washed out with the foulest-tasting concoction they could find."

"And your father knew of this?" Weir was stunned that a child could be treated to such abuse.

"What did he care?"

"Had he no feeling for you at all?"

"The only person he ever loved was Alicia Jamar, his mistress. Within a year after he married my mother, Alicia was carrying his child, a child he wanted to inherit all that was his. He was finally able to marry her after my mother died and he publicly acknowledged the boy, my half-brother, Trace. He thought by doing so, Trace could be declared his heir instead of me." A slow, taunting smile touched Syn-Jern's full lips. "But Viragonian law forbade it since I was firstborn."

"It's a wonder he didn't try to have you killed."

The smile grew. "Oh, but he did."

Weir flinched. "How old were you?"

"Nine, ten. I don't remember."

Weir let out a long breath. "What happened?"

Syn-Jern was quiet for a moment, his mind going back to that day. He tried not to think about what had happened on the road to the Serenian capitol at Boreas Keep so long ago, but in his darkest moments, the memory came back full-blown, a vivid reminder that he wasn't like other men. And never would be.

"On the day they buried my mother, Giles Sorn sent a messenger to Ciona. The man said my father wanted me with him. At first I was overcome with happiness, thinking that, at last, someone wanted me, that I was going to fit somewhere." He drew in a deep breath, held it, and then let it out slowly. "That was the first day I heard the words: 'mistress' and 'half-brother'. I didn't know what they meant, but one of the cooks enlightened me."

"That must have come as quite a shock."

"I don't think I really understood the significance of it until the man tried to kill me on the way." He hitched up his cords and sat down beside Weir although he didn't look at Saur as he continued his story. "We stopped by a stream to water the horses. He asked me if I knew how to swim. I didn't even know what the word meant."

Weir thought he knew what was coming. "He tried to drown you."

Syn-Jern nodded.

"And you did to him what you did to Patrick this morning."

*Kasella had come at him, a smile on his face. They'd wrestled, Kasella had come out on top, as he usually did. Syn-Jern had been pinned firmly to the ground, squirming beneath Patrick's lighter weight. They'd both been laughing then, but the laughter soon turned to abject terror for Patrick.*

"I didn't know what I'd done," Syn-Jern explained, seeing the messenger writhing on the ground, his eyes bulging from his head, his fingers clawing at a throat closing. "All I could remember doing was struggling in the water, trying to breath, going under time and time again as the bastard pushed me down into the stream. Sometimes I wake up at night and I can still feel that water clogging my nostrils, flowing down my throat."

*Patrick won the second toss. The men gathered around the training yard had cheered, taunted Syn-Jern, spurring him on with their good-natured insults. He flew through the air, landing with a gasp on the hard ground, and Patrick howled with laughter.*

*"If you could see your face, Sorn!" he chuckled, slapping his knees.*

*He sprang up, plowing into Patrick's belly, sending the Ionarian crashing to the ground; he'd flipped him over, dragging one of Kasella's arms up his back, pinning his right shoulder to the dirt.*

*"If you could see your face, Kasella!" he taunted in Patrick's ear before being bucked off a wildly lurching Ionarian.*

Syn-Jern closed his eyes. The image of what had happened long ago was blending with what had occurred only that morning. Even though the outcomes had been vastly different, the same raw, overwhelming power had been behind both events.

"One moment he was holding me under, the next there was blood everywhere, bubbling in the water, washing up over the banks of the stream. The man was gasping for breath, digging at his throat, and then he just simply ceased to be."

*They'd struggled with one another for over an hour, the men clapping, cheering, and calling out ribald comments to them. Syn-Jern won two tosses, Patrick three out of the five, coming up the winner. Things were going fine until Patrick forgot.*

"How'd you get out of the water?"

"The water wasn't deep, only a foot maybe. After I'd seen what I'd done, I staggered out of the stream. I ran until I could run no further and then I just collapsed. A farmer found me and took me back to Tern Keep."

*"What you need is a good drenching, Sorn!" Patrick shouted. Everyone was in such a good mood, no one really noticed the instant pallor come over Syn-Jern's face nor the wildness enter into his eyes.*

*"Throw him in the pond, Kasella!"* one of the men shouted. *"Wet him down!"*

"What happened when you got back to Tern Keep?"

Syn-Jern shook his head. "I don't remember. I didn't want to remember. They kept asking me about the man I had left with. They wanted to know where he was, why I had been found alone on the road to Boreas. I couldn't tell them because I guess I'd blocked what I'd done out of my mind."

*They struggled, Syn-Jern protesting in a strident, terrified voice no one could hear over the laughter as Patrick picked him up and slung him over his shoulder. He pummeled the Ionarian's back as Kasella ran toward the pond, intent on tossing Syn-Jern in.*

"They never found him?"

Syn-Jern shook his head. "There was nothing left to find. I totally destroyed him with that godawful power."

*"Patrick, don't!"* he screamed, struggling wildly then.

*"You stink, Sorn," Paddy taunted. He ran toward the water, Syn-Jern jiggling painfully up and down on Kasella's shoulder. "You need a bath, boy!"*

"Who took care of you when you got back to Ciona?" Weir asked. He watched as Syn-Jern ran a shaky hand through the thick gold of his hair.

"Someone sent a message to my father."

Syn-Jern drew his knees up and circled them within the perimeter of his arms. Not because he was cold, but to keep them from trembling as his arms and hands were doing at that moment. He had come so close to killing Patrick Kasella that morning. So very close.

Too close.

"He came himself to get me. It was the first time I had ever seen him and I was more than a little afraid of him. He was so big and ugly and he looked at me with such hatred. I remember him bending over me, looking me up and down, and saying: 'You aren't much, are you, boy?' He didn't touch me; he never did, although once he broke my nose. That day, he had one of his bodyguards bring me along behind him. We rode to Boreas that evening and I was given a room at one of the inns while my father visited with the Prince. The next morning we rode to Holy Dale, my mother's ancestral home. My grandmother was staying with friends in Chale. No one told her I was being brought to Holy Dale. She thought I was in a boarding school in Ionary, so she left before I could even meet her." He looked away. "I did meet my stepmother and stepbrother though."

"The meeting must not have been all that pleasant."

Syn-Jern let out a snort of disdain. "You might say that. My stepmother called me into her solar and made it quite clear to me that I wasn't wanted. She reminded me I was only there at her sufferance and if I didn't 'tow the line', she'd see to it I was sent to the orphanage in Oceania."

"It wasn't bad at all," Weir told him. "The Sisters were very kind and loving."

"Anything would have been better than what I was forced to endure, Saur."

"Was life worse there in Virago than it had been for you at Ciona?"

His life had been a living hell at Holy Dale Keep. As bad as things had been for him in Ciona, they were ten times worse under the care of his father and stepmother. He had felt his first real pain at Holy Dale.

"What of your grandmother? She didn't notice you were being misused?" Weir inquired.

Syn-Jern shook his head. "She thought I was at school. Whenever she sent word she was returning to Holy Dale, I was shipped back to Tern Keep. I was twenty-one the first time I met her." His voice lowered. "And that was at my trial."

"If life was so bad for you, why didn't you run away?" Weir asked.

"I didn't dare. I remember rebelling only once." He closed his eyes, remembering. "I couldn't sit down for three days when my father's man got through with me. My rump looked like raw meat and felt worse." He looked at Weir. "Alicia and Trace got to watch what Higgins did to me. It wasn't just the humiliation of having my britches pulled down and my ass whipped that hurt so much. It was their laughter while he was doing it. That and Alicia promising me more of the same if I so much as dared to disobey her again."

"What the hell had you done to warrant such a whipping?"

That slow, self-deprecating smile returned. "I had refused to drown the kittens she ordered me to kill." The smile slid away. "I couldn't kill the kittens, but I could kill humans without a qualm. I've killed four people, Saur."

"Is that what sent you to the Labyrinth? Another killing like that first one?" Weir asked, his eyes searching Syn-Jern's.

"Not exactly although that was self-defense, as well. I can't prove it, but I believe my brother was the one who set the bastard on me. His name was Otis Playe and he was a mean son of a bitch. Something happened just before the killing, something I'd rather not go into, and Trace had been involved with that. I think he hired the man who tried to kill me."

"But you got to him first," Weir said.

"Aye."

"How did it happen?"

Syn-Jern let out a long breath. "I was at Holy Dale. Even though I was treated like shit there, I grew to love that land as I'd never loved Tern Keep. I thought of it as my own since I believed I would inherit it one day from my maternal grandmother. It was going to be my home forever." A dark look crossed Sorn's handsome face. "And it would have been if the Tribunal had not confiscated it. I should have known I'd never own Holy Dale."

"I know the feeling. Go on."

The Viragonian shook himself. "I felt strange right after supper and, looking back on it now, I think Otis must have put something in my wine. He was one of the stewards at the manse. At any rate, I went up to my room to go to bed, to sleep off the illness. There was a steaming tub of bath water sitting in the middle of the room. I remember thinking that odd for I hadn't asked for one, and didn't use it. Instead, I lay down, sick as a damned dog, my head spinning like a top, and the next thing I know, I'm in the tub, staring up through water at a man trying to drown me."

"You killed him."

"Eventually. It took awhile, but I finally managed to fight back. When I finally came to myself, the man was lying on the floor by the tub." Syn-Jern frowned. "I'd strangled him."

"Are you sure you did it?" Weir asked.

"When Trace and his companion opened the door, my hands were still around the man's neck." A short laugh of contempt came from Syn-Jern's lips.

"With witnesses to prove it, eh?"

"Aye," came the bitter reply. "Convenient, huh?"

"Did your brother testify against you?"

"He didn't. He had his companion do it." Syn-Jern leaned back on the rock. "He wanted to inherit the title and the lands. He had a very good incentive for doing so." His eyes gleamed with bitterness. "He wanted me hanged for the murder, even had his witness testify I'd made threats against the man beforehand. What he didn't count on was my grandmother coming home in the middle of the trial."

"That must have put a kink in his chain," Weir chuckled.

"It did. Grandmere took one look at me in the tribunal hall that day and started shouting at the top of her lungs in Viragonian, which I didn't speak. I remember thinking: here is one more woman who hates me. I was backing away from her, but she reached out, grabbed my arm, and pulled me to her. She was looking at my neck and I thought: the woman is measuring me for a gods-be-damned noose." He shook his head. "I underestimated her. She insisted the Chief Tribunalist have me examined. There were bruises all over my neck and chest where the man had held me under the water. There were scratches down my hands and arms. It was obvious we'd been fighting. I had no reason to kill him, but he'd made the mistake of telling one of the cook's helpers that he'd like to see me dead. He was the one who had the water drawn up. It came out at the trial that I bathed in the morning, not in the evening so there would have been no reason for me to have asked for the water to be drawn." He lifted one shoulder with disdain. "Ergo, a lighter sentence of manslaughter instead of out and out murder."

"It's a wonder you didn't destroy him like you did the first man who tried to kill you." Weir shivered. "Like you almost did Paddy this morning."

ꕤ

They were almost to the water when the true panic had set in, when the terrible darkness had spread over Syn-Jern Sorn and he had dredged up from the pit of him the monster he had tried to keep at bay since he was eighteen years old.

"Kasella!" he thundered. His body jerked so violently his own teeth clicked together sharply as he flew off Patrick's shoulder.

Shocked eyes, gaping mouths, stilled breaths greeted his action. Men backed away from him, horror stamped on their pale features. Patrick was stunned; he couldn't move, couldn't speak. He simply stared at the man before him, rocked to the very foundations of his beliefs.

"My god!" Patrick whispered, staring up at Syn-Jern Sorn. "Oh, my god!"

Men stumbled away; their hands busy making the sign against what they were seeing. Some stopped dead in their tracks, full realization of what they were witnessing making them unaware of anything save the apparition before their disbelieving eyes.

"I told you not to do it, Kasella!" he bellowed. "Now, you'll see! Now, you'll pay!"

He was hovering above the ground, his feet a good two feet off the grass. His eyes were dark as sin, a blue-black that was deeper than the farthest pit of hell. The look on his face was evil, malevolent, and the voice that had issued from the drawn back lips was deeper than Syn-Jern Sorn's own soft Viragonian brogue; it was a voice from the Abyss.

"I will destroy you, Kasella!" it hissed.

Patrick backed away, too, just as the others had, but he had gone no more than two steps when he was suddenly lifted off the ground and flung hard against a nearby tree. He hit the trunk with brutal force and slid to the ground.

"Syn-Jern, no!" Weir shouted, moving forward only to be thrust back by an invisible hand. He stared at Syn-Jern, saw the rigid finger pointed his way.

"Stay out of this, Saur, or you will be next!"

Patrick was jerked to his feet by the same invisible hands that had stopped Weir from interfering. He was thrown across the training yard, punched and pounded by vicious blows the men could hear, but not see. Blood spurted from Kasella's nose, dripped down his chin. His lips split, his eyes swelled nearly shut. He was receiving a beating such as these men had never seen, all done by a force none of them could see.

"Syn-Jern, stop! You're killing him!"

It was Genny's pleading that finally pierced the blood-red fog that had seized his mind. One moment he was two feet off the ground, the next he was crumpled on the grass, his face buried in his hands, his body trembling so violently he could barely catch his breath. He turned hopeless eyes to Weir Saur.

"Now, do you see? Do you understand why I don't fight back?"

ᘓᘐ

"What happened when you were eighteen?" Weir had to know.

Syn-Jern took in a long breath, let it out, and turned to face Weir.

"That's when I killed my father and Alicia."

## Chapter Two

HER HANDS WERE SOFT, GENTLE ON HIS FACE. HER FINGERTIPS SMELLED OF lemon oil for she'd been dusting the furniture when they brought him in. Her lovely face was full of compassion.

And fire.

"He could have killed you, Patrick!" she said through clenched teeth as she washed away the dried blood under his nose.

"But he didn't," Patrick answered, wincing as his broken nose throbbed under her careful scrutiny.

"I warned you he was dangerous, but you and Weir wouldn't listen!" She clucked her tongue, amazed at the rapid swelling around his right eye. She bent closer to him, studying the bruised and scraped flesh. "Maybe now the two of you will get rid of that bastard."

"No," Paddy managed to say before a gasp of pain took his breath. Even though her fingers had stilled instantly at his sound of pain, he could feel the pressure on his aching cheek and turned his head away from her touch.

"Men!" she spat, getting up from the side of the bed where she had been sitting. She picked up what was left of the roll of bandages, with which she had tightly wrapped his bruised ribs and spun them into a thick tube, her hands turning the material viciously over and over until the last inch was confined. "I suppose you think what he did to you was justified." Her lips pressed into a prim, unforgiving line.

"I knew better," Paddy grunted, trying to heave himself up in the bed only to find pain waiting to lash out at him. He stopped, sighed, and lay back down. "He had every right to fight back." He glanced at her. "That's what being a man is all about, Genny."

Her snort left no doubt as to what she thought of Kasella's remark. She ran a straight pin through the material to secure it then tossed the roll into the medicine bag on the nightstand.

"Genny?" he asked softly, "Please try to understand. This man has been through hell; I added to that hell this morning. I deserved what I got."

She jerked her head around, stared down at him. Her flashing eyes widened. "He could have killed you!"

"But he didn't!" Paddy said, forcefully.

"Well," she hissed, "it wasn't from lack of trying on his part!" She snapped the medicine bag shut, picked it up, and thrust it under her arm. Her face was set, a stony vessel of anger serving up a dish of hot revenge. "Maybe next time he'll finish the job." She stalked to the door, peered back over her shoulder at him. "Maybe next time none of you will be able to stop him!"

Weir passed his sister on the gravel walkway leading from their hut to the storage sheds. He opened his mouth to speak to her, but the look she gave him as she hurried past made him snap his lips shut. He shook his head. Genny was going to be more difficult than ever, now.

He opened the door to the hut he shared with his sister, smelled the heavy scent of lemon oil and frowned. He had always associated the odor to the orphanage where it was his job to polish all the armoires. It wasn't a job he relished doing.

"Paddy?" he called out.

"In here."

Weir sighed. She'd put him in his room, he thought. Not either of the two guest rooms built off the main room, but in his room at the back of the hut, under the only shady tree in the compound. Somehow he'd known she'd put Patrick there.

Shrugging out of his shirt as he entered his sleeping chamber, he glanced at Paddy's face and whistled. "He beat the shit out of you, didn't he?"

"Do I look as bad as I feel?"

"Think about Cookie's meatloaf and you'll know how you look," Weir chuckled as he drew a fresh shirt from the armoire. "Want a mirror?"

"No."

"Probably just as well," Weir mumbled as he pulled the fresh shirt over his head. "Nothing major broken or smashed, I hope." He ran his fingers through his hair to bring it back to some semblance of order.

"Only my gods-be-damned pride." Paddy took a deep breath and managed to gasp his way up in the bed until he was leaning, panting, against the headboard. He frowned. "I made a mistake."

"A rather bad mistake, I'd say." Weir sat down gingerly on the foot of the bed. "One I don't suppose you'd care to make again?"

Patrick threw him a disgruntled look. "Did you talk to him?"

Weir nodded. "He feels bad about it. As I suspected, that anger isn't something he can control."

"God, I hope not!" Patrick growled. "If he could direct that power at will, he'd be the dangerous man Genny thinks he is."

Weir looked down at the woven mat that covered the wood flooring. "Well, he's killed with it before." He raised his eyes to Paddy's. "He was responsible for four deaths with that power of his."

Patrick flinched. He'd come closer than he'd thought that morning.

"Paddy." Weir didn't know how to say what had to be said. He took his time, thinking of the right words, not wanting the wrong impression to settle on Patrick's mind. He chose his words very carefully, then looked across the room, unable to meet Paddy's gaze. "One of the people he killed was his father."

Patrick stared at his friend. "How could he? He wasn't with them that day, was he?"

Weir shook his head. He finally turned his worried gray gaze to Patrick. He drew in a ragged breath and then exhaled in a rush of words: "Apparently he doesn't have to be anywhere nearby. He can send his thoughts like we can send carrier pigeons. He directs the anger where he wants it to go and it destroys. That's how he killed his father and stepmother."

Kasella knew the story, of course, of how Giles Sorn and his pregnant wife had died in the explosion on board the Lady Tasha. Of the twenty-seven crewmembers and four passengers on board the brigantine, all survived save the Duke and his lady. There was never a trace of the Sorns found among the wreckage.

"But why would he kill his parents? What the hell had they done to him?"

Weir looked at him. "Well, for starters, either Giles Sorn or his second wife had hired a man to kill Syn-Jern right after Syn-Jern's mother died, when he was nine. The bastard tried to drown him."

A shadow passed over Patrick's face. "To kill his own son? Why in the god's name did he want Syn-Jern dead?"

"So Trace could inherit instead of Syn-Jern. They're half-brothers and apparently the old man hated Syn-Jern's mother and loved Trace's. There were a lot of so-called 'accidents' that befell him over the next few years, but the man must have led as charmed a life back then as he does now; all the mishaps failed."

"Did he know what was happening? I mean, did he suspect what his father was trying to do?"

"He says he didn't. At least not until he overheard one of the servants talking about the 'accident' that the Duke had paid to have happen while he and his wife were sailing to Oceania on the Lady Tasha." Weir stood up and walked to the window, pulled the curtain back and stared out. "He was supposed to fall from the balcony of the manor house." He looked back at Paddy. "His father would stop at nothing to have Syn-Jern out of his life."

Patrick understood. "So when that realization hit him, he directed that lethal anger at his father."

"I think there was more to it, but I didn't press him. He didn't know he'd actually killed them until news came of the explosion." Weir shrugged his wide shoulders. "To him, it's like a wish fulfillment, something he thinks about and then when it happens, he knows he caused it. He was horrified at what he'd done the first time it happened, when he was nine, but this second time revolted him. He had killed his own father, had committed patricide."

"Sounds to me like the bastard deserved it." Patrick eyed Weir. "I would imagine you think so."

"Oh, he deserved it, all right. There's no doubt about that."

"What happened today brought it all back to him, didn't it?" A thought crossed Paddy's mind. "Why didn't he use it when that son-of-a-bitch Janssen had him keelhauled?"

Weir stared blindly out into the compound. "He said he was terrified of going under the water, of having it close over him, but then he realized that if he drowned, he'd finally be free of all the pain. He just gave up, wanting it all to end."

Patrick nodded. "I can understand that. He was more than ready for you to kill him that morning when you found out who he was. He was so gods-be-damned calm about it. Too calm. I think he really did want to die."

"But not anymore." Weir turned from the window. He fused his gaze with Paddy's.

"He's made up his mind to go after his brother and that High Priest. He asked what it would take to get his own ship."

"He wants to go a'pirating?"

"He wants his manhood back, Paddy. And the only way he sees himself gaining it, is if the people who helped to destroy him, pay for it."

"Did you ask him if this power only comes when he's threatened like that? Does the water have something to do with what triggers it?"

"I don't understand..."

"Think about it, Weir! If he can learn to control that power, to direct it, he'd be formidable!" Patrick pushed himself higher in the bed, his enthusiasm overriding the agony of his bruised ribs. "He'd be a man to reckon with!"

Weir shook his head. "He doesn't want to use it, Paddy. He's afraid of it."

"But if he can harness it, would it have to go full circle? Would he have to kill with it?"

"I've wondered about that."

Both men jumped. They turned guiltily to see Syn-Jern standing in the doorway.

"The only way to control it is if I learn from someone who knows exactly what it is I have." He advanced into the room, blanching with guilt as he looked at Patrick's face. He was about to apologize when Patrick held up a hand.

"I was at fault and I don't blame you. We won't mention it again."

Syn-Jern looked at him for a long moment without speaking. The two men understood one another; they'd been in the same hell; they'd lived the same hell.

"What can we do to help, Syn-Jern?" Weir asked, drawing Sorn's regard.

"I've heard there is a man in Chrystallus. He is a magic-sayer and I'm told he was once of the Domination. If I can get to Chrystallus, maybe he can help me."

"And if he can't?" Patrick asked.

Syn-Jern shook his head. "Then I'll ask him what I can do to rid myself of this curse."

"What if you can't rid yourself of it?" Weir questioned.

A slight smile touched Syn-Jern's full lips. "Then I learn to swim."

## Chapter Three

TO SAIL FROM MONTYNE CAY TO THE FAR EAST WAS A JOURNEY THAT would take at least four months. Provisions for such a journey had to be gathered, a crew picked who were willing to make what would be something more than just a cruise. Most of the men about the Cay were there to make their livings from raiding the ships of the Seven Kingdoms; they could not be expected to board a ship bound for a foreign port without any real assurance of gold in their pockets. Weir Saur thought it unlikely that many men would agree to sign on with just promise of an occasional pilfering amongst the ships that chanced upon on the high seas, but he gave in to Tarnes' suggestion of putting up a poster to ask for volunteers.

"Let the men know it's for Syn-Jern," Tarnes told him, "and see how many you get that want to go along. You'll be turning them away; just you wait and see!"

Weir hadn't been so sure. Since that day on the training grounds, most of the men of Montyne Cay walked a wide circle around Syn-Jern Sorn. Oh, they greeted him friendly enough, but there was a wariness in their attitudes, a superstitious gleam in eyes careful not to stare openly at him, that were sure signs they feared the man to some extent.

"It ain't fear," Stevens grumbled to Weir. "It be respect!"

"Nay, it be fear of the NightWind," Neevens disagreed. "Sorn be one of that kind."

Whatever the reason, Syn-Jern was totally unaware of the way the village men felt about him. He worked hard to learn to box, a task Tarnes cheerfully taught him. He had to strive hard to learn the more complex moves of swordplay from Weir; but in the end, he surprised even himself when he won a rather lengthy duel with Saur.

Jarl Stevens taught him some rather lethal tricks with daggers, and Neevens, despite his obvious fear of the man, had provided some handy tips on how to use a whip to good advantage.

His training under Patrick Kasella took on an entirely different tone after that fateful morning. The martial arts that Paddy had been trying to teach him in an offhand way, afraid to put too much on Syn-Jern, escalated at a rapid pace after that. Within another month's time, Syn-Jern was as proficient, if not more so, than Kasella, himself.

The men who trained him clapped him on the back, complimented his learning, but Syn-Jern Sorn had no idea what the others felt about him. Despite the new awareness of his abilities, he still had a poor self-image of himself. And he thought others saw him in the same way. To add to his impression was Genevieve Saur's constant belittling and contemptuous looks aimed his way.

"You can't make a silk purse out of a sow's ear!" was one of her favorite epitaphs each time Syn-Jern tried something new and inevitably failed the first time around. That he continued to try until he had the lesson down pat, didn't change Genny's opinion of him, or his of himself.

"I'm not a quick learner," he sighed to Paddy one evening.

"Maybe not, but you do learn, Syn-Jern. That's what counts."

"Maybe the reason he doesn't learn all that fast is because he's dimwitted. Did that ever occur to you, Patrick?" Genny had taunted.

It was the first time since Syn-Jern's arrival at Montyne Cay that any of them had seen tears in his eyes. Genny's thoughtless words lashed out at the man's fragile self-pride and knocked it to the ground. No one there could know that his own mother had often made the same remark about him in his hearing.

Syn-Jern looked over at her with such a look of longing; both Weir and Patrick were stunned by the obvious emotions crossing their new friend's face. When he pushed back his chair and fled the table, neither man could look at the other.

"Could he be falling in love with her!" Patrick asked in an astonished voice later that evening as the two men had walked along the beach.

"He'd do better to embrace a Viper than love our Genny," Weir snarled, his anger at his sister having formed a red haze of fury around his vision. "The man's never had a woman ever speak to him with kindness! I could wring Genevieve's neck!"

Patrick recognized the danger behind Genny's actions. "And she's hurting him just like his mother did!"

"Damn her!" Weir spat, kicking at the sand. "I've talked to that little bitch until I'm blue in the face, and I can't make her understand what he must be feeling! I've forgiven him for being Giles Sorn's son; why the hell can't she?"

"He doesn't need anyone tearing him down, Weir; he desperately needs someone to build him up. Genny can ruin everything with the wrong words."

But when Patrick had tried talking to Genny, he'd gotten no further than her brother had.

"Suck up to him all you want, Patrick Kasella! He's my enemy and he always will be! Take the fool to Chrystallus, if you want. Leave him there for all I care; but don't expect me to lick his boots like you and Weir do!" Her anger was like a glowing ember threatening to erupt into a full-fledged forest fire. She flicked her gaze over him. "You know, I never realized it before, but the two of you could pass for brothers." She sniffed with disdain. "More's the pity for you, Kasella, for looking like the bastard."

"Why the hell can't you understand?" Patrick shouted. "He needs our help, damn it, and all you can do is insult him! He had nothing to do with what happened to your father. Weir knows that; why can't you see it?"

"I'm not a fool like my brother!" she snapped, slamming the door behind her exit.

ജ്ഞ

Preparing to sail within the next few days, the Wind Lass had a full compliment of crew.

Tarnes had been correct: Weir turned away more men than he would have needed to man two ships. There was even a waiting list of sailors who were more than eager to set off for Chrystallus with Syn-Jern Sorn, just in case a man got ill or for some reason changed his mind about going.

"It's like this, Cap'n," one man explained as he stood before Weir and Patrick. "We all seen how he's come along. We feel kinda like godparents to him, you know? There's been some of us who's taught him a thing or two. Mind ya, he's got a long way to go *afore* he can be a real pirate like us." The man puffed out his scrawny chest. "But he's learning. You have to admire the lad, now, don't you, Cap'n?"

"He may have been sired by old Duke Sorn; but the lad ain't nothing like that jackanapes!" another stated. "This boy's got heart! You see how he can climb that rigging?"

"And he be charmed, he be!" one of the Chalean sailors commented. "He be one of the Chosen! A man ain't afeared to sail with the likes of him! Why we had a full-blasted gale headed our way when we brought him aboard the Lass! Remember how the sea just went calm like all of a sudden?"

"That's cause he's a NightWind," Neevens told anyone who'd listen. "They be charmed, that's a certainty!"

It was true Syn-Jern had learned a lot from the pirates, but most of it he had already learned, and forgotten, as a young man in the Storm Warrior Society of his homeland: riding, the essentials of swordplay, the use of various weapons. In order to win his spurs, he had endured and done well enough at a variety of events on the tournament grounds. But he'd never won an event and he'd always suspected it was his father's influence, and money, that had eventually forced the judges to pass him when he was a boy; and his own wealth and quasi-social position in young adulthood. It would have been an embarrassment had he not been awarded his spurs.

Yet he had not learned the intricacies of knighthood. He had never learned how to use his sword with finesse, how to think each move in advance. His horsemanship was fair to middling, but under the expert tutelage of a Viragonian warrior, he came into his own on the back of a mighty gray stallion Weir gave him just a few days after the incident at the training ground.

"Sometimes it's just having the right horse, or the right weapon, Syn-Jern," the warrior said wisely. "If the weapon doesn't fit your hand like it was molded there, you can't fight as well with it as you can with one that feels like a natural extension of your own flesh."

"What are you going to call him?" Stevens asked, keeping well away from the mighty hooves that pawed at the ground near Syn-Jern's feet.

Syn-Jern's eyes shone with love and admiration as he stroked the horse's withers. "His name is Windchance," he whispered. He looked at Stevens. "It was the chance of the wind that brought me here. Without that storm that blew the Tamarind off course, I'd probably be back in the Labyrinth right now."

No one asked how he had escaped the penal colony and Syn-Jern did not volunteer the information; but the men of Montyne Cay found the fact that he had escaped the hellhole of Tyber's Isle, to be one more positive thing about the young man.

"You got to admire the lad, you do," Stevens swore. "Like I always say: you can't keep a good man down long!"

On the morning of the day they were to set sail for Chrystallus on the evening's tide, Syn-Jern set out on his own away from the compound in search of the mysterious sound he kept hearing from the jungle. He left the beach behind, walking deeper than he ever had before into the interior of Montyne Bay's inland. Before long he was out of sight of the beachside village and entering a forest so thick and lush, he had to fight his way through the foliage and undergrowth.

Pushing aside low-hanging branches of mango trees, he ducked under the rosy-red fruits and smiled as the early morning dew fell silently on his naked back and shoulders. The day was humid, so thick it was hard to breathe in the closeness amongst the foliage. Sweat dripped down his brow, ran from beneath his arms, and he swatted at the insects that came to taste him. His booted feet crunched over fallen dried palm fronds and squished tropical fruits that had partially splattered on the ground. The further he pushed into the forest, the thicker the growth around him, but in the distance, he could hear what he had gone there to find and so he struggled with the trees and shrubs and bushes, going deeper into the green-black lushness of the tropical forest.

Genevieve Saur followed close behind.

When she saw him sneaking away from the compound, furtively looking about him to see if he was being watched, the hair along her arms stirred.

"Just what the hell are you up to?" she'd whispered beneath her breath.

Falling in behind him, she was surprised when he set off into the grove of fruit trees. As he made his way deeper still into the stand of trees, she thought she'd found at last why he was there.

"You're going to meet someone, aren't you, Sorn?" Her lip curled. "Some whore from the village, no doubt."

Genny had not believed her brother or Patrick's adamant and emphatic assurances that Syn-Jern Sorn was not sleeping with one of the village women.

"He's a man, isn't he?" she scoffed. "No, let me rephrase that: he has the proper equipment, doesn't he?"

For a moment her quarry seemed to disappear in a black veil of foliage, but when Genny stumbled her way across roots and fallen branches, she caught sight of him ahead of her where the growth was beginning to thin out. So intent was she on following him and finding out just exactly what he was up to, she didn't hear the sound that had been beckoning Syn-Jern Sorn since the day he had arrived at Montyne Cay.

He wasn't really sure when he became aware of being followed. He hadn't heard anyone behind him, but his sixth sense seemed to be coming alive the deeper into the forest he walked, and he could almost feel an invisible set of eyes watching him. He hid behind a tree at one point, hoping to catch sight of his pursuer, but he could see nothing moving among the mango trees and sweet shrubs.

"You know I'm following you, don't you, Sorn?" Genny thought aloud as she crouched under a wild hog plum tree. She saw him looking her way and held her breath. When his vision swept away, she let the air out of her lungs slowly, softly. She stayed in that one position, her thighs cramping her, until she saw him shrug. "That's right," she thought, a jealousy she did not understand making her livid with rage. "Go on. Go meet your mistress, you son-of-a-bitch!"

He knew someone was there. He could almost smell them. But for some reason he found hard to understand, he wasn't afraid. Whoever was trailing him didn't mean him any harm; he was sure of that. He knew he would have sensed danger had it been following him. Making the decision to go on into the sparser reaches of the forest, he turned his back on his bird dog and started the slight climb upward toward the sound that had intrigued him for months.

"Where the hell are you going?" she thought as she clawed her way up a steep incline of black, rotted and compacted leaves. Her booted toes dug into the soft ground covering and squished wetly. The smell was musty and not all that pleasant and she wrinkled her nose with disgust as her right foot slipped and she slid down on her knees into the muck.

Syn-Jern had just reached the top of the incline when he heard a soft explosion of salty language and stopped dead still in his tracks. His head whipped around and he peered back down the rolling mound of leaves, slippery bank and twisted, exposed roots. He couldn't see anyone, but took the one tailing him to be a young boy for the voice had been high-pitched and not all that accustomed to using foul language.

He frowned. It must be one of the village boys who often seemed to stroll by him more often than was necessary.

He made the decision to lose the boy on one of the many switchback paths that appeared to spiral further upward. He slipped easily onto one of the paths for a few feet, doubled back and stepped gingerly over a thick root that was protruding from the ground like a varicose vein on an old woman's leg. He balanced his way across the root and then stepped silently onto another pathway. He picked up his pace and hurried on; eager to find his way to the mysterious sound that beckoned him.

Genny stood up and dusted the rotting leaves and slime from her cords. Her mouth was twisted in a hateful line of revulsion as black goo came away on her palms.

"Ugh!" she spat, wiping her hands on a nearby tree trunk. She scraped the fecund-smelling goo off her hands, looked up the incline with a malevolent gleam of pure vengeance, and dug her toes into the slick leaf compaction once more.

He was almost there. He could hear it clearly now. He cocked his blond head to one side. What could cause such a sound, he thought? It wasn't a threatening sound, but a pleasant, calming sound and he could hardly wait to see what could inspire such longing in him.

Reaching the top of the incline, Genny almost lost her balance and tumbled backward as she took her last step. Cartwheeling her arms, crying out with more fury than frustration, she was able to stumble forward, away from the precarious position in which she had almost been thrust. Her anger turned to deep, irrational rage as she swung her head about. She saw where his boots had left light indention in one of several branching pathways, no doubt caused by the many deer and small animals on the peninsula. She started toward that path, but her eye caught sight of deeper tracks to her right and she walked to that section of ground and peered closely. There were no tracks going to the path, but tracks going up the pathway. She looked back along the ground leading from the first pathway to the one where she was standing. A tight, sneering smile touched her mouth.

"You walked along the root, didn't you, you bastard?" she said softly. "You wanted me to follow that pathway, didn't you?" She looked up the pathway he had obviously taken.

"You're not as smart as you think you are!"

There was a sharp bend in the pathway and the sound was loud, very loud there. He struggled up, gripping a thick vine that draped down from one of the tall trees overhead, and pulled himself up a small ledge, swung clumsily around the bend, and—

The sight took his breath away. His blue-black eyes opened wide, his mouth dropped open. He would later swear the heart inside his chest even ceased to beat. So stunned was he by what he was seeing, he sat down heavily on the loamy soil and stared with rapt attention.

The going was hard up the path the bastard had taken, she thought, as she heaved her light frame along the black ground. Now and again she had to fumble for protruding roots, a draping vine, and even a small shrub, to keep from tumbling back down the pathway. Her legs and thighs were cramping; her shirt was plastered to her panting chest. Sweat drizzled into her eyes and the salt stung her. Insects darted at her, bumped into her face and neck. Something was crawling inside her boot, but she was too afraid to stop long enough to dislodge whatever it was for fear she'd fall for sure. With every step she took she prayed whatever was making its home in her boot wasn't deadly.

"Godawful son-of-a-bitching bastard!" she seethed as she crawled up the last few feet of the pathway and spied the sharp turning in the course. She reached out for one of the thicker vines.

He'd never seen anything so lovely in his life. From top to bottom, the sight was one of extraordinary beauty. The sound, one he had only sensed in the village below, was a mighty roar here where he sat. He sighed, taking in the calming influence, the pleasant smell, and the awe-inspiring sight that seemed to have called him to view it.

When she finally was able to pivot herself around the bend in the pathway, after several unsuccessful attempts that had left her dangling and spinning from the vine, she landed with a crash behind him, almost falling right on top of him where he sat.

Startled by the movement behind him even though he couldn't hear it for the sound rushing in front of him, Syn-Jern turned and gaped at Genevieve Saur as she struggled to her feet.

"What the hell are you doing here?" he asked, stunned as her angry face lifted.

Genny was about to lie into him, to call him every name she could think of. She opened her mouth to do just that when her attention was caught, and held, by the sight just beyond him. Her head tilted upward until her neck could go no further on her shoulders.

He stood up, watching her expression, somehow pleased by it. She was as transfixed with the sight as he was. When her head finally lowered, her eyes found his, and he could see the same awe registering on her face that he knew must be on his own.

"Beautiful, isn't it?" he shouted to be heard. She shook her head, not understanding him. He walked closer to her, leaned toward her. "Beautiful?"

She could only nod as she tore her gaze from him and scanned the lovely, breathtaking scene from top to bottom and back again. She stepped around him, walked closer to the rim where he had been sitting and peered cautiously over the side. She gasped and stepped back, almost collided with him.

"Careful!" he yelled. He wasn't even thinking when he put his hands on her upper arms and pulled her back, away from the sheer drop before them.

Genevieve was so awed by the sight she didn't feel his hands on her, only nodded as he drew her away from any danger that could be lurking near the drop off.

"Waterfall," she murmured.

"What?"

She cleared her throat, turned to look up at him. She raised her voice. "It's a waterfall."

He nodded and turned back to the cascading water. He'd heard of such things; it was said Virago was a land that boasted as many as a thousand of the natural wonders, but he'd never seen one. He'd never even seen a picture of a waterfall in a book.

"How high do you think it is?" he shouted.

Genny lifted her gaze upward. "At least two thousand, maybe three thousand feet," she yelled back.

He eased around her and leaned over to look down into the half-moon shaped cove where the waterfall fell. White water rolled and dipped, surged and leapt over the rocks at the base of the cliff, swept eastward toward a wide stream with bubbling waves and ripples that rushed away behind a turning in the stream. The sound was deafening, a roar that defied description, and he was mesmerized by the way the water leapt and danced in the small cove.

She stared at his back, thinking how easy it would be to push him over the edge. No one would know. No one would ever find him in the rapids down below, and if they did, there would be precious little left to identify once his body had been tumbled and dragged over the sharp rocks. Her fingers flexed at her sides. She licked her lips, took in small, sharp little breaths, and took a step forward.

He took that moment to turn to her, his face bright with excitement. "It's the most beautiful..." he started to tell her when he noticed the look on her face.

He blinked.

For a long moment they stared at one another. He was so close to the edge there was no way he could get around her if she reached out to push him. They both knew he was vulnerable, in greater danger than he had been since her brother had found him. Her face was set, cold, her loathing of him evident in the way she looked at him. She was standing rigidly, poised, and coiled like a spring to rush at him. Her hatred of him was like a stench in the air around them.

"What are you waiting for?" he whispered, knowing that even though she couldn't hear him, she knew what he was saying. "Do it."

Genny didn't want to see the pain in his eyes. She didn't want to see the exact moment that he placed his life in her hands. She didn't want to hear the loss of hope in his voice, but despite not being able to actually hear his words, she felt them. She knew if she were to reach out to push him, he wouldn't resist. He wouldn't try to take her with him when he fell. His hands were hanging loosely at his sides, he was watching her, his fear on his face, but he would make no move to save himself from her.

"What kind of man are you?" she shouted at him. His silent stare ripped into her deeply than any dagger could have. "Damn you! Damn you to hell!"

He watched her turn, saw her fling herself at the vine that had brought her to the place where they were standing, saw her swing out into space, out of his sight, and he ran after her. He reached the decline just as she slid down the vine and landed on her back at the bottom. He didn't think as he leapt for another vine to follow her down. The pithy fiber burnt his palms as he dropped hand over hand down it, but he barely noticed. Just as he reached the bottom, he saw her running at a hard clip down the pathway away from him.

"Genny!" he called after her, afraid she'd tumble and fall over some hidden root, hurt herself badly in her headlong rush to get away from him, to erase him from her sight.

She could hear him thundering after her as she skirted the trees, ducked under low-hanging branches and slid on her rump down mounds of rotting vegetation. She could hear him calling her name and the sound was like a steel blade digging into her heart.

"Genny, wait!"

She thought it was sweat running into her eyes, blinding her, but it wasn't. It was her tears. Her anger pushed her forward, faster. She'd had him in her sights and had let him go! She cursed as she ran. He could have been at the bottom of the cove, drowning, if she'd only had the courage to push!

"Genny!"

One moment she was running, the next she was falling into space, her arms waving as she dropped like a lead weight. She didn't even have time to cry out, to make a sound before she landed with a horrible thud that knocked the breath from her lungs.

He saw her go over and his breath stopped. He shouted her name and plunged into the section of mango grove where she had been running. Carefully, he skidded to a stop, reaching out to grab hold of a tree branch just in time. The branch halted his forward rush and kept him from falling. He scrambled to hold on to it, swinging back from the drop off, crashing hard into the side of the steep hole. But the branch snapped with a sharp crack and he went sliding belly-first down the side of the hole.

She rolled to her side, doubled up, trying to breathe. Her eyes were watering, her lungs parching. She heard him crashing down the side of the hole where she had fallen and snapped her head around to see him tumbling sideways toward her. She managed to crab-walk away from him as he landed with a soft thud at her feet.

He was unconscious for well over two hours.

Genny was beginning to think he would never wake up. There was a thin trickle of blood at his right temple and he was lying so still, she was positive he had suffered some severe internal damage. Not wanting to even so much as touch him for fear she'd bash his head in with one of the many large rocks strewn about, she repeatedly called his name, cursed him, insulted him, and finally fell into a sullen silence when he didn't respond. When his lids flickered, when he groaned, she heaved a sigh of relief.

"Wake up!" she hissed at him, tossing a stick at his chest.

Syn-Jern opened his eyes and stared up into a canopy of thick black leaves. The sun was low in the sky, the shadows around him creeping in. He felt something strike his cheek and turned his head that way to see Genevieve Saur glaring at him.

"Just how the hell do you suppose we get out of here?" she snarled.

## Chapter Four

"HAVE YOU SEEN GENNY?" WEIR ASKED ONE OF THE VILLAGE WOMEN AS she scrubbed her clothing at one of the large cook pots.

The woman glanced up and shook her head.

"I haven't seen Syn-Jern this morning, either," Patrick remarked.

"They gods-be-damned sure ain't together!" Stevens spat as he pushed away from a tall palm. "He most likely went looking for that sound he thought he heard."

"What sound?" Paddy asked.

"Angel Falls, I reckon," the washerwoman told him. She smiled coyly at Paddy. "It be a waterfall, Milord. Would you like to go see it?"

Paddy frowned. "Not with you."

"If you see Genny, tell her I need her on board before sunset," Weir informed the others.

"That is if she's going."

"She'll be going!" Stevens growled.

Patrick fell into step beside his friend as Weir headed for the ship. "Think she followed him."

Weir's scowl was dark. "I know damned well the little busybody followed him!"

"You don't think she'd...well, you know, do something to him, do you?"

Weir stopped dead still in his tracks and turned to stare at his old friend. "You don't think she would, do you?"

"I don't know, Weir. She doesn't like him." Patrick chewed on his lip. "Do you think we should try and find them?"

They stared at one another for a moment.

"Let's go," Weir snarled.

ꕥ

He tried to sit up.

It was a mistake.

"Oh, my god!" he gasped, his left hand going to his right rib cage.

Genny looked at him with scorn. "Did you get a boo-boo?"

It felt as though his entire right side had caved in. If there weren't any broken ribs, it would be a miracle. He could feel something grating inside him as he tried once more to sit up.

"Shit!" he spat.

"Oh, for crying out loud!" Genny snapped, coming to her knees. "What the hell's wrong?"

He managed to turn his head further toward her and fixed her with a look that could have passed for pure astonishment. "I think I've broken some ribs."

"Is that all?" she mocked. She locked her gaze with his and lifted one side of her mouth in a smirk. "Serves you right for what you did to Paddy!"

He groaned, more for exasperation with her than actual pain, although he had plenty of that. He tried to take a deep breath only to find the expansion of his ribs an excruciating agony. He gasped and quickly let his breath out as far as it would go.

"Get up and get us out of here," Genny told him, standing up and dusting the clinging leaves and soil from her cords. When he didn't respond, she walked over to him and stared down at him. She nudged his thigh with her boot. "I said get up, Sorn."

He looked at her. "Go away."

Her eyebrows shot up. "Go...away?" she asked, her tone of voice letting him know she thought she had misunderstood him.

"Aye. Go away." He was panting with pain and unable to understand why the woman just stood there, standing with her hands on her hips, glowering at him.

"Get up." It was a curt, staccato burst of command.

He stared at her. "I can't."

"Aye, you can!" she retaliated. She nudged him again with her boot. "It'll be dark soon, and we're set to sail at moonrise."

"Then go," he told her. The thought of asking her to tell someone where he was crossed his mind, but he knew she probably wouldn't do it. Eventually someone would come looking for him.

Genny's mouth dropped open and she sputtered. "I can't get up that incline by myself! You got me in this predicament and you're going to get me out!"

"I got you in this predicament?" he asked in shocked disbelief.

"Aye, you did! Now get the hell up and get me out of it!"

"You followed me! Remember?" he snapped at her. Not only was his side hurting, his head was throbbing. He put up a hand to his forehead, felt something wet, pulled his fingers down, and stared at the crimson staining his fingers. "I'm bleeding."

"Oh, for the love of Alel! It's only a slight scratch!" She bent over and grabbed his wrist and tried to jerk him up.

"Shit!" he screeched again, jerking his hand back, wishing he hadn't for the pain doubled in his chest. He gaped at her. "What the hell did you do that for?"

"I told you to get up, Sorn!" She looked about the hole in that they had tumbled. "It's getting dark!"

"You're going to have to help me get up."

Genny snorted. "In your dreams, Sorn!"

No one had ever accused Syn-Jern Sorn of having a temper, he certainly never had exhibited one before; but the infuriating demoness standing over him could bring out the worst in any man. He glared at her in the late afternoon light and ground his teeth together.

"If you want out of this gods-be-damned hole, then you're going to have to help me up. It's your choice, Lady Genevieve."

She didn't want to touch him. Just thinking of doing so made her flesh crawl. But she didn't think the clumsy bastard could get up on his own. Chances were he'd need help getting up the incline, as well. Sighing heavily, hatefully, she extended her hand. When he didn't immediately take it, she shook it.

"Well? I don't have all night, Sorn!"

He wanted to scream at the bitch, refuse the hand she was grudgingly holding out to him, but he couldn't be so choosy. Instead, with supreme effort, a whole lot of pain, and a great amount of sweat, he managed to grip her fingers, then clasp her slender hand in his own. He was surprised by her strength as she dug her boots into the soft earth and pulled him up with a grunt.

"God, but you're heavy!" she snarled, stepping back from him.

He ignored her insult, only one of a hundred or more over the past seven months, and looked around them. The incline wasn't as steep as he'd thought, but it would be hell climbing to the top with his ribs throbbing and grating together as they were.

"Well?" Genny sneered. "What the hell are you waiting for? An engraved invitation, Duke Syn-Jern?"

He flicked his eyes over her before looking back to the clump of vines he'd been surveying. "I'm no longer a Duke."

"Pity, that!" she snipped.

He walked gingerly over to the vines and reached up to tug on them. The effort brought fresh sweat and pain to his face. He groaned again, putting his right hand to his ribcage.

"You're such a baby!" she snapped at him.

He squeezed his lips tightly shut to keep from shouting at her.

"Sorn?" she spat, the one word full of contempt.

"I hurt, woman," he told her.

"Well, so did Paddy!" she reminded him.

He turned around and looked at her. When he saw the way she was staring back at him, he let out a tired, defeated sigh.

"I'll hold the vine steady if you can climb up it," she taunted.

"And then what?" he asked, not sure he could climb.

"Then you can pull me up."

He snorted. Another mistake. The giving in to his ill humor made his ribcage spiral with bursts of fiery pain.

"Oh, for the love of Alel!" she shouted. Her footsteps were heavy and full of scorn as she tramped over to the vine and jerked it out of his hands. "I'll climb it myself!"

He had just enough time to get out of her way before she dug the toes of her boots into the soft slide of the incline and began to climb up with ease. He stood there, staring at her, watching her pull herself up with hardly any effort.

"You little imp," he said under his breath. He was still staring at her as she gained the top and looked down at him with triumphant. Genny could see the anger on his face and it pleased her. She hadn't really been sure why she was taunting him so for she was perfectly aware that he'd been hurt in the fall. Her motives had seemed clear to her at first: torment the man as his family had tormented hers. But his obvious hurt tempered her vengeance. When he didn't seem inclined to get up, she began to realize that only insults would penetrate the self-pity the man seemed to be steeped in.

"You intend to stay there all night?" she called down to him. "Coward that you are?"

Maybe it was the scoffing in her voice or the put down that made him grip the vine and try desperately to ignore the excruciating agony in his ribs. Or maybe it was just the thought of letting another woman get the best of him that made him try to climb out of the hole. Whatever it was, it worked. Despite a great deal of panting, sweating, grunting, and whimpering with pain; slipping and sliding more downward than going upward, he managed to reach the top just as the sun was bobbing on the horizon.

"You ought to get someone to teach you how to climb!" she spat at him as he staggered away from the lip of the hill and sat down heavily on a fallen palm trunk.

"Can you find your way back by yourself?" he asked, having had all he could take of her vitriolic tongue.

"Would I have been waiting around for you if I could?" she asked, knowing full well she could have if need be.

He sighed, pushed himself up with some difficulty, and with a slight grunt, flung out his left hand in a gentlemanly manner. "Then allow me, Mam'selle." He called on his last reserves of strength and began to walk toward the path that had led him into the grove.

ꕤ

"I hear it, but I don't know which way to go," Patrick grumbled. He and Weir had been following several different animal paths into the heart of the mango grove, but all of them had ended up leading into dead-end walls of thick, impassable foliage.

"It's getting dark, Paddy," Weir said in a worried voice. "Maybe we should go back to the village and see if they're back."

Patrick nodded. All the two of them needed to do was get lost in the overgrowth and have to have the village out searching for them as well.

"If they're not back by the time we to sail, we'll just have to come looking for them with torches," Patrick advised.

ꕤ

It had taken him over two hours to reach the waterfall, he thought as he led the way down an almost non-existent path then another hour on the top running after her. He totaled that up and figured he was right in assuming that by the time he fell into the hole, they'd been in the jungle nearly two and half-hours.

"How long was I out?" he managed to ask her through the pain stabbing into his side.

"Two, three hours, I guess," she shot back, her voice letting him know she'd been very unhappy about him sleeping so long.

He nodded. That made five hours. They'd been walking for thirty minutes or so now for the sun was barely on the rim of the horizon. He could just make it out through the lush fronds. That meant they had at least an hour to an hour and a half of trekking through a dark grove, unable to see their way.

"You've screwed us royally, haven't you?" she taunted.

Never had he wanted to strangle a woman in his life. If truth had been told, Syn-Jern was afraid of women. They'd made him afraid of them all his life. But this one he could make an exception for.

"Did you hear that?"

"I heard you," he mumbled. He was sweating fiercely and without thinking began unbuttoning his shirt.

"Listen!" she insisted.

"All I hear is your wicked little mouth flapping!" he pronounced, stripping the shirt from his body.

"No, stupid!" she hissed, reaching out to pull on his belt. As she did, her fingernails dug into his flesh.

"Damn it, woman! That hurt!" he groaned, twisting away.

Genny's eyes widened as she took in the heavily muscled chest only a foot from her face. Unconsciously, she licked her lips.

"I think you drew blood," he mumbled, craning his neck to look at his back. "I'll probably get gangrene and—"

"Shut up and listen!" she told him, trying to ignore the crisp hair between his nipples.

He let out a long breath. He listened as he had been ordered to do and heard faint voices.

"Someone from the village?" she asked.

He listened closely. He couldn't make out the words, but he could make out the accent. He turned toward the sound.

"What are you waiting for?" She prodded his bare back with a stiff finger. "Call out to them or I will."

"No."

His answer wasn't at all what she wanted to hear. Disgust at him roiled in her gut and she opened her mouth to shout, but found her lips firmly covered by his hand as he pulled her to him, slamming her body into his, and dragged her back into a thick clump of bushes.

He was in agony as she squirmed against him, her elbows digging into his stomach as her fingers pried at the fingers he had clamped tightly over her mouth. He was panting from his effort to control her and couldn't speak, couldn't warn her. It was all he could do not to scream when her teeth bit into the fleshy part of his palm.

Genny could feel his sweaty chest against her own damp shirt and the touch was too much to bear. He smelled of wet, rotting leaves and a manly odor, not all that unpleasant a smell, but something she didn't want on her. She could taste his blood on her lips and his warm breath in her ear only made her clamp her teeth into him deeper.

"Leave off, woman!" he hissed, dragging in his breath. Pain was now eating into his palm as it nibbled at his ribs. "Those aren't our men out there!"

She stopped biting him, but kept his flesh in her mouth, not letting him pull his palm free of her teeth. She also stopped moving in his grasp and cocked her ear toward the sound of voices that were closer now.

Syn-Jern didn't dare pull her any further back into the camouflage of the bushes. The men advancing on them would hear any sound they made now. He prayed the girl would heed the warning in his voice as he whispered to her once more.

"Serenians."

Beside herself and Weir, Tarnes was the only other Serenian on Montyne Cay. If these men were Serenians, and she knew now they must be for she could hear the accent of her homeland, they were invaders.

Or worse: part of the armada the village had always feared would one day arrive.

She let go of his palm, heard his sigh of relief, but could still taste his blood on her lips. The bite must have gone deeper than she'd realized for her lips were slick with a salty wetness.

"All right?" he whispered as he moved his hand slightly away from her mouth.

Genny nodded and his hand came away. She was about to turn her head up, to try to speak to him, when the bushes moved only a few feet from where they hid, and she saw five men pass their hiding place. With the luck of the gods, none of them looked their way.

"Ain't nothing on this, Commander," they heard one of the men grumble. "We've made reconnaissance runs over this way before. If there was a village, we'd have found it by now."

"There was a jolly boat beached back there, mister!" a gruff, uncompromising voice snarled. "If there isn't a village, there is a survivor from the Tamarind. We can only hope it was one of our men."

Syn-Jern tensed. These were not invaders, an advance unit of the armada. These men were Tribunal Transporters.

Genny realized the spot they were in, as well. Tarnes had warned Weir not to tow home the three Tamarind jolly boats that were seaworthy. Weir hadn't listened. He'd awarded one to each of the three highest bidders and no doubt the one these men had found on the western shore of the peninsula was kept there by a man wanting an escape route if the armada ever came to Montyne Cay.

"Well, keep looking for anything that might suggest we've a survivor. The light will be gone soon and we'll go back to the ship to make the tide."

The voices and the footsteps moved further away from Genny and Syn-Jern, but neither moved, too afraid that the least sound would give them away.

Syn-Jern's heart was thundering in his chest. He knew a fear so dark, so primitive, it was like being buried alive. He had forgotten the pain in his ribs and the throbbing pain in his palm. Here was another pain: the pain of memory; the pain of ten long years at hard labor; of terrible humiliating abuse, starvation, and inhuman loneliness.

Genny could feel his heart against her back. The man was clammy with sweat; he was trembling from head to toe. She could hear his quick little intakes of breath, the panting of an animal gone to ground.

And she almost felt sorry for him.

The voices died away; the sounds of movement ceased. A cautious turning of their heads found no prying eye looking for them.

"Are they gone?" she whispered.

He shook his head, not knowing. He eased away from her, feeling the cotton of her shirt sticking to his bare chest.

"You've got to get back to the village and warn them," he told her.

"Me?" The one word was a mere hissing of breath but it conveyed to him her surprise and fear of going on alone.

"Listen to me!" he whispered. "With my ribs like this, I can't make good time. You can. You've got to get back and let them know these bastards are close by."

She turned around and faced him, looked up into his face and was stunned to see stark terror registering. He was quivering so violently; his teeth were clicking together.

"They're on the other side of the peninsula," she reminded him. "Weir won't sail without us. If those men sail at the tide..."

"Damn it, woman, think!" he spat at her. "Two of the other ships are also sailing at the tide! They'll cross paths down by the reef! Do you want that?"

Genny flinched. She hadn't thought of that. "What if they catch me?"

For a long moment he didn't speak, just looked into her face, searching, not finding what he truly wanted to see there. He shook his head. "They won't."

Why she trusted his words she didn't know, but trust them she did. She made up her mind. "Don't leave this spot," she warned him. "I can find my way back here after those motherless bastards are gone. Do you hear?"

He nodded. His gaze swept her face and then he seemed to change before her very eyes. A raw, animal brightness came over his face. "Go," he said, his lips drawn back over his teeth. "Now!"

She slipped away from him, as quietly as she could. Her boots made hardly any sound at all as she threaded her way under low branches and faded from sight. He heard her for a moment more and then there was no sound of her leaving at all. He was beginning to relax, beginning to feel everything was going to be all right, when he heard a crash, a soft, feminine sound, and knew she'd fallen.

"What was that?"

His head snapped around toward the shout from beyond the stand of taller palms. They'd heard!

"Over there! Through that clump of bushes!"

For one heart-stopping moment he stood there, his head turning from side to side, his breathing harsh, drawing into his lungs so quickly he could feel himself getting lightheaded. Adrenaline was pumping through his system; sweat was oozing out of every pour.

"Do you see anything?"

The voice was close, too close, to where he knew Genevieve had fallen. If they caught her, there was no doubt in his mind what they would do first before asking questions.

"I hear running!"

"Go, Genny," he whispered. "Run, girl, run!"

"Which way is the sound coming from?"

He knew it wouldn't be long before they caught up with her if they kept on the same path they were going. If they caught her...

Syn-Jern stepped out from where he was hiding. He took a deep breath and bellowed as though he were in great pain.

Genny stopped, spun around. The sound that had brought her up short came again and she heard a voice shout: a voice only a few feet from her.

"Over here! He must have fallen!"

"Syn-Jern, no!" she hissed. She looked toward the path that led back to the village, looked back to the place she figured Syn-Jern to be. She hesitated, listening to the voices moving away from her, knew he'd sacrificed himself so she could get away. Her world whipped to a halt when she heard a gruff voice call out in triumphant:

"I've got him!"

## Chapter Five

THERE WAS SO MUCH PAIN IN HIS BODY HE COULD BARELY MOVE. THEY dragged him up from the ground where they had found him kneeling and thrust a torch to his face.

"Who are you?" the man with the gruff voice snarled at him. "Where is the rest of the crew of the Tamarind?"

He tried very hard not to groan, not to show the pain he was feeling. He knew better. Men such as these fed on pain, thrived on it, devoured it. To show pain before them was to invite more.

"I'm the only survivor," he managed to whisper through teeth clenched hard against the agony in his side.

The two men holding him by his upper arms pulled him up straighter and his groan of pain was like a burst of sunshine on the gruff-speaking man in charge.

"You hurt?"

He shook his head, tried to block out the ripping, tearing agony now spreading all the way down his right hip.

"Aye, but you are, aren't you?" The man ran his attention down Syn-Jern's naked chest and noticed the way the man before him leaned to the right. He snaked out a hard, callused hand and placed it none too gently on Syn-Jern's right ribcage. The instant flare of a groan seemed to please the gruff man.

"Favoring his side, is he, Commander?" one of the men holding Syn-Jern laughed.

"It appears that way, Mister Hawkins."

Syn-Jern's gut clenched. "Don't," he begged, fearing what this man's knowledge might do to him.

"What you afraid of, boy?" the guard on his right giggled. He twisted Syn-Jern's arm cruelly and had to brace himself quickly for the young man's legs went out from under him with the pain. "Here now! Stand yourself up!" He yanked fiercely on Syn-Jern's arm and cast a quick, sadistic grin to the man in charge when the prisoner screamed in agony.

"It appears our survivor hasn't fared all that well, Mister Hawkins," the gruff man chortled. "Let's get him back to the ship and see if we can't make him feel better."

"No," Syn-Jern whispered.

"You got reason to fear us, boy?" Hawkins snarled in his ear. "Maybe you jumped ship, eh? Maybe there was a mutiny on the Tamarind and you was the only one to get out of it alive?"

The Commander of the Tribunal Transporters was peering closely into the prisoner's face and he recognized fear when he saw it. After all, he'd shipped many a prisoner to the Labyrinth and that was where fear was a priceless commodity. A sudden thought came into his head and he suddenly reached out his left hand to grip Syn-Jern's right arm, pulling it up and outward, turning it over so that the underside of the prisoner's arm was facing upward.

Syn-Jern screamed again, his ribs an excruciating band of burning fire all along the right side of his body. His knees buckled and he was dimly aware of the men having trouble keeping him from sagging to the ground.

"Hold that torch down here!" the Commander ordered as he bent forward over Syn-Jern's right wrist. He peered closely at the dirty flesh that was smeared with caked mud. Once the torchlight illuminated the extended arm, he used his thumb to rub at the mud.

"Is he marked, Commander?" Hawkins asked.

A slow, malevolent smile touched the gruff man's lips. There was a look on his face that would have rivaled any demons this side of hell. "Aye, you're marked, aren't you?" The smile grew as he noticed pale lips begin to tremble with sheer panic. He brought his other hand up to grip, to open, Syn-Jern's clutched fist and bend the fingers back, ignoring the groan his action caused. The fingers of his callused right hand patted the tattoo on the prisoner's wrist, trailed down into the flexing palm, probed.

"Please," came the feeble cry for leniency as he felt the man's index finger making a tiny circle in his palm.

The Commander clucked his tongue, shook his head as though chastising a wayward child. "You've run away before, haven't you?"

Syn-Jern wanted to cry. "Please." His voice was lost and it sounded so young and so terribly without hope.

The Commander nodded. He removed his hand from Syn-Jern's palm and reached up to caress the pale face.

"Don't worry," the gruff man said in a soothing voice. "We're going to take you home."

He chuckled as Syn-Jern whimpered. "Now, don't you worry! I'm sure the Commandant will be only too happy to see you."

"We gonna get to crucify him, Commander?" Hawkins asked. His voice was eager, almost panting with glee.

The Commander gently stroked Syn-Jern's face. He smiled. "Of course."

## Chapter Six

SHE CAME STUMBLING INTO THE VILLAGE, HER LONG DARK HAIR FLOWING behind her, her gray eyes huge in a face gone pale with fear. She'd been running for nearly an hour, crashing through the jungle, dodging trees and low-hung branches she had only narrowly missed in her headlong rush for help. She'd dared not call out, scream for help, for she knew she would be heard. Her feet could go no faster in the muck of rotting foliage, scattered branches, up-thrust roots, and creeping vines. Before she'd gone very far, a stitch of pain whipped up her left side and brought even more tears. By the time she stumbled into the clearing where the huts of Montyne Cay lay scattered in a half-moon sweep before the moonlit sea, she was panting, exhausted, and more afraid than she had ever been in her life.

"Get Saur!" she heard someone shout as she began to plummet forward. Strong hands reached out to break her fall, lift her gasping, trembling body from the ground.

"Genny!"

She turned her head and saw her brother running toward her, Paddy close at his heels. Her lips moved before her straining throat could call out.

"What happened?" Weir was at her side.

"Syn-Jern..." she gasped, one hand going out to her brother in pleading. "Must...help...Syn-Jern..."

The man holding Weir Saur's sister could feel the young woman quivering in his arms. He looked to Patrick Kasella for direction and the Ionarian leapt forward, whipped Genny out of his arms.

"Where the hell were you?" Weir shouted at her.

"You've...got...to...help...him," she whispered, her breath not having returned, her exhaustion making her entire body numb with fear.

"Where is he, Genny?" Patrick asked as he shifted her light weight in his arms. He was staring down at her, his lips pursed. "What happened out there."

From the tone of his voice, Genny knew he thought she had harmed Syn-Jern in some way. She shook her head violently. "Have...him. Captured...him."

"Who? What are you talking about?" Weir hissed, reaching out to grasp her arm.

"Transporters..." she managed to say. "Serenian."

Patrick's blood ran cold. He gripped her closer to him. "Where? Here? Here on the peninsula?"

"Found...the...jolly...boat."

Weir blanched white, shifted his eyes to Tarnes who was standing behind Patrick. There was no accusation on the old man's face, but there was a look that Weir understood all too well.

"Where is the ship docked?" Patrick asked her.

She shook her head. "Never...saw...it."

"We've got to find him!" Jarl Stevens reminded them. "They'll see that damned tattoo on the boy and you know what they'll do to him!"

Patrick knew. He swung Genny down, shoved her gracelessly into Norbert Tarnes arms. "Who'll go with us?" he called out for every man on Montyne Cay had gathered around them by this time.

"Me!"

"I'll go."

"What are we waiting for?"

"Let's go after the lad!"

Genny pulled away from Tarnes and grabbed Patrick's arm.

"You...don't...know...where!"

He didn't even think before he reacted. His hand shot out and he gripped Genny's shoulder in a punishing, painful clasp, spun her around, and shoved her toward the jungle. "Show us!"

# Chapter Seven

THE FIRST LASH TOOK HIM LOW ACROSS THE SMALL OF HIS BACK. THE second trailed from the nape of his neck to his left shoulder. The third cut a skipping line close beside the second.

"Ain't he a pretty sight!" one of the crewmembers giggled as the fourth and fifth lashes tattooed an X from shoulder to hip, opposite shoulder to opposite hip.

It wasn't so much that he could feel the lashing: his back had been covered with built-up scar tissue long ago. And it wasn't even that he could feel the godawful tearing in his palms anymore, either; that had long ago subsided to a dull ache. What hurt him the most was the pull of his body as he sagged from the yardarm.

"Make him scream, Hawk!" someone called out. "Make him scream!"

The spikes through the backs of his hands as he was nailed to the wood had hurt far worse than the first time he'd been crucified. That time, the Captain of the Vortex had hammered the dull spikes through his palms. The pain had been bad, but not nearly as bad as this time.

"Bet you can't stripe him wrist to shoulder, Hawkins!"

The sailor would have lost the bet.

"How 'bout straight across his shoulders!"

Hawkins showed his expertise with admirable skill.

His ribs were a pain separate from everything else. The sagging of his body was putting more and more pressure on ribs he knew were broken. If they hadn't been before they'd dragged him on board, they sure as hell were when they'd kicked him a few times.

"Open your mouth and scream, pretty boy!"

"Cut his ass down and I'll give him something to scream about!" one of the older crewmembers leered as he rubbed the filthy crotch of his tattered breeches.

His breathing was beginning to fade, now. It wouldn't be long before he passed out. He hadn't been able to draw a decent breath into his lungs since the tenth lash had curled around his left forearm.

He was suffocating and he knew it.

"What's the matter, Your Lordship? Cat got your tongue?"

The howling laughter at the remark jarred through his brain, penetrated the white fog of his agony. His eyes flickered open and he stared sightlessly ahead of him. Tiny darts of red light played just outside the perimeter of his vision.

"Slap that lash up side his pretty face, Hawk! He didn't shave so close this morning!"

The Commander had been standing close by, his feet planted firmly apart, his arms crossed over his chest. He thoroughly enjoyed watching Hawkins wield the cat-'o-nine. The man was an expert. He'd once seen Hawkins flay a man alive, inch by bloody inch, scream by blood-curdling scream, until there was nothing left but a pulpy ooze running the decks. There was nothing like observing a man who knew his job and did it well.

But the last remark cut through the Commander's pleasure and he frowned. He turned his head toward the speaker.

"What did you say, Jamison?"

The sailor cut a quick look to the Commander and then at his fellow shipmates. "I just told him to..."

"You said something about him not having shaved?"

Jamison ducked his head, not seeing what harm the remark could have caused. "Well, he ain't got no beard, just a wee bit of stubble, Commander; I don't see—"

"Stop!"

Hawkins arm stilled in mid-strike and he jerked his head toward the Commander. Blood from the whip's thongs slipped down the rawhide and trickled down his upheld arm. He lowered it, shook off the telltale red wetness.

The Commander trod heavily to the prisoner, grabbed a handful of thick blond hair, and dragged the man's head back.

"How many others are back there?" he bellowed into Syn-Jern's pain-ravaged face. When there was no answer, he twisted his fingers viciously in the thick mass. "How many?"

He knew he was moments away from dying. He could feel the wings of death flapping around him, fanning the air, waiting to take him. He tried to focus on the swimming face hovering over him, but the effort was too great. His lids slipped closed.

"Damn you! How many?" He gave the prisoner's head a cruel shake. "You weren't alone! I want to know how many?"

"Sail ho!"

With his fingers still clutched savagely in Syn-Jern's hair, the Commander jerked in surprise, turned, and looked up at the watch.

"Where away?"

"Off the larboard beam, sir!"

"Pirates," the Commander spat, letting go of the prisoner's hair. He walked to the rail and snatched the spyglass from his First Mate's hand. Training the glass to the place where the watch had told him the sails would be, he found the sweeping canvas of a brig, every sheet to the wind, bearing down on them.

"These waters are full of pirates, Commander," Hawkins informed him as he joined him at the rail.

"Well," the Commander said, drawing himself up. "We'll see to that scurvy bunch first and then head back to that damned cove. Our man wasn't alone there and I'd stake my life on it!"

# Chapter Eight

WEIR STOOD AT THE RAIL, FOCUSED SHARPLY ON THE BRIG LIT BY THE HIGH -riding moon. He didn't need to use his glass to know the crew of the prison transport ship was scurrying about the rigging, pouring on every spare inch of canvas the ship had.

"Run you bastards," he swore under his breath. "Run all you want. We'll catch you."

Patrick gripped the shroud beside him, his knuckles white and standing out sharply against the tan of his flesh. His heart was in his throat.

"They're running 'fore the wind," Tarnes spat as he took his place by the men. "She's full-rigged."

"And she'll be forty fathoms beneath the sea when I catch her!" Weir snarled.

Jarl Stevens nodded. "A right good place for the black bitch."

"She's got two hour on us," Neevens reminded the men. "Maybe more."

"We will catch her!" Weir shouted.

Neevens nodded. He had no doubt of that. If the Wind Lass didn't, someone else would.

"He's going to be all right," Tarnes said to no one in particular. "The boy will be all right."

But none of them were really sure of that. When thirty men had finally reached the spot where Genny had last seen Syn-Jern, there was no trace of him or the men who had captured him. When they finally wound their way down to the hidden cove where the jolly boat had been beached, the sight that had greeted them was one of pure frustration and galling fury.

"She's set sail!" Weir Saur seethed.

Only a half mile or so out to sea, the prison ship was tacking south, her sails gleaming an ivory white in the glow of the rising moon.

"What do we do now?" someone asked.

Weir Saur answered for most of them: "We go after him!"

"Aye!" the men shouted.

It seemed to Patrick to take less time to get back to the village than it had to go in search of Syn-Jern. "We're going to fetch him back," Weir told those assembled in the village common yard that had not gone with them into the jungle. He stalked past the villagers and headed for the Wind Lass, his crew close on his heels.

"What can we do, Cap'n Saur?" one of the pirates inquired. "We like the boy."

Patrick answered for his friend. "You can pray, Spaulding."

"Hell, lad!" the man shot back. "We can do better than that!"

Genny tried to board the ship, but Weir's bitter words stopped her.

"Hell, no, you aren't going!" He shoved her at one of the men who would be staying behind. "Keep my sister here!"

"Weir!" she shouted at him, struggling with the tall, thickly muscled man who had a tight, uncompromising hold on her. "I have to go! It's my fault they caught him!" She was sobbing. "He tried to save me; I have to help!"

"You've done enough already!" her brother snarled. His face was hard, furious beyond anything she had ever seen and she had actually backed away from the scorn. "You'd better hope he's alive, Genevieve!"

"Weir, please!" she begged, her words following him even after they weighed anchor.

He could hear her shouts across the water. "Weir! I have to be there! Weir!"

He turned a deaf ear to her, the sight of her struggling with his man. He resolutely put her guilt behind him and faced the open sea.

"They'll already have done it to him," Jarl sighed as he ran a wrinkled hand over his whiskered face.

"Stow that!" Patrick bellowed. The expression he turned on the old man was lethal. "We don't need your comments, Stevens!"

"What we need is the luck of the Chales," Tarnes murmured. He let out a long sigh.

"That boy don't deserve any more pain in this life time."

Paddy's face dimpled with frustration. They had a good wind; they had expert seamen on board. They had anger and right on their side, but none of that would matter if Syn-Jern Sorn were dead or dying. He looked up into the shrouds and, for the first time in a long, long time, he prayed. "Keep him safe. Please keep him safe until we can get to him."

"We're gaining on her!" the helmsman shouted. "The bitch wants to turn and fight!"

Weir turned his head and looked aft. A grim smile of satisfaction spread over his tight lips as he looked at the fleet of pirate ships riding in his wake. Facing the prison ship once more, he nodded. "Come dawn, that bitch will be history!"

## Chapter Nine

SYN-JERN OPENED HIS EYES TO THE NOISE CRASHING AROUND HIM. Vaguely he could make out men pouring over the sides of the ship, daggers clutched between snarling lips. He was floating in a lassitude of pain, beginning to sink beneath waves of disinterest. Whatever was happening around him had little or no meaning to a man who had one foot in the hereafter. The sounds of men fighting, dying, came to him as though he were already a full fathom under death's waiting waves; the screams, the snarls, the shouts of victory were muted, wavering, distorted.

"Weir! Can you get to him?" Patrick Kasella shouted as he lunged forward, his saber neatly skewering his opponent, who turned a surprised look of disbelief on his executioner.

"No!" Weir sidestepped a well-aimed parry. "Tarnes!"

Busy with a man of his own, Tarnes couldn't answer. He shook his head vigorously. He was getting to old for this, he thought grimly. He managed to gut his foe, but the effort it took was telling on him. He staggered against the railing and nearly went down on the slippery blood and gore running the decks.

Something bumped into Syn-Jern's legs and he gasped, coming awake with a renewed throb of pain in his hands. Dragging his tired eyes open took a great effort; sliding them down to the deck to see what had struck him took even more out of him. What he saw dimly registered on his numb mind, but it wasn't enough to pull him from languor into which he had slipped. The gaping mouth of the dead man lying crumpled at his feet confused him; but he wasn't interested enough to try to hang on to the flitting question of what was happening around him. He licked his dry, cracked lips, tasted blood, and fainted once more.

"Kill that bastard, Dixon!" Paddy bellowed at the sailor who was only a few feet behind his own opponent. The sailor was valiantly trying to spear the prison guard who was between him and Syn-Jern. "Gut him!"

Weir glanced over his shoulder and saw the sailor feign to the right, saw the prison guard go in low, trying to thrust his saber through Dixon's lower belly. He had little time to gasp as Dixon spun around a mast and skewered the guard in his left side.

Paddy finished his man off and rushed forward, colliding sharply with Harding as the sailor engaged another guard who had popped up to replace his fallen comrade. He didn't dare shove Harding closer to the man, so instead, he ducked under the sailor's left elbow and came up hard against the railing behind the yardarm where Syn-Jern was hanging. He spared a glance around him to make sure no enemy was close by and then stood up.

"Syn-Jern?" he whispered, reaching out a trembling hand to touch the man's face.

Around them, men fought on, died, shouted with triumph, screamed in pain. The sound of battle coming to an end, winding down, had no impact on Syn-Jern, who was unconscious. Paddy heard them only peripherally, as though from a great distance, as he stared into his friend's too white face. He turned a vicious snarl to the heavens when his gaze was torn to the blood running down Syn-Jern's naked chest and sides.

"Is he alive?" somebody asked.

Paddy didn't hear. He gently eased Syn-Jern's head back, felt for the pulse along the column of his neck. Holding his breath, his fingertips pressed to Syn-Jern's throat, he felt the faint thump of blood pushing through the carotid artery.

"We've got to get him down!" another voice whispered close to Paddy's ear. "He's suffocating!"

Paddy turned his head slowly, his gaze meeting Jarl's. He stared at the old man, not understanding what had been said to him, seeing the lips move, but not hearing the words. He swung his head back just as slowly to Syn-Jern's lax face.

"Kasella!" Jarl said more forcefully. "We've got to get the lad down! Move out of the way!"

Paddy felt hands on him, easing him to one side, but he found he couldn't move of his own volition. He was pushed away from Syn-Jern, men moved into the vacuum he had left, but still he couldn't seem to force himself to become involved in what was taking place before him. Idly, he watched the men use a crowbar to pry loose the thick iron spikes that had been driven through the backs of Syn-Jern's hands. He winced as blood rushed from the gaping wounds, trickled down the unconscious man's raised arms.

"Easy with him!" he heard someone say. "The lad's coming around."

Patrick Kasella watched the torn lips open, heard a low groan. "It'll be all right," Paddy heard himself say. "We'll take you home."

The cracked lips tried to form words, and couldn't.

"Be careful with him!" Weir shouted to the men who were supporting Syn-Jern. He reached out a hand to steady Stevens as the old man staggered beneath the weight of Syn-Jern's limp body.

"Get a plank. A wide one," Tarnes yelled to one of the sailors who had boarded the prison ship. "We can rig up a gurney to swing him from this bitch to the Wind Lass."

"I have such an apparatus already on board my ship," a voice shouted. "We can take him on board the Silver Dawn."

Weir glanced around at the speaker. "I'll go with you, then."

The captain of the Silver Dawn nodded. "Of course."

Patrick could not drag himself out of the lethargy into which he had sank. He stared at Syn-Jern's limp form being supported by Tarnes and Stevens, looked down at the puddle of blood at his feet, wincing at the knowledge that it was Syn-Jern's blood that stained the deck. "Hurry," he whispered, clearing his throat to be heard as he said the word again.

Weir looked at his friend, understanding the horror stamped on Paddy's face. He walked to Kasella and laid a reassuring hand on the man's taut shoulder.

"He's going to be fine, Patrick. Just fine."

"We can't let him die, Weir."

"We won't."

"He's one of us," Paddy said.

"Aye. He is."

Very gently, with infinite care, Stevens and Tarnes eased Syn-Jern around to allow Harding and another sailor to take his ankles. With held breaths, the men at his feet lifted Syn-Jern, and walked carefully toward the leeward rail where the Silver Dawn was riding anchor. Men moved silently out of their way, their own eyes filled with concern for the semi-conscious man.

"Easy," the Captain of the Silver Dawn yelled over to his ship as a wide, padded gurney swung across from the hastily rigged boom. He craned his neck to look up at the arcing gurney as it was lowered over the rail of the prison ship. "Let her down a little more!"

Two men from the boarding party grabbed the gurney as it slid down and steadied it as Stevens, Tarnes and the others began to lower Syn-Jern, face down onto the padded gurney.

"Steady!" Weir breathed, watching with held breath as his men placed Syn-Jern as easily as they could onto the planking.

Not a man on board left alive could have prevented himself from flinching when a loud, prolonged groan of agony was torn from Syn-Jern Sorn as his arms were lifted above his head and placed carefully on the gurney.

"Strap him down," the captain of the Silver Dawn ordered and Tarnes took a wide leather strap from one of the men to loop it under the gurney and buckle it just above Syn-Jern's hips. "All right! Lift her up slowly!"

The men followed the gurney as it rose, as it swung back from the prison ship and over to the Silver Dawn. Once it was hovering above the decks of the other ship, once it had lowered out of sight beyond the railing, they looked at Patrick Kasella who was kneeling on the prison ship's deck, tears streaming down his ashen cheeks.

"Paddy?" Weir called softly to his friend. "Do you want to go with him?"

Paddy could only nod. He was trembling so violently he could barely catch his breath. He felt gentle hands on him, lifting him up as though he were an invalid, an old, old man, helping him to his feet, helping to steady him.

"I love him," Paddy said in a soft, breathless voice.

Weir nodded. "I know."

Paddy searched his friend's face, looking for true understanding. "Weir?" he asked in a small, tight voice.

"I know, Paddy."

Tarnes turned away from the sight of the two men as Weir guided Patrick to the plank now braced between the Silver Dawn and the prison ship. He'd always had his suspicions about Patrick Kasella, but now they were confirmed. He wondered why it didn't make any difference in how much affection he bore Paddy.

## Chapter Ten

He knelt beside the bunk, Syn-Jern's limp hand clasped in his own, careful not to do any more damage to the ravaged hand. Reaching up with trembling fingers, he smoothed the damp, oily hair from a brow fever-hot and so dry to the touch, his fingertips made a faint scratching sound across Syn-Jern's forehead.

"Hold on, my friend," he whispered. "We'll be home soon."

From his place at the foot of the bunk, Weir watched Patrick Kasella.

Anyone could see the pain in Paddy's soul, feel the anger seeping from him like the escaping gas of a volcano about to erupt. When Paddy turned his face to look at him, Weir flinched, for he understood, if never before, how much his friend cared for Syn-Jern Sorn.

"He isn't to know," Paddy said quietly, his gaze steady on Weir. "I don't want him to ever know."

Weir nodded, unable to speak. He would never have guessed that Patrick Kasella's true nature was so vastly different from his own.

Not that it mattered, Weir thought. The fact that Paddy preferred his companionship from an alternate source did not, and would not, affect their friendship. Nothing had changed except Weir's concern for a man whose love would never be acknowledged.

Paddy's voice was soft, almost wary as he spoke to his old friend. "I will understand if you want to put distance between us, Weir."

"Why would I do that?"

"Don't pretend you don't understand what I'm trying to say to you."

"Nothing's changed, Paddy," Weir told him.

He looked at Weir. "You may not think so; you may not want to believe it's so, but things will never be the same between you and me ever again."

Weir shook his head. He looked down at the planking, then looked up through the sweep of his long lashes. "If life has taught me anything, Kasella, it's taught me tolerance. I think none the less of you this morning than I did yesterday morning, or the morning before that. You are still my friend, and I still respect you. You saw Genny and me through some real bad times. Do you think I'm the kind of man who would abandon you when you're the one who needs the comforting now?"

A fleeting smile trembled on Paddy's lips and he slowly tore his gaze from Weir. He sighed. "No, I know you're not," he answered.

Weir pushed away from the cabin wall and walked to his friend, laying an encouraging hand on Patrick's tired shoulder. "Go rest awhile. I'll watch him." He looked down at Syn-Jern's still face. "If he wakes up, I'll call you."

At the ship's rail a few moments later, Patrick leaned his elbows on the sea-slick teak and turned his head to glance back at the three ships trailing along in the wake of the Silver Dawn. On her larboard side was still another pirate ship cresting the waves. He watched as her running lights were extinguished in the brightening of the early morning light. He didn't have to go to the windward rail to know there was another ship flanking the Silver Dawn. Six ships had sailed from Montyne Cay the evening before.

"How's the lad?" Tarnes asked as he ambled out from the shadows on deck.

Paddy shrugged. "The fever's raging." He threw his head back and stared up at the last stars twinkling out of the sky. "They hurt him really bad."

Tarnes pulled the pipe from between his teeth and leaned out over the railing beside Patrick. "Could have been worse," he remarked as he tapped the bowl of the pipe against his left hand. "They could have killed him."

Patrick watched the ashes from Tarnes' pipe scatter, falling down into the flowing water beneath them. Ashes into the sea, he thought with a twist of pain. He'd once cast the remains of someone he had loved into the waves. Pushing away from the rail, he turned, put his arms behind him, and braced his hands on the teak.

"You don't know how good it made me feel when that gods-be-damned transport went down. Seeing that was like retribution of a sort. That was the ship I sailed on to Tyber's Isle."

Tarnes nodded, slipped his empty pipe into the pocket of his wool coat. "I'd thought as much." He looked out over the waves, jerked his chin toward the ship off their bow. "Done a lot of our men good, I'd say, to see the bitch go down."

Patrick glanced over at the ship. "I'll never forget them helping us," he said.

"They was only doing what they knew needed doing." Tarnes cast a quick look to Paddy. "They went after one of their own."

ജ്ഞ

Genny's heart lurched when the first cry of 'sail ho' came. She flew from her hut, her feet digging into the sand as she ran with the others to the beach. Shielding her eyes to the glare of the early afternoon sun, she strained to see the unmistakable bulk of the Wind Lass on the incoming tide. She dodged around some of the others, stood on tiptoe, her heart in her throat as she sought to find her brother's ship among the bobbing sails coming their way.

"There's the Dawn!" a woman standing a few feet from Genny yelled out. "That's Rolland's ship!"

Genny glanced at the woman, happy for Meggie Spaulding, hoping the smile and happy look would not vanish once the barkantine dropped anchor. She craned her neck to see the other ships.

"Don't look like none's been damaged," she heard a sailor remark.

"That's a good sign," another answered.

"What's that they're running up?"

Genny took a few steps forward until her bare toes were in the sliding waves. She squinted, looking for what the others were pointing to. At last she found a red triangle snap of fabric being hoisted on board one of the ships.

"They're signaling for a stretcher!" someone shouted.

Genny felt bitter bile rising up in her throat. She heard a moan from behind her and turned to see Meggie Spaulding in the arms of another woman. Turning her attention to the scurrying of some of the men around her, she watched as four men rushed forward into the waves with a canvas sling attached to two long, stout poles.

"There's his jolly boat being lowered," Meggie said in a low, lost voice.

The boat crashed down into the water and two sailors shimmied down into it, stood looking up at the tall ship riding beside them.

"They're lowering a gurney looks like."

How she knew it was Syn-Jern, Genny would never know. But as she watched the pyramid-shaped cables swing out from the rail, their burden of tightly-wrapped canvas dropping gently down toward the jolly boat, she felt her knees grow weak.

"It's him," Meggie whispered. "It's my Rolland."

"Nay," a woman hushed her. "It could be the lad."

Meggie's voice lowered even more. "Pray to God, it is." She glanced at Genny with anger. "And pray to God he lives." Her spine stiffened when Genny looked her way. "If'n any man lost his life or limb for having to go after the boy, there'll be hell to pay, there will."

Genny could feel the censure, the animosity aimed her way. No one had spoken to her since one of the sailors had escorted her to her hut and remained outside the door until her brother's ship was well out to sea. They all blamed her for Syn-Jern's capture.

"You've caused enough damage, you have!" the man mumbled as he shut the door to her pale face. "That boy never did a thing to you or yours!"

She'd had all night and most of the following day to regret her actions. It was true. Syn-Jern Sorn had done nothing to her or Weir. He could not be held accountable for what his vile father had done any more than she or Weir could be held responsible for their father gambling away money that should have gone to pay their estate taxes. She only hoped she would get the chance to tell him so.

"Get that stretcher out as far as you can!" one of the men on the jolly boat yelled out and Genny's eyes closed.

"We don't want to bring the boat any closer to shore. He doesn't need to be bounced around," one of the women said.

"Weir," she whispered.

"How bad's he hurt?" a young boy asked.

"Bad enough," came the reply and she recognized Tarnes' gruff bark. "Hurry that up!"

Holding her breath, Genny watched the men transferring their human cargo from the jolly boat, over the side to the waiting stretcher.

"Be careful with him!" Weir shouted as he jumped over the side and waded toward the men holding the stretcher.

Those on shore moved back, two lines opening as the stretcher-bearer's slogged through the breaking waves and trod heavily to shore with their burden. Genny stood still, her heart slamming painfully in her chest as Weir's eyes found hers. The look on his face told her she would not be welcome should she venture toward him. When the cold orbs flicked away from her, she hung her head, her face red with shame and guilt.

"We've got the medical hut ready for him."

"Take him on in," Weir answered. "I'll be right there." He sloshed through the waves to where his sister stood. "Genny?"

She flinched at the tone of his voice, steeled herself to meet him as she raised her head, but she wasn't prepared for the fury staring back at her.

"You keep away from him, do you hear me?" he snarled at her. Reaching out, he grabbed her arm to shake to her, to make his point. "Do you?" When she nodded, unable to say anything, he jabbed his finger into her shoulder with a painful thrust that made her whimper. "You've done enough harm. You damned near got him killed."

It wasn't so much the pain in her throbbing shoulder that bothered her as it was the disappointment and anger directed toward her from her only living relative. She lowered her head.

"Stupid bitch!" he snapped, turning on his heel and stalking away from her. "I can see why the man fears women like you!"

Looking up through the camouflage of her lashes, she knew the inhabitants of Montyne Cay had already judged her and found her guilty. Her shoulders sagged.

"Get back to your hut," she heard a familiar voice say and she glanced around to see Paddy walking from the waves. He kept his gaze steady on the medical hut at the far end of the compound.

"Is he going to be all right?" she asked, taking a step toward Paddy.

He didn't answer her. He walked past her, his shoulders hunched, hands thrust into the pockets of his wet cords.

"Is he, Patrick?" she called after him. "Is he going to be all right?"

"What do you care?" one of the women snapped at her as she and the others began to drift away toward the huts. "You hate him, don't you?"

"Aye, she hated him enough to put the Tribunal on him!"

"No!" Genny denied. "That wasn't what happened!"

"You followed him out yonder and got him caught!" one of the women charged. "If'n you hadn't been there, he'd have been able to hide good enough they wouldn't have found him!"

"Ain't he had enough people betraying him in his life? You be just one in the line, I'm reckoning!"

Genny could see the hostility on every face turned her way. With a sob, she lifted her skirts and ran for her hut.

"Her brother ought to take a stick to her," she heard one of the women say.

"Someone ought to!"

"Maybe when the lad is up and about."

"Aye! He should be the one to punish her!"

Genny rushed into her hut and slammed the flimsy door behind her, throwing the bolt used during inclement weather to lock it. Standing in the middle of the room, she brought up her hands and covered her face, and the tears began in earnest.

## Chapter Eleven

"HOW IS HE?"

Patrick Kasella ran a weary hand over his tired eyes and sighed. "The fever broke early this morning, but he hasn't awakened yet."

Weir looked at his friend. "Have you had any sleep, Paddy?"

Paddy shrugged. "There'll be time to sleep when I know he's going to be all right." He leaned back in his chair and shot out his long legs. "I'm not going anywhere."

A crooked smile twitched over Weir's lips. "Wasn't asking you to," he quipped. He drew up a straw-back chair and straddled it, leaned his arms over its back. "I'll just sit a spell if that's all right with you."

Paddy glanced at him and a rueful grin spread over his chiseled lips. "Maybe I can tolerate your company, Saur."

"As long as I can tolerate yours," Weir chuckled.

Late into the afternoon, a small groan came from the man lying on his stomach on the cot. Both Weir and Paddy stood as Tarnes bent over the bed and laid a gentle hand on Syn-Jern Sorn's shoulder, holding their breath as the old tar spoke in a quiet, soft voice.

"Syn-Jern? Can you hear me, son?" Another muffled grunt came from bed and Tarnes lowered his head to the young man's parted lips. "What do you need, son?"

"W...a...t...e...r."

Tarnes straightened and took the tumbler of cool water Paddy had thrust out at him. Very gently, he lifted Syn-Jern's head and put the rim of the tumbler to lips parched and cracked with the fever that had ridden him for days.

"Not much now," Tarnes warned. "Just a little at first."

Weir glanced at Patrick Kasella's face and saw tears. He looked away.

"That's enough for now." Tarnes handed the tumbler back to Paddy and eased Syn-Jern's head back down on the cot. He smoothed a recalcitrant lock of lank hair from Syn-Jern's moist brow. "Maybe you can stomach a wee bit of broth in awhile, eh?"

"You're going to be fine," Paddy said as he bent over to lay a hand on Syn-Jern's leg. "Just fine." As Tarnes moved out of the way, he eased up along the cot and laid a trembling hand on Syn-Jern's cheek. "We'll see to that, my friend."

Weir jerked his chin in the direction of the door and Tarnes nodded, casting one final look at his patient. He glanced at Paddy, watched the young man settle once more into the chair placed beside Syn-Jern's cot. He sighed. "You need rest, Patrick," he warned.

Paddy nodded. "I'll let you know when he wakes up again."

Outside in the muted rose light of sunset, Tarnes let out another ragged sigh. "He's going to make his own self sick if he don't watch it."

"A battalion of Temple guards couldn't drag him away from Syn-Jern right now," Weir pointed out. He thrust his hands into the pockets of his cords and looked out over the silver gleam of water. "Has there been talk?"

"About what?"

Weir looked back at the old sailor.

Tarnes shrugged. "Most of the men on Montyne Cay don't give a damn about that sort of thing," he reminded Weir, "and those that do, wouldn't open their traps about it." The rheumy eyes narrowed. "Least ways, they'd better not."

"I never would have guessed it about him, Tarnes," Weir said. "Genny's been running after him since she was old enough to know there was a difference between men and women."

Tarnes nodded. "That should have told you something right there, lad." He saw Weir flinch. "You ever see Paddy with a women?"

Weir shook his head in denial."

"Didn't you ever wonder why?"

Weir lifted one shoulder. "I just thought he was being discreet. That he didn't want his private life held up for public consumption."

"I had my suspicions, you see," Tarnes explained, digging into his pocket for the pipe he was rarely without. He stuck the steam between his teeth. "Not that it matters all that much to me. What Paddy does is his own business, but—"

"But, what?"

Tarnes shook his head. "That lad lying in there ain't of the same bent." He took the pipe from his mouth and pointed the stem toward the medical hut. "That lad is in love with your sister."

Weir flinched, again, then shuddered. "Even if he is, she's the last woman I'd let near him!"

Tarnes chuckled. "Son, I don't know of no way you can keep two lovebirds apart 'less you ship one to the Outer Kingdom!"

"Genny doesn't love him," Weir snapped. "She damned near got him transported back to the Labyrinth!"

Tarnes chuckled again. "Aye, she does." He grinned as the young man sneered. "She don't know it yet, but she does."

Paddy could hear their voices outside the hut for they had not walked far from the door. Even though the words hurt him, cut into his heart like surgical steel, he knew what Tarnes said was true.

"Do you love her, Syn-Jern?" he asked the man sleeping fitfully on the cot. "Do you love Genny Saur?" He ran the backs of his fingers down Syn-Jern's damp cheek. "If you do, I'll make sure you get her." He stroked the too-lean cheek. "I'll move heaven and earth to see you do."

## Chapter Twelve

HE LAY WATCHING A COCKROACH CRAWLING UP THE WALL OF THE HUT. His breathing was shallow, controlled, for a headache like none he had ever known was throbbing at his temples with a vengeance. All his life he had suffered from such debilitating headaches, but the one he was enduring at that moment was far worse than any other had been. The pain was excruciating, the nausea burning up his throat. He tried to concentrate his distorted vision on the meandering insect, but the fog was already gathering at the edges of his sight and he knew before too long the distortion of sound in his right ear would begin, as well. Then the nausea would erupt.

Trying to lift his head, the pain intensified and he gasped, easing his head back to the flat surface of the mattress. He gathered in two fistfuls of sheet, wincing at the pull of the wounds that were closing in his hands. He tried to will away the awful agony in his head, but he knew he wouldn't be able to.

"Are you awake?"

He tried to focus on Norbert Tarnes' smiling face, but the old man's features were swimming in a sea of fog.

"Think you can eat something, lad?"

The thought of food made him gag and he swallowed convulsively to force the burning bile back down his throat.

"You've got to eat something, Syn-Jern," Tarnes admonished. "How about some fresh mango slices, huh?"

He retched, hot liquid gushing from his mouth even as he tried to clamp his lips shut against the flow. His fingers dug into the sheet and he gasped with the pain from his wounds, sucking down his windpipe some of the noxious fluid that was in the process of escaping. He choked, coughed, trying to raise his head to keep from suffocating.

"Stevens!" Tarnes yelled, lunging forward to lift Syn-Jern's head as more bile poured from his lips. "Get in here!"

Jarl Stevens rushed into the hut. One look sent him hurrying to the pitcher of water on the table in front of the window. He poured water into a bowl and grabbed a cloth from the dry sink. Hurrying to Tarnes, he dropped the rag into the water and then set the bowl on the bedside table behind Tarnes.

"Is it your head, lad?" Stevens asked, wringing the rag out. He glanced up at Tarnes.

"The boy has headaches. He had one on ship."

Tarnes' lips tightened. "I bet they made the most of that!" he spat.

Stevens nodded. "Them bastards liked nothing better than to torment a sick man." He watched Tarnes washing away the slick fluid from Syn-Jern's lips and cheek. "Want me to get some men in here to lift him up? That cot's gonna need cleaning."

Tarnes held Syn-Jern's head up from the blotch of smelly liquid coating the mattress. "Aye. See if someone's got some laudanum, too, while you're at it." He turned to Syn-Jern. "Will that help, lad? The laudanum?"

Syn-Jern tried to nod, but the pain was too much and he ground his teeth together.

"Just try to hang on," Tarnes told him gently. "We'll get you fixed up."

Weir followed close on Stevens' heel as the old man wobbled into the medical hut with three other sailors.

"What happened?"

"He just got sick, is all," Tarnes remarked. He nodded toward the men. "Ease him up, boys. He's got a mighty bad headache." He looked to Stevens. "Did you get the—"

"Right here," Stevens interrupted, handing a small dark green vial toward Tarnes.

Weir helped the other men lift Syn-Jern from the cot, wincing as a helpless groan escaped the man's hoarse throat. Stevens and Tarnes stripped the cot bare, rushed to wipe the mattress and then flip it over before throwing a hastily draped sheet over the ticking.

"B...a...c...k," Syn-Jern whispered.

"Don't hurt his back!" Weir snarled, but he heard Syn-Jern's weak voice once more.

"L...a...y...on...b...a...c...k."

"Son, I don't know," Tarnes said, glancing over the barely scabbed lash marks covering the young man's flesh.

"W...o...n...'t...f...e...e...l."

Weir looked at Tarnes. "Tarnes?"

The old salt shook his head. "He's gonna break them scabs open, but maybe with all that scar tissue he won't feel it." He nodded. "Lay him on his side and then ease him over."

His gasp of pain was more from the movement the motion brought to his aching head than any physical, bodily pain he felt, but the gentle hands on him were comforting as they eased him to his back, helped position him on the cot.

"You want a pillow, son?" Stevens asked.

"Please."

Very slowly Tarnes raised his head and Stevens placed the thick goose-down pillow beneath his head.

"That better?" Stevens asked.

"Aye." It was a whisper of relieved sound.

Tarnes took a tumbler of water from the bedside table and poured a measure of the laudanum into it, swirling the liquids to mix them. He held it to Syn-Jern's lips.

"Here you go, son. Drink it all."

The bitterness of the concoction made him swallow convulsively to get it down, but almost immediately his tongue went numb and he knew relief from the godawful agony in his head was only a few more swallows away.

"Not the best tasting brew in the world, eh?" Stevens grinned, watching the grimace of distaste flicker over Syn-Jern's pale face.

"My father used to have headaches," Weir said to no one in particular. "They can be hell."

Syn-Jern sighed deeply as the lassitude of the laudanum began to take effect. He could feel it spreading throughout his body, easing him, and numbing him to the pain in his head and the nausea in his throat. He eased his head to the left, away from the light at the window.

"Cover that window with something!" Stevens mumbled to one of the sailors and the man hastened to do his bidding.

"You want anything else, lad?" Tarnes asked, wiping Syn-Jern's face with a cool cloth. He nodded, no longer feeling the pain that had been piercing his temples. "What do you need?"

The words he spoke were soft, slurred, but clear enough for every man there to hear:

"Revenge."

## Chapter Thirteen

"HE WANTS TO SEE YOU," WEIR INFORMED HIS SISTER.

Genny looked down at her clenched hands. "Is he angry with me?" She looked up at her brother's contemptuous snort.

"Don't keep him waiting. He's not well."

Genny had spent most of the time since Syn-Jern Sorn had been back sitting alone in her hut. She thankfully accepted Tarnes' accompanying her to and from the well, down to the common garden where the inhabitants of Montyne Cay worked individual plots of vegetables. Tarnes provided her with salt pork and eggs, milk from his own cow, and freshly baked bread from the lady friend with whom he kept company. Other than Tarnes, no one had come to see her. She was being shunned as only those on Montyne Cay, those of the pirate subculture, could shun a person who, in their eyes, had betrayed the code of conduct that was an unwritten law on the Cay. Genny felt the loneliness almost as much as she felt the censure and condemnation by the others. It was the loneliness that hurt most.

"The nerve of the bitch," she had heard someone comment on the only occasion when she had asked of Syn-Jern's health.

"As if she gives a rat's arse! He could have died for all that she-devil cared!"

Walking from her hut to the medical that morning, Genny could feel the hostility following her. She heard whispers, sly and scornful laughs, taunting clucks of tongues, but she walked on, her face burning a dull red in the harsh morning sun. When she at last came to the door of the medical hut, she stopped, afraid of going in, fearful of the man's reaction to her leaving him at the mercy of the Serenian Transporters.

"Well, don't just stand there, you stupid cow!"

Genny turned to face the harsh feminine voice that had spat at her. Seeing Meggie Spaulding standing only a foot or two away, four of her closest cronies flanking her ample bulk, brought instant alarm to Genny's belly. She flinched, stepped back when Meggie took a step toward her.

"What you afraid of, dearie?" Meggie cooed. "Think we might give you the lesson you so rightly deserve?" She came closer, her rolling gait, her shifting hips suggestively moving beneath the long sweep of her cheap gown.

"I don't want any trouble with you, Meg," Genny told her, eyeing the other women who had moved closer to her as well. "There's no cause for it."

"No cause for it?" Meggie snorted, swinging her head to look at her friends.

"Did you hear her, now?" Her beady eyes jerked back to Genny. "You'd best be reconsidering that, missy! As we see it, we got cause enough to yank you bald-headed!" She took a threatening step forward just as the door to the hut opened and Patrick Kasella reached out to take Genny's arm.

"Get inside," he mumbled to her as he drew her toward him. He swung his glower over the women standing at the hut's entrance. "You women get back to your chores."

"You tell her for us that it ain't over with," Meggie told him, lifting her chin high in the air. "We'll settle up with her some other time."

"You won't do anything of the sort!" Paddy growled. He stepped back into the hut and shut the door in the women's faces.

"That's what you think." Meggie hissed. Turning on her heel, she tossed her head and she and the others walked briskly away.

The inside of the hut was dark, smelling of lemon and disinfectant. It took a moment for Genny to adjust to the low light. She could make out the cot at the far side of the hut, but even as she strained to see the man lying upon it, she could distinguish no discerning features on the face turned toward her.

"He's had a bad headache for two days now. The light makes it worse," Paddy explained to her as his fingers closed around her upper arm and he began to draw her toward the cot. "Don't talk loud and don't upset him."

"I wasn't planning on..." She stopped as Paddy's fingers tightened on her arm.

"And don't argue!" he whispered.

"Leave her be, Paddy."

Genny jumped, the sound of the soft, gently chiding voice bringing home forcefully to her the position this man now held among the people on Montyne Cay. Men had risked their lives and ships for him; they respected him, loved him.

"Genny?" His voice was weak, a touch of uncertainty in the one word.

"Aye." She could feel Paddy's fingers digging into her flesh and she winced. She looked up at him and found his face carefully devoid of all emotion.

"I'll be right outside," he informed her, and with one final squeeze of her arm, he turned crisply on his heel and left the hut, shutting the door behind him.

There was a long moment of silence as Genny stood there, wishing herself anywhere else but where she was. Slowly she turned her head from the soft white block of light the opening of the door had caused.

"Will you come closer, Milady?" he asked.

She nodded. Her feet felt leaden as she walked to the cot. Nervously she licked her lips, fidgeted with the folds of her skirt, her fingers making tiny grabs at the stiff muslin, plucking at it. When she was only a foot from his cot, she could see him studying her.

"You weren't hurt, were you?" he asked. "I heard you cry out and knew you must have fallen. I was afraid they'd heard you, too."

She couldn't answer. Shaking her head in denial was the best she could do.

"I wanted to thank you."

She flinched, blinking with surprise. She stared at him. "Thank me for what?" she breathed.

"For saving my life."

Never in her wildest moments of fantasy would she have dreamed these would be the words he would say to her when next they confronted one another. She wasn't sure she had understood him. Shaking her head to clear it, she narrowed her eyes at him and searched his face.

"I nearly got you killed!" she said.

"If you hadn't been in the forest with me," he explained in a soft, reassuring voice, "no one would have known what had happened to me. I'd have simply disappeared. No one would have known about the transport. And they would have come back, Genevieve. Those bastards would have came back and attacked the Cay with everything they had."

"But you let them catch you to save me!" she protested. "If I hadn't been there, you could have hid! You could have gotten away from them! You didn't have to let them know you were there!"

He reached out for her, wanting, needing to take her hand, but she jerked away from him, not so much because she feared his touch, but because she felt guilt riding her like a cruel master. She stepped back, out of his reach. "Because of me, they caught you; and because of me, they punished you!" she cried.

"It doesn't matter," he said in a tired voice, hurt that she wouldn't let him take her hand.

"Yes it does!" she said forcefully. "If you hadn't been worried about me, you wouldn't have been hurt!"

"Genny," he began in a reasonable voice, wanting now to calm her more than anything else, "you could have left me when I fell down into that hole with you. You didn't have to stay until I woke up. If you'd gone back to the compound, the chances are they'd have found me anyway. They'd already found the jolly boat on the beach. They knew someone was on the Cay."

Tears were falling down her cheeks. She batted them angrily away and glared at him.

"Stop trying to make excuses for me!"

"I'm not making excuses for you, Genny." He let out a tired breath. His head was pounding again. "I'm only telling you that I don't blame you for what happened. I've told Weir and Paddy that, too. They don't want to listen to what I say anymore than you do."

"I almost got you killed!" She came forward, knelt by his cot and, not thinking of what she was doing, took his hand in hers, and brought it to her flushed cheek. "They hurt you because of me." She felt the scab in the center of his palm and turned her lips to it.

His free hand trembled as he brought it up to lay it on the silky sweep of her hair. Gently he stroked the soft tresses, his callused fingers catching on the silken strands.

"There's nothing to forgive," he whispered to her as he felt her lips against the flesh of his palm. "I would have been lost had you not been there with me."

She looked up at him. "I never meant to hurt you."

"I know," he told her, smiling as best he could around the agony filling his temples. "I know you didn't."

"I will never hurt you again," she promised him, pressing his palm to her cheek. "I swear to you I will never hurt you ever again, Syn-Jern."

His gaze lingered on her face, so beautiful, so dear to him. "I need to rest, now," he told her, taking his hand away from her, easing the one she held captive from her grip.

"Can I get you anything? Water? Anything?"

He shook his head. The pain was becoming an excruciating band tightening around his forehead. "Just get Tarnes for me. Please?"

She got up, looked back at him as she put her hand on the door. "Syn-Jern?"

It took him a moment to answer her, and when he did, his voice sounded strained. "Aye?"

"Thank you," she said.

"For what?"

"For not hating me."

He heard the door close softly behind her and turned toward the sound. He could still smell her essence wafting about the room: the musty scent of frangipani lingering to tease his nostrils. He breathed in the smell, letting the aroma fill his senses. It was a smell that reminded him of the shrubs around his boyhood home.

"God, help me," he whispered to the still room. "It isn't hate I bear you, Sweeting."

## Chapter Fourteen

THREE WEEKS HAD PASSED.

"You aren't going and that's final!" Weir shouted at his sister. He stormed away from her, not wanting to listen to her foolishness any longer.

"I will!" Genny yelled after him. Stamping her foot on the loose sand, she hiked up her skirts and stalked off into the camouflage of the jungle. Angrily she batted the wide green leaves out of her way as she heaped curses on her brother's handsome head.

Meggie Spaulding watched Genny Saur until the girl was lost among the emerald foliage.

The fat woman turned her head, caught the eye of her sister-in-law, Cherie, and nodded. She saw Cherie nudge another woman, who in turn, called out to a third, before they began to drift toward Meggie.

"Where you reckon she's going?" Cherie asked, drying her hands on her apron.

Meggie shrugged. "Off alone as she's wont to." Her beefy face crinkled with amusement. "Where no one ain't apt to hear her."

Nell Roderick, Kylan Roderick's sister, elbowed Ky's Chalean wife. "What you think, Bridie? You up to a wee walk?"

Bridget Roderick grinned. "Aye, I'm of a mind to take the air, I am."

Reaching into her voluminous apron pocket, Meggie pulled out a pair of sharp shears. She clicked the blades together. "I'm of a mind to take a walk, myself!"

Norbert Tarnes scratched his head when Cherie Spaulding asked to borrow a pot of tar from the ship's store, but he did not ask what she wanted with it.

Likewise, Ky Roderick did not question his wife when she left with a bag of goose feathers.

Jarl Stevens was sitting on a log, whittling, as the four women trooped by. He glanced up as they passed. He stopped whittling, stared after them as they disappeared into the jungle. For a long moment he sat there, watching the spot where the women had entered the thick undergrowth. Finally, he shrugged his thin shoulders, and put blade to wood once more.

From the doorway of his hut, Syn-Jern waited until the women were hidden by the jungle foliage before, as quietly as he could, he followed close behind, never letting them out of his sight. He could hear every word they said and the more he heard, the less he liked it. He'd been waiting for something like this to happen.

"These bitches are like piranha, Syn-Jern," Patrick Kasella had told him. "They'll eat their own!"

Syn-Jern stopped, drawing in a silent breath as the women came to a halt. He squinted with frustration as they put their heads together for he couldn't hear what was being said. The one named Nell pointed, the others nodded, and then each of them took a different pathway from where they stood. After a moment's hesitation, Syn-Jern followed the big woman, Meggie, for he knew she was the instigator of most of the trouble among the pirate women.

Lost in her anger, exasperated with men in general, Genny Saur didn't hear the stealthy approach of her enemies. She sat with chin in hand, legs crossed beneath her, and stared at the ground. Her brain was filled with plan after plan to be on the Wind Lass when Weir set sail that night; but just as a plan formed, she quickly rejected it. He'd expect her to stowaway; he'd set men to looking in any case. He'd expect her to disguise herself; he'd check every manjack who boarded the Lass. He'd expect her to try bulldozing her way aboard; he'd be prepared for that, too.

"How the hell am I going to get aboard her?" she mumbled.

"You ain't."

Genny jumped, her head going up at the intrusion. Seeing Nellie Roderick making her way into the clearing brought a snort of pique. "You scared the hell outta me, Nell."

Nell smiled. "Did I now?" She came to stand before Genny. "I didn't think nothin' scared you, Lady Genny."

Perhaps it was the contempt with that Nell spoke that set off alarm bells in Genny's head; but most likely it was the sly smirk on the other woman's face. Whatever caused it, Genny unfolded her legs and stood up, her gaze automatically searching around her.

"What do you want, Nell?" Genny asked.

Nell folded her arms over her ample bosom. "I reckon a little talk between us is in order." Her lips twitched. "Amongst other things."

Genny lifted her chin. "Such as what?"

"Such as keeping away from Lord Syn-Jern," Nell snarled.

One dark brow lifted in challenge. "Oh? And why would I want to do that?"

Nell shrugged. "Consider it a warning, I'm thinking. I'm going after that man and it wouldn't be healthy for you to get in my way."

Fury shot through Genny Saur and she took a step toward the other woman. "You think he'd even look at you, Nell Roderick." She tossed her head. "Ugly little wart that you are!"

A low growl of hatred started deep in Nell's throat, but before she could mouth the vulgarities that came to mind, another voice spoke up from the jungle thicket.

"You think he looks at you, Miss High and Mighty?"

Genny spun around, tensing as Bridie Roderick stepped out of the greenery. She glanced down at the muslin bag clutched in the larger woman's hand.

"Well, he sure as hell won't be looking at her when we're done with her," Cherie Spaulding giggled as she joined them in the clearing. The pot of tar she carried gave off a pungent odor in the full heat of the afternoon sun.

Irrational fear drove straight through Genny's heart and she turned, ready to bolt into the jungle, but found her way blocked by the bulk of Meggie Spaulding's large body. Her eyes went wide when Meggie held up the shears for her to see. Genny's hand went automatically to her long hair.

"You've always been so damned proud of that hair of yours, ain't you?" Meggie sneered. She clicked the shear blades together. "Let's see how you look without it!"

Genny whirled, ran straight at Nell, the smallest of the four women. If she could get past Nell, she thought she might have a chance of outrunning the bigger women. Cursing herself for making such a stupid mistake, for coming out into the jungle alone, she plowed past Nell, felt the woman's fingers snag her sleeve, but kept going even as the material tore.

"Get that bitch!" Meggie roared.

Crashing through the slick plants, feeling them lashing at her cheeks and arms as she ran, Genny could hear the women running after her. She dodged the thick trunks of the banana trees, jumped over protruding roots and fallen logs. Glancing back once, she saw Bridie close on her heels and was stunned to know the Chalean could move that fast.

Digging her feet into the lush matting of undergrowth, Genny increased her speed until she found a clear path through that she knew she could make good time back to the camp. If she hadn't looked back again, straining to see how close her pursuers were, she would have seen the air root that snaked across the path. As she ran into it, felt it catch across her shin, she knew she was going to trip, saw the ground coming up to meet her.

Bridie lunged, threw her entire one hundred and seventy pounds full length on the younger woman who was trying to scramble up from the ground. She heard the breath whoosh out of Genny Saur and, despite the pain in her own midsection where it had hit the smaller girl's wiggling rump, gave a whoop of victory.

"Hold her, Bridie!" Nell ordered.

Genny clawed at the ground, wriggling furiously in her effort to get free.

Bridie's meaty arms were clamped around her waist, the woman's weight pinning her down. She felt hands on her ankles, kicked out, and heard Cherie's bellow of rage as her foot connected with the older woman's arm.

"Hold her!" Cherie shouted.

Shrieking like a mad woman, Genny cursed them, bucked in their rigid grasps even as her legs were pinned to the jungle floor along with her upper body. She tried reaching behind her, to grab a handful of Bridie Roderick's coarse red hair, but found her wrist caught and held in Nell's strong, washerwoman's grip.

"Let go of me!" Genny screeched, barely able to breathe for Bridie was crushing her into the softness of the decaying leaves. A snarl of pure fury exploded from her throat when she felt hands in her hair, dragging the heavy mass upward. "No!"

Meggie squatted over her victim, shears ready, and was about to slip the blades around that thick black hair when, with an 'oomph' of surprise, she was lifted free of the ground, turned around and set heavily down on her feet. She opened her mouth to bellow her rage, when she found herself staring into two unforgiving, ice-cold midnight eyes.

"What you waiting for, Meg?" Bridie grunted as she pressed her weight on the wiggling woman beneath her.

Fear shot through Meggie Spaulding as she stared into Syn-Jern Sorn's set face. She backed away, the tales of what had happened to Patrick Kasella slithering through her mind like a pit Viper.

"Didn't mean no harm, Milord," she whispered, dropping the shears as though it was a red-hot coal. She wiped her hand on the bodice of her dress and continued backing away from the anger she was seeing. "Just having a little fun."

Nell had been so intent on holding Genny's hands, she hadn't seen the long leather-clad legs that were almost touching her shoulder. As she finally realized the dusty boots she had glanced back at could not possibly be Meggie's rundown castoffs; she slowly lifted head and looked up. Her face paled and she snatched her imprisoning hands away from Genny Saur. "Oh!" she mouthed, scrambling up and out of the way of the angry man glaring back at her.

"I'll gut you, Bridie Roderick!" Genny squealed, arcing her hand back to try once more for a handful of her enemy's red hair.

Bridie, not realizing what was happening, shifted her weight on Genny in an attempt to stop her wiggling. The older woman was grunting with the effort, sweating, and couldn't understand why it was taking so long to cut the little bitch's hair. "Get on with it, Meg!" she panted. "I can't hold her forever!"

Nell was already up, her Oceanian sixth sense having alerted her to the change in the other. When she'd glanced up, found Meggie standing fearfully beside Lord Sorn, her mouth had dropped open and she'd sprung up from the ground like a puppet whose strings had been jerked.

"Go," he said and the one word was so soft, so deadly threatening, it was like the boom of thunder in the women's ears.

Cherie bowled Meggie out of her way as she made for the pathway back to camp. Nell, walking backward, afraid to let the infuriated warrior out of her sight, tripped and fell over another air root, scrambled up, holding her hand out to stave off his vengeance, and then ran pell-mell back the way they'd come. Meggie's mouth opened once, twice, and she had almost found her voice when Syn-Jern raised his hand and pointed at her fleeing accomplices.

"Go!" he grated out, the word only a fraction louder than the first command.

Meggie made a mewling sound and then turned to run as fast as her bulk would allow.

Unaware of what was happening around them, Genny and Bridie continued to struggle on the ground. Vile threats and vulgar name calling filled the air along with grunts and pants and screeches of fury until Bridie felt an iron band wrap itself around her waist and she was plucked off Genny Saur.

Bridie grunted, bucked in the all-too obvious male arms she thought belonged to her husband for there wasn't another man on Montyne Cay who could lift her so easily. She tried to butt him with her head, but found herself sailing through the air, flung away as easily as though she were a mere babe in arms. As she scrambled to her feet, eyes blazing with self-righteous fury, a tiny squeal of surprise was the only sound she could make as she realized her attacker was Lord Syn-Jern Sorn.

Genny shot up once she was free of the weight that had been holding her down. She stood there, breasts heaving, glaring at Bridget Roderick. Her heart was thundering in her chest, her face filthy from sweat and the detritus strewn on the jungle floor, and her fists clenched tightly at her side. Instinct told her to jump on the older woman and do her damnedest to claw her eyes out, pull every last strand of ugly red hair out of her head.

"Calm down, Genny," Syn-Jern warned her, reading her thoughts.

"Do you know what those bitches were going to do?" she yelled at him.

"Aye," he answered. He locked his angry attention on Bridie. "And I know they'd damned well better not try it again."

"No, Milord," Bridie managed to croak. She was backing away from the retaliation she saw forming on Genny's face.

"You stay where you are!" he snapped, pointing at Bridget.

"Yes, Milord!" Bridie gasped.

Genny took a step forward, every nerve in her body goading her to attack. Her fists had unclenched and her fingers were drawing into wicked claws.

"Don't," Syn-Jern warned her, swinging his gaze her way and impaling her where she stood. "I'll handle this."

"This is between me and her!" Genny snarled.

Syn-Jern ignored her outburst and walked to the Roderick woman. He stood there, towering over her, and glared down into her frightened face. "Do you know what I did to Kasella?" he grated.

Bridie's face blanched white as snow and she began to tremble so violently her teeth clicked together.

"Do you, woman?" he growled.

Bridget Roderick nodded, too afraid to speak.

"And do you realize that whole incident came about because he made me mad?"

Another nod. A soft whimper.

"That I wasn't even aware I was doing it?"

The whimper became a groan of terror.

Syn-Jern bent over her, almost nose to nose, and fused his gaze with hers. "Can you imagine what I might be capable of, if I set my mind to it, to someone who makes me really angry, Madame Roderick?"

Bridie thought her knees would buckle, but she managed to hold her ground. Shake her head.

Lord Syn-Jern Sorn straightened up, folded his arms, and continued to regard the pirate woman with unwavering intensity. "What I did to Kasella was done to protect myself." He cast a quick glance at Genny, then returned that glower to Bridie. "What I'd do to anyone foolish enough to harm that woman over there doesn't bear thought."

Bridie's eyes flared wide. "She is under your protection, Milord?" she questioned. She looked at Genny with newfound respect.

"Aye, Madame Roderick," he replied, his gaze narrowing dangerously. "She is."

Genny stared at him, her lips parting with shock. His words drove through her lower body like summer lightning and set her belly to quivering. She found herself once more impaled by those blue-black orbs as he turned his head and looked at her.

"Isn't that so, Mam'selle?" he asked.

Genny blinked, felt the heavy pounding in her chest, and then nodded slowly. "Aye, Milord Syn-Jern. I suppose it is."

Syn-Jern drew in a long breath, exhaled slowly, then turned his attention once more to Bridie. "You tell your friends, Madame Roderick, that should any one of them ever feel the need to bedevil this lady again, they'll have me to answer to." His brows drew together fiercely. "Is that understood?"

"P...perfectly, Your Lordship," Bridie assured him, dipping a quick curtsy.

"And you tell them for me that since I can't seem to trust them to behave in a civilized manner toward the lady, she will be accompanying us on the voyage."

"I will?" Genny gasped.

He didn't look her way, but kept glaring at Bridie. "You will do that, won't you, Madame Roderick?"

"Aye, Your Lordship," Bridie agreed. "I will tell them what you said!"

He cocked his head to one side. "Then what are you waiting for?"

Bridie curtsied again and then hurried away, her head down and her plump legs pumping as fast as they could under her soiled gown.

Silence settled over the place where Syn-Jern and Genny stood. Even the jungle birds and beasts were still, seeming to hold their breaths for what was to come. When at last Syn-Jern looked at her, Genny saw uncertainty in his gaze.

Gone was the warrior authority he had shown the women. Gone was the deadly glower that had put the fear of the gods' in their hearts.

"Did you mean it?" Genny asked.

"About you going with us?"

"Aye."

He thrust his hands into the pockets of his leather breeches, hunched his shoulders. "Do you want to go?"

"Very much," she told him.

He shrugged. "Then, you can go."

Genny bit her lip, watched him, surprised that he didn't look away, or that she couldn't. Finally, she made up her mind.

"And the part about me being under your protection?"

His face turned hard. "What of it?"

Blood was pounding in her temples. "Did you mean that, too?"

"What if I did?"

Genny smiled shyly. "It would please me."

"Consider it so, then," he said softly then turned to go back to the village. When he realized Genny was not walking behind him, he stopped, smiled, then held out his hand.

Genny's smile widened and she hurried to him, settling her hand snugly in his.

ஐ

The pain had scarred him deeper than the cut of any lash; it had seared him with a sting that had mutilated his flesh upon the placing of the Maze tattoo on his left wrist. It had destroyed a part of his soul, and the man he had been, along with it. Constant, relentless pain over the years he had been incarcerated in the Labyrinth had nearly driven him to madness. Fear of his captors, terror of the threat they posed, had nudged him toward a bottomless pit of despair from which he'd striven hard to escape. When he had been captured the first time, fear had catapulted him to the very brink of the Abyss. With the second capture, he'd been flung so close to the flames of utter destruction he had barely been able to pull back in time.

As he walked back to the camp, he made a vow to himself—one he meant to see kept: never again would he allow the vagaries of fate to shatter his world and bring him to his knees. When he finally had it set a'right, tilted correctly on its axis, he intended to see it stayed that way.

He knew there were obstacles. One walked closely beside him. Another two waited in camp. In Virago, there were several more that would, for the moment, have to wait their turn. But one thing was certain in Syn-Jern Sorn's mind: Each one of the obstacles standing in his way to happiness would be overcome.

Starting with the one walking closely beside him.

## Chapter Fifteen

WEIR RISKED ANOTHER LOOK AT HIS SISTER'S CONTENT FACE AND SHOOK his head in frustration. "She's being too good," he remarked to Patrick.

Paddy agreed. "Two days out of the Cay and I've yet to hear the first argument from her." He pretended to shudder. "It's unnatural Saur."

Norbert Tarnes chuckled. "It's to be expected. She's put herself on her best behavior, I'll warrant."

A frown drew Weir's thick brows together. "For what?" he questioned.

"Not for what, Cap'n. For who!" Jarl Stevens replied.

"Syn-Jern?" Weir asked dryly.

"Who else?" Tarnes returned.

"He hasn't spared her hardly a glance since we weighed anchor," Weir protested.

"Hardly even acknowledges she's on board."

"Oh, the lad's aware of her, Cap'n," Stevens grunted. "Can't take his eyes off'n her."

Patrick quirked a brow. "If he's been watching her, I haven't seen him doing it."

"He's doing it right now," Tarnes guffawed. He pointed with his pipe stem.

The men looked aft and, sure enough, caught their shipmate staring avidly at the slender girl. When he became aware of their scrutiny, he turned away, the high flush of the wind, or his embarrassment, staining his cheeks.

"Well, I'll be a horned toad's wart," Weir mumbled. "He was watching her!"

"Gonna do more than watch her, is my guess," Tarnes quipped. He smiled crookedly at Weir's look of annoyance. "You can't keep her a little girl forever, son."

"Nor the hounds at bay for much longer," Patrick warned. "If not Syn-Jern, then some other buck who's gonna take notice that Genevieve isn't a child anymore."

"Hell," Weir groaned. "I don't know nothing about being a parent. What do I do?"

"Let nature take its course is my advice, Cap'n," Stevens advised. "The lad's a good man and since he's interested and the lass don't seem to be disinclined to take notice of him, I'd say just sit back and watch the sparks fly."

"Well, I don't want no sparks flying!" Weir snapped.

"Don't see as how you can prevent it, son," Tarnes told him. "Looks to me like the fire's being fanned pretty hot. And it don't look like either one of them is doing anything to tamp the flames."

Syn-Jern was coiling a length of heavy hemp around his bare arm and shoulder. The months at the Cay had turned his body to a rich, deep bronze color and had put distinct delineation in the rippling flesh. The man had gained forty pounds, all of it sleek muscles that bunched under the only garment he wore above his waist: a sheen of sweat.

"Have you ever seen Genny wear a skirt when she's been with us on the Lass, Weir?" Paddy asked, keeping his avid gaze on Syn-Jern.

Weir sighed heavily. "You know I haven't. And I've never seen her take so damned much time doing her hair every morning, either!"

"Or wearing perfumes and the like?" Tarnes put in.

"Perfume?" Weir groaned.

"Lavender, I think," Tarnes replied. "Or lilac. I don't know the difference 'tween the two."

"Lilac," Stevens assured him. "I smelled it."

"Why would she..." Weir began, then shook his head. He knew why his sister was doing all the strange things everyone had been mentioning to him since the Wind Lass set sail for Chrystallus.

"He's noticed her," Patrick commented under his breath.

"Hell, man!" Stevens snorted. "He knew the very moment the lass moved away from the rail!"

Weir watched as Syn-Jern laid aside the coil of rope and stood talking to Genny. Although neither he nor the men sitting with him could hear what was being said, the unmistakable body language told him all he needed to know.

Genny wrapping a tress of hair around and around her finger: *"Am I interrupting?"*

Syn-Jern shaking his head and digging his hands into the pockets of his cords: *"No, not at all."*

Genny swaying just a little to the pitch and roll of the ship, her skirts swishing around her bare feet: *"Nice day, isn't it?"*

Syn-Jern glancing up at the rigging, squinting into the sun: *"Aye. Hot, though."* He, lifting a hand to arm away a film of sweat from his brow.

She, watching that arm as hungrily as a starving woman at a banquet set for her alone: *"Can I get you some water?"*

He, raking his gaze down her shapely figure: *"You can get me anything you'd like, Milady."*

Genny smiling up at him through her lashes: *"You can have anything you want, Milord."*

"Stop!" Weir growled, startling the men around him and causing Syn-Jern and Genny to look his way.

Syn-Jern smiled as his companion's brother tripped heavily down the ladder to the cabins below decks. His eyes met Genny's and he laughed. "I don't think he likes me talking to you, Sweeting," he said.

Genny tore her gaze from the thick pelt of hair covering Syn-Jern's chest. "Weir still sees me as a child." Her hands clenched into fists within the hidden folds of her muslin skirt. "He doesn't want to see I've become a woman."

"A man would have to be blind not to notice," he replied.

Her heart did a funny little flip in her chest and she found herself staring into his swarthy face, caught and held by the heat of his intense gaze.

"Are you afraid of my brother, Lord Sorn?" she asked breathlessly.

"No."

The one word was an invitation and she knew it. A quiver began in her belly and spread down her thighs, lingering for a moment in a place that almost brought a groan from her parted lips. She swallowed.

Syn-Jern folded his arms over his naked chest and regarded her. The sun had kissed her dusky complexion and left roses in her high cheekbones. The wind blew loose strands of sleek black hair and set it to fluttering against her temples. Nature had expertly endowed Genevieve Saur from the top of her shining hair to the tips of the toes peeking from the hem of her skirt. If he but put his hands on her waist, there was no doubt in his mind that he could circle it with room to spare. Should he put his hands on the lush ripeness of her jutting breasts, he could...

Mentally shaking himself, Syn-Jern turned away, braced his suddenly sweating palms on the mahogany rail, and stared at the ocean. "Did you want something, Milady?" he asked.

"Like what?" she asked, her gaze roaming over the perfection of his profile from bold nose to cleft chin to rippling hair and back again before finally settling on his full lips.

Heat flooded Syn-Jern's lower body for he could feel her assessing him. He wanted nothing more than to turn, jerk her to him, and mold his fevered body to hers. It didn't matter that half the crew was watching them. It didn't matter that her brother was only a whistle away, no doubt pacing the deck and wondering how to handle Syn-Jern should the need arise.

"Did you have a reason for seeking me out?" he inquired.

Genny watched the vein in the side of his neck pumping furiously and her woman's intuition told her he was just as affected by her nearness as she was by his. That impish demoness that resides in every woman reared its trouble-making little head.

"Do I need a reason to seek you out, Milord?" the demoness asked in a husky voice.

Syn-Jern made the mistake of allowing his gaze to dip to her mouth where her tongue darted to wet her lips. A groan started deep in his chest and he had to force himself to stand still.

"Do you know what you're doing?" he whispered. He stared at the moist fullness of her mouth, unaware that his breathing had become shallow and too fast.

"What am I doing?" she whispered, fascinated by the rise and fall of his thick, wide chest and the tiny droplets of sweat that clung like flashing diamonds to the crisp hair matted there.

"You're playing with fire, Genny Saur," he told her.

She moved closer, oblivious to the stares that were aimed their way. Her hand trembling, she put it on his damp chest.

Syn-Jern closed his eyes, squeezed them tightly shut. "Oh, god, woman, for the love of Alel, don't!" But he made no move to step back or remove her hand from his flesh.

"Why not?" she asked. Her palm smoothed over his skin. Before he could unman himself before her and the entire crew, he snatched her hand from him, but kept it imprisoned in his own fierce grip. "You're not supposed to do that!" he reprimanded her.

"Why not?" Her fingers moved within his grasp until she was holding his hand. "Don't you like it?"

He thought his knees would buckle. It had been ten long years, almost eleven, since he'd bedded a woman. His body was sending signals his brain refused to heed and he trembled violently.

"A young girl like you shouldn't..."

"I'm not a little girl, Syn-Jern," she said in a husky tone.

His name on her lips was a caress, a tender stroke that was nearly his undoing. He let go of her hand, moved away, putting distance, safety, and the obstruction of a stack of canvas between them. When she made to follow him, he held his hand out to stop her.

"Lady, stay!" he grated.

Genny raised one dark eyebrow. "I am not a canine to be ordered to heel, Milord!"

He shook his head. "There was no insult intended, but unless you wish to get an up close and personal view of what you've done to me, I suggest you stay put!"

"What have I done?" she asked, her innocence showing in her puzzled expression. "I but touched you, Milord Sorn."

"And in the doing gave rise to a problem, Milady," he whimpered.

Genny's brows shifted toward one another. "In what way have I caused you a problem?"

There wasn't a man on deck who wasn't aware of Syn-Jern's predicament nor would a single one of them have gone to his aid.

"Milord?" Genny questioned, craning her neck to see why he was standing so awkwardly behind the camouflage of the canvas.

"Go away, Genny!" he begged her. "Just go away."

Her feelings hurt, Genny's face crinkled. "Have I offended you in some way?"

"Dammit! You've aroused me, lady!" he hissed. His hands were before him in a desperate attempt to hide the evidence from her. When her gaze slid downward, his own personal male demon pulled his hands away and allowed her to see what her innocent touch had wrought.

"Now, do you understand?" the demon demanded.

Genny wasn't as naive as most of the men thought her to be. She'd listened when the women of Montyne Cay spoke of their husbands and lovers; and although she didn't understand most of what they were discussing, she did recognize the telltale signs of a man's sexual need. Seeing the thick bulge in Syn-Jern's breeches brought a crimson heat to her face. "Oh," was all she could say.

"Aye," Syn-Jern agreed. "Now, go away!"

She forced her gaze to his face. Past the panting chest. Past the wildly throbbing hollow at the base of his throat. Past his parted lips to the hot need blazing in his midnight eyes. For a long moment she simply stared at him, thinking him the most perfectly beautiful male she had ever seen; then she smiled, her lips stretching seductively into an invitation as old as time, itself.

Syn-Jern blushed to the tips of his own bare toes. His manhood leapt. His heart thumped so hard he thought it would burst from his heaving chest. "You can't be serious!" he gasped.

"I am not a child, Syn-Jern Sorn," she told him. Her gaze was as hot as the fires under a crucible. She slipped her tongue along the smoothness of her upper lip. She took two steps, stopped, and looked over her shoulder. She raked him with a look that belied her inexperience and youth. "I am a full-grown woman who knows precisely what she wants." A tiny smile tugged at her lips. "And this woman wants you, Syn-Jern Sorn."

The crewmen had long ago stopped what they were doing to watch the man and woman sparring. Even though they could not hear the words being spoken, there was no way they could miss what had been offered.

"Sweet Merciful Alel!" Tarnes breathed, fanning himself with his cap.

"Is that our Genny?" Neevens asked in an awed voice.

Stevens clamped his mouth shut, oblivious to the ache his sagging jaws had begun to cause. He watched his young friend, took in the way Sorn was standing, smiled at the moment he knew the lad had made up his mind. "Go for it, laddie," he whispered. "Just go for it."

Patrick frowned. He wasn't quite sure what had just happened between Genny and Syn-Jern, but he knew he should be hurrying down to Weir's cabin to inform him. He would never know what kept him, and the rest of the men, right where they were as Syn-Jern skirted the stack of canvas and followed Genevieve Saur.

"Ought somebody to do something?" Neevens asked of no one in particular.

"Like what?" Stevens scoffed. "They're grown."

"She's a girl!" Tarnes protested. "Spent most of her life in a blasted convent."

"All the more reason to leave her alone."

"And he's been shut away from women for ten years!"

Stevens threw out a dismissive hand. "Like I said: all the more reason to leave him alone."

"But..." Tarnes looked from Patrick to Neevens to Patrick again. "What do we do?"

Patrick gave a fatalistic shrug. "We leave them alone."

## Chapter Sixteen

WEIR STARED AT THE DOOR TO HIS CABIN. HE HAD HEARD THE CREAKING of the hatchway ladder. First, the light steps that could belong to no one but his sister; then the heavier tread—bootless—of someone following her. With the opening of his sister's cabin door, the poignant silence that followed, the squeak of wood planking, the gentle closing of the door, Weir Saur knew Genevieve was not alone.

He sat there, wondering if he should intervene, giving himself a dozen reasons why he should, a dozen reasons why he should not. There was a thump and he flinched, then he laid on his cot to stare at the beams overhead.

No sounds came from Genny's cabin: no squeaking of the bed; no giggles; no muted voices, hushed and guilty; no thumping against the wall that separated the cabins.

But he knew Syn-Jern Sorn was next door. As surely as he drew in a ragged breath and released it, he knew the man was there.

If he should get up, go to Genny's cabin, demand entrance, he knew one of two things could happen:

One. He could prevent from happening what he knew was about to happen and possibly save his sister from making a terrible mistake. She would listen to reason; send Sorn from her cabin; contritely beg her brother's pardon for her momentary lapse of good judgment and morals; return to the naive, untried, and virginal woman-child he had rescued from Galrath Convent.

Or...

Two. Syn-Jern would call him out; fight for his right to be with Genevieve; become his lifelong enemy; remove Genny from all contact with her brother; and keep the lady's heart forever.

Or...

"You can just leave them the hell alone," Weir snarled.

Should he intervene, Weir knew, neither Genny nor Syn-Jern would ever forgive him. They were both adults; they knew what they wanted.

"And they want each other," Weir's little voice reminded him, "else they would not be where they are at this moment."

Not that he minded his sister's attraction to Sorn. If truth were told, he welcomed it. He liked Syn-Jern. He admired the man.

But right was right, he decided as he lay there.

ꙮ

There had been no thought in Syn-Jern's mind at all as he followed Genny Saur. His body, or a part of it at any rate, had put his bare feet to plank and carried him along without hindrance from his brain. Nor had he made any effort to circumvent what he knew was going to happen the moment he went below and found her waiting—impatiently, he thought—outside her cabin door. And he hadn't hesitated as he went to her, waiting as she stepped back into the haven of her cabin, her face bright with expectancy. Neither had he entertained the notion of leaving well enough alone as he closed her cabin door and quietly shot the bolt. As he stood there facing her, his body on fire with a need he knew would have to be quenched else he would go stark raving mad, there was no doubt in his mind that before it was all over, Genny Saur would be his.

"Are you sure?" he asked her as he watched her lift her hands to the laces of her bodice.

"Aye," Genny whispered and began to work the buttons that held her gown in place.

He was trembling when he gently brushed aside her hands and took on the task himself. The fabric parted and the creamy swelling of her breasts made him draw in a labored breath. His manhood stirred, growing rock-hard in the confines of his too-tight breeches.

Genny put her hands on his, pressed them to her chest, and delighted in the soft groan of his need as his fingers molded her breasts.

"Weir will have me flayed alive," he whispered, but his hands were moving on her, easing inside the bodice to cup the hot, firm globes that beckoned him.

She moved so close he could feel her body heat through their clothing. Her head fell back as he placed his thumbs on the peaks of her breasts and rubbed gently.

The swan-like arch of her neck invited his lips and he dipped his head, his mouth fastening greedily on the pulse point at the base of her neck. Her helpless sigh of passion inflamed him even more and he ran his hands around her, beneath the confines of the gown, tearing fabric, pulling loose seams, and not caring. He pressed her to him, ground his hips against her, allowed her to feel the essence of him.

Genny put her arms around his neck. She brought his mouth to hers and as his lips closed over her own, his tongue began its ravaging. She clasped his strong neck, lifted her legs, and draped them around his lean hips.

"My, god, Genny!" he gasped against her mouth. He was straining to hold her up for his legs were as rubbery as a newborn colt's. "Where the hell did you learn that?"

"Do not dilly-dally, Milord!" she warned him, her body sliding further up his as she arched her hips.

Never in his wildest dreams had he thought to be the one conquered in this business. He was not prepared for her aggression, nor was he able to think straight as her breasts flattened against his chest and her mouth began a ravishing of its own. From the moment her tongue darted boldly past his lips, he was lost.

"Now!" he heard her demand and it was all he could do to stagger to the bunk with her.

They fell with him on top, his weight a useless lump as his shaft strained to be free of its imprisonment.

"Take off your damned breeches, Sorn!" she ordered him, dragging one hand from his neck to pluck at the offending obstruction of his buttons. Her fingers grabbed him through the fabric, pulling.

"Lady, easy!" he rasped. "You're going to..."

"Shuck your breeches!" she demanded. Her fingers were scorching him.

Syn-Jern stood on quivering legs as his hands made quick business of unbuttoning his fly. Barely had he freed himself before Genny was on her knees, reaching out to take possession of what she saw.

"You...are...going...to...make...me..." He couldn't finish for her lips were now around him and he found he could no longer breathe. He buried his hands in her hair and held her head to him as her mouth did for him what no woman's mouth ever had. "Oh, Genny!"

So this was what the women of Montyne Cay had said was the ultimate power over their men, Genny thought as she drew on the rigid flesh in her mouth. She'd heard that a woman's expertise in this particular phase of lovemaking could make her man do just about anything. From the gasps and groans and whimpers coming from Syn-Jern, Genny could well understand that to be a truth.

"Lady..." He was pleading, his entire body quivering beneath her touch as she molded his taut ass in her hands and squeezed roughly. "I...am...going...to..."

Genny suckled him, drawing from him a wetness that was not altogether unpleasant to the taste. She experimented with her tongue, dragging it around the swollen head of his shaft, making lightning stabs into the tiny slit that emitted the slightly salty essence of him.

"Genny!"

If she were surprised by the sudden jerking of his shaft, the explosion of fluid that shot from her lover, she gave no evidence of it. She relaxed her tongue, allowed the liquid to flow smoothly down her throat, swallowed instinctively, drawing every last drop of fluid from her lover's manhood.

Syn-Jern dragged in a shuddering breath as her lips left him. He lowered his head, stared at her with absolute astonishment. He was panting from what she had done to him, shocked to the very foundations of his soul, yet when he opened his mouth to ask her where in the hell she'd learned such tricks, she smiled shyly at him.

"If I'd have allowed you to take me as you were, Milord Syn-Jern, you'd have hurt me for sure...I've listened well when the other women talk to one another." She looked down at the coverlet. "I am a virgin, Syn-Jern."

"You..." he breathed raggedly. "I...we..."

Her eyes lifted to his. "The next time I won't interfere," she said in a contrite tone. "I'll just lay here and..."

"The hell you will!" he grated.

Genny found herself on her back, her skirts yanked up to her waist. She tried to sit up, but found his heavy hand in the center of her chest, pushing her down.

"Be still!" he snarled.

"Milord," she started to reason with him, but when his mouth latched onto the very core of her, she squealed—half in protest, half in absolute terror. "What are you doing?"

"Two can play this game!" he said, pulling his mouth from her just long enough to thrust his hands beneath her hips and lift her to his lips.

"Syn-Jern!"

From the moment his tongue darted inside her, Genny Saur's brain ceased to function. Her body took over. She arched her hips, pressing against his questing mouth. She grabbed handfuls of his thick hair and dug her nails into the sleek curls.

Syn-Jern had never entertained the desire to make love to a woman in this fashion. He had always thought the act disgusting. Having always been fastidious in his person before his deportation to Tyber's Isle, he had overcome a lot of pre-conceived notions of what was allowed and what wasn't; but oral sex had never held any appeal to him.

Until now.

*"So much for your ideas of sex, Sorn,"* he thought.

Her taste filled his mouth and he drew on the tender nub that seemed to excite her so much. Running his tongue along the pulsing point, he inhaled the musty scent of her sex, finding his body growing hard once more.

"I...need..." she said and he lifted his head to look at her.

"You need what, Milady?" he whispered huskily.

"I...need..." Her fingers tensed in his hair. She wiggled her hips, lifted them. "I want..."

He knew well enough what his lady wanted and he removed one hand from her smooth rump and insinuated it between her thighs.

"Oh!" she gasped, trying to clamp her legs shut around the intrusion.

"Unh, unh," he told her, using his elbow to pry her left leg away. Before she could try to shut him out again, he inserted his middle finger inside the hot, wet slit of her womanhood and probed gently. Her juices flowed over his questing finger and he probed deeper, finding—and rejoicing at—the unbroken barrier of her maidenhead. His finger wiggled inside her.

"Sorn!" Genny shouted. "Damn it, do it!"

Syn-Jern laughed and removed his hand. Settling his weight gently atop her, he guided his shaft to her and pushed inside gently.

"Will you just…" Genny hissed.

Praying he wouldn't hurt her overly much, he accommodated his lady's need. He stilled when she sucked in her breath, then began to move inside her. Despite his gentleness, she began wiggling against him, grinding her sex around his, and gripping him tightly with her inner muscle. At first he tried to shorten his thrusts in order not to hurt her, but her mindless wiggling, her nails raking down his tensed arms as he poised over her, drove him to a frenzy that had his shaft pumping with fury between her legs.

"Aye, Milord!" she encouraged. "Aye!"

When he felt her quivering around him, the slick wet heat of her bursting into fulfillment, he could not hold his own back any longer. He drove deeper, going to the hilt in one final jab that brought a scream of pleasure from her lips and a grunt of satisfaction from his as he held himself hard against the very core of her. The scream brought everything to a standstill above decks.

It brought Weir Saur upright in his bunk.

ഇ

Weir was waiting for him when he came out of Genny's cabin. Saur was standing in the gangway—arms crossed over his wide chest, his shoulder against the bulkhead, one booted ankle crossed over the other. There was a gleam in the man's eye, a tight frown on his lips.

"Weir," Syn-Jern said in acknowledgment. He had automatically tensed when he'd found Genny's brother outside her door.

"Sorn," Weir returned with an upward flick of his left eyebrow.

Syn-Jern ran a hand through his tousled hair. He had no idea what to say to the man. Did he apologize for what had happened? Did he try to explain it? Could he make Saur understand how it was between him and his sister before the man ran him through with the serviceable dagger strapped to his thigh.

Weir's lips twitched with annoyance as he instinctively read those thoughts going through the other man's mind.

"Ten minutes, Sorn," Weir said into the silence.

A puzzled look crossed Syn-Jern's face. "I beg your pardon?"

"Ten minutes," Weir repeated. He jabbed his chin toward Genny's door. "I want her presentable and on deck in ten minutes." He unfolded his arms, nearly smiling as Sorn stepped back.

Syn-Jern stared at his woman's brother, held his gaze, and then lifted his chin in defiance. "I won't let you hurt her, Saur."

Weir nodded. "I have no intention of hurting her, Sorn," he answered. He took a step toward Syn-Jern. "Nor you, for that matter, but I am going to make you marry her."

He swept his regard down Syn-Jern, then looked him in the eye. "You have nine minutes to have her up top or I'll send men to drag you there!"

ꝏꝏ

As the sun set on that August day, the twentieth day of the month, in the Year of the Windflower, Syn-Jern Sorn of Holy Dale Keep, Virago, took Genevieve Saur to wife with the entire compliment of the Wind Lass's crew as witnesses.

Weiren Saur, brother of the bride, performed the Joining. The best man was Patrick Sean Kasella and Norbert Tarnes gave the bride away.

## Chapter Seventeen

WEIR SAUR NODDED POLITELY. "GOOD MORN, SYN."

Syn-Jern glanced at the dawn sky. "Is it?"

Weir shrugged and began to re-roll the map he'd been studying. "You know what they say about 'red sky in the morning'?"

"Aye. 'Sailors take warning'," Syn-Jern replied.

"We're in for a blow, I'm thinking," Neevens put in from the wheel.

"How bad?" Syn-Jern asked.

"Bad enough," Weir answered. He returned the map to its leather sheath. "There's a small island about five nautical miles to the larboard. I think we should set course for it until the storm's over."

"I agree," Syn-Jern said. Since his marriage, he had become much more cautious and extremely protective.

"Is Genny up?"

Syn-Jern shook his head. "Lazy woman, your sister."

"You can't keep the girl up all night, Sorn, and expect her to be bright-eyed and bushy-tailed the next day," Patrick said moodily.

"Get laid, Kasella," Syn-Jern answered sweetly.

"No one here to lay him," Neevens guffawed.

It was a measure of the men's respect for Paddy that they now joked about his sexual preference. He took it in stride, recognizing it for what it was: acceptance without question.

"It's been a long voyage, Neevens," Patrick said in a menacing voice. "Better keep your doors locked!"

Weir and Syn-Jern laughed at Neevens' instant blush. The man ducked his head and pursed his lips tightly together.

"I'll go see if I can get Genny up," Syn-Jern said.

"You sure you ain't going to see if she can get you up, Sorn!" someone called out.

Syn-Jern snorted and made his way to the hatchway.

ƐƆCƷ

"Land ho!"

The gale had started by the time the Wind Lass dropped anchor around eight bells that morning. The wind was howling like a Chalean banshee—rocking the barkantine roughly in the heaving swells—as the crew began to lower the jolly boats. It took strength to fight the lashing waves, row the boats toward the dark outline of the shore. The spit of land toward which they moved was high. Crags of black volcanic rock jutted into the water, the waves breaking over their slick surfaces and shooting plumes of spray high into the air. Palm trees swayed dangerously to and fro in the lash of the wind.

"Get to higher ground!" Patrick shouted as his boat ran the shallows. He was out almost instantly, helping the other eleven men with him to pull the jolly to safety.

The entire crew of the Wind Lass made it to the beach, staggering against the fierce onslaught of the gale winds, squinting against the stinging intrusion of salt water and sand. They were soaked by the time they found shelter in a shallow cave, all thirty of them wedged tightly inside the opening. The air inside the cave was rank. It reeked of offal and the entire crew had to stoop to keep from banging their heads on the ceiling.

Overhead the rain lashed down in sheets of icy cold and the wind whipped around their wet clothing to stick the fabric to shivering bodies.

"There's got to be more caves around here!" Weir shouted to be heard above the wind's roar. He circumnavigated the tight area, ran his hands along the rock, but it appeared the cave had only one entrance and exit.

"When it lets up, we'll go look!" Syn-Jern yelled back.

"From the sound of that storm, it ain't gonna let up no time soon, lad!" Tarnes warned. The old salt had seen many a bad storm and this one was going to be one to tell his great-great grandchildren about.

If he lived through it.

Syn-Jern sheltered Genny with his body. He could feel her trembling—more from her fear of lightning and thunder than actual cold—and put his arms around her. He put his lips to her temple and kissed her; her arms went around him to hold him as close as space would allow.

"I can barely breathe in here!" Patrick shouted.

"We need to find other shelter or we'll all suffocate!" Weir replied.

"Genny?" Syn-Jern spoke against his wife's ear. "I've got to see what else I can find. This place is starting to close in on me!"

Genny knew Syn-Jern was claustrophobic, had been since his imprisonment. She could feel his unease, the rigidity of his body. Despite every instinct, she knew she would have to let him go; let him seek out a more spacious haven. With one final hug, she slipped her arms from him, looked up into his jittery face, and told him to go.

Syn-Jern needed no further prodding. He squeezed between Weir and Neevens and was out of the cave before anyone could stop him.

"Damn it, Sorn! Get back here!" Weir bellowed, but he knew his words had been snatched away by the wind.

"I'd better go after him!" Patrick yelled.

Outside the safety of the cave, the rain slashed against the two men like razor-sharp blades. Debris hit them as they bent into the wind. The crack of lightning, spirals slamming into the island, unnerved the both of them: an added incentive to quickly find other shelter. A dark sweep of foliage soon blocked their view of the cave where the others hovered.

Reaching out to grab at Syn-Jern's shoulder, Patrick pointed to the right. "The land curves upward over there!" he shouted.

Syn-Jern nodded his understanding and headed that way. Slipping on the slick undergrowth, he grabbed a thick aerial root and levered himself up the incline. The rain had plastered his hair to his forehead, obscuring his vision.

"You try that way," Syn-Jern ordered once he'd gained the top. He jerked a thumb over his shoulder. "I'll look over there."

"Be careful!" Paddy cautioned.

The men moved away from one another, cautiously watching where they put their feet in the thick growth.

Looking about him, shielding his eyes from the onslaught of the pelting rain, Paddy moved toward a darker blotch of rock outlined against the gunmetal sky. With the howling wind and lashing debris being flung around him, he didn't hear the cut-off scream that came from the direction Syn-Jern Sorn had taken.

## Chapter Eighteen

SYN-JERN HADN'T SEEN THE HOLE HE'D STEPPED INTO. ONE MOMENT HE was making his way to what he knew had to be the entrance of a cave, the next he was plummeting through space. Loose roots rimming the hole lashed at him as he fell, scratching and gouging the flesh on his arms and neck. He felt something sharp cut him, cursed when his head slammed painfully into a ledge. Lucky for him, the ledge gave way as soon as he hit it. When he landed, flat on his back, the breath knocked out of him, he lay there, and stared back up at the faint glimmer of light that was the world outside.

"Wonderful," he gasped, knowing he was in trouble. That glimmer of light had to be at least ten to twelve feet up.

Coughing, spitting dirt that he'd sucked into his mouth when he'd screamed, he turned to his side and lay there trying to get his wind back. The mud beneath his cheek was cloying, cold, and he felt something crawling beneath it.

"Help!" he yelled, knowing damned well no one could hear him but feeling the urge to ask for assistance anyway. "Patrick!"

His shout had been a mistake for the reverberations brought instant results.

Scrambling from the ground as dirt cascaded around him, Syn-Jern knew a moment of sheer panic. Full realization set in that he could be buried alive inside the shaft. His intense fear of closed in places turned his insides to jelly and he stumbled forward, seeking a way out.

He put his hands up, touching nothing as he swept his arms from side to side. Beneath his feet, the ground slanted upward so he inched forward, feeling the way with the toe of his boot.

It was cold, penetratingly cold, in the cave and the air bore a strange odor he couldn't identify. As he made his way blindly through the darkness, he began to shiver.

And pray.

ஐ

The cave was deep, wide, but most important of all, dry. There was a shaft leading up at an angle that would make an ideal flue. All Patrick needed to do was gather some dried palm fronds, wood, anything combustible and he could have a fire going. Searching his pockets, he found his flint and kissed the box, thanking his lucky stars he'd had enough sense to bring it along.

It didn't take Patrick long to have a halfway decent fire blazing. The light from the flame jumped over the dry walls of the cave to assure him there were no beasties with whom he and the crew would have to share the night's lodging. Above the din of the storm still raging outside, he could hear the chatter of bats further back in the depths of the cave, but he didn't worry about that. If the little creatures stayed where they were, he'd make damned sure he stayed where he was!

Waiting until the fire was going well, Kasella took a deep breath and ventured once more into the pounding rain.

ஜ۩ஜ

Was it warmer than before? Syn-Jern wondered as he stopped and sniffed the thick air around him. The odor he'd smelled was stronger and he thought the air was, indeed, not as cold. He squinted, his night vision almost useless in the ebony space in which he walked. He was lucky he hadn't tripped over anything, yet; plunged through some gaping hole in the ground that would close in around him and squeeze the air from his lungs.

"Knock it off, Sorn!" he said aloud, his imagination beginning to play tricks on him.

He continued, hearing a whoosh of air that told him he wasn't far from some kind of air vent in the ground. Now and again, he felt a draft and knew he was moving in the right direction. He could no longer hear the storm but every once in awhile, he could feel the trembling of the walls around him and would hold his breath lest the rock come showering down upon his head.

The smell was nearly overpowering. His forehead crinkled. What was that odor? It almost smelled like...

Incense!

As the word registered, he thought he heard whispering and stopped dead still in his tracks.

ஜ۩ஜ

"It's about ten minutes from here," Patrick shouted to Weir. He'd spent at least half an hour searching for Syn-Jern then decided the man had probably found a cave of his own and had gone back for the others. Paddy felt a slight tremor of worry when he found that was not the case.

"Where's Syn?" Genny yelled.

Patrick shrugged. "Still looking I guess. Once I get us back to the shelter, I'll find him."

For some unfathomable reason, Genny wasn't afraid for her husband. She felt calm in the face of Patrick's obvious unease and wondered why. It was as though she knew that wherever Syn-Jern was, he was safe and would return to her none the worse for wear.

"I found a stream close by the cave, too," she heard Patrick explaining. "We won't have any trouble finding foods. There's plenty of edible fruit."

Weir motioned the others to follow them into the storm, but cautioned with a stern bellow for everyone to 'stay close to one another'. Without a backward glance, the crew left the damp of their cramped haven and ventured into the gathering dusk.

ꕥ

An errant breath of warm air touched Syn-Jern's cheek and he inhaled sharply. Wood smoke! He could smell the unmistakable odor of wood smoke! Peering closely through the dark gray of his surroundings, he thought he could see a spark of light ahead of him. With his heart thumping expectantly in his chest, he set a path toward that distant flash of light.

ꕥ

"He's probably found another cave," Patrick said, looking out of their shelter's entrance at a storm that had suddenly intensified to a full-fledge hurricane. Such fierce weather was not fit for man or beast and he was worried.

"He's all right," Genny assured her brother's friend.

"How do you know that?" Weir asked for the tenth time since they'd taken shelter before the roaring fire.

"I don't know," she said, thoughtfully. "I just do." She smiled. "I think I'd know if he was in trouble."

ꕥ

The light was a campfire and Syn-Jern made his way to it like a drowning man to a broken spar. He squatted before the heat, his hands thrust toward the flames, and soaked in the warmth.

There were furs laying in a circle before the fire, giving mute evidence that someone had been here. And recently. Despite his repeated calls, no one answered and he was beginning to think they were either afraid of him or waiting to ascertain whether or not he proved a threat.

"I'm from the Wind Lass," he said. "We dropped anchor to wait out the storm."

No one answered.

"We mean you no harm; we're just sailors from Ionary on our way to Chrystallus."

Still there was no answer.

"We're not pirates. We..."

It was pointed.

It was sharp.

It drew his blood.

Syn-Jern became perfectly still, ceasing even to breathe. His eyes shifted slowly to the right and he saw the gleam of the blade poised as his throat. The slightest move and the blade would sever his jugular.

ĐƆƆʓ

"We're going to have to go look for the little brat!" Stevens said. He stomped around the cave, his thin shoulders hunched forward, his jaw jutting. "We been here near on three hours and ain't seen hide nor hair!"

"He's safe," Genny repeated.

"Why hasn't he come looking for us, then?" Paddy snapped.

"The rain?" Genny reminded him. She pointed beyond the cave's entrance. "It's dark out there, Patrick. Would you have him stumbling about in that?"

"I want him in here!" Patrick shot back.

"If I'm not worried about him, Paddy," she said in a reasonable voice, "why are you?"

"Maybe you don't love him like…"

Genny turned from the man hovering over her. Everyone, with perhaps the exception of Syn-Jern, knew how Kasella felt. And even though Patrick would rather have had his fingernails pulled out with hot pinchers than let Syn-Jern know, the man had no such qualms about the others knowing his secret.

Not even Syn-Jern's wife.

"Sit down, Paddy," Weir said quietly.

"I can't!" came the growl.

"Then go out there and look for him!" Tarnes snapped. "You're worrying me to death with all your pacing, boy." He looked at Stevens. "And you go with him!"

"They're not going anywhere," Weir replied.

Patrick's nerves were near the breaking point and if Syn-Jern didn't show up soon, he was going to go look for the man despite their Captain's orders.

Genny felt sorry for Patrick. She understood his irritation and his fear, but she was quite content where she sat by the fire, nibbling on papaya and mango slices. Once more she tried to bring up some concern about her husband and couldn't. She took that as a good sign that he was perfectly safe.

ĐƆƆʓ

"I'm unarmed," Syn-Jern whispered.

"Put your hands behind you."

Syn-Jern blinked with surprise and almost made the fatal mistake of turning his head to see the speaker. If he had, he'd have impaled his throat on the sharp tip of the spear. As it was, he was shoved roughly to the side, caught unaware, and went sprawling on the cave floor with a none-too-light weight perched on his back.

"You're women," he accused, his face stained with embarrassment.

"I said to put your hands behind you!"

He complied quickly for even though the spear point was gone, a dagger blade now lay across his windpipe. In the length of time it took his attacker to push him down and straddle him, his head was pulled back by the hair, exposing his throat to the blade's bite.

The constriction of the leather strap around his wrists as a second attacker tied his hands behind his back was painful; it cut into his flesh and made him wince.

"Put your legs together."

He didn't wait for that order to come again, but drew his ankles close and felt them being tied just as tightly as his wrists. When he was bound, he was jerked from the cave's floor as easily as if he had been a sack of feathers and dragged backwards.

ꟿ

He had no sense of time as he sat slumped against the cave wall. He tried to flex his wrists, but the bonds held and only got tighter as he strained.

"You will cut the circulation off altogether if you persist," one of his captors warned.

He believed it for his fingers were starting to become numb already.

"Can I have some water?" he asked.

The bigger of the two women who had taken him prisoner dipped a gourd in a bucket of water.

"Get on your knees."

Syn-Jern clenched his jaws. "Why is that necessary?"

His captor turned away.

"Wait!" He was thirsty, as well as cramped in the position he was sitting. Swallowing his anger, and his humiliation, he struggled until he was kneeling.

The gourd was brought to his lips and he drank deeply, emptying the vessel. As it was removed from his mouth, he licked his lips and looked up with a plea that could not be mistaken.

"You want more?"

"What do I have to do to get it?" he grated, seeing humor in the dark faces peering at him.

A slight smile stretched thick lips. "Just say 'please'." The smile became a grin. "You can do that, can't you, pretty one?"

He had to bite his tongue to keep from saying something he knew he'd regret. "Please," he mumbled through clenched teeth. As he drank, he studied his captors.

They looked like mother and daughter with the same dusky coloring. They wore their long, coarse black hair gathered at the crown of their heads and hanging to their shoulders in many thick plaits. They had high cheekbones, thick lips, and long, graceful necks that were adorned with row after row of silver chains. They were wearing short white gowns that barely covered their upturned rumps.

"Who are you?" he asked and when they did not answer, he rephrased his question.

"We are Necromanian," the older informed him. "But we are of a sect that encompasses many nationalities and races."

"What sect?"

"She will tell you when she arrives."

"She?" he grumbled. "Is this how you women get your kicks?" he snapped. "Taking men hostage?"

"Only those She bids us take."

"Lucky me," he mumbled.

"She singled you out," the older woman told him. "You should be grateful."

"Well, I'm not!" He strained against his bonds, grunting with frustration and pain when the knots held and tightened even more.

"Stop doing that, Milord, or we will be forced to stake you to the ground!" the older one warned.

Syn-Jern blew an angry breath from his nose, but did not reply. These women were a mystery to him.

If they'd wanted to hurt him they certainly could have before now. If it was their intention to kill him, he knew he'd sense the danger; but they appeared reasonable enough, for female bandits. They had not turned venomous looks on him or, with the exception of making conditions whereby he could take water, they had not misused him.

"What's her name?" he asked.

"The Great Lady?"

"Whoever," he scoffed.

"Rowena," the older one stated.

"Rowena what?"

"Simply Rowena."

"Well," he grumbled, "does Simply Rowena intend on getting here any time soon?"

"What is your hurry, Milord?" the younger one asked.

"I've got to piss," he threw at her.

The women exchanged glances, frowned, then looked at him.

"You'll have to hold it."

He squinted dangerously at them. "The hell I will."

The older one shrugged. "Then piss."

Syn-Jern's teeth came together. "In my breeches, woman?"

"If you feel the need," she replied.

He would have made the worst kind of vulgar reply had not the arrival of a dozen more women silenced him. They filed into the cave, their silent attention locked on him.

"What the hell is this?" he demanded, the hair on his arms stirring.

"Milord Syn-Jern?" one asked, stepping in front of the others.

He was stunned she knew his name, but tried not to show it. He stared at her, caught, and held by her extraordinary beauty.

The woman was tall—at least as tall as he—and she was exquisitely curved in all the right places. Her flaming red hair, cascading almost to the floor of the cave, glowed around her ivory face. Emerald green eyes held him prisoner behind thick red-gold lashes. Lush, red lips—full and moist—parted to show small white teeth. She wore an abbreviated gown that fell just below her shapely derriere and plunged to a breathtaking V between full, spectacular breasts.

"You are Syn-Jern Sorn, Duke of Holy Dale, are you not?" Her voice was as lovely as she was.

"Maybe," he answered. "Who are you?"

"I am your mistress, Rowena."

☙❧

Genny turned in her sleep and mumbled. She dragged her coat to her, mindless of the dampness that clung to the fabric.

She was dreaming of a place she'd never been, but one she seemed to know well. It was a land that could come and go in the twinkling of an eye. A shadowy place. A land of shadows.

A shadow land.

"Syn-Jern," she whispered, nuzzling the coat against her fevered cheek. "Be careful."

☙❧

"Mistress?" he snorted. "I think not."

"Oh, but I am," she said. "We have known one another for centuries."

"I don't know you!" he snarled.

"Not as well as you once did, but that will be remedied," Rowena replied. She nodded and the women behind her moved as one.

Syn-Jern tensed as two of the women moved behind him, but he felt their hands on him, untying his wrists and thought fleetingly of trying to escape; but there were too many of them and he had no weapon. Two more moved to untie his ankles.

"Have I made an enemy of you, Simply Rowena?" he asked, never taking his eyes from the women kneeling at his feet.

Rowena smiled. "I have always thought you entertaining, Milord Syn-Jern," she said.

"I'm so glad. I...," he answered. He would have said more, but he was suddenly yanked flat on his back and the women converged on him: two dragging his legs apart, pressing his ankles and knees to the ground; two flinging his arms wide and forcing his wrists and shoulders into the sand. Before he could voice his denial, they had him pinned securely, spread-eagled.

"What the hell are you doing?" he shouted.

"Cradle his head, Olivia," Rowena commanded the older of his original captors. Her hands moved to the wide belt at her waist. "We don't want him to hurt himself."

"Get the hell off me, woman!" Syn-Jern demanded. He tried to jerk his head from the woman who knelt above him, but found his cheeks firmly grasped in two smooth, cool palms, his head held firmly in the woman's silk-clad lap.

"We aren't going to hurt you, Milord," Rowena said as she let her gown fall to the ground. "Merely satisfy you."

He stared at her, her naked body gleaming in the light cast from the campfire. Surely the woman didn't mean to...

"Don't you dare!" he seethed as she dropped to her knees between his spread legs.

"Throughout history, Milord," Rowena informed him as she bent forward and put her hands on the buttons of his fly, "the Daughters have had Consorts to do their bidding. In many of my former lives, I chose you; I do so again."

"Get your hands off me, woman!" he shouted and started to struggle wildly.

Rowena sighed and lifted her gaze to Olivia. The older woman slapped a confining hand down over Syn-Jern's mouth.

Smiling at the muffled threats, Rowena returned her attention to his fly and finished undoing the buttons. She freed him from the confines of his clothing and caressed him.

"You are as manly in this life as you have been in all the others, Syn-Jern," she said breathless.

Syn-Jern was wriggling fiercely in an attempt to get free. Even as she positioned herself above him, her womanhood poised over an erection he would have sworn there that was no way in hell for him to achieve, he could not believe that he was going to be raped by a woman.

"Do not take this so personally, Milord Syn-Jern," she said as she slid her hot, warm body onto his. "You have always belonged to the Daughterhood of the Multitude. Your body is ours! Just as the males of your bloodline will always be ours."

## Chapter Nineteen

He was at the rail, staring moodily out to sea. His back was rigid, his face set, his hands tightly gripping the mahogany rail. He hadn't said one word in over two hours nor had he taken his attention from the rolling sea. He had made sure everyone on board understood he wanted to be alone in his self-imposed vigil.

It had been the morning after the storm when the silences began; the gloomy moods set in.

"Syn!" Genny had squealed and ran to her husband. She threw her arms around his neck and showered kisses on his cheek.

"That's enough," Syn-Jern told her, then gently pushed her away.

"Where were you?" she asked, searching his face before he turned away.

"Waiting out the storm," he answered.

"We were worried about you," Weir explained. "We didn't know if you had gotten hurt or—"

"I am fine! " he said in a curt tone.

Patrick stood, arms akimbo, and stared down his friend. "Then why are you acting like you've something to hide?"

The anger that had erupted from Syn-Jern Sorn then had stunned everyone, left mouths dropped open with shock. He had thrown a true temper tantrum, turning the air blue with his curses, and then stomped out of the cave.

Genny stood where she was, her mouth open at the outburst. She exchanged a look with her brother.

"Something ain't right," Weir said.

Genny clamped her lips shut then took out after her husband.

When the others made their way to the beach, they'd found Syn-Jern pacing the sand, plowing agitated fingers through his hair.

"We have to leave this place," Syn-Jern demanded. "Now. Right this minute!"

"May I ask why?" Weir queried.

"Because I said so, that's why!" Syn-Jern bellowed.

"What is wrong with you?" Genny demanded.

"Nothing!" Syn-Jern snapped, then squeezed his eyes shut, seemed to be trying to get a hold on his temper. "Nothing, Genny. I just want to leave."

Now well out to sea, watching Syn-Jern Sorn crouched at the rail, the crew kept their distance.

"Something happened to him on that island," Stevens told Tarnes. They were less than a day's sail from Chrystallus and making good time.

Tarnes nodded as he studied Syn-Jern. He took the pipe from his teeth. "Been right snotty of late."

"With all of us 'cept his lady," Neevens commented.

"Tried that snappishness with her," Tarnes informed them. He sniffed. "She put him in his place."

"Well, the closer we get to Chrystallus, the worse he seems to be getting," Stevens said.

"Maybe it's just nerves."

Genny heard the men as she passed. They weren't gossiping about Syn-Jern, as he had accused them of doing only the day before. They were simply worried about him. Just as she was worried. Though his mood swings were a nuisance, they had not carried over into their relationship. In their cabin, he was as attentive and pleasant as he had been before the storm. His lovemaking certainly hadn't suffered, if anything, he was nearly as insatiable as she.

"Are you worried about something, Syn?" she'd asked him that morning, before the darkness had come over him again and he'd gone up top.

"No." He'd looked at her, his brows drawn together. "Do I seem worried?"

She thought about it for a moment and decided maybe worried was the wrong word to describe the vigils at the rail. "You seem distracted, Milord."

"I've a lot on my mind," he'd replied. "I've got things to do."

A small niggling of worry flitted through Genny. "You still intend to return to Virago?"

That had been his plan from the very moment ten years before when he'd been sentenced to Tyber's Isle. Now, it had become not just a dream; it had become as necessary to his peace of mind as Genny was to his happiness.

"I've got to go back, Genny. I've got to reclaim what those bastards took from me. And it isn't just me they've cheated and abused; there are others who need help in fighting the Tribunal."

"No one has ever successfully gone against the Tribunal of Virago, Syn-Jern," she reminded him.

"There's always the first time."

"What of the Hesars?" she asked, knowing how much he hated Prince Innis and the royal family.

"What of them?" Syn-Jern's tone of voice had been thick with contempt.

"Even if you are able to reclaim your lands from the Tribunal, do you believe Prince Innis will allow you to live peacefully? You were sent to prison for manslaughter. Patrick told me that was a mandatory twenty year sentence."

"Ten years in the Labyrinth is equal to thirty in the real world," he told her. "I served every year I was given, Genny."

"But you only served ten—"

"Ten was all I was given," he interrupted. "It was involuntary manslaughter, self-defense."

"Then why did you escape if your sentence was up?" she asked. They had never talked about his stay on Tyber's Isle. It was something he never discussed with anyone, not even Paddy.

"Because they were not going to release me!" he shouted. "Innis Hesar didn't want me released because Trace and his gods-be-damned wife didn't want me released! The three of them meant to see me rot in that damned penal colony so I could not reclaim what was rightfully mine!"

"Wouldn't your grandmother have protested when you did not return?" she asked. "Surely she would have counted every day and known the exact moment you were to be home."

"My grandmother died two years ago. There was no one left to champion me, Genny."

"Then, how do you expect to fight the Tribunal, Syn-Jern?" she protested.

He had gripped her arm in a punishing hold. "There are still court records, Genevieve. Records that registered my sentence. There were people there that day in the courtyard when my back was laid bare and the lash nearly crippled me! There will be those who remember just how long I was to stay in Innis Hesar's hell! They will remember and they will help me regain all that was lost! Holy Dale is mine and mine it will be again!"

"Who?" Genny asked. "Who will help you?"

The darkness had shut down his face, had hardened his mouth. "They are waiting for me to return," was his answer and he'd turned and left her.

# PART THREE

## Chapter One

"THE MAN YOU SEEK IS CALLED PRETORIUS," THE LITTLE CHRYSTALLUSIAN woman answered, her face creased with a respectful smile. "You may find him in the town of Misawa, near Shiku Pass. The Wind be at your back, Milords." She bowed deeply and continued on her way, a large basket of figs perched precariously atop her graying hair.

"Friendly people, aren't they?" Weir inquired of no one in particular.

"Very courteous," Patrick agreed.

"How far is this Shiku Pass?" Syn-Jern asked of their guide.

"One day's journey, boss," the wizened fellow replied. "It is in the central highlands. Very steep climb. Dangerous traveling."

"And expensive, as well, eh?" Syn-Jern snorted.

"Ah, so it is!" the man answered. "Much expensive."

Weir grinned. He liked the man they'd hired to guide them. The little fellow's face was so wrinkled from his constant smiling that Patrick had nicknamed him 'The Prune'. His name was Koji. He was close to sixty with short-cropped white hair that lay slicked back from his high forehead. His eyes were tiny, a dark, rich brown, and he wouldn't weigh more than a hundred pounds soaking wet.

"I am expert guide," he'd assured them, jabbing a bony finer into his equally bony chest. "Know all places in Chrystallus! Know every personage of honor, as well!"

"Do you know the Serenian sorcerer who hides here from the men of the Domination?" Syn-Jern had asked.

Koji had shaken his head. "Him, I have not heard of." Thinking he would not be hired for his lack of knowledge, his merry face had lost its perpetual smile. "But if you need to find such a one, I will ask."

"How expensive, Koji?" Patrick asked.

"Ten, maybe twenty more Ya," Koji said sorrowfully. "Depends on how much snow is in the Pass."

"Twenty more Y..." Patrick stopped his outraged cry when Syn-Jern laid his hand on Paddy's shoulder.

"Pay the man, Paddy."

"But, Syn..."

"What choice do we have?"

Grumbling, whispering uncomplimentary epithets about The Prune's ancestors, Patrick dug into his purse and counted ten golden Ya. He slapped them into the waiting hand of their guide. "That's all you're going to get, you sniveling little thief!"

Koji hefted the coins, shrugged, and then pocketed them in his vest. "It will suffice." His smile returned. "For now!"

ꝏꝏ

Preparations were being made for the treacherous climb into the mountains. Horses and mules were purchased, provisions acquired. Heavier clothing than the men had brought along was procured. It was decided that since Genny had not been feeling well since their landing that morning, she would stay at an inn on the outskirts of Nyotoka, the Imperial capitol. For her protection, Neevens would remain behind, as well.

It was while Weir, Syn-Jern, and Paddy were bargaining for thick wool coats in the bazaar that they were approached by a phalanx of Imperial guards, spears in hand.

"Uh, oh," Weir whispered. "I think we've got trouble."

Syn-Jern turned to see the military guard coming toward them. He tensed, the years he'd spent in prison making him wary and more than a little afraid. Patrick had become rigid, as well, his hand going to the knife at his waist.

The guards stopped a few feet away, parted, and a man of imposing height and obvious authority stepped forward. He bowed deeply and when he straightened, his gaze went unerringly to Syn-Jern Sorn.

"I am Masarawa, Chief Guard of the Imperial Palace of Binh Tae. I have been ordered by his Imperial Majesty, Emperor Akito Shimota, to invite you to the Palace." He flung his arm toward the opening between the guards. "Please be so good as to follow me."

Weir looked at Patrick; they both looked at Syn-Jern.

"I believe you have the wrong men, my friend," Syn-Jern answered. "We are privateers from—"

"Montyne Cay," Masarawa interrupted. He smiled in a condescending way. "I have the correct personages, Duke Sorn. I never make mistakes."

Syn-Jern's left eyebrow crooked. "Really?" he drawled. He glanced at Weir and Paddy, saw the same unease on their faces as he was feeling. "And just why would your Emperor want us to come to his palace?"

The Imperial Chief Guard shook his head. "His Highness does not make me privy to his thoughts, Your Grace. He orders; I obey." He indicated the path again. "Now, if you please."

"What if we don't want to go with you?" Weir asked.

Masarawa smiled nastily. "I shall arrest you and take you there anyway. If you resist, I will have my men beat you to the ground."

"Is that what your Emperor ordered?" Patrick snarled.

"No, it is not, but when my Emperor orders me to do something, I do it even should it mean I will be punished later for going beyond what he desired," the man replied.

Once more he pointed to the pathway between the guards. "Either go with us or be carried. As for me, I do not care which choice you make, Overlander!"

"We aren't going anywhere with you," Syn-Jern replied. "We don't know you from Alel's house cat and, to tell the truth, you don't look like someone we could trust."

The Imperial Chief Guard blinked. "What?" he gasped, his training and manners gone.

"You heard me." A lethal smile slowly formed on Sorn's angry face. "I damned well didn't stutter."

Masarawa frowned darkly. "You dare to suggest I am not to be trusted, Overlander?" the Chrystallusian sneered. He raised his hand, would have backhanded Syn-Jern, but the Viragonian caught Masarawa's wrist in an iron grip, twisted, and sent the surprised Chief Guard flying head over heels.

Weir whistled even as he drew the dagger from the sheath at his thigh. He barely noticed Patrick doing the same. The guards, seeing their leader down, rushed forward with a chorus of yells. Weir and Paddy had little time to protect themselves; they were surrounded, blade spears at their chests, their weapons yanked from their hands.

Syn-Jern turned, his eyes flaring wide with rage at the sight of his friends taken captive, but before he could summon the uncontrollable demon that lurked inside him, something hard and unforgiving slammed heavily against the back of his head and he went down.

## Chapter Two

"ONE HUNDRED LASHES," THE WOMAN SAID AS SHE WASHED THE CAKED blood from Syn-Jern Sorn's head.

He was still trying to swim up through the undulating water that had enveloped him. The sound of the woman's musical voice was distorted, warped, and the pain in his head was excruciating.

"Detention for one year." Her fingers were gentle. "Perhaps longer."

"W...where am I?" he asked. The sound of his own voice was an agony he'd just as soon forego. He tried to lift a hand to his throbbing forehead, but the woman pushed it down again.

"The Imperial Palace." She smoothed the hair from his eyes. "Lie still. The physicians say you have a concussion."

Pain was nothing new to Syn-Jern, but the intense pounding and the nausea that was hiding in his throat combined to make him wish that whoever had hit him, had done a better job and killed him. He groaned. "Alel, Iluvia, and Orion! What the hell did he hit me with?"

"You are a stubborn man, Milord Syn-Jern," she sighed, pushing his hands to the coverlet once more. "You must lie still."

It took a great deal of effort to try to focus on the woman hovering over him. He was seeing double and the ceiling had the tendency to lurch to the right without warning.

"God, I hurt," he moaned.

"The physicians do not wish to give you something for your pain. They do not want you to fall asleep again. We must keep you awake."

Syn-Jern didn't want to stay awake. He wanted to sleep, to get rid of the pain in his head; but every time he closed his eyes, the woman beside him would gently coax him into full consciousness.

"Stay awake, Milord Syn-Jern," she warned. The back of her hand caressed his cheek. "I can't let you sleep."

His anger surfaced. "Aye, don't let me know any relief from this godawful agony before you lash me" he grated through clenched teeth.

"Lash you?" she asked. "No one is going to lash you, Milord Syn-Jern! I was speaking of your attacker."

He tried hard to see her, to make out her shifting features, but her face wouldn't hold in one position for long. The movement made him deathly sick to his stomach and he barely had time to flip over to his side, away from her, before hot bile spewed from him.

"Lin Su!" he heard her call out. "He is ill again."

Someone wiped his mouth, washed his face, his fevered brow, gave him water to drink. He was lifted in rock-hard arms and held against a chest as solid as granite as the linens on his bed were changed. The cool air on his flesh told him he was naked and the thought shamed him even as he was covered with a downy comforter that smelled of sandalwood.

"Where are m...my damned clothes?" he managed to ask.

"That is not a concern at the moment," the woman told him.

Syn-Jern fought hard to remember what it was she'd said about the lashing.

"It is Masarawa who will be lashed," she said as though she'd read his mind. "After his detention, he will be stripped of rank and drummed out of the Guard."

"My men?" he gasped, suddenly remembering Weir and Paddy.

"Your friends are sleeping in the chamber beside your own," she assured him. "They are well. No harm was done them at the marketplace. The Emperor was infuriated by what happened. He has lost face and for that, many will pay. The guards who arrested your friends have been let go."

"I don't understand," he sighed. "What does he want with us? We're nobodies."

"That is not true, Milord Syn-Jern," she told him. "You are a very important man, indeed."

He tried once more, unsuccessfully, to look at her, then finally gave up. His eyes wouldn't cooperate and neither would his brain.

"I need to send word to my wife..." he began but she laid cool fingers over his lips.

"Your lady is ensconced in a chamber across the corridor. Our physicians are taking care of her."

Syn-Jern's face paled. "Why? What's wrong with my wife?" He tried to sit up but a mountain of flesh moved to block the light.

"Calm yourself, Milord," a deep, gruff voice commanded. "Your lady suffers no more than what any woman suffers in her condition."

"What condition?" Syn-Jern screeched. "If Genny's been hurt...If you bastards have done something to my woman..."

"It is what you have done to her, Milord," the husky voice answered in an amused voice. "Your lady is with child!"

## Chapter Three

Syn-Jern looked up as the door to his chamber opened. He had been expecting either Paddy or Weir, but the gentleman who stood in the doorway could be none other than the Emperor, himself.

"May I visit?" the Emperor asked quietly.

Unable to get out of bed for his head was still throbbing painfully and his vision blurred, Syn-Jern blushed with embarrassment. "I'd be honored, Your Highness," he answered.

Emperor Akito Shimota gently closed the door. He swept his arm toward a chair. "May I?"

"Of course!" Syn-Jern felt ill at ease that he was indisposed in the presence of so august a person as the Emperor of Chrystallus.

The Emperor sat gingerly on the very edge of the damask-covered chair, his feet planted firmly on the floor, and rested his palms on his knees. "You are feeling better?" he inquired politely.

"A little," Syn-Jern acknowledged. "I don't think I'll be doing any handstands any time soon, though."

Akito Shimota frowned. "I wish to render my most abject apologies, Lord Syn-Jern. The enormity of Masarawa's perfidy has filled me with great shame."

"I don't blame you for what that bas..." Syn-Jern cleared his throat. "The man thought he was carrying out your wishes by bringing us here at any cost."

"It was not my wish that he do either you or your men harm, Duke Sorn. I requested your presence; you were free to decline if you so desired. I thought I made that clear to Masarawa." He looked away, thoroughly ashamed. "I see I did not."

Syn-Jern wanted to put the man at ease. "Maybe it was my abrasive personality that caused it. I hinted the man wasn't to be trusted."

Twin black brows leapt upward. "Truly?" The Emperor almost smiled. "No man has ever dared question Masarawa's trustworthiness."

"Well, I didn't know him from Alel's house cat," Syn-Jern admitted.

A smile finally tugged at the corners of Akito's small mouth. "And would not have cared had you known?"

Syn-Jern smiled, too. "Probably not. I've never been accused of having a whole lot of tact and diplomacy, Your Highness."

"I have heard many intriguing things about you, Syn-Jern." His forehead puckered. "May I call you by your given name?"

"My friends call me Syn," was the reply.

"I am Akito," the Emperor offered. "Please to call me such."

Syn-Jern turned a deathly white color. "I wouldn't presume to call you..."

Akito fanned his hand in dismissal of the objection. "I detest titles and men who feel the need to employ them." He leaned forward, lowered his voice. "I find most of those who do so are only out to curry favor with the Imperial House and are not to be trusted." He sat back and crossed his arms over the elaborate silk robe he wore. "My family has often bemoaned my lack of courtliness. My father expressed his doubts to my mother that I would ever be sensible enough to sit the Lotus throne. Call me Akito," he said.

Syn-Jern liked this small man with his long black braid and wicked grin. Everything about Akito Shimota bespoke warmth and friendliness.

"You said you'd heard about me?" Syn-Jern asked, feeling more comfortable in the man's presence. "What have you heard?"

"That you have set yourself the task of destroying the Viragonian Tribunal."

Surprise lifted Syn-Jern's forehead. "Who told you that?"

Akito smiled. "I have spies everywhere, even in Virago."

Syn-Jern flinched. "Spies who knew I was on my way here?"

"No," Akito was quick to tell him. "As far as I am aware, no one in Virago knows your whereabouts at this moment, although I am told the whole of the Tribunal and Palace Guards are on the lookout for you there."

Syn-Jern's face groaned. "Oh, that's wonderful."

"Not to worry," Akito stated. "By the time we are finished with you, no man will be able to stand against you, Syn."

"By the time you're..." Syn-Jern squinted. "What exactly does that mean?"

"I married a Chalean," Akito said, dropping the statement into the conversation as though Syn-Jern had asked about his guest's marital status.

Syn-Jern stared at the man. What did Akito's choice of a wife have to do with anything?

"I joined with her much against my parents' advice, I might add," Akito continued. He shrugged elaborately, twisting his lips as he did. "Another example of what my father liked to call 'Akito's infernal rebelliousness'." The Emperor chuckled. "But he later recanted after he'd spent time with my lady. He came to love her as I do."

Syn-Jern could think of nothing to say. He suspected there was a reason the man had brought this up so he just listened quietly, keeping his thoughts to himself.

"We have been extremely happy, she and I." Akito smiled wistfully. "Our marriage is nearing its silver anniversary."

"But you can't be more than thirty!" Syn-Jern protested.

"On the contrary," Akito beamed. "I will be fifty on my next birthday and my Lady-Wife will be forty-two."

Syn-Jern shook his head. "Must be something in the water here."

Akito threw back his head and laughed. "See," he said, pointing at Syn-Jern, "that is why you will have your people's support when you return to your homeland. You have not lost your sense of humor despite your imprisonment in the Labyrinth."

"You know about that?" Syn-Jern was stunned.

"I know all about you, Syn-Jern," Akito confessed.

"From your spies." It was an accusation.

"Yes, from them, but also from your friends and your very beautiful Lady-Wife. They dined with me last evening and we had a long, long talk. Until my physicians insisted the Lady Genny retire for the night." The smile slipped slowly from the Emperor's face. "May I extend my congratulations on her impending motherhood?"

There was something in the way Akito expressed his sentiments that made Syn-Jern uneasy.

"We have not been so lucky, my wife and I," he said, looking down at the hands he had folded tightly in his lap. "We have tried, but there will never be issue from our union. I fear the fault lies with me, not her."

Syn-Jern's heart went out to the man. "I am sorry."

"I, too," Akito answered. "But we have decided to adopt a boy and girl from my wife's country. Twins, I am told."

When there was a long silence, Akito looked up guiltily. "Please," he asked, his eyes contrite, "do not think I will hold their lineage against these children. I would never do such a thing."

"I'm sure you wouldn't," Syn-Jern agreed.

"I will love them and cherish them as though they had sprang from own loins!" Akito stressed, seeming to need Syn-Jern's approval. "I would never abuse them in any way. You must believe that!"

"I do."

Akito shivered. "Do you, Syn-Jern? Do you believe I will be a good father to these children?"

"Aye," Syn-Jern replied, knowing he meant it.

The Emperor seemed to relax. His smile returned, albeit tremulously, and he unclenched his hands. "So," he said, changing the subject again. "When you are well, we will begin your training."

Syn-Jern blinked. "I beg your pardon?"

"Pretorius and I." There was smug satisfaction on Akito's ivory face.

"Pretorius?" Syn-Jern felt a shiver of apprehension travel down his spine. "You know him?"

"Naturally," Akito responded. "He taught me the precepts of your Storm Warrior Society, as well as the dogma of the Serenian Wind Warriors. He is an excellent teacher."

There was a quiet knock at the door.

"I believe that would be my Lady-Wife," Akito whispered conspiratorially. "She wonders what is taking me so long. She has been away for several weeks, visiting her sisters. Now she wants my full attention." He grinned. "And her nosiness demands she find out all she can about you!"

"I can't receive Her Highness like this!" Syn-Jern gasped. He could feel his nakedness from the tips of his toes to his burning face. "I don't have anything on under these covers!"

The Emperor snorted. "It matters not." He padded to the door and opened it quietly. "His head still bothers him," he heard Akito explaining, "but I believe he is ready." There was a soft mumble, then the rustle of silk.

The Empress of Chrystallus came into the room, touched her husband's arm lightly, and then glided silently to Syn-Jern's bed. Her smile was bright and warm and her touch as she reached out to lay it along Sorn's cheek, was cool and possessive.

"Good morn, Lord Syn-Jern," she whispered. "Remember me?"

"Rowena!" Syn-Jern breathed, his entire world coming to a halt.

She grinned. "Aye, Milord. Simply Rowena."

# Chapter Four

GENEVIEVE SORN WAS NOT HAPPY. SHE'D BEEN WAITING TO SEE HER husband for well over two hours. Lin Su, the personal bodyguard His Highness, the Emperor, had been assigned to Syn-Jern, and had assured her his new master was fine.

"He took a small amount of broth upon waking; drank two cups of tea." Lin Su inclined his head. "At the moment, His Imperial Majesty is visiting with him, Lady Sorn. They would not wish to be disturbed."

The mountain of a man that was Lin Su made for an excellent obstacle for he would not allow Genny to enter Syn-Jern's chamber, neither would he knock to announce her.

"And just when do you suppose they will be through with their chat?" Genny snapped.

Lin Su shrugged massive shoulders. "It is not my place to anticipate such things, Lady Sorn." His lips twitched beneath the camouflage of his thin mustache and he returned her hostile gaze with a complaisant one of his own. "Perhaps, soon, though."

Genny was not amused. She stamped her foot with frustration and was about to turn away when the monolith standing before her had dropped to the floor like the rock he was, his forehead pressed close to the carpeting.

"What the hell are you doing?" Genny gasped.

"Showing obeisance," came the answer.

Genny turned, her eyes going wide at the sight of the titian-haired woman walking toward her. Towering over Genny by a good foot, the woman took advantage of the younger woman's shock by pushing Genny none-too gently aside and rapping softly on Syn-Jern's chamber door.

"Who are you?" Genny demanded.

The woman ignored her as the Emperor opened the door. When the door closed in her face, Genny took a step toward it, reached out to take the handle, just as Lin Su leapt to his feet and caught her hand.

"You may not, Milady," he informed her.

Genny tried to snatch her hand away, but the giant had it locked firmly, if gently, in his huge paw. "Let go of me!" she snarled. "I want to see my husband!"

"Perhaps you should lie down, Lady Sorn," he said, pulling her toward her own chamber door.

"I don't want to lie down!" she hissed.

"I think perhaps you should rest now, Lady Sorn," he repeated and put his giant paw of a hand on Genny's neck. Almost instantly, Genny collapsed in the big man's arms.

The Emperor took that precise moment to exit Syn-Jern's room. "Is she ill?" Akito asked, rushing forward.

"Nay, Highness," Lin Su assured him. "Only sleeping."

Akito looked at the big man. "With help from you?"

"She wished to enter the Duke's chamber; I could not allow it."

"No," Akito agreed. "It would be most unwise at the moment."

ꟗ

"Does he know what you did?" Syn-Jern grumbled.

Rowena smiled sweetly. "Akito is privy to all I do, Milord Syn-Jern."

"Including my rape?" he snapped.

"Your seduction," she corrected.

"Nay, Lady!" he hissed. "My rape!"

The Empress sighed. "Call it what you will."

"It was rape!" he stressed. His hands clenched the bedcovers.

"It was necessary."

"For what?" he barked.

"Milord Syn-Jern," she said with a long exhalation of breath, "please do not shout. I am not hard of hearing."

He narrowed his eyes. "What will you do? Call another one of your Necromanian she-devils to gag me?"

She met his glower directly. "If need be to insure your cooperation."

Without the first moment's hesitation, he flung the covers from his legs, ignoring her short gasp, and stood there, weaving for a moment, looking for his clothes. "I want my gods-be-damned clothes, woman!" he demanded.

Rowena dragged her gaze from the thick nest of blond curls at the juncture of his thighs. "No doubt you do, but until the physicians have assured me you are well enough to dress yourself, you shall not have them."

"I want my clothes!"

Her chin came up. "You certainly won't get them using that tone with me, Milord Syn-Jern." She stared him down until he turned away, yanked the sheet from the bed, and draped it around his body. "Where do you think you can go?" she asked as he headed for the door.

Syn-Jern jerked the door open, ran up against the obstruction that was Lin Su. He pushed with his free hand since his left was holding the sheet. "Move," he ordered.

Lin Su looked past him, saw his Empress shake her head. "I am sorry, Duke

Sorn. You may not leave." He splayed his hand in the center of Syn-Jern's chest and pushed gently.

"Go to hell!" Syn-Jern snarled and tried to get past the man. He found himself lifted in a firm bear hug, taken back into the chamber, and deposited in the middle of the floor and the sheet torn from his body despite every effort to retain it.

Syn-Jern bellowed as the giant left him with nothing to wear, taking the sheet with him as he left the room and closed the door.

With a growl of pure animal fury, Syn-Jern turned on Rowena. "Am I your prisoner again?"

"No."

"Then let me out of this room!"

"Not until we have talked." Rowena settled back on the settee and regarded him. She patted the seat beside her. "I promise not to molest you."

Despite the fact that he was entirely naked, Syn-Jern stood, arms akimbo, and stared at her.

Rowena could feel a light sheen of sweat glistening on her upper lip and had to look away. "Do you remember that evening on the island?" she asked.

He snorted. "I don't think any man would ever forget being set on by a bunch of female sex fiends, Madame!"

"No one touched you but me," she reminded him.

"Aye, but the rest of your demonesses held me down for you, didn't they?" he accused.

"And enjoyed it, too," Rowena sighed. "Surely you are aware of the power you have over females, Syn-Jern."

"Oh, aye!" he spat. "They flocked around me like flies in Virago!"

Rowena winced. "Since that time, Milord."

He laughed scornfully. "Must be the scars on my hide that attracts you bitches now, eh?"

"Do you remember that evening?" she countered, wanting to take his mind from the mutilation of his flesh.

"Of course, I do!"

"Then you remember our conversation," she said.

"I remember it all," he answered bitterly.

ꟷ

When Rowena had finished with him, the women holding him backed away, allowed him to get up, hide from their view. He was mortally ashamed of what had happened; sick with the knowledge that he'd been taken against his will. He felt unclean, used, soiled beyond redemption and his first thought had been of Genny and how his wife would view what had happened.

"She need never know," Rowena told him.

"I'll know!' he spat at her. He glared at the woman who had raped him.

"It was not rape," she said then.

"If not rape, then what would you call it?"

"A necessity," Rowena named it.

"For whom?" He was enraged by her calm words.

"For us."

The answer further infuriated him. He swept the women with a defiant leer. "Am I to be taken by every one of you sluts?" He looked pointedly at their spears and the daggers thrust into the belts of their short gowns. "You'll have to kill me first for I'll damned sure do as much damage to as many of you as I can before it's through!"

"I believe he would, Lady," Olivia remarked.

"You better believe I will!" he roared. "I will—"

"What do you know of the Daughters of the Multitude, Milord Syn-Jern?" she asked, interrupting.

"That you're a bunch of whores," he sneered.

There was a low mumble of resentment, but Rowena held up her hand for quiet. She turned the full authority of her gaze on him. "Was your grandmother, Monique, a whore, then, Milord Syn-Jern?"

Syn-Jern swore at her.

"She was one of us," Rowena told him. "Surely you heard tales of her powers when you were a boy."

"That's neither here nor there," he hissed. "If Grandmere was one of your sect, she certainly never felt the need to..."

"His name was Justin," Rowena stated. "Justin McGregor, the first king of Serenia after the Holocaust. King Doran's father."

If the fury in those midnight blue orbs could have snuffed the life from his tormentress, she would have died in an explosion of light.

"That's a gods-be-damned lie!" he whispered.

"You no doubt heard the rumors of her affair with the Serenian prince, did you not?" Rowena challenged. "We certainly heard about it as far away as Chale. Of course that was before my time, you understand. Before I accepted the mantel of The Great Lady from Monique."

"They may have been lovers," he threw at her, "but she certainly did not rape him!"

"She most certainly did!" Rowena shot back. "Here!" She pointed to the cave's floor. "Where you were taken, Tristan Syn-Jern Sorn!"

"Every Consort has been taken in such a way since the Daughterhood was established," another of the women informed him.

"Whether he was willing or not," Olivia put in.

"And you're proud of that?" he bellowed. "Well, I'll promise you this much: as soon as I am able, I intend to warn sailors about that gods-be-damned little cave of yours. I—"

"Did you think you came to this place by chance, Milord Syn-Jern?" Rowena asked him. She stared into his sullen face. "Do you think the storm came up all on its own?" She shook her head. "You were brought here, my lover. You were ordered here by us!"

"For what purpose?" He came to his feet, oblivious to the spears.

"For the same reason Justin McGregor was brought here," Rowena replied. "And Olan Hesar before him. And before them, there were Jean-Claude Montyne; Severn Taborn; Liam Brell; Raine Wynth, and Ruan Cree. One royal son after another; one country after another; one generation after another in the hopes that we could find the one man destined to be our Champion!"

"They wouldn't do your bidding, eh?" he scoffed.

"None had the Power. That self-same Power with which you were born," Olivia explained.

"Power?" he questioned, incredulously. "That power I neither want nor can control? Is that what you desire? You want a killing machine to champion you?"

"We want a warrior who can help us crush the Domination and its hold over our peoples!" Olivia shouted. "You wield such power, Milord Syn-Jern, whether you wish to or not!"

"The Domination?" Syn-Jern shuddered violently. "No man would be stupid enough to go up against that filthy bunch."

"Who do you think controls the Tribunals of Virago and Serenia, Syn-Jern?" Rowena challenged. "Of Chale and Ionary? Necroman and Oceania?" She spat on the cave floor. "The Brotherhood of the Domination, that's who!"

"They were behind the theft of your land, Duke Sorn," Olivia said. "Behind the death of Trevor Saur."

"They are like cockroaches," Rowena hissed. "Step on one and another crawls out of the woodwork." She jabbed him in the chest with a rigid finger. "We need an exterminator, Milord Syn-Jern. A man who can stand up to them and crush them." She jabbed him again. "A champion who, with the very use of his mind, can completely devastate their ranks!" She jabbed again. "Are you that man?"

"Poke your finger at me one more time and I'll break it," he warned her, batting her hand away.

"Legends say one day there will come a warrior to crush the Domination. When, we do not know; but he will come." Rowena fused her stare with his.

"It may be you; it may not. But with every male child born on the night of the winter's Solstice, we make our search."

"That's it?" he asked, his jaw dropping open with disbelief. "You chose me because I happened to have had the misfortune of being born on the 21st of December?"

"Don't be ridiculous!" Rowena snarled. "There were other considerations, as well."

"Such as?"

"Where the child was born. How. To whom. How he was forced to grow up. What interest the Domination shows in him."

"And they showed great interest in you, Milord Syn-Jern," Olivia told him.

"Who says so?" he demanded.

"Demonicus," Rowena answered.

Syn-Jern could not argue that point. The priest had shown far too much interest in him since he had been old enough to know there were men like Demonicus Voire.

"Fight for us, Syn-Jern," Rowena begged, watching as he vacillated between believing her and rebelling. "Be our champion. You have been in ages past. Be so, now!"

"I..." He plowed his fingers through his hair. "Why didn't you just ask?" he growled. "Was what you did necessary? Was it supposed to bind me to you, Rowena?"

"Do not let your male pride get in the way of what you know must be done," Olivia cautioned him. "You will return to Virago to fight for what was taken from you. Why not simply go a step further and seek out the root of the evil instead of merely lopping off the branches?"

"Branches that will grow back and strengthen. Branches that will drop seed to breed more evil!" Rowena added.

Syn-Jern was not a stupid man and he understood their concerns. Everyone knew the Multitude fought the Domination, had for hundreds of years. Since the Holocaust. The Multitude was powerful, perhaps even more so than the Domination, and even though he'd never had dealings with the Daughters, he had always respected their fight with the evil the women had vowed to terminate. To hear that his beloved grandmother was one of them made him less inclined to argue.

"Join us, Milord Syn-Jern," Rowena begged. "We need you."

Something happened then that Syn-Jern Sorn would remember to the day he died and beyond. His Grandmother came to him, stood right before him in a halo of light; and what she had said, what she had told him, what she had made him promise, had brought the darkness, the moodiness, and silences that so worried his wife and friends.

"Syn-Jern?" Rowena asked, bringing him back to the present.

He looked at her, really looked at her, and perfect understanding hit him like a ton of rock. "You're pregnant," he breathed.

Rowena started. "Why do you say that?"

His gaze moved down her, held at her belly. "You wanted a child and you took it from me. That was what it was all about. It had nothing to do with the other part, nothing at all to do with that. You raped me to get with child." Even as she was shaking her head in denial, he nodded. "Aye, you did. Akito could not give you a babe so you—" He stopped, the Emperor's words coming back to him. "Twins?" he asked in a husky whisper. "You are carrying twins?"

Rowena opened her mouth to lie, but she could not. Instead, she lifted one shoulder in acceptance of his accusation. "With my powers combined with yours, I knew a male child would be almost invincible. If you could not or would not aid us, I would bring him up to do so." She smiled. "I did not, however, count on there being a girl child, as well. You are most potent, Milord Syn-Jern."

His hand trembled as he raked his fingers through his hair, a habit that endeared him to her. "If I can't control the damned thing—"

"We will teach you," she said quickly, reaching out to take his hand. "Pretorius and I. Even Akito. He has some limited magik, himself, he can teach."

Syn-Jern shook his head. "I don't know..."

"You made a promise to Monique," she reminded him.

"Aye," he sighed. And so he had.

## Chapter Five

"WHAT DID THAT WOMAN WANT WITH YOU?" GENNY DEMANDED LATER that morning.

Syn-Jern drew in a long breath. "We have to talk, Genevieve."

"Aye," his wife agreed. "That we do, Syn-Jern!" She came to his bed and stood there, angrily tapping her foot. "Who was that woman?"

He bit his lip. "The Empress Rowena."

Genny's eyebrow shot up. "Really?" she asked in a droll voice. "And just what did she want with you?"

There was guilt on her husband's face and he fidgeted with the covers. "Genny..." he began, but she cut him off.

"You look like a small boy caught with his hand in the candy jar, Milord. Do you know that ugly redhead?"

Surprise lifted Syn-Jern's brows. "Ugly? Rowena?" At his wife's narrowed gaze and constricted lips, he grinned. "You're jealous!"

"I am not!" she protested with a snort.

He looked at her closely. She was angry; her body was rigid; her eyes flashing; his grin widened. "You are jealous!"

"If it pleases you to think so, then fantasize all you will about my so-called jealousy, Syn-Jern, but if you do not tell me what that woman was doing in here, I will seek her out myself!"

The grin on Syn-Jern's face wavered. "I'm not sure that would be such a wise idea, Genny."

"Oh, you don't, do you?"

"No, not at all." He took his wife's hand. "Besides, she means nothing to me."

"Is that so?" she inquired in a voice that was too sweet by far. She sat beside him. "You know, Milord, I have often heard it said that in order for a woman not to mean something to a man, he must first have had dealings with her on a personal level."

The grin slipped from his face. "Now, Genny—"

"And in order for him to have had dealings with her on a personal level, he had to first know her."

"Well..."

Genny took his chin in a bruising grip. "Do you know that bitch, Syn-Jern?"

"We had met..."

"Where?"

"Genny..." He yelped as she jerked viciously on his chin. "Damn it, woman; that hurts!" he grumbled, pulling away.

"Syn-Jern!" she warned in a tone that brooked no further delay in his explanation.

He flexed his aching jaw. "All right!" he mumbled. "I've been trying to think of a way to tell you..."

"Thinking up lies to tell me?" she countered.

"No!" he snapped. "I don't want there to be lies or secrets between us, Genevieve, but this was not something easily told or confessed."

Genny drew back. "Confessed?" she pounced on the word. "Confession constitutes transgression, Milord Syn-Jern."

"I did nothing wrong!" he defended.

"You knew that woman." It was an accusation. "Before Chrystallus."

Syn-Jern's forehead creased. "Aye. I had encountered her."

"Encountered," she said flatly. "In what way, Milord?"

"Will you make me a promise?" he asked worriedly.

"No."

"Genny, please," he pleaded. "If you want to hear this, then let me tell it without you jumping on every word I say." His voice turned irritable. "It's hard enough to tell you this without having you sitting there waiting to slap the hell out of me if I say something you don't like!"

His wife folded her arms and stared at him, one brow lifted. "All right. I'll hold my tongue, and my hand, until you've finished."

He wasn't so sure she would; he wanted the ground rules understood. "You won't interrupt until I'm done?" When she shook her head, he took a deep breath, held it, then let it out slowly. "We met on the island."

"What island?"

"Genny!" he snapped. "You promised—"

She held up her hand. "Explain with names, dates and times, Syn-Jern, and there will be no reason for me to interrupt for clarification."

"I don't know the name of the gods-be-damned island, Genny," he snapped. "It was where we stayed during the hurricane."

That answer was not what his wife had been expecting, but she managed to hold her tongue, nodding for him to go on.

"It was while we were apart." At her arch look that told him she understood that much, he ducked his head. "I was captured by her women." When there was no outburst, he looked up, searched his wife's face for disbelief or humor; there was none.

"Go on," she said but there was no inflection in her voice to let him know what she'd felt at his words.

"There were a dozen or more of them. They had weapons they damned sure knew how to use and..." He blushed. "I didn't have a chance."

Genny continued to stare at him. Her look was disconcerting, accusing, but she did not speak.

He winced. "They tied me up."

"All night?" she asked sarcastically.

"Well, no," he answered, guiltily. "Not all night."

"I see."

Her tone told him she saw something that wasn't there. "They had weapons, Genny. Spears, daggers, swords..."

"So you've indicated." She crossed her legs. "These were warrior women, I take it?"

"Aye!" he said, grabbing at the word. "And very good warrior women. They overpowered me before I had time to react. The two Necromanian women who tied me up—"

"Necromanian?"

"Aye. They were Necromanian, Oceanian, and Ionarian. Rowena is Chalean. I don't know if there were any Viragonian women there, but one or two had Serenian accents."

"A conference of all nationalities on that little un-named island," she mumbled. "How quaint."

Syn-Jern cocked an annoyed brow at her. "You said you wouldn't interrupt."

"Sorry. Go on."

"These women are all part of the Multitude." He searched her face. "The Daughters of the Multitude?"

"I know who they are, Milord. All women know of their sect."

"They were there for some kind of gathering. The place is sacred to them."

"One of their Shadowlands," Genny acknowledged. She remembered her dream. "I've heard tales of such places."

"I was still tied up when Rowena arrived," he hurried to say.

"She's their Great Lady or some such title." Syn-Jern hesitated. "You're not going to like this," he finally said.

"You slept with her," Genny said flatly. "I've heard such women have powers they can use over men."

He shook his head. "No, not exactly."

"Not exactly?" came the growl.

His face flooded with color. "I had been tied up, Genny, but they untied me then..." He couldn't look at her. "They held me down. Then..."

"Then what, Milord?" she asked, her voice a lethal whisper.

"She raped me," he answered in a small voice.

When the explosion didn't happen, he risked looking at his wife. She was sitting on the edge of the bed, staring at him, her face perfectly blank. For what seemed like hours, she just sat there, unblinking, staring, her breath easy and controlled, her hands relaxed in her lap.

"Genny?" he questioned, worried. "Say something."

She didn't.

"Genny, please," he begged. He didn't dare touch her for fear she'd claw his eyes out. His lovely wife had a violent temper he'd seen in action too many times. Her unexpected calmness in the face of his confession was unnerving. "Genny?"

Genny stood. Her face was devoid of expression, her head cocked slightly to one side.

The silence was torture.

"This is why I didn't want to tell you," he said, coming to his knees on the mattress. "I was afraid of your reaction." He reached out to her, but she stepped back.

Genny looked down at his nakedness then settled her gaze on his hurt face, but she could not find words. If her life had depended on it, she could not have uttered one syllable. She just pointed at his nudity.

Syn-Jern snatched the sheet up to cover himself, suddenly mortally ashamed. The sheet was a barrier he wanted to hide behind, to protect himself from the look on his wife's face. He was of a mind to fling the damned silk fabric over his head, lie down, curl up, and die.

But life isn't as easy as that and if he wanted to salvage the moment, he had to make her see why he'd kept this piece of vile news from her.

"They held me down, Genny. I couldn't get away. I tried, but I couldn't. There were too many of them and she had planned this for a long time."

"She? This Rowena?" she asked.

Encouraged that she had spoken, he nodded. He scrambled from the bed, dragging the sheet with him. "I should have told you what happened that morning, but..."

"Aye," she said. "You should have." She squinted dangerously. "That was four days ago, Milord. Why have you said nothing before now?"

His heart was thudding madly in his chest. "Because I didn't want to see you looking at me the way you're looking at me right now!"

"How am I looking at you?" she asked.

"Like every woman who's ever known me has looked at me," he answered. "With contempt. With utter hatred." His voice broke. "With disgust."

She shook her head, ignoring his words. "Did you go looking for that woman that day?"

"No!" he said. "I had no idea they were even on that damned island. If I had..." He shivered. "If I had known what would happen, I sure as hell wouldn't have left Patrick Kasella's side!"

"Did you help that woman in any way to do what she did to you?"

He stared at her. "I fought them, Genny! I—"

"They held you down," Genny said in a matter of fact voice.

"Aye, then—"

"Then this Rowena person did what?"

His face flamed. He tore his gaze from her. "She straddled me."

"Straddled you, then impaled herself upon you?"

Syn-Jern flinched. "Aye."

"Is that all?" she asked, suspecting it wasn't.

"Well..."

"That isn't all." Genny clenched her hands. "What else? Tell me all of it before you lose your nerve."

His mortification couldn't have been any worse if he'd been forced to run stark naked through the streets with a red bow tied around his shaft.

"She's pregnant," he said in a voice so soft, so low, it was no more than a breath of sound, but his wife heard it, nevertheless.

"She told you so?" Genny snarled.

He searched her face for any sign of forgiveness. "Aye. This morning."

"And being The Great Lady, she would know," Genny said on a long breath. "Boy or girl?"

There was nothing left to do but answer her questions. "One of each."

"Twins?" Genny rasped. "And just precisely what is it she intends for you to do about the matter?" A horrible thought interrupted. "Does her husband know?"

Syn-Jern nodded miserably. "And isn't all that damned happy about it, either." He shrugged. "But the man desperately wants children and he can't give her any."

"So she steals them from another woman's husband!" Genny snapped. "I take it since her husband knows of her perfidy, she has no plans for you to acknowledge the babes as your own."

He closed his eyes to the bitterness in his wife's voice. "She has absolved me of any responsibility."

Genny's mouth twisted. "Isn't that thoughtful of her. So, does that also mean she has absolved you of any further recourse with her, as well?"

"Not exactly," he whispered.

Genny came to him in a rush of fury. "What exactly does it mean, then, Syn-Jern?" She pummeled his chest, staggering him. "Does she mean for you to be at her beck and call to do stud service for her again?"

He caught her wrists, held her even though she struggled wildly against him. "No, Genny! She doesn't want anything like that." She kicked him on the shins and he yelped with pain.

"Then what?" she shouted, tears falling down her cheeks. "What does she want from you?"

Despite her struggling, he drew her to his chest and held her, stilling her angry fists, kissing the top of her head, feeling her trembling down the entire length of his body.

"Shush, now," he soothed, running his hand down her back. "I am yours. Don't you know that?"

"She raped you!" Genny cried, her body sagging against her husband. She clung to his neck, her anger replaced by abject sorrow. "She raped you."

"Genny, stop," he said. "You'll make yourself sick." He cradled her, planting small kisses at her temple. On her forehead.

"What does she want with you?" Genny whispered, fearing the worst.

"My sword arm, Sweeting," he said. "Just that, nothing more."

Genny pushed away. She could see the pain on his face as he took in her ravaged visage. He would have spoken, but she put her hand over his lips.

"As her Consort? Oh, Merciful Alel, Syn-Jern, you can't—"

"Her champion and nothing more," he said firmly. "I made her swear on her honor."

"A woman who would take what is not hers has no honor!" Genny hissed.

"Listen to me," he said, pulling them both to the floor and kneeling there with her. "I love you, Genny Sorn. You are my life. If I were to lose you, I couldn't bear it, lady. Do you think I would do anything to jeopardize how you feel about me?" He shook his head vehemently. "I spent my entire life searching for you. I knew I'd found what I had been craving from the moment I saw you on the Wind Lass." He squeezed her arms. "I knew I would do anything, try anything, endure anything, to make you mine. I swore I would move heaven and earth to have you. Do you think I'd ever allow anyone or anything to come between us."

"She will..." Genny began, but he shushed her.

"Have my sword arm and nothing more," he stressed. "The Multitude needs a warrior to help them fight the spread of the Domination's evil, Genny. I would be stupid not to accept her offer of help to do what I had already planned: to crush the Viragonian Tribunal, if I can. Rowena's help in doing that is all either she or I want from this unholy union of ours. This I swear to you on the child you carry within you! Our child!"

"You know?" she gasped. She had not known how to tell him.

"Aye," he said, smiling. "I know."

Genny's face crinkled. "She told you?"

"No, Lin Su did," he replied and pulled her to him. The sheet slipped from his lower body and the feel of her against him was glorious. "It pleases me beyond telling, Sweeting."

"You aren't angry?" she asked in a small voice.

"Why would I be? I have never been happier."

"I can't tell you what sex it will be," she pouted.

"Nor would I want you to if you could," he laughed. "That would take the mystery from it, Dearling."

"Truly?"

"Whatever it will be—boy or girl—what matter as long as it is healthy?" He smoothed the hair from her damp cheeks. "I love you. Don't you know that?"

"I won't have her putting her hands on you, Syn-Jern Sorn!" Genny snarled.

"She will not. I swear it to you."

"Nor being anywhere near you, either!"

"There is no reason for me to be—" He stopped, thinking, then bit his lip.

"What?" Genny barked.

"That might be a problem."

His wife pushed at his chest. "What kind of problem?"

"She intends to join with Pretorius in teaching me how to harness the powers within me."

Genny could see the usefulness of having the Multitude's most powerful sorceress instructing her husband. After all, when Syn-Jern went against the Tribunal, and in essence the Domination, he would need all the strength at his command.

"As long as I sit in on the lessons, she may do so," she decided, eyeing her husband closely.

Syn-Jern smiled. "Agreed although Rowena may object."

Genny ground her teeth. "Let that homely red-haired husband molester object all she will!" she told him. "You are mine, Syn-Jern Sorn and the gods help any woman foolish enough to try to take you away from me. For any reason!"

# Chapter Six

HE WAS WELL OVER SIX FEET TALL, THIN AS A RAIL, WITH LONG ARMS AND crippled arthritic fingers that curled painfully toward his large palms. His shock of long white hair was thinning, but sleek, worn combed straight back from his high forehead. His nose was beak-like; his cheekbones bony and protruding with deep eye sockets where pale blue orbs, the color of frost on a winter's day, held little warmth, but mirrored the man's vast intelligence. He walked with a rigid control of his thin shoulders and stiffness to his long, stick-like legs.

"I am Pretorius," he said in a deep, husky voice as he entered the room. He did not extend his twisted hand for greeting, but bowed elegantly in the Chrystallusian fashion.

"Forgive us for not sending word of our arrival, Master," Koji said respectfully, bowing just a fraction lower than their host.

"I knew you were coming," Pretorius answered as he nodded his head at Syn-Jern Sorn. He swept his arm to the thick cushions scattered about the room. "Please, sit. Refreshments have been ordered."

Syn-Jern bowed, motioned for Weir and Patrick to sit before he did. Koji had warned them to let him do the talking, get the social amenities out of the way before they got down to the real business of why they were there.

"You had an uneventful journey through the Pass?" their host inquired as he folded his lanky frame upon a cushion and tucked his crippled hands into the sleeves of his emerald green silk robe.

"We made excellent time, Master," Koji informed him. "The snows have not deepened so much as yet."

"That is good." Pretorius did not look at the young woman who silently entered the room. "Had you come later in the season, it would have been more difficult to reach me."

The girl placed a teakwood tray on a low table that sat in the center of the ring of cushions. The smell of strong tea filled the little room as she poured a small porcelain cup and extended it with respect to Pretorius. When he sniffed the tea, then nodded, she handed the cup to Syn-Jern.

"It is rice tea," Pretorius explained. "A special recipe I find relaxing."

"Thank you," Syn-Jern told the girl.

"Was your summer productive, Master?" Koji asked as he received his cup of tea.

"Ah, most productive. Our pantries are filled to overflowing." He waited until each of his guests had tried their tea before sipping his own.

"A bountiful harvest is most appreciated," Koji said wisely.

"Just as the destruction of a crop is devastating to the soul," Pretorius sighed. He put aside his cup and looked directly at Syn-Jern. "And the loss of one's property a bitter brew to swallow, is it not, Lord Syn-Jern?"

"Aye, Master Pretorius," Syn-Jern agreed. "A very bitter brew." He knew the talk would now get to the heart of the matter.

"I, of course, will help you in what you have set yourself to do," Pretorius informed his guest. "There was never a question of that." He frowned slightly. "Even if my tutoring will be augmented by those of whom I am not particularly fond."

"The Multitude?" Patrick questioned and received a fierce shake of the head from Koji.

Paddy blushed, remembering he was not to speak unless first spoken to.

Syn-Jern shot Paddy a withering look. "Can this power I have be controlled well enough to do us any good, Master?"

"With proper training, it can," Pretorius answered. "But it will take a great deal of time and work for you to learn to harness that raw magik lurking within you." He took up his teacup again. "Two years should suffice."

"Two years?" Weir gasped, forgetting he, too, had been warned to be silent. "We don't have—" He grunted as Syn-Jern's elbow dug into his ribs.

"You may not have two years, Lord Saur, but in order for your friend to best achieve the expertise with which to fight his enemies, he will need two years of training."

Weir took the opportunity to speak since the older man had addressed him. "What do we do while Syn's in training?"

Pretorius shrugged. "Stay here. Learn, also." He arched a white-blond brow at his guest. "There are things you could learn, as well." He drained his cup and handed it to the young woman to re-fill. "If you desire to be a good pirate, you have come to the perfect place to learn. Our pirates are the most formidable in all the world."

"Well, that's all well and good, but—"

"As for you, Lord Kasella," Pretorius interrupted. "We have a young man here from your own neck of the woods who is in training with one of our fencing instructors. Perhaps you have heard of him? His name is Robyn Brell."

Patrick's mouth sagged open. "Prince Robyn Brell? The Heir-Apparent?"

"One and the same," Pretorius acknowledged. "For some time now, we have taught fencing to the heirs of the royal house of Brell."

Patrick turned to Syn-Jern and smiled. "I think I'll stay."

"I am pleased," Pretorius said. He looked at Weir.

Weir shook his head. "I can't. I've got a ship and men to look after. They can't be expected to cool their heels here. They've got families back on Montyne Cay. Families who need them."

"A suggestion?" Pretorius injected.

"We would welcome any advice you give," Syn-Jern said.

"Allow those who wish to return to Montyne Cay to do so. The Emperor will provide them with a ship suitable to sail home." He inclined his head. "A small gift of appreciation from the Chrystallusian people for the task you have set for yourself, Lord Syn-Jern."

Syn-Jern put his cup aside. "You think I'm doing the right thing in fighting for what was mine?"

"Most assuredly, I do," Pretorius replied. He, also, put his cup aside and held up his hands, palms outward. "Do you know what these are, Milord Syn-Jern?"

Patrick and Weir exchanged a shocked look; Koji merely nodded for he'd seen such marks many times before.

"Nail holes," Syn-Jern said softly.

"Yes," Pretorius sighed.

"When were you there?" Paddy asked.

"Oh," their host answered wistfully, "many years before any of you were born." He switched his gaze to Koji. "Well, most of you, at any rate."

"Where were you sentenced?" Weir demanded.

"In Serenia." He smiled at Syn-Jern. "I, too, killed a man with my power, Syn-Jern. And just as you, I was sickened by what I had done. I swore to learn to control it, but there was no one who could teach me. When, in a fit of jealous rage, I killed my lover, I was sentenced to deportation."

"You are from a royal family?" Weir asked quietly.

Their host was silent for a moment, then lifted one shoulder as though the answer was of little consequence. "I am of the Boreal line, yes." He held Weir's stare. "You understand, of course, that Pretorius is not my true name?"

His mind working furiously. Weir tried to remember his Serenian history. He could think of no member of the McGregor family who had been sentenced to Tyber's Isle for murder.

"As I have said," Pretorius reminded him, "it was long before your time, Lord Saur."

There was a faint tick of a smile on the man's thin lips. "Have you not a connection to the McGregor, as well?"

"We are distant cousins," Weir answered sourly.

"Yes, I know," Pretorius told him and this time there was a slight, obvious smile. "One day your family will be even closer to the McGregor clan." He dipped his head. "As close as brothers."

Weir shook his head. "There has never been any love lost between the Saurs and the royal family, Master Pretorius. I doubt there will ever be any closeness."

"You'd be surprised," Pretorius said with a twitch of his lips. "Even one drop of blood can be sacred among families."

"How long were you imprisoned before you escaped?" Syn-Jern wanted to know.

"Five years," Pretorius replied. "Out of the lifetime I was given." He frowned. "I was caught right at the landing site the first time and taken back. I never made it off the Isle." He snorted. "The second time I learned my lesson and made good my escape."

"And you came here?" Syn-Jern asked, intrigued.

"There was a man here, then. A very wise and powerful man named Yulin. He took me under his wing and taught me all he knew. Between us, we established a training camp for those of like mind who wished to see the Domination destroyed." He ground his teeth. "Cockroaches that they are."

Syn-Jern smiled. "That's the second time I've heard those bastards likened to cockroaches."

Pretorius finished his second cup of tea, then relaxed. "I can scry into the future, Milord Syn-Jern. It is not a talent I use often or at any great length; nor do I ever read my own destiny. Sometimes the things a man knows about what is in his future can alter his present, and in the knowing, make that future come into being."

"And what do you see for us?" Patrick asked.

"Glory for some, Lord Kasella; a high price to pay for others."

"But will we accomplish what we set out to do?" Syn-Jern questioned.

"Some will; some won't," Pretorius said mysteriously. "But, all in all, your venture will turn out well."

"At what price will we succeed, though?" Paddy asked.

Pretorius turned his enigmatic gaze on the young Chalean. "Love and loyalty sometimes require great sacrifices, willingly given, lovingly so, but done completely without regret." He looked at Syn-Jern. "You have a question, Milord?"

"I guess what I want to know is if what we accomplish will do any good. Will it make a difference?"

"Most assuredly so," Pretorius nodded. "The Domination will lose power for three generations before rearing its tentacles again."

Syn-Jern frowned. "But we won't destroy it?"

"No, I am afraid not. That distinction lies with a young man yet to be born and he will pay a very great price for his victory." Pretorius shuddered. "Men never learn," he whispered. "So much pain and suffering. So much tragedy for my family."

"Then this warrior," Weir asked, sitting forward on his cushion, "will come from our homeland of Serenia?"

Pretorius nodded grimly. "Aye, Lord Weir. He will be The Chosen. The Dark Overlord of the Wind." He mentally shook himself and turned his full attention to Syn-Jern.

"What's it to be, Milord? Do you train with us or not?"

"Do I have a choice?" Syn-Jern asked lightly.

"We all have choices, Syn-Jern Sorn," Pretorius told him.

"If I am to reclaim what was mine..." He looked at Weir. "What belonged to others before the Tribunal gobbled it up, then I don't see any other choice but to learn to use this damned power I don't want and didn't ask for."

Pretorius smiled the first true smile. "Good. Be here at first light in the morning. We will begin your training then!"

# PART FOUR

## Chapter One

SYN-JERN PACED THE FLOOR OF THE IMPERIAL PALACE LIKE A CAGED TIGER. Now and again, he would look up, listen and, upon hearing only silence, stalk from one end of the hallway to the other.

"He's going to wear the carpet down to the matting," Patrick commented with a snort.

"Shut up," Weir snapped. He was sitting on a chair, his hands dangling between his spread knees, his eyes glued to the intricate pattern on the carpet runner.

"What good does he think it does to…" Patrick began only to have Weir grasp him painfully on the knee.

"Shut up!" Weir insisted.

Realizing his friend's nerves were stretched thin, Patrick nodded and reached down to ease Weir's hand from his leg.

"Why is it taking so gods-be-damned long?" Syn-Jern grumbled as he passed the two men

"Why don't you sit down?" Patrick countered, turning his head to follow Syn-Jern.

"It shouldn't take this long, should it?" Syn-Jern asked as he walked back the other way.

"How the hell would we know?" Patrick queried.

"First time is always a mite long," Tarnes commented, drawing on his pipe. "Ain't uncommon for it to be twenty hours or more."

Three sets of horrified eyes shot to Norbert Tarnes. One set belonged to a man who groaned with irritation; one, to a man who shuddered hard then swallowed convulsively. The third man nearly passed out as he assimilated the information and had to stop in mid-stride to grab a marble column for support.

"Twenty hours?" Syn-Jern repeated, his face pale. His attention went to the door of his wife's room and held. "Twenty hours?"

"Or more," Tarnes reiterated. He leaned back in his chair, exchanging a knowing look with Jarl Stevens. "Might be tomorrow a'fore she has the bantling."

The men watched as Syn-Jern Sorn sank slowly to his haunches, squatting there in the middle of hallway and looking as though he would throw up that morning's meal.

"Hell, son," Stevens piped up. "Women are used to this sort of thing." He looked at Tarnes, who was nodding in agreement. "The gods made 'em to birth our children."

"She was in pain," Weir whispered, having been the one to find his sister just after she had gone into labor. Tears filled his green eyes. "She hurt." He lifted his head and looked directly at Syn-Jern. "She hurt," he repeated, his jaw set.

Syn-Jern flinched. Not because his brother-in-law was blaming him for Genny's predicament, but because he blamed himself. When news reached him on the training field that his wife was in labor, he had whooped with joy.

It was only as he sped across the pasture to the palace that he began to understand the seriousness of what was happening. Never having been around females giving birth, he had, nevertheless, seen horses straining to push their young from heaving bodies; he had some idea of the birthing process. But as he ran, he remembered one such animal panting in pain and he pulled up short, his eyes wide in his sweaty face.

"Pain," he had said, and the word was like a red-hot prod against his heart.

The thought of the woman he loved being subjected even to a bruise cut him to the quick. Knowing there was nothing he could do to relieve her torment, was a torture more severe than any he'd ever experienced.

"Milady, I would gladly take the pain from you," he whispered.

He started walking toward the palace, his heart racing. When he reached the outer courtyard, a servant ran to him, bowing and bobbing like a cork on the water.

"Your Lady has been taken to her room, Your Grace. You must hurry!"

Loping after the servant, he had hoped it would all be over by the time he arrived, but one look at Weir Saur's face told him that was not going to be the case.

"Where the hell were you?" Weir threw at him.

"Training…field," Syn-Jern replied, out of breath. He looked from Weir's angry face to the stoic expression on Patrick's.

"They say it will take awhile," Patrick explained.

Now, hunkered down outside his wife's room, Syn-Jern strained to hear even the smallest sound, but only silence filled the long, gilded corridor.

"Have any of you been over to the ship Master Pretorius is having fitted out for us?" Neevens asked, drawing everyone's attention.

"Not now," Weir hissed. "We aren't concerned with the gods-be-damned white ship right now!"

Neevens looked at Tarnes, then Stevens, then shrugged as the older men cast him a warning look.

Syn-Jern put his hands to his neck and threaded his fingers behind it. He rocked on his heels, making tiny little hopeless sounds that irritated Kasella more than the waiting.

"Will you stop that?" Patrick threw at his friend. "You're starting to—"

The loud, piercing scream unnerved every man there, even the seasoned salts. Weir and Kasella stood up slowly, their mutual stares going to Genny's husband. Syn-Jern was on his knees, his entire body shuddering. When the second scream peeled from the room, he threw back his head and howled in unison.

"Sweet Merciful Alel!" Neevens prayed, crossing himself. "The NightWinds."

"Shut up!" Saur, Kasella, Stevens, and Tarnes shouted in unison.

The third ululating shriek brought Sorn to his feet. "Genny!" Syn-Jern cried out, his hand out in pleading. He stumbled to the door, but Patrick stopped him before he could go into Genny's room.

"You don't want to do that," Kasella warned as another scream erupted from behind the closed portal.

"Milady!" Syn-Jern bellowed, trying to get past his friend. He touched the door. He locked gazes with Kasella. "I have to go to her."

"No, you don't," Patrick disagreed. "She doesn't need you right now."

"I have to help her!" Syn-Jern said.

"You've helped her enough," Weir Saur snarled.

Syn-Jern opened his mouth to reply, but the next sound—the mewling cry of a newborn babe—made his knees weak and he would have collapsed had Patrick not grabbed him.

"Easy there," Kasella grunted, steadying his friend.

Tarnes sat down and popped his ever-present pipe in his mouth. Even though the obnoxious thing wasn't lit, he drew on it as if it were. He smiled around the stem as Stevens and Neevens walked over to him.

"A shiny gold piece says it's a girl," Stevens quipped.

"Two says it's a boy," Neevens replied.

"I'll match your one," Tarnes stated. "It's a boy."

Patrick held Syn-Jern's gaze. "Now, you can go in, Milord," he said, smiling and stepped aside to open the door for his friend.

Syn-Jern was hesitant to enter the room. He could see the Imperial Physician standing beside Genny's bed, wiping his hands on a towel. On the other side of the bed was an elderly woman cradling a bundle in her arms, her head bent over her burden as she crooned in the lyrical Chrystallusian tongue. Another older woman, carrying a pile of soiled linen, glanced shyly at him as she made her way from the room.

"You may enter, Lord Sorn," the Healer said softly.

Syn-Jern shuffled uneasily into the room, his hands thrust deep into the pockets of his cords. He cast a quick glance to the Healer and when the man nodded easily, everyone in the room, and outside in the corridor, heard Syn-Jern's sigh of relief.

Healer Ju'lin stepped back to allow his patient's husband to take his place at his wife's bedside. In passing, he patted the nervous man gently on the back, meeting the worried eyes calmly. "She sleeps, Milord, but she came through the birthing extremely well for a first timer." He nodded toward the elderly woman. "Would you like to see your son?"

Syn-Jern drew in a harsh gasp. "Son?" he questioned.

"Aye, Milord," Healer Ju'lin acknowledged.

The elderly woman, whom Syn-Jern learned was the Healer's wife, eased the cover from the baby's face, and smiled when she heard his father's groan of awe. "Would you like to hold him, Milord Sorn?" she asked shyly.

He didn't know if he should; but the old woman didn't give him time to protest for she was presenting him with the precious bundle, settling it firmly in his arms.

"As the old saying goes, Milord," she said with a low chuckle, "he will not break."

The sweetest thing in the world to Syn-Jern Sorn at that moment was the negligent weight of his firstborn. The wizened little face that peered at him from the folds of the blanket was red and wrinkled like an apple left too long in a jar of water. But the crystal blue eyes that stared into his own were alive and inquisitive and the rosebud lips were puckered as though in deep thought.

His right hand trembling, Syn-Jern lifted one finger to the tiny fist and almost instantly, the little hand gripped his finger. Syn-Jern's smile could have lit the darkest night. He looked up at the older woman and then at the Healer, pride rampant on his beaming face.

"What will you call him, Milord?" the Healer inquired.

Syn-Jern's eyes widened. "I don't know," he said. "We have not talked of names. I think—"

"Dermot Patrick Weir Sorn," was the sleepy mumble.

She was smiling lazily, her rumpled hair a dark halo fanned on the pillow. She was pale, but there were two bright patches of color high on her cheekbones. Her voice was tired, but there was nothing weary in the way she held out her arms for her child.

Syn-Jern eased onto the mattress, turning so he could hand this wonderful gift to the woman he loved. He felt as though his heart would burst with pride when she bared her breast and put the infant to nurse. Tears slid silently down his cheeks, yet he was unaware of their passing. He touched Genny's arm.

"Thank you, Milady," he said, as unaware of the raw emotion in his words as he was of the droplets of moisture falling from his eyes.

"Does the name agree with you, Milord?" she asked, searching his gaze.

He nodded, too overcome at that moment to answer. When she extended her hand, he took it, bringing her palm to his lips and kissing her gently in the center of that soft flesh. He cradled her hand against his chest, not realizing she could feel the hard tattoo of his excited heart.

"I want to give you many children," Genny whispered, her tired eyes closing.

"There will be time to talk of that later," the Healer said in his professional tone. He laid a hand on Syn-Jern's shoulder, indicating he was to let his lady rest.

"I love you," Genny said as she fell in a healing sleep.

He gently let go of her hand, laying it beside her on the bed. He stood, bent over her, and placed the softest of kisses on her damp brow. When he straightened, he kissed his fingertips and laid them just as tenderly on his son's wisp of dark curls. "I love you both," he said.

In the corridor, each of the men came to him, congratulated him on the birth of his firstborn, then quietly left, allowing him time to get accustomed to the magnitude of what had happened this day. When he was alone, Syn-Jern closed his eyes tightly, his shoulders slumped, and he covered his face with his hands.

ꕥ

When news came to the Empress Rowena of the birth of Lord Sorn's child, she rubbed the blossoming mound of her own belly and smiled. "A fine strapping son you will be, Dermot Sorn," she whispered. "And a faithful brother and friend to your little brother and sister."

"They will get to know one another?" her husband inquired.

Rowena nodded. "Aye, for they will grow up here together." Her lovely face crinkled with worry. "This will be the only safe place for his family."

Emperor Akito knelt beside his wife and laid his head in her lap. He loved to have her stroke his hair for her touch soothed the concerns that kept him awake most every night.

"Why does your Sisterhood put these men through such torment, Rowena?" he asked.

His wife's fingers threaded gently through Akito's thick black hair. "They are tested with fire, my husband, because they are the Chosen. They are Princes of the Wind and each in turn must know the burn of that harsh element. We protect them as best we can, but in the end, it is their strength, or lack thereof, that will fulfill their destinies."

Akito shuddered. "I would not like to be one of your Chosen Ones, Milady," he said with heartfelt sincerity.

"And I am thankful you are not," his wife told him.

## Chapter Two

PATRICK, WEIR, AND SYN-JERN SAT LOOKING OUT TO SEA, WATCHING THE terns swooping over the waters. The sky was a soft gray, anticipating rain, and the light breeze that rippled their hair was pleasantly cool. The men had been sitting on the promontory for over two hours, keeping track of the workers who were putting the finishing touches on Weir Saur's new ship, The Revenge. The black hull gleamed in the lowering light and the black shrouds, though furled, looked intimidating even from a distance.

"What did she say again?" Weir asked, following the path one squawking tern was making as it stitched the sky.

Syn-Jern sighed. "She thinks I'm not letting her go with us because I am tired of her. Was she dropped on her head when she was born?"

Patrick snorted with amusement, then sobered when his two companions sent him a warning look. "Sorry," he mumbled.

"It's the other woman," Weir said, nodding.

Syn-Jern's forehead crinkled. "What other woman?" he asked.

Weir Saur shrugged. "Whatever woman you had before her," he stated.

"Or women," Patrick amended. When Syn-Jern turned a confused look to him, Patrick lifted his hands from the ground and spread them wide in an attitude of 'you-should-know; not-I'. "There was one who betrayed you, wasn't there?"

Syn-Jern stared at him for a moment, then a light passed quickly over his face, and he looked away. "Oh," he said. The second word dropped like a rock into the conversation, "Her."

"Aye, her," Weir stated. He craned his neck so he look past Patrick to where Syn-Jern sat propped on his elbows on the grass. "We've been training here for two years, Syn and in all that time you've said nothing of her to us." He exchanged a look with Patrick, then returned his attention to Syn-Jern. "Have you told Genny about her."

"Sweet Merciful Alel, no!" Syn-Jern muttered.

"You'd better," Patrick advised, "else it's going to be hell leaving her here imagining you in Virago humping some skack there."

"He humps one skack," Weir snarled, emphasizing the Viragonian slang word, "and that will be the last skacking he will ever do!"

Syn-Jern locked gazes with his brother-in-law then smiled nastily. "Skack you," he said sweetly.

"You know precisely what I mean, Syn-Jern," Weir warned.

"You'd better tell her about the woman," Patrick said.

"Aye, he'd better," Weir agreed in a menacing tone.

Syn-Jern sighed. He hadn't thought about Rosa-Lynn in a long, long time and the thought of her now made his stomach churn.

"Go tell her, now," Weir ordered. He glanced at the ship that would be taking them to Virago on the morning tide two days hence. "Give her time to accept what you've got to tell her before you go."

ℰ𝒪𝒞ℬ

Genny looked up as her husband poked his head into the nursery. She put a finger to her lips, warning him their child was sleeping. Covering her son, she tiptoed from the room, easing the door closed.

"How is the rash" Syn-Jern asked.

"Under control," she replied. She went to her dressing table and sat. Her eyes met her husband's in the mirror. "Don't you think you need to get dressed?" she asked, then wrinkled her nose. "After you bathe?"

Syn-Jern frowned, then lifted his arm to sniff. His lip curled. "Aye, a bath is definitely in order I think."

"Aye, so do I," his wife replied. She picked up her brush and began to pull it through her hair, not in the least surprised when her husband eased it from her hand and began to draw the bristles down her long tresses. She watched his face as he worked. "You have something to talk to me about, Syn-Jern?" she asked quietly.

His gaze locked with hers reflected in the mirror. "You know me too well, Milady," he complained.

"No, I know your moods," she replied, retrieving the brush.

Syn-Jern thrust his hands into the pockets of his breeches. For a long time, neither spoke, then he sighed deeply, walked to the window, and stared down at the courtyard.

"All right," his wife said, laying the brush on the dressing table. "Out with it, Syni," she said with exasperation. "What have the three of you done now?"

He looked around. "Nothing," he said, surprised. When she cocked her head to one side in warning, he shrugged. "Really, we've done nothing."

Genny searched the innocent expression on her unruly husband's face for a moment then decided he was being truthful. "All right," she sighed. "What are you three about to do that you know I won't like?"

He grinned. "You can't chastise me, Genevieve, until I've actually committed the crime."

She frowned. "Out with it, Syn-Jern!"

Her husband chuckled. "Your trust in my ability to be a grown-up leaves a lot to be desired, Genny," he told her.

"Humpf," Genny snorted in reply, "your ability to be a grown-up is often in question, Milord."

He didn't reply to her taunt. Instead, he pulled his hands from his pockets and sat on the wide window seat. Stretching out on the plump cushion, he lifted his knees and rested his arms on them. "We do need to talk, Sweeting," he said quietly.

In the three years she had known this enigmatic man, she had become accustomed to his moody silences for they were not brooding, melancholy silences, but rather were of the reflective and introspective kind. His quietness was a good indication of something bothering him for usually he was sparring either verbally or physically with Paddy or Weir. He had a wonderful sense of humor and loved to tell jokes that were not always suitable for mixed company. Possessing a beautiful singing voice to accompany a remarkable ability on the guitar, it was not unusual to hear him singing or playing to the children gathered outside the solarium for their morning lessons. Much of the time he was either laughing and joking with the men of Weir's crew or teasing the servants until the entire Imperial Palace rang with laughter.

So when he became silent, Genny knew he was troubled.

She also knew he would broach the subject of what was pestering him in his own good time. But she wasn't prepared for what he had to say.

"Her name was Rosa-Lynn," he said quietly.

Genny turned on the seat and gave him her full attention. "Who?" she asked, her heart doing a funny thump in her chest.

He was looking out the window, his head against the wall. 'The woman in Virago." He closed his eyes. "My betrothed." When his wife made no comment, he turned to her. She was staring back at him with a carefully blank expression.

"Go on," she said after a moment or two had passed and it seemed he needed to be prompted.

He could not look at her as he told the tale; he was too ashamed. So, he returned his gaze to the window and the light rain that was beginning to plink against the pane. He lifted his left hand and touched the glass with the knuckle of his index finger, traveling the path of a raindrop as it fell down the pane.

"Did you love her?" she queried, not really wanting to know the answer to that question, but understanding she had to ask.

"With all my heart," he said softly. He drew in a long, shaky breath then exhaled slowly. "And I thought she loved me." He gave a small, self-deprecating snort. "Shows how much I knew women back then."

Genny could not resist. "And you think you know us now, Milord?" she asked in a light, teasing tone.

"No, Genny," he said, shaking his head. "And no man ever will."

"Humpf," was his wife's reply to that. She stood and walked to the window seat, then sat in front of him, wrapping her hand around his calf. She rested her cheek against his knee. "So," she said, "tell me of this vixen who didn't have sense enough to keep the treasure Alel cast her way."

Syn-Jern put his hand on her head and stroked the midnight silk of her hair. "Do you know how much I love you?" he whispered.

The demoness that exists in every woman's soul answered him: "More than you loved this Rosa-Lynn person, I hope."

He threaded his fingers through her hair and anchored her head as he searched deep green eyes in which jealousy ran rampant. "More than my own life, Milady," he swore to her. He stretched out his legs and pulled her onto his lap, settling her against his chest as he enfolded her in his arms. He kissed her hair then rested his chin atop her head.

"I will tell you the whole of it, Genny," he said seriously. "All I ask it that you say nothing until I am done." He craned his neck to look down at her. "Is that a deal?"

She nodded, unwilling to speak for fear the green-eyed monster would issue a challenge of its own.

He was quiet for a bit, then drew in a long breath, exhaled, and began to tell her things of that he had not spoken in over ten years…

"She was the eldest daughter of Gerard Montyne, Duke of Delinshire, and Shanell Du Mer, the sister of the Chalean King. Her beauty was so exquisite, it took away my breath: hair the color of an autumn sunset, eyes that were gray one moment and, in a different light, a shimmering silver blue the next. She was tiny, her hands and feet like those of a porcelain doll. So delicate and fragile-looking, she brought out the protective instinct in me. Her voice was husky and sensual, eliciting thoughts I knew I should not be having. When she touched me, I felt powerful and capable of doing anything I set my mind to; and when she allowed me to lie with her, I thought I knew what it was to be a man.

"Montyne had inherited a hunting lodge from a maiden great aunt and the land bordered Holy Dale. Although not as beautiful as Sorn land, it was ripe with wildlife and there was a wide stream that fed off Talbert's Pond to the north of the Sorn manor house. The land was valuable, but Montyne was not satisfied. He wanted to incorporate the lands surrounding the lodge and make for himself a demesne that would outshine Innis Hesar's.

"At first he tried to buy the lands from my father, but father refused to even discuss the matter. It wasn't so much that he wanted to keep Holy Dale as it was to thwart Duke Gerard. There has always been bad blood between the Montynes and the Sorns simply because the Montynes were friends with the Hesars. The bad blood between the Sorns and Hesars started over a century ago.

"When his offer to buy Holy Dale was rejected, the Duke set out to take the land anyway he could get it. After learning I was to inherit, he thought he saw a way by connecting our two families in marriage. I will believe till my dying day that he ordered his own daughter to seduce me, the son of his enemy, simply to get his hands on Holy Dale.

"I was a lonely child, growing up without the love of either parent. I became a lonelier young boy shunned by most of the staff and hated by those who were forced to care for me. By the time I reached puberty, I had such low self-esteem; I often entertained the thought of joining a monastery. My reasoning was simple: I was leading a life of monastic depravation already. Why not take the necessary steps to remove myself from everyone's way? No one wanted me; no one loved me; no one wanted me around. I had almost convinced myself to apply to the Order of St. Regis or else take a blade and end my own miserable existence.

"But then Rosa-Lynn came."

"You are Lord Syntian, are you not?" the young girl asked.

"Syn-Jern," he corrected, surprised by the question. He had been on his way to the stables to saddle his nag when the girl stepped in front of him, blocking his path.

"Syn-Jern," she repeated, seeming to savor the pronunciation. She smiled. "I like it."

Syn-Jern ducked his head. "Thank you." He stepped around her, but glanced sideways to find her staring boldly as she fell into step alongside him. Unnerved by the saucy grin she tossed his way he looked away again.

"I am Dorrie," the girl informed him. "I am Lady Rosa-Lynn's maid."

He knew the Duke of Delinshire had arrived that morning with his eldest daughter, though he had yet to meet either of them. While his hunting lodge was being renovated, the Duke and his daughter would stay at Holy Dale. Begrudgingly, Syn-Jern's father and half-brother, Trace, would entertain the Duke; his stepmother would surely plan a party of some kind for the Duke's daughter simply to put on a show.

But he knew he would not be invited to attend any more than he had been asked to be there to help receive Holy Dale's guests.

"Where is your mistress?" he asked, wondering why the little chit was running around on her own.

"Waiting for you by Talbert's Pond," she giggled.

"Not me, Mam'selle," he denied, shaking his head. "My brother, perhaps, but not me."

"Aye, it was you she sent me to fetch, Milord," the girl responded and her knowing look was not lost even on an inexperienced lad such as Syn-Jern.

"She does not know me," he said. "Why would she send you to fetch me?"

The girl cocked her head to one side. When Syn-Jern also stopped and looked around, he was stunned to the toes of his scuffed boots as her gaze crawled over him.

"Have you looked in a mirror lately, Milord?" she drawled, then shocked him even more as she licked her full upper lip.

Syn-Jern felt his cock leap at her action and her words drove like steel spikes into his brain. He stared at her, amazed at the lascivious look that had settled on her young face. She was assessing him as though he were worthy of her attention—and since this was the first time any female had looked at him in such a way, he was instantly aroused. Feeling the rigid tumescence of his shaft bulging against his breeches, he hastily covered his crotch with his gloved hands.

"Do not hide it, Milord Syn-Jern," the wench whispered. She walked to him, her young hips swaying like those of a much older, experienced female. When she stood before him, she smiled coyly, then boldly reached out to push his hands away.

"Mam'selle, you should not..." he began only to gasp in shock when she molded her fingers over his crotch and rubbed slowly.

"When Milady has had her fill of you," the girl said in a throaty voice, "come find me, Milord, and I will let you ride me until you are well satisfied."

He jumped from her scorching touch. The chit could be no more than thirteen years of age if she were a day. Barely out of the cradle and here she wanted to hop into a man's bed!

Not that he was really a man, yet, he thought. He was all of twenty and one, but he was not a man in the sexual way. A virgin, he thought to remain one into his dotage since no maid or even tavern whore had ever looked at him like this saucy baggage.

"What's wrong, Milord?" she taunted and reached for him again, but Syn-Jern moved out of her way, shaking his head in denial of her intent.

"You are a child," he protested although every part—especially the one throbbing so desperately beneath the fabric of his cords—urged him to accept what she was offering.

"I've had many a man, Milord," the girl chuckled. She looked at him through the fringe of her eyelashes. "I've made many a man, as well."

Her words made his manhood harder than ever and he backed away, his hands cupped protectively around his privates. "Go away, Mam'selle," he ordered. "You are playing with fire."

She grinned in challenge. "Do I stoke your fires, Milord?" she asked. "Have I started a flame in your loins." She licked her lips once more. "I will gladly quench those flames with the juices of my—"

"Be quiet!" he said. Her voice was driving him insane with need and her bold statements had him on the verge of shaming himself. It was all he could do to turn and walk away as fast as his rigid shaft would allow.

"She waits for you by the river, Milord!" the girl called after him.

"She can wait all the gods-be-damned day," Syn-Jern said under his breath. His teeth were clenched for he was in acute pain. The pull of the corduroy on his aroused cock was both pleasurable and irritating at the same time. By the time he reached the sanctuary of the stables—relieved to find no one else there—he could do only one thing to alleviate the pressure. He went into one of the stalls, shut the door, released his bulging shaft, and took matters into his own hands. When he was finished, he was ashamed of himself.

Slumping to the floor, he sat there with his head in his hands. He didn't even glance up when the door to the stall opened. "May I please have some privacy?" he mumbled, squeezing his eyes shut.

"You may have whatever you desire, Milord."

Syn-Jern opened his eyes and lifted his head. Very slowly, his gaze traveled from the hem of a pale green gown, past a tiny waist, behind that two alabaster arms were clutched. His attention moved over a high-thrusting bosom to a slender, swan-like neck framed with tendrils of titian curls. When at last he saw her face, he drew in his breath and held it, so taken by the loveliness of her delicate face, he could not breathe.

"I sent for you, Syn-Jern," this glorious vision said. "I am not accustomed to being kept waiting for my men. Have you no care for a lady's desires, Milord?"

He couldn't have answered her if his life depended upon it.

"You should not make a lady come to you, Syni," she said in a throaty purr. She placed her hands on the laces of her bodice. "Nor should you allow one to be left unattended." Her fingers plucked at the laces that held her gown over her bosom.

He sat staring at her as she disrobed. His eyes wide, his body trembling, he could do no more than that. When all that separated her from the air was a thin silk ribbon circling her slender neck, he began to sweat.

"So," he heard her say. "Do you like what you see, Milord Syni?"

She was more beautiful than any painting adorning the walls of Holy Dale manse. Her flesh appeared more luscious than a strawberry shortbread cake plumped high with mounds of fresh cream. The curvaceous body before him was more enticing than a cool pond on a scorching summer's day. She was everything he had ever dreamed in a woman: an ideal he never expected to see much less possess.

"Is this a habit you will always have, Milord?" she inquired on a long sigh.

"What?" he managed to ask, his heart thudding so hard in his chest, he was sure she could hear it.

"This propensity to keep a woman waiting for you to pleasure her?" she replied and lifted her arms. She spread her hands wide so that her perfect breasts arched high against her chest. "Do you not like what you see, Milord?"

His mouth was as dry as a stone quarry, although his palms were slick with sweat, itching to mold her breasts. He licked his lips. "Aye, Milady," he whispered. "You are most beautiful."

"Beautiful enough for you to ride?" she queried.

He groaned, knowing full well that the thoughts flashing through his fevered mind were wrong, wicked, and totally inappropriate. She was the daughter of his father's neighbor; a guest in his home; a person of royal rank. He was about to tell her all that when she moved, dropping down on the hay as gracefully as any swan gliding across Talbert's Pond.

"If the mountain will not come to Rosa-Lynn," she said in a breathy whisper, "Rosa-Lynn will come to the mountain."

What happened next was the stuff of any young man's fevered dreams: this beautiful, sensuous, glorious woman seduced him. She put her hands on his flesh, massaged him, flicked open the buttons of his cords, and drew him out to stroke. He could not have stopped her had he the desire to do so for she so expertly manipulated him and his ego.

When he thought about it later in his bed alone, she had controlled the moment from the time she entered the stall until she left him—weak and sated—lying on the hay. He thought he had seen admiration in her knowing eyes when she saw him naked. He wanted to believe she found him as desirable as he found her. He prayed that her silky words of enticement had been true.

"You are all I have ever desired in a mate, Syn-Jern Sorn," she told him. Her fingers plied his limp flesh, kneading it until it began to rise once more. "Your shaft is a wicked blade cutting a swath through this lonely heart of mine."

She worked him well for over two hours: straddling him; drawing on his eager flesh; leading him to heights he never knew existed. So intense was their sexual union, he was sore by the time she dismounted and stood to retrieve her gown.

"You do things to me no other man ever has," she said as she dressed. "I can not wait to have you again."

He lay there, propped on his elbows, marveling at what she was saying. "You wish to make love with me again?" he asked in surprise. This being his first time, he knew he had lacked the finesse that would come with age and practice. He doubted he had satisfied her for he had seen disappointment flit through her lovely eyes before she hid them from him.

"If I were not expected at your stepmother's tea this afternoon, Syni, I would ride you until you dropped," she said, grinning at his look of stunned surprise. Dressed once more, she smoothed her skirt. "But that will have to wait for later tonight, don't you think?"

He was incapable of thought. He simply lay there, smiling like a fool when she turned, blew him a kiss, then left with a saucy laugh trailing in her wake.

Later than night when the door to his room opened quietly and Rosa-Lynn joined him, he folded aside the coverlet, opened his arms, and gave her his soul.

"By Alel's mercy," Syn-Jern sighed, "I really thought she loved me."

Genny said nothing, knowing there was more. She stroked the strong arm surrounding her, giving him time to gather his thoughts. His breath was ruffling her hair as they reclined on the window seat. She could feel the strong beat of his heart; smell the cinnamon scent of his cologne. When he began his tale again, she closed her eyes for there was pain in his gentle voice.

The Duke and his daughter remained at Holy Dale for two weeks. During the day, Giles Sorn and his son, Trace, would take Gerard Montyne hunting or into Wixenstead Village to one of the waterfront gambling dens. Rosa-Lynn was forced to sit with Syn-Jern's stepmother and carry on idle chitchat that bored the younger woman to tears.

But when servant and master, alike, retired for the night, Syn-Jern's door would creak open and there—framed against the pale light in the hall—would be his lover.

Into the wee hours of the morning, she lay with him, whispering love lies in his ear. Her practiced, knowing hands roamed his eager body and taught him things he could but wonder where she had learned.

And he believed every falsehood she told him.

"You take me to heights I have only dreamed of attaining, Syni," she vowed. "No man will ever satisfy me as you do."

He was fool enough to take her words as gospel truth and stupid enough to think she meant them.

"When we are wed," she would sigh, "we will unite our lands and make for ourselves a veritable kingdom!"

Syn-Jern loved Holy Dale, but he had no grand desire to be lord and master over all he surveyed. The lands surrounding his home were lush and vibrant with wildlife and fertile for planting; but he had no great wish to be the wealthiest man in Wixenstead Parish.

"Do you have no ambition, Syn-Jern?" she threw at him one night when storms were raging inland from the coast.

He watched the lightning reflected in her silver eyes and thought he caught a glimpse of a demoness lurking in those seductive depths.

"I have all I want, Milady." He nuzzled her neck, unable to see the look of distaste cross her lovely face as his lips pressed against her flesh.

She pushed him away. "But I don't," she protested.

He smiled, thinking her pouting lips adorable. "What more do you wish from life, Milady? When we are married, you will be mistress of Holy Dale. When Father is gone, you will be Duchess of—"

"I know all that, Syn-Jern," she snapped. "I am not some stupid tart whose skirts you've flung over her pointed little head!"

The venom in her words stung him. She was the only woman with whom he'd ever lain.

He was deeply in love with her—and because he was—could not see her as she truly was.

"I deserve a grand house with acres and acres of land surrounding it," she said, her teeth clenched. "I want fine Rysalian horses to breed and race for purses so heavy it will take a fleet of Serenian ships to carry them! I want dozens of servants to jump at my beck and call and I want seamstresses and cobblers there at a moment's notice should I desire a new dress or pair of slippers." She dug her nails into his arm. "I want handsome men dancing attendance on me at fancy balls and beautiful women envying me the fine possessions surrounding me!"

He winced as her nails pierced his flesh. "I can not give you all that," he said, trying to ease his arm from her grip.

"You will!" she swore and raked his arm, drawing blood.

"My god, Rosa-Lynn!" he gasped, jerking away. He sat up, holding his injured arm and stared at her as the strobe of the lightning flashed through the room.

"Come here, Syn-Jern," she hissed, her lips drawn back over pearly teeth. She reached for him.

"I think not," he said and swung his legs from the bed, intending to rise.

"I said come here!" she spat and twisted toward him, her fingers becoming talons as they arched down his back from shoulder to hips.

The pain took away his breath as her nails raked his bare flesh. He yelped, spinning around to find her on her knees on the mattress, her hair wild, her eyes flared with what could only be hatred.

"Are you insane?" he asked, the sting of the scratches making him flex his shoulders.

It was the wrong thing to say.

She flew at him like a were-tigress, her nails going for his eyes this time. He barely had time to grab her wrists to keep her from blinding him. The weight and momentum of her body sent them body crashing to the floor, hers pinning him beneath her as she struggled to ram her knee into his groin.

"Rosa-Lynn!" he gasped, struggling to get her under control. Her shrieks and wild thrashing would soon have the entire household barging into his room if he did not quiet her.

Then he discovered the one thing that could melt Rosa-Lynn Montyne's heart.

"I hurt her," he said and Genny could hear the shame in his voice. "I managed to roll atop her, pin her down, getting my legs between hers to keep her from battering my shaft to pulp. I had her wrists in a grip strong enough to break them, but still she struggled. She called me the vilest names, spat at me, tried to sink her teeth into my shoulder. At one point, she butted me in the chin. My teeth clicked together and a tooth was chipped. The force of the blow almost knocked her out, but still she fought me. I had long furrows down my calves where she gouged me with her toe nails."

Genny felt her anger rising in leaps and bounds. That anyone could do that to her husband set her killer instincts into high gear. She wished with all her might that Rosa-Lynn were there at that moment. If she had been, Genny would have taken a dagger to the bitch's black heart, cut it out, and presented it on a silver platter to Syn-Jern.

"It seemed the more I tried to restrain her, the worse she became until…" His voice tapered off a moment and he was quiet for so long, Genny looked up at him to make sure he hadn't fallen asleep.

He was awake, but he was staring into the distance, seeing something that made his eyes dark with memory. Then he shuddered, closed his eyes, and exhaled heavily. He swallowed, then opened his eyes to stare once more at a past he surely wished he could forget.

"I began to realize she was becoming aroused by the struggle. I could smell the heat of her. When I looked into her eyes, I could see the desire. There was such blatant need in that look, such carnal lust." He drew in a long breath, let it out in a wavering sigh. "And the gods help me," he said, "I kissed her."

He jammed his mouth over hers, thrusting his tongue into the warm recess as she had taught him. Grinding against her lower body, he jerked her arms above her head, pinned the wrists together with one hand, and moved the other to a heaving breast. Cruelly squeezing that pliable flesh, he pinched and pulled at her nipple until it swelled in his fingers. Even then, he continued to punish the turgid bud until he felt slickness on his flesh. At that point, he did not care if it was sweat or blood oozing. All he cared about was ramming his cock inside her and riding her until she screamed for mercy.

And that was what he did.

He took her in every way he could, jamming his flesh into hers with no care at all for how much he hurt her. He pummeled her; thrusting with an abandon of which he would not have imagined being capable.

Like two wild animals, they went at one another. When it was all over and the last shudder had wracked his body, he lay bruised and bleeding atop her, her arms and legs wrapped around his sweaty body.

"I've made a man of you at last," he heard her say as he fell asleep atop her. "Fancy that."

Syn-Jern stopped talking. The afternoon light was fading and as the storm overtook the horizon. "We may be in for bad weather."

Genny rubbed his arm, but remained silent, knowing there was more to his story.

"When I woke the next morning," he continued, "she was gone. She and her father had left at the crack of dawn for their hunting lodge." He shifted, grunting as he positioned himself more comfortably on the window seat. "And like an idiot, I moped about the manse all day until my libido got the better of me and I saddled my horse and rode to Fairworth, the Montyne lodge."

An unsmiling servant who informed him the Duke was not receiving visitors met him at the door. When he asked if the servant would take a missive to the Lady Rosa-Lynn, the man said he would not, then shut the door in Syn-Jern's face. Accustomed to such rude behavior, Syn-Jern simply turned around, climbed on his horse, and rode back to Holy Dale.

Two hours later, all hell broke loose.

"Syn-Jern Sorn!" his father bellowed at the top of his lungs.

Syn-Jern exited the library, his forehead crinkled with puzzlement at the furious tone of his father's voice. "Aye, Milord?" he inquired, looking past his sire to the man's smug wife.

"How dare you?" the elder Sorn screamed, rushing to his son. "Do you have any notion of what you have done?"

Syn-Jern was not prepared for the vicious backhand that knocked him against the wall. He hit the doorframe and slid to the floor, his nose bleeding profusely.

"Do you know what you've done?" his father repeated, bending over him.

He knew his father was going to hit him again, but he also knew better than to try to block the blow. Blood sprayed the wall beside him and he put a hand to a nose that was broken with the second hit.

"I could kill you, Syn-Jern!"

"Giles," the Duchess of Winterset cautioned her irate husband. "Be careful what you say."

Giles Sorn stood there, his entire body quivering with outrage. His eyes bulged from his porcine face and his meaty fists opened and closed at his sides. "You worthless little bastard! You have ruined us!" he hissed.

Over the protection of his fingers, Syn-Jern saw his half-brother leaning insolently against the banister. Trace was grinning hatefully, his eyes glistening with spite. He fingered his dark mustache, twirling one tip around his forefinger. "You've done it now, haven't you, big brother?" he chuckled.

"Get up!" Syn-Jern's father demanded. When his son hesitated, he took a step closer, intending to kick the boy if need be to propel him into action.

Syn-Jern scrambled to his feet, edging sideways from the deadly menace emblazoned on his father's beefy face. "What am I supposed to have done?" he asked, his hand cupped full of his own blood.

"Delved one time too many into the sweet jar, I'd say," Trace chortled.

Giles Sorn pointed a rigid finger at his beloved son. "Stay out of this Trace Edward or I swear before all that's holy I will wed you to the chit!"

Syn-Jern's heart did a funny little flip in his chest. "Are you speaking of Rosa-Lynn, Father?" he asked, not daring to hope there would be a union between them.

"You have gone and plumped her full of your vile seed, you thankless whelp!" his father threw at him. "She is with child and Montyne is demanding satisfaction!"

"We are lucky he isn't calling you out," the Duchess sniffed. "As 'tis, all he wants is for you to marry the little tart."

The pot calling the kettle black, Syn-Jern thought as he looked into his stepmother's bold eyes.

"You do not fit in here," the Duchess remarked, sensing her stepson's thoughts. "You never have. It will be a blessing to have you gone from this manse."

"Aye," Giles Sorn snarled. "Getting rid of him is not the problem!"

"I think you need to explain in language the dolt can understand, Papa," Trace taunted.

"From the looks of him, he is lost in the ether!"

It was true: Syn-Jern had no idea what was happening. Obviously his father was irate. Any father would be to learn his son had impregnated an innocent girl. But he knew, all too well, there was nothing innocent about Rosa-Lynn Montyne. If truth were told, he suspected she could teach his lascivious stepmother a thing or two. Yet, having to marry the beauty was not such a terrible thing. So what was the problem? He was willing to marry her. Apparently the matter had been settled at Fairworth and, even if Rosa-Lynn was not accommodating to the plan her father had put forth, at least she would do as she was told.

Just as Syn-Jern would do as he was told in the matter. So he asked himself again: what was the problem?

"The conniving bastard wants land as dowry!" Sorn shouted, his face red with fury. "And Holy Dale as recompense for the rape!"

"Rape?" Syn-Jern repeated, stunned. "What rape?"

"The gal is only fifteen, big brother," Trace said, clucking his tongue in mock dismay. "You soiled a mere child now you'll have to pay dearly for it."

Syn-Jern blinked. Fifteen? How could that be? She seemed older; she looked older.

Hell, she acted far older than his twenty-one years! And, inexperienced as he was, he had known she was no virgin when he took her the first time.

"Montyne is willing to keep quiet about your perfidy," Syn-Jern's father spat, "but he will do so at a great price to Sorn holdings!"

"You had better pray the Tribunal does not get wind of it," Trace remarked, "else you'll have their whip applied most diligently to your tender back Syn-Jern."

"Shut up, Trace Edward!" Sorn shrieked and his wife rushed to his side lest he have a stroke.

"Giles, please!" the Duchess pleaded. "Calm yourself! The situation is not as bad as it seems at the moment." She cast her stepson a vicious look. "He will marry the bitch and that will be the end of it."

"Montyne is taking my land, Alicia!" Sorn whined. "He is taking my beloved Holy Dale."

Syn-Jern wanted to tell his father the land was not his anyway. The land belonged to Syn-Jern's grandmother, Monique, though if the Viragonian Tribunal saw fit, they could take it at any given time. As his maternal grandmother's only living heir, he, and he alone, was entitled to the land.

"We have Tern Keep," the Duchess reminded her husband. "We will have the Saur lands to add to our own before the week is out. What more do we need?"

"But I like it here!" the Duke whimpered. "I want Holy Dale!" Syn-Jern's father said, stomping his foot much like a young boy denied a toy would do. He glared at his oldest son. "I have you to thank for being put off my own property, you vile little demon!"

"Tell him when the Joining is to be and let us end this unpleasant conversation, Giles," the Duchess suggested. "I grow tired of seeing his ugly face." She cast Syn-Jern an insulting look.

Even as the details of his impending marriage were spelled out to him in scathing, sarcastic language, Syn-Jern merely stood there, cautioning himself not to let his joy show. That he would have Rosa-Lynn as his wife was well worth all the vitriolic aspersions hurled his way this day. He had to school himself not to grin like an idiot as the Joining plans were made.

Within two weeks, he would be husbanded to Rosa-Lynn Montyne in the traditional midnight ceremony that would make them one.

"I was looking forward to the Joining," Syn-Jern recalled softly. "I honestly believed I could make her happy."

"You really thought she loved you, didn't you?" Genny asked.

He didn't answer for a bolt of lightning streaked across the darkened sky. "Let's not sit here and tempt fate, okay?" he muttered.

They went to the settee. Genny sat at one end, Syn-Jern at the other, facing one another. He held out his hand and she entwined her fingers with his along the settee's tall back.

"Aye," he said, squeezing her fingers. "I did believe she loved me." He smiled wistfully. "But then, I did not know what love truly was until I met you."

"And now you do," his wife stated with certainty.

"And now I do," he repeated. He waited for her to say something else and when she did not, he moved so he could lay down, his head in her lap. Her fingers threaded through his thick golden hair and he sighed with pleasure.

"Would you like to take a nap?" she asked.

"Not sleepy," he said, his yawn betraying the lie.

Genny smiled and continued to massage his scalp, luxuriating in the silky feel of his blond curls. She glanced to the window as light flared then thunder shook the glass panes. Even as she watched, the rain began to pound against the window with force.

"It rained the day before the Joining," he said, drawing his wife's attention back to him. "It rained as though the gods and their ladies were crying for us."

Given strict instructions that he was not to make matters worse by presenting himself to his future father-in-law, Syn-Jern stayed at Holy Dale for the entire two weeks of his engagement. The banns had been announced at the Temple at Tempest Keep, the capitol of Virago, so both the Viragonian Tribunal and King Innis Hesar officially sanctioned the engagement. According to tradition, there was to be a party on the eve of the Joining so members of the royal court could congratulate the couple and offer gifts. Several days before the party, the Duchess traveled to Fairworth to lend her considerable talents toward making sure only the best food and beverages were served at the Joining supper.

Since Duke Montyne's wife was in the family way herself, and restricted from traveling to Virago for the Joining, Alicia Sorn took over the duties of surrogate mother to her future daughter-in-law and helped the girl pick out a suitable pattern for a wedding gown. All the arrangements had been made by the time Giles Sorn informed his son it was time to leave for Montyne's hunting lodge.

"Do you realize what an insult this is to the Duke to have to give his daughter into marriage from a hunting lodge!" Syn-Jern's father snapped as the carriage taking them to Fairworth bumped along the rocky road.

"Don't see why he didn't have it at Delinshire," Trace grunted, casting his half-brother a repulsive look.

"The chit is with child, is why!" his father responded with a hiss. "By the gods, she might even be showing by now!"

"I don't think—" Syn-Jern started to say, but his father's angry kick cut him off.

"No, young sir, you did not think!" Giles Sorn growled, his jowls wobbling with anger. "Had you thought, we would not be at this very moment on our way to that reprobate's lodge to hand over the keys to Holy Dale to him and his slattern offspring!"

"Should have kept the old Cyclops in your breeches, old man," Trace snickered.

"Pray do not be vulgar, Trace Edward," their father reprimanded.

"Your apology, Father," Trace said, bowing his head in recognition of his father's authority. He glanced at his brother and grinned maliciously.

Upon arrival at the lodge, the Duke and his beloved son were shown over-zealous respect from the servants. Their luggage was carried with haste to their assigned chambers. But Syn-Jern was left to his own devices, following in his kinsfolk's wake as they climbed the stairs to the guest quarters.

"Who the devil are you?" the steward asked, putting a hand out to keep Syn-Jern from going up the stairs. Before Syn-Jern could answer, the old man turned him around and pointed him back the way he'd come. "No servants allowed above stairs," he said with a sniff.

"I am…" Syn-Jern tried to say, but the old man would have none of his back-talk.

"Do as you are told and fetch your master's belongings. Hop to, now. Do not keep me waiting or I'll take a strap to your backside!"

"I say, Syni, but are you having a rough time of it already?" Trace called from the balcony.

Syn-Jern looked up to see his father and brother smirking. "Will you kindly tell this gentleman who I am, Father?"

The servant blinked, then turned his attention to the balcony.

"He's the groom," Giles Sorn said with an audible sigh.

A pair of wintry gray eyes shifted from the balcony to Syn-Jern's embarrassed face and held. "Oh, I see," was all the steward said. His gaze crawled down the length of Syn-Jern and up again before he pivoted on his heel and, without an apology, walked back the way he'd come.

"Don't think he likes you, Syn-Jern," Trace laughed and elbowed his father, who joined in the mirth at his eldest son's expense.

Syn-Jern stood where he was, looking up at his father and brother. He was humiliated and felt the censure of eyes regarding him as Montyne's servants flitted to and fro. He made no move to climb the stairs, not even when his father and brother turned their backs on him and left the railing, their laughing taunting him.

Digging his hands into his pockets, he hunched his shoulders and remained there at the foot of the stairs, hoping someone would take pity on him and show him where he needed to go. His defensive posture was lost on the servants for they ignored him.

For fifteen minutes or so, he stood watching the bustling servants escorting guests up the stairs. No one paid any attention to him, so he finally sat on the bottom step, partially in the way, but even then, servant and guest stepped around him, barely glancing his way. No doubt, he thought with a sinking feeling in the pit of his gut, they knew who he was and were snubbing him.

After an hour had passed and no one had come to show him to his room, he stood, sighed, and began to climb the stairs in search of his father.

"You!"

The single word—spoken with an explosion of rage—brought Syn-Jern to a stop and he turned, his hand on the stair rail. He saw his future father-in-law glaring at him.

"Your Grace," he said, bowing his head in greeting.

"I want a word with you, boy!" the Duke of Delinshire snapped before spinning on his heel and stalking away.

Syn-Jern turned and hurried down the stairs, craning his neck to see which way the Duke had gone. When at last he caught sight of the man's coat tails disappearing in a room down the long corridor that led from the entry, he ran to catch up.

"Shut the gods-be-damned door!" Duke Montyne growled as Syn-Jern came into the room.

The Duke was an imposing man with a thatch of thick white hair. His black eyes were small, but intense, peering from a face set now with a heavy scowl. Tall, and exceptionally handsome in his youth, he was a virile man with numerous bastard offspring flitting around his keep at Delinshire. As he stood by the fireplace, tapping a leather quirt against the palm of his right hand, he cocked his chin toward a chair, indicating Syn-Jern was to sit.

Syn-Jern seated himself, knowing better than to say anything. He waited expectantly, his eyes wary.

"On the table beside you," Montyne said, pointing with the quirt, "you will find the papers my tribunal lawyer drew up regarding the transfer of ownership of Holy Dale and its surrounding acreage from you to my daughter, Rosa-Lynn. The ownership will be relinquished to her upon the blessing of your Joining this eve. Do you understand?"

Syn-Jern nodded. It didn't matter whose name was on the paper for according to Viragonian law property must pass from mother to child.

"Well, are you are as stupid as you look or is it you do not know how to sign your name?" Montyne snapped.

"I know how to write, Your Grace," Syn-Jern answered.

"Then do it!" the Duke shouted, striking the hearth with his quirt.

He took the paper, started to read it, but jumped when Montyne's quirt whistled through the air and landed with a slap against the paper, pinning it to the table. He looked up quickly to see his future father-in-law glaring at him with such a venomous glower, he drew in his breath.

"Are you questioning my honesty, Sorn?" the Duke demanded, pressing the quirt to its breaking point.

"No, milord!" Syn-Jern answered.

"Then sign the gods-be-damned thing and get the hell out of my sight!"

Syn-Jern did as he was told.

"You've no backbone at all, have you?" Montyne insulted him.

Syn-Jern flinched, then looked the man in the eye. "I've never been allowed to have one, Your Grace," he replied.

Montyne stared at him for a good long while, then snorted with disgust. "Get out of my home until it is time for you to do right by my daughter. Your presence offends me."

Standing, Syn-Jern lifted his chin. "Where am I to dress, Your Grace? Am I to wed your daughter clothed in what I wearing?"

Montyne sighed heavily then stalked to the door and yelled, "Playe!"

The older servant who had kept Syn-Jern from climbing the stairs appeared in the doorway almost as though he knew he would be needed.

"Aye, Your Grace? What is your pleasure, Milord?" Playe inquired.

"Take this bastard to the garçonniere then fetch his Joining togs. I'll not have him in my home one moment longer than is absolutely necessary!"

"As you wish, Your Grace," the servant said, bowing. He turned his insolent eyes on Syn-Jern. "Well, do not dawdle, Lord Sorn. Come with me!"

The door of the Duke's study slammed behind Syn-Jern's departure and he stopped, looking back with complete confusion.

"Pray do keep up else I will leave you here!" Playe grated as he continued down the corridor.

The garçonniere was in actuality only a one-room shack about a quarter of a mile from the manse. The place had few amenities and smelled of neglect and mildew. Other than a tarnished brass bed with a sagging mattress and well-worn coverlet, there was a porcelain chamber pot, a straight back chair, wobbly table with a chipped pitcher and ewer, and a single window sans curtain.

"If we'd known you would be staying here," Playe sniggered, "we would have spruced it up a mite." He folded his arms over his chest and glared at Syn-Jern. "What's your pleasure, Milord?"

Syn-Jern would not give the old bastard the satisfaction of knowing he was not only angry about the accommodations, but also heartsick that he was being treated as he was. "If you'll just bring my—"

"I'll have my son drop them off," Playe interrupted. His left eyebrow crooked in challenge. "Sometime today."

Syn-Jern's nails were digging into his palm, but he managed to nod his head politely. "That will be fine." Then his own little demon raised its pointed head in kind. "They won't be able to start the Joining without me, now, will they?" When Playe's superior grin slipped a notch, Syn-Jern's smile could have lit the darkest room. "Whenever you get me the clothes, I'll get dressed and we can get the ball rolling, eh? Don't want her to have the brat without benefit of a name, now, do we?"

Playe narrowed his mean eyes, curled his lip, then spun around, slamming the door behind him.

"That entire family was hard on doors," Syn-Jern chuckled and his wife wondered how he could possibly find amusement in the way he had been treated. Left up to her, the entire Montyne family, and every one of their insolent servants, would be tarred and feathered for having treated her husband so rudely.

They listened to the rain pounding against the palace windows for a bit, then Syn-Jern turned on his side, the back of his head against his wife's belly. Genny could not help but wonder if that was because he did not want her to see his face as he finished his tale.

"I must have been tired," he said, wedging his right hand under his wife's thigh and draping his left over her leg. "I remember stretching out on that lumpy mattress, but then the next thing I remember, it was ten of the clock and I could hear laughter and music coming from the lodge."

"They started the party without you?" she gasped.

"That is the Viragonian way," he said with a shrug. "The bride and groom don't show up until a few minutes before midnight, the traditional hour of Joining."

"Humpf," was his wife's comment, her usual answer to statements that annoyed her.

"Anyway, I got up and looked around, thinking Playe's son had brought my clothes to me while I slept, but they weren't there. I was furious, but what else could I do but go looking for them? So, I left the garçonniere and started back through the woods."

She stroked his shoulder in an attempt to relax him for his body was suddenly tense.

He walked in the direction he thought they'd come earlier, but soon found he was hopelessly lost in a maze of shrubbery. Frustrated, he met dead end after dead end, cursing each time he stumbled into a thorny hedge. Able to hear the music and laughter clearly off to his right, he stopped, took a long, deep breath, then tried another pathway, only to come up against still another blockage.

"How the hell do I get out of here?" he growled. He started back the way he'd come and tried one more pathway. This one led him to the back of the stables. He could hear the snort of horses and smell the ripe stench of fresh manure. Trying to fan the thick branches apart to crawl through did him no good. The thorns of the bayberry poked into his flesh and he gave up, determined to find his way out of the labyrinth no matter how long it took him.

"I've often wondered if losing my way in the maze that night wasn't an omen," he said, "of things to come."

"Obviously you escaped that maze just as you did the one on Tyber's Isle," she replied.

"Aye," he acknowledged, lifting his hand and looking at the scar in the center of his palm. He flexed his fingers. His voice was very soft, very thin when he added, "and with just as much pain."

After twenty minutes of bumbling his way through the brambles, he came to an opening behind the stables. Relieved, he was dusting debris from his cords when he heard Rosa-Lynn's voice. Not having seen nor spoken to her in the last two weeks, he was eager to hold her, kiss her, and make love with her. He didn't question why his wife-to-be would be in the stables at that time of the evening. Instead, he grinned like a child about to be given a treat and headed for the stable doors. When he heard his half-brother's unmistakable throaty laughter, he stopped dead still in his tracks.

"I crept into the stable, being as quiet as I could, but with all the noise they were making, I doubt they would have heard an army tramping inside," he said, his voice filled with hurt. "They were in one of the stalls, as naked as the day they were born, and she was doing to him the things she had done to me."

Genny closed her eyes to the pain she was hearing. In her mind's eye, she could see Syn-Jern standing there, spying on the woman he loved and the brother he despised as they cuckolded him. What shame and humiliation he suffered, she could only imagine. He had grown quiet and she kept the silence between them, instinctively knowing the worst was yet to come.

"I let them finish what they were doing and was about to confront them with their perfidy when Rosa-Lynn asked Trace how she was going to be able to deny me my husbandry rights."

"The mere thought of that spineless eel climbing atop me makes me want to puke!" Rosa-Lynn said fiercely. "Every time he lays his hands on me, I positively cringe!"

"Then don't let him touch you," Trace replied.

"How am I to stop him, Trace?" she returned. "I will be Joined to the hideous creature."

"Once the deeds are noted in the Tribunal log, we'll have no further use for him, Dearling. You can cry your pending motherhood. He's such a stupid twit, he'll believe anything you tell him," Trace laughed as he stroked his mistress' breast.

"It takes four months to get the deeds noted," Rosa-Lynn pouted. "I can not possibly live with that creature for four months!"

"You won't have to," Trace assured her. "Go visit somebody."

"Like who?" she flung at him.

"Oh, I don't know," he drawled. "Mayhaps the father of your babe? Where is it he lives again? Tern Keep?"

Syn-Jern stiffened. Under Serenian law, Tern Keep would be the inheritance of Duke Giles Sorn's second born: Trace Edward Sorn.

"We have not picked a name for our child," Rosa-Lynn giggled. "Do you have a preference?"

As he stood in the shadows of the stable listening to his brother and the woman he loved discussing their coming child, Syn-Jern felt sick to his stomach. The terrible things the two said about him were nearly as disabling as the knowledge that the child Rosa-Lynn carried was not his, but Trace's. Knowing if he were to confront them at that point—after all he had learned—he would kill them both with his bare hands, he thought it best to leave.

Being as quiet as he could, he left the stable and started walking. It was nearly five miles to Holy Dale, fifteen to Wixenstead Village.

He opted for the village.

"I had a few coins with me," he explained. "Enough to get me roaring drunk at one of the seediest taverns on the waterfront and a bed with one of the whores who worked there."

"Good for you," his wife said firmly.

Syn-Jern craned his neck and looked at her. "That doesn't bother you, Milady?"

"Not in the least," she replied. "Go on."

He chuckled, then laid his head in her lap again. "I must have done right by the bawd for she served me breakfast in bed the next morning, though I didn't have the money to pay for the food or the stomach to eat it. I had a blazing hangover that was causing me considerable grief when the door to her room burst open and there stood my father."

"Get your ass out of that bed, now!" Duke Sorn bellowed, stomping to the bed and flinging the covers from his son's naked body.

"Have pity on him, Your Grace," the whore begged. "He's been sick, he has!"

"And he will be sicker still when I am finished with him!" Syn-Jern's father promised.

The shouts were excruciating stabs of pain in his temples and Syn-Jern tried to hide his head under the pillow only to be jerked to a sitting position when his father yanked the pillow away, grabbed a handful of his hair and pulled.

"Merciful Alel, that hurts!" Syn-Jern shrieked.

"You ain't seen hurt yet, boy!" another voice snarled from the doorway. Duke Montyne came into the room and helped Giles Sorn drag his son from the whore's bed.

They took him down the stairs and through the tavern, ignoring the whistles and hoots of the customers watching the spectacle. It wasn't everyday a naked man was dragged through the streets of Wixenstead Village by two members of the royalty then thrown into a carriage and carted out of town.

Twice, he threw up in the carriage for the harrowing ride was torture on his aching head and queasy stomach. Once he splattered his father's boots and was rewarded by a backhand slap that tore open his lip.

"I won't marry her," he managed to say as he huddled in the corner of the carriage, shivering with cold and humiliation.

"Aye, you will," his father corrected.

"I will not."

The Duke of Delinshire said nothing. His beady black eyes were fastened on Syn-Jern as he tapped the riding quirt he carried with him at all times against his dusty boot.

"Have you no shame," Giles Sorn threw at his son. "Do you have any ken what you have caused by running out on your Joining?"

"It's not my baby," he said, swallowing the last of the bile threatening to spew.

Duke Sorn looked to Montyne, but Rosa-Lynn's father ignored him. Sorn had his doubts about the parentage of the child. He suspected Trace was the culprit, but wasn't about to say so. He had no doubt between them, Rosa-Lynn and Trace would find a way to get rid of Syn-Jern. Then, after his grandson was born—he refused to acknowledge that it might be a girl-child—he would find a way to relieve Trace of his cumbersome wife so Holy Dale would revert to the Sorns.

"I will not marry her," Syn-Jern repeated stubbornly.

"You aren't being given a choice, young man," his father grated.

"You can all go to hell," Syn-Jern told them.

"I bet that went over big," Genny gasped.

"It got me something I didn't count on," Syn-Jern replied. His grip tightened on his wife's legs. "I should have kept my gods-be-damned mouth shut."

The long silence that had settled on the carriage ended when Montyne lifted his hand and rapped on the partition separating them from the driver. Almost instantly, the carriage ground to a halt and the driver hopped down, putting a hand to his cap as he appeared at the door.

"Aye, Your Grace?"

Montyne didn't look at his driver. He was staring sullenly at Syn-Jern. "Fetch me the rope you keep in the boot."

"Aye, Milord!" the driver responded, going for the rope that was used to pull the carriage out of the mud should it get stuck.

Sorn's eyebrows arched. "What are you planning, Gerry?"

The Duke of Delinshire ignored the question. Instead, he turned the quirt over and jammed the handle none-too gently under Syn-Jern's chin to lift his face. "You listen to me, boy," he said, his voice thick with evil. "I will give you the choice your father will not."

Syn-Jern tried avoid the sharp prick of the quirt's handle, but the Duke of Delinshire had anticipated his move and slapped the side of the quirt firmly, but now hard, against Syn-Jern's cheek to keep him from doing so.

"As I said," the Duke growled, "I will give you the choice of two evils."

"And that being what?" Syn-Jern shot back, his nakedness and his anger making him reckless.

"You can get out of this carriage and walk behind it tied to the axle so every manjack and humping skack between here and Fairworth can see how little a man you are or…"

He ran the handle of the quirt down Syn-Jern's cheek, over his shoulder and down to his hip. "You can suffer my anger and be done with it."

"What does that mean, Gerry?" Sorn asked.

Montyne leaned toward Syn-Jern. "You may be right when you say the brat isn't yours. I've no illusions about my daughter's purity. Her mother's a whore and so is she. I don't care one whit about either of them, but I wanted Holy Dale and I didn't particularly care how I went about getting it. Despite wanting the land as much as I still do, I am not willing to pay the price to have it. I do not want you for a son-in-law so I will allow you to beg off the Joining if you will submit yourself to my anger." He trailed the quirt's handle down Syn-Jern's leg to his knee. "And it will be a steadfast anger, I can assure you."

Syn-Jern looked at the quirt resting on his knee. Then lifted his eyes to Montyne. He saw infinite savagery in the man's beady gaze.

"If you think walking behind the carriage will be the easiest route," Montyne said pleasantly as he leaned back in the seat, "you might wish to reconsider. I have known Ferris to be a wild and reckless driver on occasion and I would imagine it would be hard to run very fast in your bare feet."

Syn-Jern turned his gaze to his father, but there was no help there. What he saw made his blood run cold for he knew his father had realized, as he had, just what other choice Montyne would give him. "You would let him do this?" he asked.

Sorn shrugged. "You jilted his daughter at the altar. You deserve whatever retribution he desires to mete out." He relaxed; knowing Holy Dale would stay in the Sorn family. The price—whatever it would be—to keep the land would be paid by Syn-Jern.

"If you think to try and run, boy, think again," the Duke of Delinshire warned. "Should you make that choice, I will bring you down and hamstring you so you will never run again, then I'll drag your naked ass through the town anyway."

Absolute terror flitted across Syn-Jern's spine and he knew he was doomed no matter what choice he made. He had no doubt he would be caught handily if he tried to run. He also knew he'd be dragged, screaming and bleeding, behind the carriage if he made that stupid choice. Having his back stripped by the quirt was certainly the lesser of the evils.

Sensing his opponent's defeat, Montyne took the leather gloves from his coat pocket and drew them on. "Get out of the carriage, go to the wheel and wait there," he ordered, fusing his eyes with Syn-Jern's.

Syn-Jern tired once more to garner his father's help. "Don't allow this, Father," he begged, tears forming in his eyes.

"You are asking the wrong person," Sorn snorted.

Knowing there was no help for him, Syn-Jern lifted his chin. "I hope you rot in hell," he told his father.

"I've no doubt he will," Montyne chuckled.

"He beat you with the quirt?" Genny whispered.

"No," her husband replied. "I told him if he wanted to whip my ass he'd have to drag me out of the carriage, but I warned him if he tried, I'd do my damnedest to break his jaw."

Genny smiled. "What did he say to that?"

Syn-Jern shrugged. "He said..."

"Well, Sorn. It's looks as though the boy might have a backbone after all."

"Apologize to His Grace this minute, Syn-Jern!" his father demanded. "Of all the gall! Telling him you would try to..."

"Leave off, Giles," Montyne snapped. "Your son and I understand one another, don't we, boy?"

Syn-Jern's eyes narrowed with hate. "I am not a boy, Duke Gerard."

Montyne's grin was mean. "No, just a cuckolded man, I'd have to say." He turned away. "Ferris! Drive on!"

"I dreaded our arrival at Fairworth. I thought people would point at me and whisper behind my back how I had left Rosa-Lynn waiting at the altar while I whored in Wixenstead." Syn-Jern sighed. "But I was in for the surprise of my life."

"Even more than finding out the woman you loved was betraying you?" Genny asked.

"Aye," her husband stated. "It seems while I was in Wixenstead, Rosa-Lynn and my brother eloped. They crossed the border into Serenia and were married by a Tribunal priest. There they were in the courtyard at Fairworth being congratulated by the same royals who had gathered to celebrate her wedding to me."

"Oh, my," Genny said. "How did that make you feel?"

"I can't say I was overly concerned considering I was sitting in the midst of a large crowd with nothing between me and them but the carriage door. I half expected Montyne to make me get out of the carriage and walk into the lodge."

"Would you have?" his wife asked.

"At that point, I think I would have done so and enjoyed the hell out of seeing the shock on the faces of the royals." He chuckled. "But I think Montyne was afraid I might just do it, so he had his men stand in front of the doors while Ferris went into the lodge to find my clothes."

"And your father?"

"Got out of the carriage, went up to his son, hugged him, patted him on the back, then welcomed Rosa-Lynn into the family."

"You must have been so hurt, Milord," she whispered, stroking his face.

"I was beginning to hate Rosa-Lynn and Trace with a blinding fury," he admitted. "As I dressed, I heard Trace telling one of the royals—some Chalean Prince—that he and his new bride would be in residence at Holy Dale if the Prince would care to call. I think it was then I realized they meant to see me ousted from my home." He closed his eyes. "I never got out of the carriage that day. I think if I had, I would have killed them both. Father must have thought so, too, for by the time I was dressed, Ferris was driving me back to Holy Dale. All the way there, I thought about how I'd been used. How stupid I had been in believing she loved me as I loved her." He locked eyes with his wife. "As much as I had loved her, then, I despise her now. My real hatred of her began when Trace brought her to live at Holy Dale."

"That must have been horrible for you," his wife said, pushing a lock of stray hair from his forehead.

"It was not pleasant, but then again my life at Holy Dale had never been pleasant. I kept out of their way, taking my meals in my room for the next two days, spending as much time as I wanted on the outside balcony. I learned Father was taking Alicia on a holiday to Oceania and I would be alone with the newlyweds. Then when father and Alicia left, I overheard one of the servants telling another that Duke Sorn had paid someone a goodly amount to push me from the balcony. He said the Duke did not want to return to find me still alive."

"Oh, Syn-Jern," Genny whispered. "How awful!"

"I went into my room and the anger got the best of me. All I could think about was my father and how much he hated me; all the pain and humiliation I'd suffered over the years; all the loneliness, the hate. At some point, I wished him and his evil wife dead." His voice became a mere breath of sound. "I had no way of knowing I was capable of dealing death from hundreds of miles away, but that is what I did. I willed them dead and they died."

"It was an accident, my love," she consoled.

"No," he said, getting up from the settee. "It was murder."

It had to be asked.

"What happened to the baby?" Genny asked.

Syn-Jern lowered his head. "When news of the Lady Diedre's sinking was sent to Holy Dale, the servants began whispering that I had caused the tragedy. Rosa-Lynn became convinced I would do the same thing to her and Trace." He looked up, his gaze bleak. "She had a miscarriage."

"She blamed you," Genny said.

"Aye," he replied. "And so did everyone else."

## Chapter Three

PATRICK KASELLA WAS ALONE IN THE TEMPLE, SITTING WITH HIS HANDS clutched between his legs. He sat staring at the statue of the golden-haired woman whose arms were stretched wide in invitation to those whose souls were troubled.

"Here I am again," he said to the statue. His blue eyes roamed the serene features of the alabaster statue, taking in the gentle smile and kind eyes; the expression of empathy the sculptor had incorporated into the beautiful face.

Since coming to these exotic shores, Paddy felt like a fish out of water. He was in his element with the rough and tumble members of Weir's crew, but here—in this lap of luxury and lushness—he was like a bull in a china shop. The only place in which he had found peace was in this little shrine the Empress Rowena had built to one of the ancient deities of their mutual homeland.

"Bless me, Mother," Paddy whispered, "for I can not rid my heart of Syn-Jern Sorn."

He hung his head, tears welling in the azure depths. His entire being ached with love for the forbidden and he was finding life more and more unbearable of late. No one ever treated him any differently than they did the other members of the crew, yet he was keenly aware of the yawning gulf that separated him from the rest of the men. His loneliness at times was a crippling pain and on the rare occasion he found solace in the arms of another like him, the experience was less than rewarding. What he sought—someone to call his and his alone—he was beginning to think he would never find.

Paddy lifted his gaze to the statue. "Help me, Lady," he pleaded. "Help me to make sense of this solitude I have been given."

Weir Saur turned from the doorway of the temple. He had come looking for Paddy, needing to make sure his second in command was on ship before the crew started boarding. The Revenge would be sailing on the evening tide; the good-byes were already being said. Obviously, now was not the time to interrupt Paddy.

"Weir!"

Weir looked to his left and saw Syn-Jern loping toward him. He smiled. "I see you must have found a locksmith."

Syn-Jern's brows drew together as he reached his brother-in-law. "I didn't know I was looking for one," he responded.

"You weren't trying to find someone to remove that leg iron named Genny?"

Weir teased and watched the instant embarrassment stain Syn-Jern's cheeks.

"Don't start," Syn-Jern sighed. For the past two days, he and Genny had been at odds since she was determined to make him let her and Dermot sail with him as far as Ciona.

"The only way you're going to be sure she stays behind is if you slip a dollop or two of tenerse in her ale," Weir chuckled. "Else, she's liable to stow away."

"The hell she will, " Syn-Jern grunted. "She knows I won't have time to worry about her safety." He clucked his tongue with irritation. "And she knows gods-be-damned well I won't allow her to bring our child along on this voyage even if I was stupid enough to let her tag along!"

"What women know and what women accept are two entirely different propositions, Syni," Weir reminded him. "When are you going to learn that, my friend?"

"She's not going," Syn-Jern stated firmly.

"I know she ain't," Weir said with equal determination.

"Where's Paddy?" Syn-Jern asked. "I was told he was with you."

Weir jerked a thumb over his shoulder. "In the temple, praying."

Syn-Jern looked past Weir and nodded. "Ionarians spend a lot of time on their knees, don't they?" he said in a respectful tone.

Weir shrugged. "I suppose so." He turned to look at the temple. "Probably wouldn't hurt either of us to ask for a little divine intervention for our endeavor. Whatcha think?"

"We're going to need all the help we can get," Syn-Jern agreed, slapping his brother-in-law on the back. "Let's go visit Paddy's Lady."

Patrick sensed movement behind him and turned, saw who had entered the temple, then looked away again. He heard Weir and Syn-Jern settling onto one of the benches then heard the creak of the kneeler being lowered. He smiled to himself. Neither of his friends was particularly religious, but then again neither knew what lay ahead for the men of the Revenge.

"Pray for us, Mother," Paddy said, his eyes once more on the gleaming white statue. "Intercede with the Blessed One to make sure Syn-Jern returns safely to his family here."

He closed his eyes. "And if one of our band must join you in the Heavens, I beg you to let his end be swift and painless."

Patrick had no illusions about the dangerousness of what he and the other men were setting out to do. They were going up against the Viragonian Tribunal and the evil sect that controlled it: the Brotherhood of the Domination.

꧁꧂

At the same time her husband was kneeling in the Temple of María, Genny Sorn was sitting in the Temple of Tethys, listening to the Empress Rowena make entreaties to The Majesty of the Multitude. Among the women gathered were those who had connections to the crew of the Revenge: lovers, and in some cases, new wives. Each woman sat quietly, face worried, heart breaking. For each knew they might never see their man again.

"Lead them, Oh, Fruitful Mother of us all, safely to their destination," the Empress chanted, her arms lifted to the heavens as incense wafted around her dark purple robe. The scent of lavender was thick in the smoky air.

"Lead them," the women gathered repeated.

"Teach them the pathways to peaceful solutions to their endeavor so they will not be placed in harm's way."

"Teach them."

"Grant them success with what they are trying to accomplish."

"Grant them."

"Protect them so they may return to us in good health and sound of limb."

"Protect them."

"Help us to accept whatever You feel must be the outcome of this venture."

"Help us," Genny whispered, her throat clogging with emotion.

Rowena lowered her arms and looked at the women gathered before her. "We who are left behind will bear the burden of waiting and worrying. Our prayers must go with these men to protect them. They must know we are behind them in all they do." She locked gazes with Genny. "They must know we will remain here, faithful to them and trusting they will remain faithful to us. That no temptation, either old or new, will sway them from our arms."

Genny tore her eyes from the Empress and looked at a girl-child nestled in the arms of a nearby servant. The child had a twin brother who, because he was male, could not enter the Temple of Tethys. Because the girl-child was the daughter of the Great Lady, herself, she had been brought to the vespers ceremony.

She was also the daughter of one of the men sailing on the evening tide.

"Fear not his love for you," Rowena told the women, but her words were for the ears of one woman, alone. "Trust in him for he will return to you and to only you."

Genny shifted her gaze from the child to its mother. Although she hated Rowena Shimota with every ounce of venom her jealous heart could muster, she knew the woman was no threat to her relationship with Syn-Jern. Why he had been chosen to provide the other half of the equation to produce the Empress' offspring, she could not—nor would she—begin to understand. That he cared nothing for the other woman was evident in the way he avoided her. But the jealousy was still a prickle in Genny's heart. Just knowing the bitch had lain with Syn-Jern was enough to make Rowena Genny's enemy for life.

As though she had read the virulent thoughts running rampant through Genny Sorn's mind, Rowena shook her head with sadness, then turned her attention to the other women. "Let us go to our men and—"

*Not your man!*

Rowena stopped, shocked by the mental thought that slammed into her with enough force to give her a mild headache. She looked at Genny Sorn with wide eyes.

*Not your man and you will stay the hell away from him!* was the warning. *Do you understand me, you ugly red-headed bitch?*

The Empress put a trembling hand to her aching temple. It had been her intention to go to the docks and say goodbye to Syn-Jern, to the father of her children, but this she had not expected. The force of the anger directed at her had surely awakened what little psychic power the Saur—

"Sorn!" was the correction.

Rowena stared at Genny.

*Touch him ever again and I will pull every hair out of your head,* was the silent promise. *Is that clear enough for you, Great Lady?*

Knowing she had a formidable enemy on her hands, Rowena wondered how she would ever calm the seas between them.

ꕥ

Taeli Masarawa held the incense stick aloft and watched the smoke wafting from its tip. Very slowly, he lowered the burning stick and placed its fiery end to the flesh of his left arm. Only the slightest flicker of an eye betrayed the pain the action caused him.

For what was a mere speck of fire when his thoughts were of the white-hot brand that had been laid upon the ravaged flesh of his back two years before?

Masarawa shrugged his thick shoulders, feeling the pull of scar tissue. In the courtyard of Binh Tae palace, his back had been laid to the bone with a hundred passes of a steel-tipped lash. The legacy of his punishment would remain with him to the funeral pyre. The disgrace of his punishment would follow Masarawa into the Afterlife.

As would the pathetic attempt his enemy had made to stop Masarawa's punishment.

"His Grace pleaded leniency for you, cur," the executioner had snarled, "but Her Imperial Highness would not allow it! You attacked Lord Sorn and you will pay for it with your hide!"

"As you will pay for all the pain I have suffered, Syn-Jern Sorn," Masarawa swore. His meaty fist crushed the incense stick, bending it in half.

The man who was once in command of the Imperial Guard sat on his heels, laid the broken incense stick aside and drew his ceremonial dagger from the folds of his kimono. With his hard eyes staring straight ahead, Masarawa extended his arm then drew the blade of his dagger across his flesh of his left palm. He doubled his fist and allowed his blood to flow into an earthen bowl on the floor before him. Slowly, his gaze fell to the dripping blood and he smiled.

"As surely as my life's blood flows, I will follow you to the ends of the Earth. Your friends will be my enemies; your enemies will be my friends. That, that you champion, I will oppose. That, that you oppose, I will champion. I will have my revenge."

ꟙ

The Emperor's eyes gleamed with admiration. "It is fine," he pronounced. "Truly fine!"

The swordmaker bowed his head respectfully. "I am honored you are pleased, Highness."

"More than pleased," Akito Shimota stated. He hefted the sword, testing its balance. "It is by far the most elegant weapon you have cast, Shin Lee."

"A weapon worthy of a great warrior," the Emperor's advisor remarked.

"It surely is," Akito agreed. He handed it reverently into the care of its creator. "And I am most pleased with the craftsmanship." He lifted the hammered steel and admired the elaborate symbols etched into its length. Reading the Chrystallusian words of power, he shuddered. "A most deadly combination."

"He will be protected with such a weapon, Highness," the advisor said.

"Even a warrior with less skill than our outlaw would make of this weapon a widowmaker," Shimota chuckled.

"Outlaw?" the advisor questioned.

The Emperor shrugged. "That is what they will call him," he said, laying the sheath aside. "As soon as he steps foot on Viragonian soil, the Brotherhood will learn of it. There will be those who will testify he served his entire sentence; we have seen to that. Even so, the lands that were his, were confiscated and he no longer has right to them. But when he begins to take back what is rightfully his, he will have the Tribunal Guards after him." The Emperor spread his hands. "He will be an outlaw."

"With a hefty bounty on his golden head," the Empress said softly.

Shimota turned to his wife. "Is he not under the protection of the Daughters?"

Rowena nodded slowly. "Aye."

"And have you not said he will return to safety here?" The Emperor liked the Viragonian and wanted nothing to happen to him.

"I said," Rowena reminded her husband, "his family will know safety here." She lowered her eyes. "I can not guarantee Syn will return to Chrystallus unscathed." Her voice lowered. "Or that he, himself, will return at all."

"But…" Shimota began, but his wife lifted her head and he saw tears glistening in her eyes.

"We can only pray the gods pay heed to our entreaties, Akito. Beyond that, there is nothing more we can do." She nodded toward the lethal sword in the hands of its creator. "Those who live by such, may die by such." Her eyes clouded. "Or have their lives snuffed out at the end of a hangman's noose."

Akito felt his heart thudding in his chest. Did his wife know more than she was telling? Was it Syn-Jern Sorn's destiny to die in that heathen land he wanted so desperately to have as his own once more?

"His people will protect him as best they can, Akito," Rowena prophesied, "but even they can do just so much to keep him safe."

"His people?" Akito questioned. "You mean his crew?"

"No," she replied. "The people of Wixenstead Village."

The advisor shook his head. "Returning to the place from whence he was handed over to the Tribunal is foolhardy. Could no one deter him from such a reckless action?"

Rowena turned her attention to her husband's advisor. "They will rally to his cause, Kym. They have had ten years under the suffocating yoke of the Tribunal. Ten years in which to come to the realization that Syn-Jern Sorn was sent to prison simply because his brother wanted his inheritance."

"But the brother does not have the lands, does he, Highness?" Kym asked.

"No, they belong to the Tribunal, but Trace Edward Sorn lives on those lands and is overseer for the Tribunal," Rowena explained. "He will not be happy to see Syni return to Virago."

"Such talk disturbs me, wife," Akito said. "Let us have no more of it. We will present this magnificent weapon to our friend this eve at the banquet in his honor and he will know what a true friend he is to us."

Rowena did not reply to her husband's words. She looked at the weapon of which he and the swordmaker were so proud and felt a shudder of distaste travel through her body. Her own words echoed back to her:

*Those who live by such, may die by such.*

She prayed that would not be the case with Syn-Jern Sorn.

## Chapter Four

"ONE LAST TIME," WEIR SIGHED. "AND NO MORE THAN THAT, GENNY!"

Genny brazenly smiled at her brother, then ran up the gangplank, threw herself into her husband's arms. Much to her brother's embarrassment and the crew's amusement, the woman Syn-Jern was leaving safely behind him in Chrystallus plastered her body and mouth to her husband's and latched on.

"For the love of Alel," Weir swore and turned away, his face flaming as the crew hooted their approval.

"You send him off real good, now, Genny-girl!" Mr. Tarnes chuckled.

"From the looks of him this mornin'," Stevens drawled, "she liked to wore him out last eve." He pointed the stem of his pipe at the couple. "Best spray 'em down, Mr. Neevens, else they'll set fire to the deck with that action there."

"Will you get that shameless hussy off this boat?" Weir snapped. He looked around at his sister and brother-in-law and snorted. "Genny, get gone!"

Syn-Jern eased his wife's mouth from his, looked into her tearful eyes, and shook his head. "I will be back, milady. Do not think otherwise."

"I want to go with you," she said stubbornly though they had been through that argument many times.

Her husband cupped her face in his callused hands. "You can not," he said softly, "and you know why you can not." He lowered his head to place a gentle kiss on her forehead, then locked gazes with her once more. "I love you with all my being, Genevieve Sorn, and I promise you I will come home to you."

She stared into his eyes for a long time, then reached up to cover his left hand with hers, turning her face to plant a kiss in his palm. Before she could begin to sob, she turned and ran down the gangplank.

"Gangplank, away!" Weir shouted.

Syn-Jern walked to the ship's rail, his heart aching at the sight of his wife standing with her back to the Revenge. He willed her to turn and face him and when she did, he moaned softly at the tears cascading down her cheeks.

"I will return to you, milady!" he called as the ship began moving backwards out of her slip. He could hear the creak of the ropes as the harbor-men with their dray horses pulled the Revenge down the length of the long dock until she could catch the winds at the mouth of the harbor.

Genny's lips were trembling and her heart breaking. It would be months, maybe as long as a year before she would see her husband again.

"I will return, Genny!" she heard him shout.

"Aye," she whispered, then yelled her last words to him: "If you don't, I'll come and get you, Syn-Jern Sorn!"

Patrick came to stand beside Syn-Jern. Genny's words made him grin. "I do believe she's liable to do just that if you don't return when she thinks you should, my friend."

Syn-Jern lifted his hand in farewell and wasn't surprised to see it trembling. He was leaving everything he loved behind: his wife and infant son. And to do what, he asked? To take back lands he had no intention of ever living on again? To throw Trace Edward and his whore out of Holy Dale? Or to simply run his half-brother through his black heart with the elegant sword Akito had given him?

"You're wondering why you're doing this," Patrick said, and when Syn-Jern turned to look at him, Kasella smiled. "We've all had the same doubts, Syni, but each of us knows this needs doing."

"And what will we be able to accomplish, Paddy?" Syn-Jern asked.

Patrick leaned on the railing, his fingers threaded together. "We'll hit the Tribunal coffers and gather enough money to pay the taxes on Weir's family estate. We can stop other men from losing their ancestral holdings in the same way. And we can clear your good name."

Syn-Jern snorted. "By the time I'm through, my 'good name' as you call it, will have a price on it!" He shook his head. "I'll be an outlaw, Paddy, and never able to return to Virago even if I want to live there." He focused on his wife as her lovely face began to blur with distance. "But Trace Sorn will not be living in the lap of luxury with his vicious slut at his side. I'll make gods-be-damned sure that my children will be able to live at Holy Dale if that is their wish. I'll make Rosa-Lynn signs the manor house, free and clear, to Dermot." He was unaware he was gripping the rail, his knuckles devoid of color. "And it will remain in Sorn hands until it crumbles to the ground. There will never be another Hesar to own Holy Dale!"

Patrick Kasella did not reply to that statement. If the eerie dream were a portent of things to come, there would be another Hesar living in Holy Dale three or four generations from now.

And that Hesar would find Holy Dale a living hell.

"Kaelan," Paddy whispered, picturing a man limping about the musty halls of the great manor house.

"What?" Syn-Jern asked.

Patrick's forehead crinkled. "Is there a staircase rising from the center of the main floor at Holy Dale and is the flooring black marble?"

Syn-Jern blinked. "Aye. Have you visited there?"

"With a huge rose-colored chandelier," Patrick continued, his mind's eye looking back on his strange dream, "hanging directly over a large mahogany table in the middle of the floor?"

"You've been there," Syn-Jern said, wondering when.

Patrick shook his head slowly. "No, I have never stepped foot inside your ancestral home."

"Then how could you know?" Syn-Jern began, but Patrick interrupted him.

"I heard you mumbling about it when you had the fever," Paddy lied. He shrugged. "How else would I know?"

Syn-Jern knew his friend was lying and wondered why. But Patrick's privacy was not to be invaded so Syn-Jern kept his thoughts to himself.

The ship was well into the harbor, now, the sails cascading down the masts to catch the wind. The sounds of a ship and her crew making ready to sail made it impossible to carry on any further conversation. Instead, Syn-Jern kept his attention on his lady until the only thing he could see was the imposing palace of Binh Tae.

"Stay safe, my love," Syn-Jern whispered. "I will come home to you."

## Chapter Five

TRACE EDWARD SORN ROLLED OVER IN HIS BED AND DRAPED A HEAVY ARM over his wife's side. He wiggled closer to the warmth of her and nuzzled his face against the nape of her neck.

"Are you sated, milord?" Rosa-Lynn sighed with annoyance.

"Aye," Trace replied sleepily.

"Then kindly turn over and let me go to sleep," his wife snapped, pushing his arm away.

"Fine," he said and flipped over, dragging the cover from his wife's shapely shoulders.

"The demon take you, Trace Sorn!" Rosa-Lynn grated, jerking the covers.

"I think she did but a few moments ago," Trace threw at her. He lifted himself on one elbow, punched his pillow into submission then plopped down again.

"You can go to hell," Rosa-Lynn said in a sweet voice.

"I am living in hell," her husband snarled.

"'Twas your choice," she told him. Snuggling into the covers, she cursed the chill of the room in which they lay; the drafty old house in general; and the ineffectual fool to whom she was married.

"It was not my fault the Tribunal insisted we remain here as wardens to the property!" Trace reminded her.

"Oh?" his wife drawled, turning over to stare at his back. "And where else were we to go, fool?"

"Tern Keep," Trace declared. "I would rather live in Tern Keep than here in this great pile of stones with only a handful of servants who curse me behind my back and mumble insurrection at every turn!"

"Tern Keep was confiscated, as well, or have you very conveniently forgotten it belonged to Syn-Jern?"

"Do not speak his name to me!" Trace thundered.

"Some plan you had!" his wife threw back at him. "Frame him for Playe's murder and he'll hang, huh?" She hit him on his shoulder. "Did you not think he would fight back when Playe held him under the water, fool?"

"He was supposed to be unconscious, bitch!" he yelled. "He was not supposed to wake up in the middle of the drowning and turn the tables on his assassin!"

"Do not yell at me, Sorn," his wife warned him in a steely voice.

"I'll do whatever the hell I feel like!" Trace responded.

"What think you the Tribunal would say if they ever learned 'twas not Syn-Jern who strangled Playe?" At her husband's threatening growl, she smiled savagely. "What think you they would say if I told them you promised to kill me if I did not testify it was Syn-Jern who strangled the slimy bastard?"

"He believed he strangled Playe," Trace said from a tightly clenched jaw. "He did not deny it."

"He woke with his hands clasped around Playe's neck, aye, but you and I both know the man was already dead!" Rosa-Lynn said.

Trace snaked out his hand and grabbed a fistful of his wife's lovely hair and yanked as hard as he could, smiling brutally at the shriek of pain his action brought. He ignored her as she gasped: "You're hurting me!" as he wound the thick lock around his wrist and pulled her face close to his.

"Open that pretty mouth and say one word of how Playe died to anyone," he snarled, "and it will be the last word you ever utter, Rosa-Lynn." He tightened his grip even more. "Do I make myself clear to you?"

"Aye!" Rosa-Lynn gasped, trying to pry his hand from her hair. She began to whimper with pain, but stopped abruptly as her husband's hand moved from her hair to her neck. Her eyes widened as he pushed her to her back and placed his other hand over her throat, his thumbs pressing into her windpipe.

"Do I make myself clear?" he repeated, his face filled with savageness.

"Aye." It was a squeak of agreement, but it was enough to lift the strong hands from her throat.

Rosa-Lynn drew in a long, shuddery breath, knowing she'd pushed her husband too far.

And there was only one way to get back in the man's good graces.

Trace put his hands behind his head and stared up at the ceiling as his wife went about soothing his anger. He counted the cracks in the plaster over his head; studied a slab of paint peeling from one corner; frowned at the tarnished appearance of the drapery rods.

As Rosa-Lynn's lips drew from him his forgiveness, he spied a spider web dangling from the ceiling to the chandelier and ground his teeth. The slovenly servants did no more than they could to maintain Holy Dale. He was forced to live in a pigsty with a sow at his side.

He lifted his head and looked down at his wife's silky hair as she worked at giving him pleasure.

He frowned even more.

Rosa-Lynn's talents—as were her beauty and usefulness—were fading.

Soon, he would have to find a female to replace her. Until then, he would just have to make do with what he had.

Trace sighed.

Being lord of the manor was not what he had thought it would be.

ஐ

Sara Gill eased from the door of the Duke's bedroom and made her way silently down the corridor. It wouldn't do to let the bastard know she'd been eavesdropping. Quickly making her way down the servants' stairs, she hurried into the kitchen and grabbed her brother, Drew's arm. "Come outside," she commanded, drawing her youngest sibling with her.

Drew tossed aside the cloth he was using to wipe the table and gladly accompanied Sara. "They be fighting again?" he asked.

"Like cats and dogs," Sara responded. "The same thing over and over again, every day." She led her brother to the stable, cast a quick look around, and then pushed him into the darkened interior. She closed the door behind them and, although there was no one about to hear, she lowered her voice to a whisper. "I want you to hightail it to the village and find Kerm. Tell him I overheard the Duke admitting to killing Otis Playe this time."

"You did?" Drew gasped, his eyes wide.

"Well, not in so many words," Sara said, opening the stable door a tad so she could make sure no one was lurking about. Satisfied they were alone, she eased the door shut and turned to her little brother. "Tell Kerm the Duke threatened to kill the Duchess if she breathed a word of what happened up there that night."

Drew whistled. "Like as not that won't set well with Her High and Mightiness," he chortled. "She'll find a way to make him forget his anger."

"She's already taken matters into her own hands on that regard," Sara sniffed. "You just go tell Kerm what I told you and be quick about it. They'll be wanting supper a'fore too long so hurry back." She sniffed again. "Won't come down for the noon meal, but they'll be starved for supper."

"I brought up the wine like he ordered me yesterday," Drew announced. "Opened the bottle so it could 'breathe' like he demanded."

"And pissed in it," Sara smiled. At her brother's blush, she patted him on the back. "You done good, Drew. If I could have, I'd have pissed in it, too!"

Drew scratched his head. "You know something, Sara?" he asked, his eyes puzzled. "There was something not altogether right about that cellar." He scratched his head some more. "I think there be a room under there."

"There is," Sara replied. She shushed him as he started to give his opinion on what might lie beneath the thick oak flooring. "Go on with you, now, and tell Kerm what I said. He needs to get word to Ferris."

"Don't see what good none of this tattling has done us so far," Drew grumbled as he pulled his cap from his pocket and settled in on his mop of flaxen hair. "Tribunal wouldn't believe a thing any of the likes of us might have to say."

"Maybe not, but the more ammunition we have, the more chance we got to have the right man sent to Tyber's Isle for killing Otis Playe."

"Won't do His Grace no good," Drew responded, thinking of the rightful owner of Holy Dale. He ducked his head. "Makes me feel bad the way we treated him."

"Oh, go on with you!" Sara snapped. "You were but a wee bairn when His Lordship was taken to prison. What would you know?"

"There's talk," Drew said stubbornly.

"Aye, well," Sara admitted, "there's always talk." She cracked the door, peered out, then pushed her brother outside. "You hurry back, you hear?"

"No wonder you can't find a husband, Sara Elizabeth Gill," Drew complained. "You're too bossy by far!"

Sara watched until her younger brother was out of sight, then walked back to the kitchen, casting a suspicious eye on the balcony window behind which the Lord and Lady of Holy Dale lay sleeping.

"And it eleven of the clock on a bright day," Sara snorted. She purposefully slammed the kitchen door behind her, knowing how much the Duke hated the sound. With a fierce look on her pretty face, she began to bang pots and pans and dishes as she prepared the noontide meal.

## Chapter Six

"IT WAS WHITE AS SNOW," KERM GILL, SARA'S ELDEST BROTHER, WHISPERED to the men sitting at his table. His voice was strained. "I tell you it was a ghost ship!" He reached for his ale, his hand trembling, and took a large gulp.

Andrew Spiel turned to the man on his left. "Whatcha think of his tale, Dano?"

"Think he's too much of the drink taken," Danny Dunne joked.

"Weren't drinkin' a gods-be-damned thing!" Kerm snapped, banging his tankard on the table. "Were as sober as sober can be when I saw it!"

"Ghost ship," the fourth man at the greasy tavern table snorted. "Right out there in Wixen Harbor."

Kerm turned and whistled for the tavern wench. When she looked his way, he pointed at his empty mug, then slumped in the chair, eyeing his drinking companions with contempt. "I don't care if'n you believe me or not, Bryce Heil!" he growled. "I know what I saw!"

The men sitting with Kerm laughed, but a stranger at the next table over stopped them in mid-guffaw when he spoke up.

"I saw her, too," the stranger said quietly in a thick Ionarian accent.

Kerm and his friends turned their attention to the stranger. The man was sitting with his arms on the table, his hands wrapped around a dented tankard. He was not looking at Kerm or his companions, but seemed to be studying the contents of his drink. He wore a long robe of coarse black material, marking him a Low Priest of one of the many Orders in Virago. His face was immobile, his profile appeared chiseled as though from stone within the cowl of the robe.

"You seen it, Brother?" Kerm queried.

The stranger nodded and raised his head to stare across the room. "She dropped anchor about half a mile down the coast from where I was camped. I saw her, but…" He turned so that one dark eye regarded them steadily; the other eye was hidden behind an eye patch. "…I saw no one on board her."

"Neither did I," Kerm whispered, shivering. He lifted his mug, realized it was empty and banged it twice. "Gloria, get me my ale, bitch!"

The tavern wench flipped him the universal symbol of comment, then flounced to the tap to draw him a fresh brew.

"I don't believe a word of it," Dano Dunne stated. He turned his head and spat on the rush-strewn floor. "A ghost ship my pimpled, hairy ass!"

"Believe what you will, friend," the stranger said ominously, "but I've seen her likes before."

"Where?" Kerm whispered.

"Down near Hellstrom Point," the stranger replied. He narrowed his one good eye. "I heard tell the ship's name is The Revenant and that she's crewed by the restless spirits of all the prisoners who've ever been transported to Tyber's Isle." He lifted his tankard, took a long sip, then settled back in his chair, bracing the tankard on his thigh. "They say that when you see her, she's come after the man who wrongly accused one of her crew and sent him to the bowels of the Labyrinth to live out his days."

"The Labyrinth," Kerm repeated. A hard shudder rippled down his lanky form. "That was where the Sorn boy was sent. Only one hereabouts ever to go to that hellish place!"

Dano Dunne, his bravura slipping at the mention of the infamous penal colony nodded. "Aye and we all know who sent the boy to Tyber's Isle, now, don't we?"

Andrew Spiel leaned over the table and spoke to the men in a lowered voice. "You think that ship's come after Sorn?"

"Wouldn't surprise me none," Kerm growled. "He sure as hell deserves the haints to come after his evil ass!"

Weir Saur dug into the pocket of his robe and drew out a silver coin. Tossing it on the table, he stood, turned once more to the men at the next table, and met each one's gaze in turn. "I'd be very careful, my sons," he suggested, "if I were the lot of you."

"Careful of what?" Andrew Spiel asked in a hushed tone.

"Not to get in the way of the NightWinds," Weir replied in a chill tone. "I'll wager they've come after one of yours."

"NightWinds!" Dano Dunne, the only Chalean in the tavern gasped. "You say them is NightWinds on board that there ship?"

Weir nodded slowly. "That's what I've heard, friend," he agreed. "And you know what they say of the NightWinds, don't you?"

Dunne's hand shot up to cross himself. "Aye, I sure as hell do!"

Andrew Spiel and Kerm exchanged a look, but it was Bryce Heil who asked what the stranger meant.

Weir locked gazes with Heil and lowered his voice to a throaty monotone. "The Talespinners say if you get in the way of a NightWind and his mission, you'll end up in the Abyss for all eternity, but..."

"But if'n you help them," Dunne interrupted, "they'll leave you alone and might even come to your aid when you're having troubles of your own!" He wrapped his arms around him as though he had suddenly developed a severe chill. "I sure as hell intend to leave them alone!"

Syn-Jern Sorn's brother-in-law leaned over the table, bracing his hands on the slick top. His hooded scrutiny moved from Heil to Dunne to Spiel, then settled on Kerm Gill. "If I were you, I'd do everything I could to help the NightWinds, my friends. I'd make gods-be-damned sure no one gets in their way and no one should come between them and the man..." He narrowed his eye. "...Or woman they've come after." He arched one thick dark brow. "That'll hold you in good stead with Them and I can't help but think that might be a good thing, don't you?"

"Surely!" Dunne was quick to agree. "Surely it would!"

"You know a lot about them things," Heil grumbled. "How come you know so much?"

Weir straightened. He did not answer the question, but turned and limped slowly to the tavern door. There he reached for a heavy staff that rested against the wall.

"You didn't answer him, Brother!" Fiels called out.

The captain of the newly christened ship, The Revenant, stopped at the door. He looked around, his silence bringing every eye in the place to him. When he knew he had everyone's attention, Weir replied, "Mayhaps that's because I am one of Them, Stanton Bryce Heil." Then he slowly smiled with such evil intent, it made the hairs on his listener's arms stand to attention. The men were so taken aback by that leering grin, not a one of them moved as the tall stranger opened the door and hobbled out into the foggy evening.

Absolute silence filled the smoky tavern as all eyes remained on the door. The fog from the harbor began to drift in through the open portal and the chill of the late evening finally brought the proprietor from behind the bar to close it. Before he did, he bravely ventured outside, turned this way and that, then hurried back inside, closing the door with a firm snap.

"Weren't a soul walking out there," the proprietor told his patrons. His thick lips trembled. "Not a living soul, anyways!"

"Sweet Merciful Alel," Dano Dunne finally breathed. Slowly, he crossed himself again and scrubbed his hands over his face. "The gods help us."

"I ain't gonna get in their way," Spiel stated, pushing from the table. "I sure as hell ain't gonna get in their way!"

"You'd better believe I ain't gonna do it, neither," Kerm echoed.

Heil's attention was still on the door. "He was as much flesh and blood as you and me, Gill," he snapped. "And I don't believe all that mumbo-jumbo he was spouting."

"Believe what you will, Stanton Bryce Heil," Dano Dunne hissed. "How did he know your name, anyways?"

Bryce owned the local livery, but few people knew his first name and no one in Wixenstead who did know it ever called him by it.

"If'n we help them," Spiel said in a low voice, "they'll do right by us." He looked at Dunne. "Ain't that the way of it, Dano?"

Dunne nodded slowly. "So's I've always heard."

"What is it we can do?" Kerm asked.

"Help 'em," Dunne stated.

"To do what?" Heil grated.

Dano Dunne glanced around, knew every manjack in the tavern felt as he did about the man out at Holy Dale. "We all know what he did."

"Can't prove it," the bar's proprietor spoke up.

"Mayhaps not," Dunne acknowledged, "but we all know just the same."

"The Sorn boy will have been out of there by now," Heil objected.

Kerm frowned. "You know that for a fact, do you?"

"Well, no, but…" Heil stopped, feeling the animosity of the others in the bar. "Hell, it ain't nothin' to me, but didn't a one of us stand up for the boy when he was accused."

"What if the boy died in that hellhole?" Spiel asked.

"We'd have heard of it," the bar's proprietor, Vin Ruck, put in.

"Mayhaps not," Dunne repeated. "Why would we have? His old granny done be gone and her ashes scattered to the Four Winds. Who else is there ever been to care about the boy one way or t'other?"

"That's the truth of it," Spiel agreed, nodding. "Surely not that witch out to Holy Dale. She stood up there and swore the boy's life away and her contracted to have been his wife at that!"

"You 'member what the stranger said?" Kerm asked in a near whisper, his eyes round in his ruddy face. "He said: 'no one should come between Them and the man or woman they've come after'."

"How'd he know about her?" Spiel whispered.

"Good question," Dunne remarked and his gaze went to the door once more. "A gods-be-damned good question."

"I ain't buying none of this!" Heil snorted. He scraped his chair back and stood. "Not a bit of it!" With that he stomped across the room, flung open the door, and left, banging the portal behind him.

"Fool," Spiel labeled their friend.

Dunne and Kerm nodded their agreement then the three men lowered their heads and began to discuss the evening's eerie events.

Bryce Heil strode briskly down the wooden planks that served to keep the villager's from walking through the mud in the streets. His boot heels made explosive little pops on the planking, the sound magnified in the fog-laden night.

Pausing beside the undertaker's establishment, he fished in his pocket for his pipe.

"How did it go?" a voice asked from the dark alley between the undertaker's and the shipping office.

Heil struck a lucifer on the seat of his gabardine britches and stuck the flame to the bowl of his pipe. He puffed the tobacco into life before fanning out the lucifer and flicking it aside.

"They bought every haunting word of it," Heil said through the restriction of his teeth clamped on the stem of the pipe. He squinted against the smoke rising up from the bowl and leaned against the side of the undertaker's building. "They won't give you any trouble, Lord NightWind."

Syn-Jern Sorn smiled. "My thanks to you, Bryce."

Heil shrugged. "The least I could do, Milord," he replied. "I'm with you in this every step of the way."

"Good man," another voice spoke from the shadowy confines of the alleyway and Heil recognized the stranger's Serenian accent.

"I am only following the McGregor's orders," Heil said, pushing away from the building. "He says your cause is just and because he does, I'll follow you to Abyss if needs be."

With that said, Heil sauntered away, a plume of smoke following in his wake.

"Nice to be appreciated," a third voice quipped.

Syn-Jern draped an arm around Prince Tiernan McGregor's shoulder. "Have I told you how appreciative I am of your help, Cousin?"

Tiernan shrugged. "I didn't have anything better to do, Syni," the Serenian chuckled.

"Not until later this week," Weir reminded the Prince.

Tiernan sighed as deeply as any Chalean ever had. "I wish you hadn't brought that up."

Syn-Jern clapped Tiernan on the back, then lowered his arm. "We need to know who this accuser is who's going to the Court of Storms, Tier. If it's Trace, we can deal with that, but if it's someone I don't know, then we may have to re-think our plans." He folded his arms over his chest. "Of course it won't make a gods-be-damned bit of difference with what the NightWinds are going to do."

Tiernan grinned, his white teeth glowing in the darkness. "By the gods but this is gonna be fun!"

"Not if your father catches us," Weir warned. "The king might not look kindly on his son and heir causing mischief over here in Virago."

"My father doesn't give a Diabolusian warthog's arse what happens in this godawful place. Any trouble we can make for Innis Hesar, the better!"

Syn-Jern wasn't so sure, but he kept his opinion to himself. He needed the help of Tiernan McGregor and McGregor's good friend, Rhian Brell, one of the best—if not the best—swordsmen of his day. He was grateful for Rowena Shimota's help to put him in touch with McGregor and Brell.

"They will aid you, Milord," Simply Rowena had assured him. "They are consorts of two Daughters who would make their lives miserable otherwise!"

"The Daughters," Syn-Jern said aloud.

Tiernan grunted. "The Daughters," he repeated on a long sigh. He sighed again. "I've a feeling we're going to need all the protection they can give us!"

ꕥ

Thousands of miles away in the palace at Binh Tae, Rowena Shimota looked up from her scrying mirror and smiled. "And you shall have it, Lord Northwind," she said, calling Tiernan by the code name chosen for him by Syn-Jern Sorn.

## Chapter Seven

KING INNIS HESAR FROWNED SHARPLY AT THE TALL MAN WHO BOWED SO elegantly before him. "What is this matter of utmost importance?"

Taeli Masarawa inclined his head. "It is in regard to a mortal enemy of yours, Highness," he said smoothly.

Hesar's frown deepened. "I have no enemies," he snapped. "Every enemy I ever had is moldering in his grave."

The Chrystallusian warrior knew better. The man had more enemies than any ruler of his time and no friends. "This is a man you sent to a living grave," Taeli quipped. "A man who has returned."

The Viragonian King was not particularly sharp of mind and riddles annoyed him since he was never able to solve them. He always surrounded himself with men of low intelligence and dull wit so he could shine in his own eyes. When anyone presented something to him that he did not understand, he became even more hateful than was normal for him.

And when he became hateful, he became ruthless.

When he became ruthless, he became deadly.

"Come to the point!" the king ordered. "I don't have all day."

"Syn-Jern Sorn," was all Taeli had to say. He saw the king sit bolt upright on his throne, his dark brown eyes wary.

"What of him?" Hesar asked in a low tone.

Taeli knew he had the king's full attention now. "He has escaped the Labyrinth, Your Highness, and is on his way here." The Chrystallusian lifted a single black brow. "To kill you and take back what he considers his."

Hesar sucked in a quick breath. "That can not be! I extended his sentence so he…" He stopped, looking at the ministers of his court who were scattered about the throne room. It would not do to have them learn he had circumvented Viragonian law so he could spend one less than memorable weekend with Trace Edward Sorn. He cleared his throat. "So he would be punished for the mischief he was causing on Tyber's Isle," he finished.

"What mischief was that, Your Highness?" Prince Tiernan McGregor asked. The Serenian delegate from the Court of the Winds disliked Innis Hesar and hated his assignment at the Court of the Storms in Virago. But for once the appointment given to him by his father as punishment would prove to cause Innis Hesar untold trouble. For that reason, and that reason alone, Tiernan was now suddenly taking his job very seriously, much to the surprise of his fellow court appointees.

Innis Hesar waved an imperious hand. "You should not concern yourself with Viragonian matters, McGregor." He turned a vicious scowl to Tiernan. "You have a hard enough time as it is handling your duties here."

Tiernan shrugged. "There is so little for me to do, I get bored." He smiled nastily at the King. "I miss the mental exercise my father, brothers and I engage in at Boreas."

A few of the ministers exchanged amused looks. McGregor hadn't come right out and accused the King of being slow-minded, but he'd come close to it on several occasions. The trouble was, Innis Hesar didn't know he was being insulted.

"I'll see if I can find you something to occupy your time, then," the king snapped.

"That would help immeasurably," McGregor replied, winking at one of the ministers.

Taeli Masarawa was a very intelligent individual and his quick wit homed in on the interplay between the obnoxious Overlander king and the Serenian nobleman. Under other circumstances, Taeli might have sought out the one called McGregor; he could well imagine the enjoyment of sparring mentally with him. But there were more important matters at hand.

Such as revenge.

"I am told Syn-Jern Sorn has also sworn to kill the man responsible for sending him to prison," Taeli said, gaining the king's attention once more. "As well as the woman who was to be Sorn's wife."

Tiernan McGregor crooked his finger at his aide and when the man bent over, McGregor whispered instructions to him. The aide nodded politely, doubled his fist, struck his chest in salute, then hurried away.

"How long has Sorn been imprisoned?" McGregor asked politely although his mind was on an entirely different subject.

"This does not concern you, Serenian!" Innis Hesar snapped. "Pray mind your own business!"

Tiernan bristled at the rebuke. "The man you are discussing was born in my country. Therefore, according to our Tribunal laws, he is a Serenian." He narrowed his blue eyes dangerously. "That makes it my business."

"Our laws state he is Viragonian, McGregor," one of the minister's said, "since citizenship is counted through the maternal line."

"We should debate this," an older minister mumbled. "I propose we put it to—"

"Silence!" Hesar shouted. If there was anything he hated worse than riddles, it was debates of any kind.

McGregor hid a smile behind his hand. If there was anything he liked better than slipping gently between the thighs of a willing maid, it was aggravating Innis Hesar.

"Might I suggest a troop of Tribunal guards be dispatched to Holy Dale Manor, Your Highness?" Taeli inquired, wanting to get the matter settled.

"For what purpose?" the king demanded.

Taeli dug his nails into the palms of his hands. It was all he could do to maintain a façade of respect while dealing with the foolish Viragonian king. "To re-arrest him, your Highness," the warrior said in as polite a tone as he could muster.

"Correct me if I am wrong in this," McGregor injected, "but wasn't his time up two years prior to this?" He snapped his fingers and another aide hurried to him, placing a document in his outstretched hand.

Innis Hesar's forehead wrinkled. "What have you got, McGregor?"

The Serenian unfolded the paper. "The court ruling on one Syn-Jern Sorn, Duke of Winterset," he responded, pretending to read the document he already knew by heart. "Ah, here it is!" He was silent so long the king let out a snort of disgust.

"Well, read it aloud, fool! What does it say?" Hesar demanded. Truth told he had forgotten what the writ of imprisonment had decreed. He wasn't even sure he had ever signed the second writ that was intended to keep Syn-Jern Sorn locked away for the remainder of his life.

"It says," McGregor drawled, "the sentence was completed two years ago." He re-rolled the parchment and laid it in his lap. "Unless there is a second writ, the man is free."

"I think not," the king grated.

McGregor turned to the group of ministers hovering nearby. "Were any of you gentlemen privy to a second writ of imprisonment?" He looked from one to the other of them. When they shook their heads in denial, he arched both brows. "None of you witnessed such a writ?"

Again the ministers shook their heads.

The Serenian turned his full scrutiny on the Viragonian king. "Surely you would not have given a verbal order to keep a man in prison long after he had served his rightful sentence, would you, Your Majesty? Is that not against Tribunal policy and Viragonian law?"

Innis saw the ministers watching him. Although they could do nothing to him if he had bent the law in such a way, now was not the time to get on the men's bad side. There were things he wanted to do and he needed their approval. "Of course not," he answered, hating McGregor with every fiber of his being.

"Then we are agreed he is a free man, are we not?" Tiernan pressed.

"Free?" Innis echoed. "I can not agree if he escaped the Labyrinth. As such, he will have to serve additional time for that." His slow mind wrestled with the problem, trying to find a way he could prolong—indefinitely—Syn-Jern's committal.

"You can not fault a man for escaping if he has served his time," the Ambassador from Chale spoke up. "What man among us would not do so?" He looked about him and was pleased as those among the assembly nodded their agreement. "Right is right, Sire."

"He has to be punished for his crime!" Innis objected, unable to come up with one good reason for having Sorn returned to the Labyrinth.

"His lands were forfeited; his title revoked," McGregor stated. "What more punishment is needed?"

"If he has committed no additional crime, then he is a free man," the Chalean ambassador proclaimed. "So it is written in the Tribunal tomes."

"Aye," the other ministers and ambassadors confirmed.

"You must declare him free, Your Grace," Tiernan prodded Innis.

"You must send him back to Tyber's Isle. He has sworn to kill his enemies!" Taeli Masarawa seethed. "And his king! That is treason!"

"That is hearsay and nothing more," McGregor said, passing off such remarks as irrelevant. He nodded as the aide he had dispatched for information came back, whispered what he had learned in his prince's ear, then took up a position beside Tiernan's chair once more.

"He is on his way here to carry out his death threats," Taeli insisted. "Will you let him murder your king in his bed?"

Innis flinched. He certainly would need to increase security to his person.

Taeli sneered at Tiernan. "Or is that what you would like to see happen, Prince McGregor?"

"Who are you?" Tiernan snapped. His gaze bored into Taeli. "And why are you here spewing this wild tale of murder and mayhem? What is in this for you?"

"He's a gods-be-damned Chrystallusian," the Ambassador from Diabolusia grunted. "And I'd like to hear why he's tale-telling myself!"

Taeli drew himself up to his full height, that was impressive. "I am the Captain of the..."

"Was," Tiernan corrected. "Was the captain of the Imperial Guard, but you were sent to prison for assaulting Syn-Jern Sorn."

There was a chorus of in-drawn breaths throughout the throne room. Narrowed gazes fell on Taeli Masarawa.

"Assaulting him where?" Innis questioned. "Here in Virago?"

"In Chrystallus where the man is living at the moment," Tiernan replied. He cocked his head toward his aide. "We are in contact with the Imperial house as you know, Your Grace, and as such, we are privy to what occurs there. When His Imperial Majesty, Emperor Shimota, learned of Syn-Jern Sorn's arrival in his homeland, he sent this man to escort him to the palace to be welcomed. Instead, Masarawa attacked Sorn, nearly killing him."

Taeli's face flamed. "You do not understand what transpired. You—"

"You," Tiernan emphasized, "rendered Syn-Jern Sorn unconscious, attacking him from behind, as it were, and sending him to bed with a severe concussion. For your—"

"You do not understand!" Taeli interrupted. "I had been given orders to—"

"For your crime," Tiernan shouted over Taeli's objection, "you were lashed and sent to prison, from which you escaped!"

The narrowed eyes of the court widened, then became flint hard as the stares became glowers of outrage.

"An escaped prisoner, you say?" Lord Diego Estevez barked. He had as much love for Chrystallusians as the McGregors had for the Hesars. He pointed a crooked finger at Taeli. "Arrest that man!"

"No!" Taeli shouted and turned to run. His escape was met with two Tribunal guards, swords drawn.

Tiernan McGregor stretched out his long legs, braced his elbows on the arms of his chair, pressed his fingertips together and rested his chin on them as he watched the Tribunal guards wrestling Masarawa to the floor. Amid the vicious Chrystallusian curses being brought down on the heads of every man in the room and the grunts of pain as meaty fists plowed into the ex-captain of the Imperial Guards' body, Tiernan was enjoying himself immensely. The clanking of heavy chains being clamped around the warrior's wrists drowned out the low chuckles of amusement coming from Tier's twitching lips. He shifted his eyes to Innis Hesar and saw that man slumped on his throne, his face worried.

"You've got plenty to worry about, you bastard," Tiernan thought to himself as a well-aimed fist knocked the light out of Taeli Masarawa's world and the Chrystallusian was dragged away. "Your troubles are just beginning."

"McGregor," the king said in a flat tone.

"Aye, Your Highness," Tiernan replied.

Innis Hesar turned his concerned gaze on the young Serenian Prince. "You say you are bored."

Tiernan nodded.

"Would a trip to Holy Dale liven things up for you?"

McGregor cautioned himself not to smile. "I would not mind the trip, Your Grace."

Innis lifted a tired hand. "Then go and report back to me the climate of Trace Sorn's village. See if there is anything to the rumor of his half-brother returning to Holy Dale to cause trouble for the crown."

Tiernan inclined his head respectfully. "As you wish, Majesty. Consider it done." He smiled slyly. "May I take one of the Tribunal ships since I will be there in an official capacity?"

"I don't care what you take," Innis snarled. "Just see to it!" With that he thrust from the chair and stalked away, his massive shoulders hunched like those of a bull.

# Chapter Eight

TRACE EDWARD SORN'S UPPER LIP WAS LIFTED IN SCORN AS HE WATCHED the Tribunal's Serenian emissary slurping soup into his mouth. With contempt, Trace lifted his napkin and blotted at his lips. "And just how long will you be staying with us, Prince…" He arched a thin brow.

"McGregor," Tiernan supplied the name. He swung his attention to the woman sitting at the far end of the table. "You set a goodly table, Your Grace," he complimented the sullen bitch. "Captain Saur and I certainly appreciate you providing us such a glorious repast, do we not, Captain?"

"Most certainly, Your Grace," Weir agreed.

Rosa-Lynn Sorn rolled her eyes and dug into the steak on her plate with a vengeance. After voicing her protest of the intrusion to her home by the Serenians, she had set about to ignore her visitors.

"As you can well imagine, Milord," Trace drawled, "we were not expecting company and my lady-wife is—"

"They are not guests, Trace Edward," Rosa-Lynn spat, grabbing her wineglass. "They have commandeered our home!" She lifted the glass and took a long, hard pull on the dark red claret.

"I believe this is a Tribunal residence," Tiernan said, fusing glares with the woman. "It belongs to the Brotherhood, not to you."

Rosa-Lynn sputtered, her eyes flashing pale fire at the man down the table from her. "How dare you?" she snarled, her lips drawn back from her teeth.

"I dare," Tiernan said in a haughty, lethal tone, "because I have, should the occasion arise, the authority to put you out on your shapely rear, Milady, if that is my desire." He smiled nastily. "Perhaps I should ask if you care to remain here or would prefer to retire to one of the convents while I am in residence." The smile vanished from his lips. "The Court of the Storms would certainly uphold any decision I make regarding the disposition of Tribunal owned property."

Trace's eyes widened. "By the gods, no!" he gasped. He knew if Rosa-Lynn was threatened with imprisonment in a convent—and that was surely what McGregor was implying—she'd tell everything she knew about the death of Otis Playe.

Rosa-Lynn's face had drained of color at the threat. The hand holding her glass of wine trembling, she returned the goblet to the table and put her hands in her lap, clutching the fingers together to keep them still. "I…I meant no insult to you, Highness," she whispered, then turned her best engaging and seductive smile on the man. "I beg your pardon."

Before Tiernan had even met the bitch, he had hated her. Knowing what she had put Syn-Jern through was enough to put the very demon in his dry tone when he said," You do not want to make an enemy of me, woman." When her suddenly worried eyes locked with his, his own narrowed into thin slits of dislike. "The last thing you want to do is make an enemy of a McGregor clansman. Do I make myself clear?"

"I..." she began, but Tiernan cut her off.

"Shut up. You are an annoying piece of tail, are you not?"

Trace blinked. No one had ever said such a thing to Rosa-Lynn and he shifted his startled gaze from his wife to the Prince then back again. Rosa-Lynn was sitting in her seat as stiff as a board. Her face was pale, her lips trembling, but she was holding her temper—a formidable task for one such as she. When her head lowered, Trace nearly hooted with laughter for he'd never thought to see the day any man humbled Rosa-Lynn Sorn.

"You have to know how to put a woman in her place and keep her there," Tiernan snapped, skewering a piece of steak and popping it into his mouth. He spoke around the gob of meat. "Obviously, you have let this one get away with murder."

Rosa-Lynn's head came up and she turned toward Trace. The venom in her stare made her husband nervous, but he knew it would be unwise to come to her defense with the prince. So instead, he kept his mouth shut, and returned to the food on his plate.

"Tell me about the bastard I was sent here to investigate," Tiernan mumbled as he stuffed bread into his mouth.

Trace's brows came together over his aquiline nose. "Beg pardon?" he asked, not having been apprised of the situation that had brought McGregor to Holy Dale's doors.

"This Sorn fella," Weir stated, looking from husband to wife, gauging the reaction. "The one sent to Tyber's Isle."

For a moment, neither husband nor wife registered the name, but when the full implication settled in, their mouths dropped open. Rosa-Lynn was actually heard to gasp as her hand flew to her throat.

"Sorn?" Trace managed to inquire. "You don't mean my half-brother, Syn-Jern, do you?"

"Aye," Tiernan grated, viciously stabbing the slab of steak on his plate. "That's the ex-prisoner's name." He popped the meat in his mouth and chewed, happy to see unease flitting across the faces of his hosts.

"Ex?" Trace stammered. "What do you mean by ex?"

"He served his sentence and has now been declared a free man," Tiernan informed them.

"Free?" Trace gasped. "Surely you are mistaken!"

Tiernan smiled nastily. "I have his free papers in my diplomatic pouch." To disabuse Sorn of the notion of trying to steal the papers and destroy them, McGregor took great pleasure in telling him the papers had already been recorded in the Temple at Wixenstead.

"Recorded," Trace repeated. He swallowed. "Where is he now?"

"The last we heard, he was in Ciona," Weir explained. "Working on a ship to get passage money to Wixenstead."

"H…he's coming here?" Rosa-Lynn asked. She looked around, expecting to see the man in question come striding into the dining room.

"Aye," Weir replied. "So we have been told."

Trace grimaced. He had hoped Syn-Jern would die a raving lunatic in the bowels of the Labyrinth, but to find he had been let out of prison was unsettling.

"Ah, come now," Tiernan barked, drawing the eyes of the husband and wife to him. "Surely the tale is worth telling!" He leaned back. "You don't hear of a Duke being sent to prison every day, now do you?" His jaw tightened. "What did he do?"

"Do?" Trace repeated, casting a quick glance to his wife before clearing his throat. "Ah, he murdered a man."

Weir's hands balled into fists on the table. "Then why wasn't he hanged?"

"What my husband meant to say," Rosa-Lynn was quick to say, drawing the captain's unwavering stare to her, "was he killed a man in self-defense."

Tiernan's left eyebrow crooked upward. "Self-defense, is it? If that's the case, why was he sent to prison in the first place?" He smiled courteously at the maid who was bringing in dessert. "Did he make an enemy of some vindictive personage?"

The husband and wife exchanged looks, then the husband spread his hands as though asking for understanding. "Well, it seems he made an enemy of King Innis," Trace said.

"Ah," Tiernan drawled. The one word was a condemnation. "That would do it." In the immediate silence that fell over the diners, he glanced around him. "More is the good fortune for you, though, eh, Your Grace?"

Trace frowned. "I don't follow."

Tiernan swept a hand over the table. "This, Your Grace." He moved his arm to indicate the surroundings behind him as well. "All of this." His gaze stabbed into Trace. "It all came to you as the new Duke, eh?"

"We are caretakers of the estate," Rosa-Lynn was quick to point out. "Nothing more than glorified landlords."

Tiernan heard the maid snort beneath her breath and when he caught her eye, he was not surprised to see contempt glittering in her hard glower.

"The lands, as you reminded us," Trace said, drawing the captain's attention from Sara Gill, "belong to the Tribunal. We are merely allowed to live here on their sufferance."

"Some living," Weir muttered and looked into the eyes of the maid as she plopped a spoonful of cream on the apple custard dessert she had shoved in front of him. The woman's lips twitched as she moved away.

"Do we have cause to worry about him?" Rosa-Lynn asked.

Weir swung his attention to the Duchess. "About whom?" he asked, knowing full well what she meant, but wanting to hear the name on the woman's lips.

"Syn-Jern," Rosa-Lynn answered, her face flushed.

"We don't believe so," Weir acknowledged. Lifting a spoonful of the delicious-smelling custard to his lips, he paused, looking down into the creamy dessert. He frowned and lifted the spoon closer to his face.

"Something wrong with the custard, Milord?" the maid inquired.

Weir slowly lifted his gaze from what appeared to be rat droppings to the innocent face of the pretty maid. He cocked an eyebrow, but said nothing. The Duke and Duchess were too busy shoveling the custard into their greedy mouths to notice their visitor's reaction to the dessert.

Sara's lips quirked into a knowing grin as the Serenian lowered his spoon to the custard cup and pushed the concoction away with a decided look of unease. She saw his scrutiny shift to the plate of food he'd consumed, then nearly burst into laughter when she saw him swallow hard.

"Can I be getting you anything else, Milord?" Tiernan heard the maid ask Weir.

Weir shook his head in denial, gorge rising up in his throat as he wondered what he might well have eaten this night. "I think I've had quite enough," he mumbled.

"I'll have some more custard," Rosa-Lynn demanded, licking her lips.

Tiernan, who realized something must be wrong with the food, reached for his own cup of dessert. "Allow me, Your Grace," he said, pushing back from the table. "I am too full to eat my own."

Sara watched the prince walk to the Viper's chair and place the custard before her. When he turned, his eyes met Sara's. The maid's eyebrows shot upward when the prince winked at her and said, "You are a fine cook, Mam'selle. I compliment you."

Tiernan sat down and lifted his goblet of wine, but before he drank, he cast a quick look to the maid.

Sara shook her head slightly to let him know there was nothing wrong with his drink. She watched him for a moment, then turned away. When she reached the door, she turned her head and gave Weir a look that was hard to interpret.

"You seem to have made a conquest there, Captain," Trace remarked.

Tiernan stretched his long legs beneath the table. "Is the wench married?"

"No," Trace replied. "Feel free to make use of her if you wish."

"Thank you," Tiernan yawned, "but I find I am too tired this evening." He looked at Weir. "Perhaps the good Captain would not mind partaking of the lady's amble talents?"

"Do you hand her over to whomever comes to call?" Weir asked in a bored tone although his hands clenched tightly on the chair arms.

"No one comes to call," Rosa-Lynn snorted in an unladylike manner.

Trace shot his wife a damning look before turning to the Serenian "Do what you will with the slut. She certainly won't dare to protest else she'll find herself out on her ear." He waved an imperious hand. "It matters not to me what you do so long as you don't use her so well she can not tend to her duties come morning."

Keeping his face carefully blank so Sorn would not see the fury that remark generated, Tiernan nodded thoughtfully. "We appreciate your hospitality, Your Grace."

"What the hell choice did you give us," Rosa-Lynn grumbled. She toyed with her wineglass for a long moment then turned to look at Weir. "How is he?"

"Are you referring to the your brother-in-law?" Tiernan inquired.

"I've not seen him since the trial, of course," Rosa-Lynn said in a low voice. "I just wondered if he—"

"What the hell difference does it make, Wife?" Trace snapped, lifting his napkin to his lips. "He is out of our lives and that is all to the good, is it not?"

Rosa-Lynn did not reply. In her mind's eye, she saw Syn-Jern as he had been that last day in the Tribunal Hall of Wixenstead Village and she heard once more his angry words:

"Why, Rosa-Lynn?" he begged as he was led away. His wrists were weighted down with thick lead manacles. He could barely walk for his ankles were banded in the same way. "I loved you and you swore my life away. Why?"

His dark golden hair had been tousled wildly about his head that day. His midnight blue eyes were filled with infinite hurt at having been betrayed. Despite all she had done to him, the tragic events she had set into motion, she knew as she looked into his bewildered face that he still loved her.

As no man ever had or ever would again, she thought as she glanced down the table to her husband.

Rosa-Lynn hung her head.

"You looked troubled, Your Grace," Tiernan told her.

Trace frowned. "My wife has a tender heart, I fear."

"Most women do," Tiernan replied. He studied the woman, wondering if her conscience was bothering her.

Trace sighed deeply. "She was with me when we found the man Syn-Jern murdered."

"I thought it was self-defense," Tiernan reminded the Duke.

Sorn flung out a dismissive hand, a habit that was beginning to wear on Tiernan McGregor. "The Tribunal called it so, but there was bad blood between the two. It is a matter of semantics, I fear."

"Well, you have nothing to worry about, I'm sure, Your Grace," Tiernan said. "Your brother—"

"Half-brother," Trace was quick to remind his visitor.

Tiernan nodded in polite acceptance of the correction. "Your half-brother would be foolish to return here to cause trouble, would he not?"

"If it pleases you, Your Grace," Weir said, yawning, "I am for bed. Tomorrow will be a long day for me." He turned to Sorn. "I must sail to Ciona to ascertain if our man is actually there and what exactly he intends."

"If you can find him," Tiernan put in.

"Aye," Weir agreed. "If I can find him." He yawned again and apologized.

Tiernan nodded toward the kitchen door as Sara entered the dining room once again. "You have my permission to bed the wench, Captain, if that is your desire."

Weir understood the silent command and grinned. He stood, took hold of Sara's arm. "You're to come with me, wench," he ordered.

Sara's back stiffened. "I am no man's—"

"Go with him else you'll have no job!" Trace snarled. "Pleasure him as he desires or you'll rue the day you ever stepped foot inside Holy Dale manor!"

Before the maid could balk, Weir snaked an arm around her waist, then buried his face in her neck, ignoring the hand that went to his chest to push Weir away. "Hush, Mam'selle, and do as you're told. Syn-Jern Sorn's life might well depend upon it!"

Sara, who was about to curse the ship captain, stilled, her stunned look going to the tall man's face.

"Pleasure him, I say," Trace growled as he walked from the room. "He'll tell me if you don't!"

Weir released the maid's waist. Before she could question him, he took her by the shoulders and stared deeply into her eyes. "We are friends with Bryce Heil, Mam'selle. He has spoken highly of you and your brother, saying you can be trusted."

A warning bell went off in Sara's mind and she clamped her lips shut.

The Serenian sighed heavily. "Mam'selle, we are not your enemy."

Sara refused to say anything to the Tribunal flunky. She glared at him, her mouth tight, her body stiff.

"Woman," Weir said with exasperation, "did you not notice Sorn's rather hasty exit just now? Do you not realize he is after finding someone to rid him of his brother once and for all?"

"There ain't a manjack in Wixenstead Village what would do that!" Sara snapped.

"Are you sure?" Weir asked, searching her eyes. "Are you absolutely sure?" When she didn't reply, he shook her gently. "So sure you'd risk Syn-Jern's life to prove it to me?"

Sara wavered. There might be a scoundrel or two bellied up to the bar at the tavern who might do anything for a copper or two. She bit her lip, thinking on the situation.

"Trust us, Mam'selle," he insisted. "That's all I ask."

Sara Elizabeth Gill was a very shrewd woman. And smart beyond her years. She knew this could well be a trap, a Tribunal ploy of some sort; but the earnest look in the eyes of the man standing before her was no lie.

Sara pulled out of his grasp and put distance between them. "Do you think me a fool, Milord? That I would believe a Tribunal transport's captain cares a fig what happens to His Grace?" She punched him in the chest with a rigid finger. "I know all about your kind."

Weir held out his hand. "If I can help keep him alive until we can prove he is an innocent man, then—"

"What?" Sara hissed. Her voice was low and urgent. "What are you saying?"

"That jackanapes and his slut are responsible for Syn-Jern Sorn having been sent to the Labyrinth twelve years ago," he said in a low voice. "All I need is proof Trace Edward Sorn killed Playe. If we can get a Magistrate here to be a witness to the confession, he can send a statement to the court. We can get Syn-Jern's sentence overturned and put the real murderer on board the Vortex bound for Tyber's Isle!"

Sara stared at the man, weighing his words for falsehoods and misleading turns. Looking into his face, she was of a certainty he was telling the truth and there was no hidden motives in what he was trying to do. Her one concern was still why he was trying to clear Syn-Jern Sorn's name.

"I see everyday the terrible things the Brotherhood of the Domination is capable of doing, Mam'selle," Weir said, once more taking Sara by the shoulders. This time she did not pull away.

"I have touched the scars in men's palms where their hands were nailed. I've seen the ravaged flesh of backs cruelly beaten with a cat-'o-nine. I've heard the ramblings of fever-ridden wretches who are reliving the horror of what was done to them." He reached up to cup Sara's chin. "I have seen this and more, Mam'selle and I am sick to heart of it. It has to be stopped. Do you understand?"

"And you think you can stop it?" she asked with a snort.

"Not alone, no," he replied. "But if we band together; if there are more who think like me; if we have a leader who knows what it is to suffer at the hands of the Tribunal, we just might put a dent in the Tribunal's armor."

"You think His Grace is the one?" Sara queried. "The one they called the Dark Overlord of the Wind? The one the Talespinners have predicted?"

"Who better?" Weir asked, never having considered the old tale.

"What is it you think he can do?" Sara demanded, having always dismissed the tall tales of the Dark Overlord.

Weir grinned. "Take from the ones who came by their riches at the expense of others and give it to those who need it to hold onto what they otherwise might lose!"

"Rob the Tribunal coffers," Sara said slowly. "That is what he intends?"

"Aye," he said, his grip tightening on her chin. "Plunder their ships and raid their caravans and do unto them what they are doing to those who get in their way!"

"Though none of us lifted a finger to help him ten years ago?"

"He doesn't blame the townsfolk for what happened to him," the Serenian replied.

"He should," Sara said, moving away so that her back was to him. "He was our rightful liege lord."

"There was nothing any of them could have done to save him, Mam'selle," he reminded her. "Do you not realize money had to have changed hands between Trace Edward Sorn and King Innis? Syn-Jern's sentence was up two years ago, but he was not pardoned. Why do you think he tried to escape?"

Sara turned. "Two years ago?" she whispered.

"Aye, but they had no intention of allowing him to ever leave the Labyrinth."

She stared at him for a long time, then nodded.

"All right, Milord. You'll get the proof you need to hang Trace Edward Sorn. My brother and I will do anything to see the bastard get his rightful due!"

Weir heaved a sigh of relief, then his face crinkled. "Do you always put rat turds in their food?" he asked.

"No always," Sara answered. "Sometimes I put piss, snot and puke in it, but there's always something special to flavor the vittles."

The Serenian's face turned green. "And tonight?" he said, swallowing. "Did you put any of that in their food tonight?"

Sara lifted her chin. "What do you think?"

Weir gagged. "I think I'm gonna be sick!" he said, slapping a hand over his mouth.

Sara Gill watched the handsome ship's captain trotting down the hall. She wasn't surprised when he didn't make it all the way to his assigned room before the sounds of violent retching echoed back to her.

## Chapter Nine

ONE WEEK AFTER WEIR SAUR'S VIOLENT NIGHT WITH HIS HEAD STUCK IN a chamber pot, the raiding of Tribunal wagon trains and couriers began. Trunk after trunk of gold was lifted from stunned guards who found themselves facing heavily armed bandits dressed entirely in white. No words were ever spoken by the masked men. Riding down on the Tribunal shipments on steeds as white as the flowing Hasdu-like garments the thieves wore, the guards were relieved not only of the gold they carried, but important papers as well.

Nor did the Tribunal ships escape the wrath of the NightWinds as every villager in Virago now named the mysterious bandits. Sailing out of a moonless night, the solid white ship seemed to materialize from thin air, her silent, menacing crew cutting a swath of terror through the sailors of the Tribunal navy. After chaining the prisoners and blindfolding them, the Tribunal sailors were put in a long boat and rowed to a second ship that carted them to only the gods knew where.

The Tribunal ships were then torched and left to burn as a warning to those who would defy the NightWind Force.

Only a handful of trusted Viragonians knew for a certainty who was behind the attacks and Sara Gill, her brothers, and Kerm's best friends were among them.

It had not been easy to bring Kerm and his drinking companions into the fold. Sara's arguing had not swayed them. It had taken Weir Saur's unexpected arrival at the secret meeting place the men went to drink and play cards of a Friday evening to convince Kerm, Dano, and Andrew that the ghost ship of the NightWinds actually belonged to Syn-Jern Sorn.

Each time she thought of it, Sara laughed. She had taken Weir Saur to the place her brother and his friends didn't know she knew about. Kerm had nearly fainted when the white clad Saur stepped from behind a huge oak tree and called him by name.

"NightWind!" Dano had proclaimed, shrieking like a woman as he made to run away.

Andrew had choked on the wine he was consuming and stumbled into the fire, setting his pant leg on fire. Hopping about the clearing like an intoxicated toad, he had finally run into a tree and knocked himself out.

A comedy of errors, Sara remembered when she thought on it.

But once the men were firmly under Bryce Heil's command, the comedy ceased and the real operation began.

While Prince Tiernan lazed at Holy Dale, supposedly sending the captain of the Revenge on missions to catch the marauding NightWinds, Weir Saur's crew was actually rendezvousing with the Revenant, captained by Norbert Tarnes. The two crews would then combine to attack Tribunal ships or drop off men who rode the night skies in flowing white robes. Tribunal prisoners were transported to Montyne Cay and left there at the mercy of the pirate confederation.

Each time another shipment was taken, another foreclosure notice failed to reach its destination before the family about to lose their property to Tribunal taxmen could pay, Sara would say a silent prayer for the man her countrymen were calling The Outlaw.

And the handsome ships' captain whose face she saw each night in her dreams.

ꕤ

Syn-Jern lifted a hand to his forehead and rubbed at the band of pain over his right eye. He was not well, but dared not mention it to McGregor's man, Heil, for fear the mission would be compromised. It was vital they reach Heathenstead by mid-afternoon else a family who took in orphaned children would lose their property to the Tribunal bullies.

"Are you all right, Milord?" Bryce Heil inquired.

"Aye," Syn-Jern responded, not daring to look at the man. "Let's saddle up."

Heil's forehead wrinkled with concern. All morning, he had been watching the leader whose own men called him The Outlaw rather than risk speaking his name for fear the wrong ear would hear. Sorn's face was infused with color and his eyes were glazed in pain. Twice, he'd seen his leader stagger as though exhausted and that worried Bryce greatly. They were a long way from the main brunt of the NightWind Force and with no way to contact them immediately. It would be days before a message could be sent to the Weir Saur, who was leading a group of NightWinds on a raid of a Tribunal warehouse in Delbenshire. Although they were only an hour or two from Holy Dale, word could not easily be sent to Tiernan without suspicion being cast on the McGregor, himself.

"I said saddle up, Heil," Syn-Jern ordered.

Heil nodded without replying. He grabbed his saddle horn and vaulted onto the back of his steed, easily controlling the massive animal with an expert squeeze of his thighs. "Milord?" he asked, seeing Sorn reel as he took his own mount.

"Aye?" Syn-Jern snapped, clenching his jaw tightly to keep his teeth from chattering.

"Milord, you must—"

Those words were the last Syn-Jern heard before his eyes rolled up in his head and he crashed sideways from his steed.

ꟾ

Sara shivered as she stood outside the entrance to the cave. She had wrapped her shawl around her, but having to hold the lantern up so the men could make their way over the rocky ground allowed chill air to flow down her arm. Her teeth were clicking together, her knees knocking, but it wasn't altogether the cold Viragonian wind that was making her tremble so. She cast wary eyes about her, praying to whatever gods might be listening that no Tribunalist was lurking about Holy Dale this night.

A soft three-note whistle came from the fog hovering about the mountain scree littered underfoot.

Sara answered the whistle with a four-note trill.

"Is the door open, Sara?" her brother, Kerm, whispered.

"Aye," Sara whispered back. "Hurry now before the Eel or his Viper comes looking for me!"

"They don't know of the cave," Kerm said.

"You'd best hope they don't!" Sara snapped. She looked past her brother to the men who were with him. "Where is he?"

Kerm jerked a thumb over his shoulder. "Andrew and Fiels is bringing him along. He ain't woke up yet."

Sara bit her lip. "How sick is he?"

Kerm shrugged his broad shoulders. "Sick enough, I reckon."

There was a crunch of stone then two men carrying a makeshift stretcher of canvas and poles came trudging out of the fog.

"Through here," Kerm ordered and took the lantern from his sister so he could light the hidden entrance to the cave.

"Lord, this boy be heavy," Fiels grumbled. "He be a tad bigger than when he left here, I'm thinkin'."

"That be twelve years ago," Andrew Spiel reminded his father. "I've growed some since then, meself."

"Ain't got no smarter, though," Fiels complained. He stumbled under the weight of their burden and would have fallen to one knee if a third man with them hadn't made a grab for the pole Fiels had in his hand.

"Will you be careful?" the man grated, taking the pole handles from the old man.

"The hell with you, Bryce Heil!" Fiels snorted, but he was relieved he no longer had the weight of the unconscious man.

Kerm Gill led them down a tight passageway cut through the mountain and into a cave where burning rushes lit the walls. "Put him there," he said, pointing to a pallet Sara had struggled to bring to the cave from the hidden room beneath the cellar of Holy Dale manor.

Bryce Heil and Andrew Spiels gently laid Syn-Jern on the pallet, rolled him until they could get the makeshift stretcher from beneath his limp body, then eased him onto his back once more.

"He's got the fever," Andrew commented.

Bryce placed a hand thick with calluses on Syn-Jern's forehead. "Aye," he agreed. "Labyrinthian Fever." He knelt on one knee, then turned to look at Sara. "Best get some quinine if you got it and lots of water, Sara. He'll get worse a'fore he gets better."

Sara cast a glance to her brother and at his nod of approval, she hitched up her skirt and headed back down the corridor. It was safer—and quieter—to go outside to fetch water from the well and quinine from the stables than to open the squeaky door to the hidden room, make the trek up the stairs into the kitchen, and hope like hell the Eel or the Viper didn't catch her.

Ten minutes later, Sara brought a pail of water and a dipper to Bryce and squatted beside him. She got a good look at the unconscious man's face for the first time and frowned. "You sure this is Syn-Jern Sorn?" She was just a child when the Lord of the manor had been dragged in chains to the harbor and man-handled on board the Boreal Star; her memories were of a larger man with hair the color of burnished gold.

"It's him, all right," Kerm answered for Bryce. "I remember him well."

Daniel Dunne wet his kerchief and began to wipe the glistening sweat from Syn-Jern's face. "I remember him, too. We're of the same age." His memories were of the young boy he wasn't allowed to play with or even smile at as they grew up on different sides of the manor walls. Dano had always felt sorry for the boy no one seemed to want around. But it would have meant a whipping if any of the servants' children made friendly overtures to the sad-eyed boy who spent most of his time on the balcony overlooking the forest.

"They say he's got the sight," Fiels mumbled. "Can kill with just a look."

"Be quiet, old man!" Kerm warned. "That's talk what can get a man burned at the stake in these times!"

Fiels sniffed, his crooked nose lifting in the air. "I heard it told that he killed a man what tried to do him in." He shrugged his frail old shoulders. "Don't know if that be the truth of it, but t'was what I heard."

"What the hell difference does it make?" Bryce countered.

Kerm lifted his head, cocked it to one side, then frowned. "I hear horses."

"No, hell you don't," Fiels guffawed.

"If he says he does, he does," Sara stated. "It's more'n likely that bastard Eel coming back from his gaming hell." She pushed to her feet. "I'll get them all settled in then bring down a meal to His Grace. Maybe he'll be awake by then."

"Make gods-be-damned sure the trapdoor is hidden before you come back here," Kerm told his sister. "Don't be coming down through it."

"I won't," Sara replied. She looked at Bryce. "You come on into the kitchen in a bit with some firewood. I'll send you down to the cellar for something and you can put the table back over the trapdoor. I dragged it out of the way to get down here, but I don't dare drag it back for fear of someone hearing. I'll come the back way when I bring his food."

Syn-Jern had been awake for quite some time, listening. A part of him was amazed these people were willing to risk the hangman's gibbet to protect him. He remembered the tall man, Daniel something; had a vague recollection of the red head that was obviously the woman's brother, but could not recall the woman at all. As for the two men who had carried him into the cave—that he'd had no idea existed—he remembered the elder as being a woodcutter in the village. None of those he remembered had ever spoken a word to him yet here they were making plans to ensure his future.

He stayed very still, feeling the fever claiming him and hoping against hope he didn't start babbling like he was known to do when the illness was on him. He felt the chills coming on and now and again he shuddered, but kept his eyes closed.

His hands were aching, the old wounds in his palm throbbing with every beat of his heart. Despite the pain, he flexed his right hand and could not stop the groan.

"You're safe, Milord," Bryce Heil said, his hand going over Syn-Jern's mouth lest the man cry out. "You're with friends."

Syn-Jern's fever-glazing eyes locked with Bryce's. He saw Bryce jerk a thumb upwards.

"You're in the cave under Holy Dale, Milord. You gotta be quiet lest they hear you. You understand?" Bryce queried.

A slight nod of his head was all Syn-Jern could do for he was beginning to shiver uncontrollably from the fever. The agony radiating through his head made him sick to his stomach, but he kept as still as he could.

"We got some nepenthe from Oceania," Kerm suggested. "It'll take the edge off the pain, Your Grace." He slid his hand under Syn-Jern's neck and lifted the damp man's head. "Here. You drink this."

He wasn't given a choice. A cup was placed at his lips and he let the sweet taste of cherries burst on his tongue. Almost immediately, his tongue became numb from the potent narcotic.

"You go back to sleep, Milord," Kerm said. "You're safe with us. We won't let nothing happen to you, Milord."

"Syn-Jern," the fever-ridden man murmured. "Call me Syn-Jern." His words slurred as the tenerse began to take hold of his mind. "The farm at Delbenshire—"

"It's been taken care of, Milord. Just rest," Bryce said. He stroked a lock of wet hair from Syn-Jern's forehead. "You've got nothing to worry about now."

"Tell the McGregor to…" Syn-Jern closed his eyes and let the drug take him where it would. As his world became muffled and slow, he thought he heard Rosa-Lynn's voice raised in shrill protest.

As sleep claimed him, he smiled.

The bitch was going to have a lot to protest in the weeks to come.

## Chapter Ten

"YOU'VE GOT TO MAKE SURE HE'S ALL RIGHT, WEIR," PATRICK SAID AS HE paced the cabin. "We've only their word that he's safe."

"He's safe," Weir sighed as he watched his old friend plow a nervous hand through his thick blond hair.

"How's his fever?" Patrick growled. He tugged at his golden curls. "Is he eating? Does he…?"

"Leave off, Kasella!" Weir snapped. "The McGregor says they are taking care of him!"

"We don't know that for sure!" Patrick threw back at him.

Weir cursed beneath his breath. "I give up with you, you stubborn Ionarian jackass. If you're that worried about him, why don't you just diddlyscamp over there, knock on the door of Holy Dale and demand to see the escaped prisoner they're harboring somewhere inside the manse?"

"In the caves," Patrick grumbled, plopping down on Weir's bunk. He cast a jaundiced look to his friend. "They've got him hidden in the caves that were used centuries ago by Viragonian pirates for storing contraband."

"You know this for a fact, do you?" Tarnes inquired. He pulled the unlit pipe from his snaggletooth mouth and pointed the stem toward Patrick. "You been scamping over there, have you?"

Patrick clamped his jaw tightly shut and refused to answer.

"Oh, Sweet Merciful Alel, you have!" Weir exploded, recognizing the militant look on Kasella's face. "You were spying on them?"

"They didn't even know I was there," Patrick mumbled, refusing to meet Weir's stunned gaze.

"By the great horned demon, you idjut!" Weir shouted. "What if you had been caught?"

"I wasn't, now, was I?" Patrick snorted.

Weir stared at Patrick, amazed at the man's bravura and—to his way of thinking—mindless stupidity. "Don't," he said through clenched teeth, "do it again!"

"Then find out for yourself how he is!" Patrick bellowed.

"The girl is going to take Tiernan and the magistrate through the hidden corridors tomorrow evening," Weir said, his eyes blazing, "and position them right beyond Sorn's bedroom wall. When he and the bitch start talking about—"

"If," Patrick snapped, "they start talking about the murder."

"They do nearly every day," Weir shot back.

"Well, it would just be our luck tomorrow won't be the day!" Patrick complained.

Weir sighed heavily with exasperation. He understood Patrick's concerns about Syn-Jern; he shared them, himself. But it wasn't going to be all that easy to make the villagers trust him enough to let him see Syn-Jern anytime soon. It would be a waiting game for awhile and Patrick had to be made to understand that.

"They could turn him over to the Tribunal," Patrick said quietly, voicing his major fear. "If they catch him, you know what will happen."

"They'd turn him over to me," Weir said. "After all, I'm the Emissary's ship captain."

"We'd better hope no penal colony transport decides to take harbor here," Tarnes told them. "Could get a might touchy if that was to happen, Cap'n."

Patrick stood. "I'm going to turn in," he announced. "I didn't sleep well last night."

"Wonder why?" Tarnes chuckled.

"Stay your ass on board this ship, Patrick," Weir ordered. When Patrick turned to glare at him, Weir nodded. "I mean it. Stay on board."

"And just what the hell am I supposed to do while the rest of you are fighting the Tribunal, Saur?" Patrick grated. "Tarnes has been captaining The Revenge for you while you're getting all the glory being the pirate captain of The Revenant, but by the gods, Saur, I want to see some action, myself!"

"Whyn't you put him to swabbing down the decks, Cap'n?" Tarnes suggested. His old eyes twinkled. "Unless you think we ought to tie him to a mast and leave him stew for a mite."

"Go to hell you pox-ridden old salt," Patrick insulted Tarnes, who thought the remark funny.

"We can't take a chance of someone seeing you who ought not to, Patrick," Weir repeated. "Someone loyal to Innis Hesar or have you forgotten who sent you to the Labyrinth, my friend?"

"There ain't nobody loyal to that queer," Tarnes snorted. His face turned red and he ducked his head. "Weren't meant as an insult to present company."

"Weren't taken as one, neither," Patrick muttered in his best Serenian brogue and yawned widely.

"Get to bed, Kasella," Weir demanded. "You're gonna need your strength for swabbing my decks come morning."

Patrick frowned, but he didn't rise to the bait. He'd swabbed many a deck in his lifetime. What was one more? With his shoulders hunched, hands dug into the pockets of his breeches, he sauntered out of the cabin.

"That be a mighty worried man, Cap'n," Tarnes proclaimed.

"Aye," Weir agreed. "Make sure you set someone to watching him. I don't want him skamping off this ship again."

ജ്ര

In his delirium, Syn-Jern was once more in the bowels of the Labyrinth. Hanging from the cross bar of the whipping post, the blood from his ravaged back was seeping into the ground. His hair was matted, clinging damply to his forehead and cheeks and neck. Flies crawled over his bearded face and lips and he didn't even have the strength to blow them away. His body odor was so bad, he could barely stand to draw a breath. Dimly, he thought he should be used to that stench by now, but he knew he never would.

He wished he could die.

They had worked him all night; the light of the harsh moon upon the rock field making it possible to see the rocks into which his pick ax bit. The sound of metal to rock had given him a savage headache, but he knew better than to speak of it. His migraines had gotten much worse during his imprisonment and the one he came down with that evening was one of the really bad ones. When he vomited on the boots of one of the guards, the retaliation had been swift.

The whip scored his back with nine fingers of fire, each gouging deeper than the one before. He thrashed in his pain, trying to avoid the drag of the cat as it clawed its way down his spine again.

"Kill me!" he begged, wishing the cat-'o-nine would finish him.

He could feel blood running down his back, soaking the waistband of his tattered breeches. The headache, the fever he could feel heating up his body, all combined to make his punishment an agony of unending duration.

"Kill me!" he pleaded with his captors. "Finish it!"

"You don't want to die, Milord," someone whispered and he felt hands lifting him, placing him on his belly on a cool board.

"Kill me," he whispered.

"We're getting you out of here, Milord," the man told him. "Hush now."

He remembered the long, winding corridor; the drip of water against limestone as the men carrying him wound their way through the bowels of the Labyrinth. He smelled the brimstone of the firepit and heard the shriek of bats deeper in the underground caverns.

"Kill me," he repeated over and over again.

"There's a ship waiting for you, Your Grace. She'll take you to Creel Point."

The last thing he remembered was someone touching his ravaged back as he screamed his way into unconsciousness.

"What's he saying?" Sara asked as she ran a wet cloth over Syn-Jern's chest and side.

"Something about the Labyrinth," Bryce replied. "I think he's reliving his escape."

"Wonder how he got away?" Kerm inquired. "I've heard tell it ain't no easy feat."

"Near impossible as best I can tell," Fiels Spiel reported. "Had to have had outside help."

"But who?" Sara queried.

Spiel shifted his bony shoulders. "Ain't no telling, gal. Somebody what knowed how to get there and how to go 'bout setting him free."

"I would imagine it was his grandmother's doing," Bryce suggested. "She had the money and the power."

"He should have been released two years ago and when he wasn't, I'll wager she sent someone after him." She looked up at Bryce. "Makes sense, doesn't it?"

Bryce nodded. "Aye. She let him stand the punishment—what choice did she have—but when he didn't come home, she must have known he wasn't going to be allowed to do so."

"He's got good King Innis to thank for that," Kerm snapped.

"We've all got good King Innis to thank for many a rotten thing in our own lives," Bryce spat.

"The gods damn the Hesars and all their kin!" Fiels Spiel said, turning his head and hawking a wad of phlegm against the cave wall.

"Nay," Bryce said. "Not the McGregors."

Fiels nodded. "Well, maybe not them."

"Genny!"

The others jumped as Syn-Jern sat bolt upright on the pallet, his eyes wild.

"Genny!"

Bryce reached him first. "It's all right, Your Grace. You're safe now."

"Genny?" The one word was a heartbreaking sound of fear.

Sara knelt on the pallet. "Your Genny is safe, Milord. She's safe." She pushed a lock of wet hair from his cheek. "And so are you."

"Genny," he whispered, the word a talisman to ward off the terrors of his delirium.

"Lay down, Milord," Bryce told him. "You've been sick."

He allowed them to push him down, half-expecting there to be agony in his torn back, but finally realizing he was a long way from the barbed whips of Tyber's Isle.

"Where," he asked, "am I?"

"In the cave beneath Holy Dale manor house, Milord," Bryce told him.

His forehead crinkled for a moment, and then memory filled in the missing pieces. "The ship?" he asked. "The Revenge?"

"She's in the harbor at Wixenstead, Milord."

Syn-Jern closed his eyes. He was sicker than he could remember being in a long while, his headache worse, and he was starving. Sara touched his face and he opened his eyes. "Aye, Milady?' he whispered.

"Here, Milord," she said and lifted a cup to his lips.

Syn-Jern smiled once more as Sara stroked his stubbled cheek. "You want to ask me something, Mam'selle?" he inquired, his words starting to slur.

"Is he married do you think, Milord? The captain of the Revenge?"

"Sara Elizabeth!" Kerm gasped.

"Well, hell in a twig house, Kermit," Sara snapped, craning her head to look at her brother, "you're the one always going on about me getting hitched!"

"T'weren't that what amazed me, you brazen wench," her brother snapped. "Leave His Grace alone with silly fool questions such as that!" He pointed his chin at Syn-Jern. "Can you not see he's in no condition to be bothered?"

Sara snorted and started to rise, but Syn-Jern reached out to take her hand in his own. When she looked down at him, he brought her palm to his cracked lips and placed a tender kiss there.

"Ah, Milord," Sara sighed, a flush speeding rapidly through her body.

"No, Sweeting," Syn-Jern said, "he's not married and he has no lady. You'd make him a fine one, though." With that, he closed his eyes again and drifted off, her hand still clutched in his.

"Come away, wench," Fiels said quietly, putting a fatherly hand on the girl's shoulder. "Let the lad sleep."

Sara eased her hand from Syn-Jern's and was glad of the help Bryce gave her in standing.

"I think you just got his blessing," Bryce said with a grin.

Sara's lips twitched. "Aye, I think I did, too."

## Chapter Eleven

ROSA-LYNN WAS HUDDLED AGAINST THE WIND BLOWING IN FROM Wixenstead Harbor. It swirled around her legs, plastering her skirts to them. The wind was so strong, she had to keep a hand on her bonnet lest the gusts pluck it from her head. Her lips trembling with the chill early morning air, she was vastly uncomfortable and ill at ease with the looks darting her way from the stevedores milling about. Doing her best to ignore the low whispers and angry snorts, she stood at the end of one long quay, her eyes tearing from the ripe wind, and stared at the black ship lying at anchor in the harbor.

Her spine as straight as the discomfort would allow, Rosa-Lynn tried to blot out the insulting words she could hear coming from the villagers who were watching her with contemptuous looks. She had no doubts about the way the villagers felt concerning her and Trace: they were hated worse than Innis Hesar. If either of them were to fall into the water, the villagers wouldn't lift a hand to save them from drowning. But Syn-Jern?

Would they do anything to help their rightful liege lord?

They certainly hadn't while Syni was living at Holy Dale, she thought. He had been as ignored as she and Trace were despised. But had that been because he was Giles Sorn's son, she wondered? Giles had been a thorn in the side of the Viragonians for many a year prior to his untimely demise on board the Tamarind. He was not a good landlord and most certainly not a man who endeared himself to anyone, least of all his eldest son, whom he had loathed.

"Syn-Jern," she whispered, her conscience pricking her in ways she never thought to experience. "How I wish I could speak with you, now."

Aye, she thought as she grimaced from a particularly rough blast of sea wind, *I stood in the dock and swore his life away, yet why can I not forget him?* His sad eyes followed her into sleep each night and his face was ever present in her dreams.

"Why, Syn?" she asked aloud. "Why can I not forget you?"

He had not been a particularly good lover; but then he had been inexperienced and unsure of himself.

He was not as handsome as Trace, but there was something endearing and sweet about his lack of sophistication that had made it possible for her to endure his fumbling lovemaking.

And he had loved her with all his heart, she remembered with a catch in her throat. She had seen that love glowing in his eyes, just as she had witnessed the deep hurt enter those midnight blue eyes at her betrayal.

Rosa-Lynn groaned. Her guilt was a cruel master these days. She had betrayed perhaps the only man who would ever truly love her; had sent him to prison to a life she knew would crush his spirit and maul his body—a body she had found more exciting than she cared to admit.

"Whore."

The word reached her ears and she turned to see if she could pick out the speaker from among the men loitering about; but every face turned her way was hostile and every mouth hard and unforgiving.

She faced the ship once more. "Oh, Syn-Jern," she whispered and it was not the wind that caused moisture to flood her eyes. "What did I do to you?"

A year ago, she thought—even a month ago—she would not have felt like this. But, since hearing of Syn-Jern's escape and the terrible retribution meted out to him by the horrid prison transporters, Rosa-Lynn Sorn's guilty conscience was becoming unbearable.

Rosa-Lynn choked off a sob and started back up the quay. Men stepped aside—not out of respect, but rather to not be contaminated by her touch.

"Harlot," they called her.

"Sorn's slut!"

A disgusted laugh hastened Rosa-Lynn's footsteps into a run and she shoved those who weren't quick enough out of her way as she fled the harbor.

"Can't run away from what you done to him, dearie!" a prostitute yelled at her. "You be the cause of all that boy's misery!"

"Aye, you run back to your whoremaster, bitch!" another prostitute taunted. "Reckon he'll give you what you got coming to you!"

Loud, raucous laughter followed Rosa-Lynn to her carriage where a coachman stood slumped against the door.

"Take me home," Rosa-Lynn cried. "Now!"

The coachman didn't reply. He yanked open the carriage door and waited for her to climb in by herself, refusing to offer her his assistance.

Seeing she would get no help, Rosa-Lynn snatched up her skirts and entered the carriage as gracefully as she could. She was barely seated before the door was slammed.

ᘓᘐ

Trace paid no attention to his wife as she rushed by him on her way up the stairs. He yawned, wondering what the dickens she was doing out of bed and dressed so early of the clock. That it was close to noon, didn't matter to Trace Edward Sorn. Anytime before two was early for him.

Lumbering slowly down the stairs, he stopped on the bottom step, watching the activity of two of the four servants he had managed to hold onto over the years and frowned. He put a hand to the banister and ran his fingertips along the rolled edge. There was dust accumulating in the crevice, just as there were dust bunnies lurking all over the manse. He raised his eyes to look at the tall mullion windows flanking the double entry doors and saw streaks of grime and fingerprints on the glass.

His frown deepened as he continued into the dining room. No doubt the dishes were not as clean as they should be, either, he thought.

When he was seated at the table, he lifted his fork, and peered closely. A snort of disgust shot from his mouth and he tossed the food-caked utensil to the table.

"Sara!" he bellowed at the top of his lungs.

The door to the kitchen opened and Sara Gill sauntered out, her shapely hips filling out her uniform nicely. "Aye, Milord?" she asked in a bored tone.

"The gods-be-damned silverware is filthy!" Trace snarled.

"Is that a fact?" she countered.

"Look for yourself, woman!" Sorn growled.

Sara took her time reaching the table. She made no move to take the fork from her master, merely looked down at it and shrugged. "Jobe's eyes ain't what they used to be," she said in way of explanation.

"Then hire someone who can see what it is they are washing from my silver!" Trace demanded. "There is caked food between the tines!"

"What folk you gonna get to work here, Milord?" she responded. "Ain't a single one what wants to do that." Her eyes narrowed as he glared at her.

"Especially not with that hellship bobbing out there in Wixenstead Harbor." She pretended to shiver. "And that ghost ship lurking about the waters of the Boreal."

"I don't want to hear that superstitious gossip, do you hear me, woman?" Trace snapped.

When he'd gone into town to hire an assassin to rid him of his hated half-brother, he stopped in his gaming club for a round or two of cards. He'd listened to what was being said down at the club, felt the appraising stares aimed his way, and dismissed the whole thing as peasant twaddle. A ghost ship, indeed! He reasoned some enterprising bandits were merely trading on foolish superstition to raid the Tribunal vaults. It was nothing to him.

"Suit yourself, Your Grace," Sara muttered. "You can believe the tales of the NightWinds or not. That is your privilege, Milord."

Trace ground his teeth. His hands itched to throttle the sassy wench, but she was the only cook he had and offending her, misusing her, would only gain him an empty belly.

"Wash these utensils yourself!" Trace ordered. "I will not have my table unclean."

Sara merely blinked at him, saying nothing. It was a tactic she used often in dealing with the son-of-a-bitch for she knew it unnerved him and made him madder still.

"Oh, go on with you!" Sorn finally proclaimed, waving her away. "It isn't worth arguing about!" He snatched up the fork and began scrubbing it with his less-than clean linen napkin

"As you wish, Milord," Sara drawled. She spun on her heel and marched back into the kitchen, a look of triumph on her pretty face.

"Wait 'til he tastes this," her helper, Jobe McCallister chortled. "You out did yourself on this meal, you did. It oughtta make him sicker than a dog."

"Shush," Sara cautioned. She glanced behind her, half-expecting the bastard to have followed her. She took a bowl and scooped some of the stew she'd made from rancid beef for Trace Sorn. "This ought to keep His Ugliness on the pot for an hour or two today."

"How is our boy?" Jobe asked as he tore a chunk of freshly baked bread from the loaf and placed it on the plate of stew destined for Syn-Jern Sorn.

"Ain't seen him this morning, but I reckon he's fine else Bryce would have come fetched me," she responded.

"You knowed the Viper went down to the docks this morn," Jobe stated.

"Aye, that was news the moment she asked Manley to hitch up the carriage," Sara replied.

"Conscience getting the better of her, I reckon," Jobe chuckled. "Wonder what she'd say if she knowed the NightWind, hisself, is right under her nose?"

"Be quiet, Jobe!" Sara warned.

Jobe clamped his lips shut. It wouldn't do for the wrong person to find out about His Lordship.

"Fix me up another plate of this swill," Sara whispered, "and I'll take it up to the Viper. And don't forget to feed the decent stuff to Prince Tiernan. We don't want him getting sick!"

Jobe winked his agreement and shuffled to the stove. He began to laugh. What Sara had made for the Eel and his slut would go a long way in making the two greedy fools pay for every wicked thing they'd ever done.

The old man sobered.

"Well, everything but killing poor Otis Playe," he muttered. He thought about that for a moment, then shrugged. No one had really liked Playe anyway so his loss was no great burden on the folks of Wixenstead Harbor.

ꕥ

Rosa-Lynn did not respond to the knock on her door. She was stretched across her bed—her face on her arms—as she had been since flinging herself on the silk coverlet half an hour before. The pale pink material was stained with her self-pitying tears.

"Milady?" Sara asked quietly as she opened the woman's door. "Are you all right?"

"Go away!" Rosa-Lynn snarled. "Can you not see I am grieving?"

Sara smiled hatefully. "I have your lunch, Milady." She bumped the door open with her hip. In her hands was a tray with a large portion of spoiled spew, a thick slice of bread slathered with butter that was less than fresh, and a salad of greens that had not been washed when they were plucked from the garden. "You need to eat."

"I'm not hungry," Rosa-Lynn declared, but she was sitting up. She licked her lips. "Is that stew?"

"Your favorite," Sara pronounced. "Made with the mushrooms you like so much."

Rosa-Lynn ran her hand under her chin. "Was the beef soaked in wine?" she asked, her stomach rumbling.

"Aye," Sara agreed. "It was soaked." In Kerm's piss, she thought wickedly.

The Viper licked her lips again and cocked her chin toward the little tray. "Set it there. Perhaps I'll have a bite or two."

Sara smiled as she placed the tray on the desk. She knew there wouldn't be a crumb left by the time the pig got through. She turned, her hands folded demurely at her waist. "Will there be anything else, Milady?" she asked.

Rosa-Lynn scooted from the bed. Her one true weakness in life was eating. As much as she consumed, Sara thought, it was a wonder the woman wasn't as big as a whaling ship.

"Is there no dessert?" the mistress of Holy Dale manse demanded.

Sara smiled. "I believe there is custard from last eve," she replied. Actually the custard was left over from three days before, but what did that matter? Sara thought.

"That will do nicely," Rosa-Lynn stated. She seated herself and began to shovel the stew into her greedy mouth.

"Enjoy," Sara said quietly and turned to go.

"Don't forget the custard!"

Sara looked behind her. "Oh, I won't, Your Grace. Have no fear on that account."

As she closed the door behind her, Sara hoped the pig would choke on her vittles.

## Chapter Twelve

"HIS GRACE TOLD ME TO TELL YOU THERE WAS A MAN RESCUED FROM ONE of the Tribunal hellships last evening, Milord," Sara said as she watched Syn-Jern eating.

Syn-Jern looked up from the wonderful stew. "That's good to know. What was his name, Mam'selle?"

"Don't know, Milord," Sara replied with a shrug. "Just another poor soul destined for Tyber's Isle, I suppose."

"He's lucky the NightWinds intercepted the ship, then."

"I hear tell he'd been whipped something awful," she informed him.

Syn-Jern laid down his spoon. "What had he done?"

Sara shook her head. "Don't suppose it matters, does it, Milord?" she asked.

"It does to me," he said and meant it. He cared about every prisoner aboard every one of those black ships that plied the waters between Ghurn Colony and Tyber's Isle.

"Aye, I imagine it does," she replied softly. She looked at his hands. "Do they pain you, Milord?"

Syn-Jern sighed. "Just when it rains like today," he said and lifted the spoon clumsily. He spilled some of the delicious stew on the front of his nightshirt and groaned.

"Here," Sara said, her smile bright. "Let me."

Although he protested, she fed him every last morsel of the food she had lovingly prepared for him.

"Did you meet with the ship's captain this morning, Kerm?" Sara asked, her blush betraying her growing fondness for Weir Saur.

"Aye," Kerm answered. He'd been there all morning, sitting with his back to the cave wall, mending a fishing net. "He's gonna bring the magistrate back out here tomorrow." He looked up with a sharp frown. "Maybe this time the Viper will goad the Eel into confessing instead of wallowing on the bed bawling like a newborn!"

Sara pursed her lips before snapping, "Weren't my fault they didn't do nothin' but ignore one another that day I led the Prince and the magistrate through the corridors."

"Aye, but did they do somethin' the day you led the good captain in there just the two of you?" Kerm grunted. He glared at Sara. "Or was the two of you the only ones doing somethin' in there in the dark?"

Syn-Jern looked from brother to sister. From the few times he'd been able to speak to Weir, he knew the man had fallen hard for the feisty Viragonian woman. Just how hard he'd had no idea until now.

"We was listening!" Sara defended herself and Weir, but the stain of guilt was coloring her cheeks.

"I'll bet you was listening," Kerm snorted. "Listening to one another moaning and groaning whilst the Serenian played hide the sausage!"

Syn-Jern sputtered with laughter, wincing at the pain such action caused in his throbbing head. He had to turn his cheek into the pillow to still the sudden vertigo that spun his world to one side.

"What I do with my man ain't none of your concern, Kermit Gill!" Sara snapped, coming to her feet. "You keep your filthy thoughts to yourself!" Flicking her skirt with disdain, she stormed down the corridor.

"Go after her, Kerm," Syn-Jern advised.

"She'll be back," Kerm predicted with a grin. "Be raining cats and dogs out there."

In less than five minutes, Kerm's prediction came true and Sara flounced back in, sat down by the fire and heaved a disgusted sigh.

"I'll tell you this much, Sara Elizabeth," Kerm said, his voice serious, "if'n he don't do right by you, I'll geld the son-of-a-bitch."

A militant look and angry grunt was Sara's answer.

"He'll do right by her," Syn-Jern said quietly and when Sara turned a softened face to him, he smiled. "I promise you he will."

"He told me you was kinfolk," Sara said.

Syn-Jern nodded. "His sister, Genny, is my wife."

"And you have a son," she added, ignoring her brother's surprised look.

"Aye," Syn-Jern sighed, "and I miss them terribly."

"Why didn't your lady come with you?" Sara wanted to know.

"Because it wouldn't have been safe, Sara," Syn-Jern explained. "When things heat up, they'll be looking for me and anyone connected to me. I couldn't take a chance that Genny would be taken and…" His eyes glazed with worry as his voice trailed off.

Sara understood his concern and let the matter drop. She wondered if he knew Genny Sorn's name was on his tongue even in his sleep.

Syn-Jern flung away the covers, got up, and stretched. The forced rest of the last week was wearing thin. He longed to be with his men, searching the countryside for people to help; raiding the coffers of the Tribunal so Viragonian men and women could provide adequate food and lodging for their families. He wanted to be riding across the green hills of this vast land, the chill wind stinging his cheeks. He ached to feel the heft of his sword in his hand as he fought the injustice heaped on his people by the Tribunal. Soon, it would be winter and the snows would begin falling. There would be little scavenging to do when the weather turned foul in this far Northland.

"I had best be getting back," Sara said and sighed. "The Eel will be scrambling back here as soon as the weather breaks."

"Where did he go?" Syn-Jern asked.

"Don't rightly know," Sara admitted. "He don't tell nobody nothin' he don't have to of late." She frowned. "Not even the Viper."

"They'd best be talkin' so's someone can hear 'em next time you take the magistrate and himself through the corridors," Kerm mumbled. "Else the magistrate will think we're pulling his leg 'bout all this." He sent Syn-Jern a worried look. "Still don't think it was all that wise to bring him through here."

Syn-Jern nodded, wondering himself if Weir and Tiernan had made the right decision in showing the local magistrate the hidden cave beneath Holy Dale. When Karl Krueger was led through the cave and up through the hidden passage into the cellar above, Syn-Jern had hidden in the shadows, instinctively knowing the Tribunal lawman did not need to know Syn-Jern Sorn was in the country.

"He might hate the Eel," Kerm remarked, "but he's still a Tribunalist through and through."

And that worried Syn-Jern more than it did Kerm Gill. He had learned Tribunalists were not to be trusted any further than they could be seen. Most were appointed, but he had learned that Krueger had paid for his own appointment and was looking for an advance up the ladder.

"You don't think he knows we've anything to do with the NightWinds, do you?" Sara asked, her concern evident in her voice.

"He may suspect it," Syn-Jern replied, "but unless our men do something to actually take money out of his own pockets, I doubt he'll cause trouble for us."

"If'n he were to turn a NightWind in, he'd sure make a name for himself in that fashion, now, wouldn't he?" Kerm suggested.

"He'd be dead before he got a chance to do that," Bryce Heil snapped and everyone jumped for they hadn't heard the man come in.

"Faith, you scared the hell outta me!" Sara told him, her heart pounding.

"Don't go sneaking up on folks like that, Heil!"

Bryce ignored her. "Got some news from our contact in Ciona, Milord," he told Syn-Jern. His broad face was set in a hard grimace. "And you ain't gonna like it."

ฆ๏ଓ

The ship docked at Creel Point and the gangplank was lowered just as lightning began to streak across the western sky.

Holding her scarf in place over her hair with one hand, Genevieve Sorn placed her free hand into the keeping of the Chrystallusian escort who was never far from her side. "Thank you, Lin Su," she said as she stepped onto the gangplank.

Lin Su, a warrior from the province of Navarre, bowed to his mistress and fell into step a pace behind her, his keen almond-shaped eyes surveying those who might hinder his lady's progress in any way. He kept one well-trained sword hand on the hilt of his akimo blade and his instincts open to the slightest trouble.

"Lady Saur? Lady Saur, over here!"

Genny turned, searching for the one who had spoken her name. Upon seeing the little man hurrying toward her, she relaxed. She waved at Weir's agent at Creel Point. "Good morn to you, Dixon," she said, smiling.

"Welcome, Lady. Welcome!" The dwarf waddled toward her, his pudgy hand adorned with rings for every finger, even his small thumbs. "I trust your journey was uneventful?"

"Tiresome, but uneventful," Genny replied. She glanced up. "I am thankful we made it to port before yonder storm."

As she spoke, thunder boomed in the distance and the wind rose.

"We had best hasten to the carriage before the onslaught starts then!" Dixon suggested and reached for Genny's arm, but found his wrist trapped in a steely constriction that made him draw in a pained breath.

"No," Genny said softly, putting a gentle hand on Lin Su's thick arm. "He is a friend and as such, he is not taking liberties."

Instantly, the band of pressure was removed from Dixon's wrist and the little man stepped back, his beady eyes narrowed at the tall warrior whose seven foot frame towered over Dixon Pait. "Who the demon are you?" the dwarf demanded.

"His name is Lin Su," Genny replied. "He is my Sentinel."

Dixon sniffed, not understanding the term, and was annoyed at having been—in his opinion—mauled by the giant. "Couldn't you tell me and the lady are friends?" he grated.

Lin Su stood like an oak tree there on the wharf, his heavily muscled arms folded over a wide chest. A smirk cocked the right side of his mouth upward, but he remained silent.

"Rude fella, ain't you?" Dixon growled, getting a creak in his neck straining to look up at the giant.

"Lin Su does not speak," Genny explained. "He is a mute."

Understanding physical differences better than most people did not, Dixon's belligerent attitude evaporated like water on a hot skillet. His moon-shaped face broke into a shy grin and he lifted one pudgy little hand to Lin Su. "Good morn to you," he said.

Lin Su did not hesitate. He engulfed Dixon's hand within the massive breadth of his own and gently squeezed. Although he did not smile—it was not in his nature to do so—his black eyes shone with friendliness. When he released Dixon's hand, he resumed his stoic stanch, arms crossed over his brawny chest.

Genny looked around her. "Where is your carriage, Dix? I've no mind to get wet."

Dixon pointed to a sleek black carriage. "This way, Milady," he replied, but made no move to take Genny's arm again as he led his visitors to the conveyance. Nor did he attempt to help Genny inside; he stood back for Lin Su to accomplish that courtesy. When the giant remained outside the carriage, Dixon frowned up at him.

"You will ride inside with us, will you not, friend?" the little man asked.

Lin Su glanced at the driver, who stared back at him with openmouthed wonder, then looked to his mistress. At her agreeing nod, Lin Su swept his hand toward the door, bidding Dixon enter first. When the little man had trouble climbing the carriage steps, Lin Su put firm hands on the dwarf's waist and propelled him gently into the cab, then climbed in behind him, taking a seat across from Genny.

"Thank you, friend," Dixon said breathlessly. "That climb gets higher each time I attempt it."

Lin Su's chin dipped slightly to the side in acknowledgment.

"I took the liberty of engaging your usual room, Milady," Dixon said, "but I did not know to book a room for your protector."

Genny patted Dixon's hand. "That isn't a problem, Dixon. Lin Su will stay in my room with me."

Dixon's eyebrows shot up and his thin lips pursed. "I do not believe Weir would approve, Milady," he said firmly. "I am not sure I can allow…"

"Then we won't tell him, now, will we?" Genny interrupted.

"Lady," Dixon stated, his face schooled into disapproving lines, "you are an unmarried woman, traveling…"

"I am a married woman, Dixon," Genny corrected, "traveling to join her husband in Virago."

"Married?" Dixon gasped. "When?" He blinked. "To whom?"

"A gentleman from Virago," Genny replied. "For security reasons, I prefer not to name him at this time."

"Security reasons," Dixon repeated, his brow creasing with worry. "Milady, this grows more and more distressing! When your brother passed through here six months back, he made no mention of your marriage." The little man put a hand to his chest. "He spoke no word at all to me of such a thing. Does he even know what you have done?"

"He knows and sanctioned it, Dixon," Genny said gently. "Have no fear on that account. He approves most highly of my Joining, believe me."

"Oh, dear, oh dear," Dixon said, his attention going to Lin Su. He studied the silent warrior for a moment, then twisted in the seat to speak earnestly to Genny. "Lady, are you in danger? Is that why you have a bodyguard?"

Genny knew Dixon could be trusted. He had been Weir's agent for many years. She bit her lip, wondering just how much to tell the little man. She didn't want to worry him, but neither did she want him hounding her for information. He could be tenacious and unrelenting when he felt stones had been left unturned.

"Lady?" Dixon questioned, his voice strained.

"Did you see any of the men with my brother when he docked here, Dixon?" she countered.

"Patrick was with him, of course. Tarnes and Neevens are like shadows of the man." He scratched his balding pate. "There was another older man I had never seen before, but I don't recall his name though Patrick introduced him." He thought, his lips pressed together, then his forehead smoothed out and his eyes widened. "By the gods, you mean the Sorn fella!" he gasped. "The one what was in the Labyrinth!"

Genny nodded slowly. "Syn-Jern Sorn," she replied.

"Oh, Milady!" Dixon groaned.

"What?" Genny asked in a defensive tone. "You object?"

"No, no," Dixon sighed. "'Tis only I have heard tales..." His words faded into silence, then he slowly looked to Lin Su. "You know him?"

Lin Su inclined his head in affirmation.

"You know the stories they tell of him?"

Lin Su lifted his hands and made gestures with his fingers.

Dixon looked to Genny for an explanation.

"He is speaking with his hands," Genny explained. "Each sign relates to a word or a letter of the alphabet. It is the way mutes speak to one another."

A look of intense excitement replaced the look of concern on Dixon's round face. "And you can interpret these signs?" he asked hurriedly.

"I have been taught, aye," Genny answered. "Patrick Kasella is fluent in the language. I believe he learned it in the Labyrinth."

"What did this fella just say?" Dixon was intrigued.

"He said the stories are exaggerated." She waited until Lin Su signed something else, then smiled. "He says the only people who should fear my husband are the ones who would do harm to those Syn-Jern Sorn holds dear."

"Fascinating," Dixon stated. "And you can understand all he says."

"It is most helpful when you do not want your conversation overheard by prying ears."

"Ah," Dixon said on a long note. His beady eyes began to gleam for he could see the advantages of such silent language in his business. Conferring with his men in a way his competitors could not 'hear' would be extremely advantageous during bidding procedures. "Would he teach me?" the dwarf asked.

"It has taken me six months to master the rudiments of the language, Dixon, and I have to insist Lin Su sign very slowly for me to follow. We will be here only a day; just until the Serenian Star arrives in port. That wouldn't give you much time to learn."

Dixon's concern over Genny had been replaced with an eagerness to learn something new he could use to make his business prosper even more. He took her hand in his and brought it to his lips. "Lady, there are only a very few words I wish to know for now," he told her.

ꟿ

Trace Sorn read the missive in his hand once more, his eyes gleaming with evil intent. Carefully, he folded the parchment in fourths and placed it in his coat pocket. For a moment or two, he sat at the gaming table, ignoring the messenger who had brought him the news, then motioned the man to come closer.

"You can vouch for the accuracy of this information?" Sorn asked.

"Aye, Milord. It came from a very reliable source," the messenger replied.

"I see." Sorn pulled at his lower lip, thoughts swirling like storm clouds in his fevered brain. "There is no mistake?"

"None, Your Grace."

Sorn stood. He bowed slightly to the two inebriated older men who were half-dozing over their jilp cards. "I must take my leave, Lord Gannon," he told the more sober of the two.

"I pass," Lord Gannon replied and threw down a card. His head dipped to his chest and he began to snore.

With a disgusted snort, Trace Sorn strode regally from the gaming room. He'd won a goodly sum of money from the two drunkards only because none of the other members of the club would play with him. Lords Gannon and Wilson were too old, too soused with mead, and, as such, oblivious to what went on around them to know or care with whom they lost the occasional gold coin.

"Find me six hungry men," Sorn said as he and his messenger left the Thorny Rose Gentleman's Club, "who will do whatever I tell them to do and not ask questions."

Lyle Drake rubbed his bewhiskered face. "Won't find any such here in Wixenstead, Milord," he countered. "I'll have to hire over to Ciona."

Sorn's upper lip lifted in scorn. "I don't care if you have to go all the way to Corinth for them; just find me six of the meanest pricks you can muster!"

"You want men what will kill if need's be?" Drake asked, licking his lips.

"Aye," Sorn snapped. "And make sure it will not matter to them if it's a woman they have to kill!"

A gleam of pure evil lit Lyle Drake's vicious eyes. "A woman you say." He reached down to scratch at his crotch. "Can we have her a'fore hand if'n we got to do her in?"

It was on the tip of Sorn's tongue to say no simply because a wisp of decency still remained in the reprobate; but then he considered who the woman in question was and her defilement mattered little to him.

"You may do whatever you wish to her," Trace Sorn granted. "Only not before you bring her to me." He pierced his minion with a steely glower. "Is that understood, Drake? You are not to touch her in any way until I give the word."

Drake nodded. "It'll be as you say, Milord."

"Good," Sorn said, his smile as cold as the nether regions of the Abyss. "Then we'll have the honey to catch the fly!"

## Chapter Thirteen

AT THAT MOMENT, WEIR SAUR WAS CURSING A BLUE STREAK TO THE heavens as he paced the deck of the Revenge. "Where the gods-be-damned hell is that woman's head?" he bellowed, frightening away a flock of seagulls sailing overhead. "We told her to stay in Chrystallus!"

Neevens spread his hands. "When has a woman in love ever done what she was told to do, Cap'n? Leastways, she didn't bring the bairn with her."

"Aye," Weir snarled. "At least she didn't do that!" But he was just as angry at his sister for leaving her babe behind as he was to find she had disobeyed both his and Syn-Jern's express orders.

"You want us to send some men to intercept her a'fore she scamps over this way?" Neevens inquired.

Weir drew in a long, calming breath. "Aye, you'd better." He raked his hand through his thick curls. "I ought to beat her black and blue for this, but I think I'll reserve the honor for Syni."

Neevens sniffed. "As if he'd lay a hand to the lass," he commented.

"He ought to!" Weir growled.

"Ought to and gonna ain't the same thing," Jarl Stevens put in.

"Send word to Syn-Jern so he won't worry and..." He stopped when he saw Neevens shaking his head. "He knows?" he gasped.

"Word came from the McGregor, Cap'n, and the McGregor got the word direct from that Kerm fellow who got it from..."

"I don't give a rat's arse where Kerm got it from!" Weir snapped. He wasn't overly fond of Sara's sullen brother. "We've got problems, then, if Syni knows that idiotic sister of mine is camped out in Ciona."

"How's that?" Stevens inquired.

Weir hung his head. "He'll gods-be-damned sure go after her."

"Even sick as he's been?" Neevens demanded.

"On his deathbed, if need's be," Weir responded.

ᘓᘐ

Genny tapped her foot on the carpet as she stared out the window of the inn. The rain was coming down with such force, she could see only a blur beyond the pane. As the lightning stitched across the gunmetal sky, she tensed, but did not leave the window. A rap on the table behind her drew her attention to her sentinel.

Lin Su, his face inscrutable, signed his feelings to her.

"I think not," Genny disagreed. Her frown tightened. "The gods are not angry with me."

A quick flurry of the warrior's hands brought a contemptuous snort from Genny Sorn. "I don't know why we've had such bad weather, but it isn't because the gods are pissed at me for coming after Syn-Jern!"

One last comment from the strong sword hand of Lin Su made her turn away.

"No, I don't want to go to sleep!"

Lin Su shook his head at his lady's stubborn attitude and pulled the blanket over his shoulders. The settee did not accommodate his tall frame well and was uncomfortable, but the only other alternative—the floor—was worse. He snuggled into the warmth of the wool blanket and closed his eyes. If his lady was inclined to spend her evening glaring at the rain, he could not stop her. He had sworn to protect her, but he'd made no vow to encourage her willfulness.

"Sleep well," he heard her tell him and smiled despite himself.

Genny slumped against the window frame, her eyes prickly with the need to sleep, but she was too wound up, too excited, and too furious with the uncooperative weather to rest. Since leaving the palace at Binh Tae, the rain clouds had followed them all the way to Ciona. She'd suffered motion sickness most of the time and that was something that had never happened on board her brother's ship. She did not want to entertain the thought that the gods were trying to keep her from joining Syn-Jern; but now that Lin Su had broached the subject, she wondered if there might not be something in his argument.

The Serenian Star had nearly sunk off the coast of Oceania and her journey had stalled for five days while repairs were made to the hull. Oceania was lovely, the weather so perfect, Genny had sighed with relief, thinking the remainder of their trip would be easy. But two hours from the harbor at Fealst, the sky became a thick layer of gray wool basted with silver threads of lightning. Half an hour later, the Serenian Star was fighting a full-blown gale as a pall of black velvet fell over the sea.

"Even if the gods are angry," Genny said aloud, knowing Lin Su was still awake and listening, "I'm still going to find my husband."

Lin Su's thick lips pursed with aggravation, but he remained still. He wasn't angry with his lady, but at the circumstances that had brought her to Serenia. If he could keep her from venturing into Virago, he would, for he felt it was not in her best interests to journey to that cold land.

"If there's not let up in the weather come morning," Genny said, "we'll just have to look into buying horses and going overland."

The Chrystallusian warrior opened his eyes. He wondered how well his lady knew the country of Virago. The Empress Rowena had given Lin Su an extensive lecture on the place and he had memorized sea routes as well as land trails. Would it be wise to tell his lady they were only a few miles from Holy Dale?

He pondered the situation for a moment, then decided it would not be. If his lady knew they were that close, she'd insist on riding out this very night, storm, or no storm. At least going by sea to Wixenstead, he would have another day or two to protect her from what he was beginning to believe was destined to be disaster.

Totally awake now, unable to sleep, the warrior stared at the ceiling, his superior tactical mind going over and over alternate plans. He had not agreed with his lady's plan to show up at Wixenstead, announce she was Captain Saur's sister and insist on meeting with him. It was a dangerous ploy, especially in light of the growing lack of communication between the NightWind force and Binh Tae palace of late. That, he thought with a sharp frown, was why the lady was here in the first place. Her worry had gotten the best of her and her coming here may have gotten her into more trouble than Lin Su could handle for her. The Emperor and Empress could not talk the strong-willed lady from traveling to this heathenish part of the world in search of her husband so the Empress had assigned Lin Su to the young woman.

"Every Daughter has a sentinel to keep watch," the Empress had told the lady. "Lin Su will be yours."

"I am not a Daughter!" the lady had snapped.

"You're close enough to being one that it doesn't matter," the Empress replied. "You'll not leave here without his shadow close at your side!"

"If it is raining tomorrow morn," Genny said, drawing Lin Su's attention back to her. "We will go by land through the Carbondale Gate."

Lin Su sighed. Perhaps the lady knew more about the country than he suspected.

"I know it will be dangerous, Lin Su," she told him, "but I am worried."

No more than I am, Lin Su thought.

ꙮ

Lyle Drake hunched over the table and lowered his voice so the four men sitting with him had to crouch toward him in order to hear. His Grace had wanted six men, but four was all Drake could find at such short notice.

"She'll be passing through the Gate right around ten of the clock. You can't miss her 'cause she'll have a hulking bastard a'ridin' with her. You are to ride down on 'em, kill the man what's with her and take her." Drake's face tightened. "You ain't to lay a mitt on her 'til His Grace says you can. Is that clear?"

One of the men rubbed his bewhiskered chin. "Not even a feel?" he asked.

Drake shook his head. "Not nothin' 'til the man gives you permission."

"I don't want these Serenian's after my arse," another of the men commented. "They see us attacking a woman, they'll send a troop after us for sure! They be protective-like of their womenfolk. Remember what happened with the Hesar woman back years ago?"

"This bitch ain't one of theirs," Drake growled.

"Don't matter," his companion returned. "Them Serenians be funny in that regard."

"You snatch her and get her deep into Virago," Drake ordered. "They won't be a'comin' after you through the Gate."

"You don't know that they won't."

"Ain't got no jurisdiction in Virago," Drake grated, proud of his use of the big word. "Can't come after you with no authority whatsoever!" He dug into the pocket of his filthy jacket. "I got ten silver pieces for each of you soon's the job is done." He drew out the pouch of coins and jiggled it. "Not a single flauthing, though, 'til you bring the bitch to the cabin I told you 'bout."

"That's too near the witch's hut for me!" another of the men piped up.

"That old biddy ain't no witch," Drake guffawed. "She's just an ugly old cripple so's you got nothin' to worry 'bout on that count." He jiggled the pouch again. "What's it to be? A single flauthing can buy a man a right good bottle of ale."

His companions stared at the pouch, licked their lips, then nodded in agreement.

"Count me in," the oldest of the four replied.

"Me, too."

"I reckon I could use a flauthing or two to last me through the bad months," another commented.

The fourth man nodded, but he wasn't as thirsty as his friends. His thoughts were of the woman and what he would do once he was given free rein of her helpless body. The mind picture he entertained brought such an evil leer to his face, the others at the table moved cautiously away.

ജ

Sara looked up at the sky as she came out of the manse the next morning. The rain had stopped, but the sky still looked angry and threatening. Her lips pursed, she resolutely set off to the stables to fetch Kerm his breakfast. He would be accompanying her to market this morn and she knew he'd be in a foul mood; he always was when he had to take her shopping.

"It's about time you brought my vittles, woman," Kerm snapped as soon as his sister pushed open the stable door.

"You know, Kerm," Sara quipped, "as mean an old bear as you are, it's a wonder you don't hibernate during the winter time!"

"It's a wonder I don't toss you o'er my knee and wallop your backside good like Pa used to do," Kerm mumbled, snatching the plate of ham, fried eggs, and mush from her. He began shoveling the food into his mouth with grim determination.

"You're just pissed that he didn't let you go with him," Sara said, understanding her brother's fury.

"He's gonna need every hand what he's got!" Kerm snarled. "What if'n someone recognizes him down at the harbor whilst he's a'waitin' for his hardheaded woman to come sailing in?"

"Bryce will watch his back," Sara replied. "So will Fiels and Dano."

"Ain't the same as having me along," Kerm complained. "I'm more've a warrior than the two of them bumpkins put together!" He poked a forkful of eggs into his mouth and chewed without relish. "And me havin' to take you to market don't set well with me at all!"

"We'll need decent food for his lady, Kermit," Sara reminded her brother. "We can't feed her the same's we feed the reptiles."

"Humpf," was Kerm's answer. He crammed the last of the ham into his mouth, then stood. "Let's get goin' so's I can get you back." He grabbed his hat, slapped it angrily against his thigh, and yanked open the stable door.

Sara clucked her tongue as she followed him. The horses were already saddled—probably had been for quite some time. She hated the massive beasts, feared them, and had never been good at riding. She had hoped Kerm would hitch the buggy, but when she asked why he hadn't, her brother had turned furious eyes on her.

"The Eel had me up 'fore dawn hitching it, woman! You didn't know he weren't to home?"

Sara had not. She frowned. "Where in tarnation did he go so early of the morn? Ain't like him to venture outta bed a'fore two of the clock!"

"Don't know and don't care where the bastard went!" Kerm spat. He stomped to his sister, put his hands on her lean waist and hefted her into the saddle. "And don't you be fallin' off again, you hear me, Sara Elizabeth?"

With that said, he vaulted onto the back of his own mount and put heavy heels to the steed's rib. Sara had no choice but to follow behind him at an uncomfortable, frightening pace.

## Chapter Fourteen

DANO WALKED THE LENGTH OF THE QUAY AND BACK AGAIN, TALKING with the sailors working on the two ships in dry dock at Wixenstead. He sauntered casually to the harbormaster's office and took his sweet time walking back to the tavern where Fiels and another man sat in the shadows of the smoky room. Ordering a jug of mead, he ambled to the hearth and held his hands to the flame, seeming not to notice Fiels and his companion.

"The Serenian Star is scheduled to dock here at eight of the clock this evening if the weather holds," Dano whispered. "She had trouble in Fealst so's she's running behind time."

Syn-Jern snorted. "When I get my hands on Genny Sorn, she'll rue the day she ever defied me."

Fiels grinned. "The most you'll do is grab her and squeeze her 'til she yelps, boy," he chuckled.

"I'll make her do more than yelp," Syn-Jern swore. He snatched the cup of black coffee from the table and drained it.

"She missed you, son," Fiels—older and wiser—commented.

Syn-Jern did not reply. He glared across the room. He narrowed his eyes at the five Tribunal guards who were having their breakfast. His palms ached at the sight of the bastards and it was all he could do not to physically attack them.

"Steady as she goes, mate," Fiels cautioned, picking up on the tension in his young companion. "We don't need no trouble with them men."

"They're here to escort the new ark priest," Dano whispered.

"What's an ark priest?" Fiels inquired.

"Arch-Prelate," Syn-Jern corrected Dano. The hairs on the backs of his arms tingled and he risked a sidelong glance at Dano. "What's the bastard's name?"

"Demonicus," Dano reported and out of the corner of his eye saw Syn-Jern stiffen.

"He's coming here?" Syn-Jern asked urgently.

"Due to arrive on the morning tide," Dano answered. "In about half an hour or so."

For the first time, fear drove straight through Syn-Jern and he reached up to pull the cowl of the robe he was wearing closer to his face. He was dressed in the robes of a StormWarrior priest, but if Demonicus saw him, the game would be up for no priests were assigned to Wixenstead and the Arch-Prelate would know that. It was one thing to explain to the locals that the priest was passing through; Weir had used the disguise, himself. But it would be folly of the worse kind to be caught by Demonicus, a man who knew Syn-Jern by sight.

"I have to go," Syn-Jern said, his face carefully concealed within the folds of the cowl. "Demonicus knows me."

Dano heard the fear in their leader's voice. He wasn't the smartest of Syn-Jern's men, but he had an agile mind that had always held him in good stead in times of need. Without missing a beat, he knew what he had to do. "Whatcha mean I cheated you last evening?" he snapped, turning from the hearth. He glared at Fiels. "I don't have to cheat to win, old man!"

"The hell you don't!" Fiels exclaimed, catching the cue. "You had an ace up your sleeve, you braying ass. I knowed you did!"

The Tribunal guards paused in their eating and looked toward the argument. None of them would intervene unless the two combatants became physical. Only one of them paid attention to the priest walking slowly to the front door.

"The Storms stay behind you, Your Grace," the Tribunal guard called out.

Syn-Jern stopped, half-turned and nodded silently in acknowledgment of the greeting. He lifted a hand in blessing to the soldier. As he left the tavern, he was smiling grimly at the heated argument between Dano and Fiels that covered his exit.

ജ

Demonicus Voire barely glanced at the Tribunal guards who fell into step behind him as he came down the gangplank. He ignored those waiting for him on the pier. His hooded gaze swept the town and his lip lifted in scorn. The village had changed little in 20 years. It had been a pest-hole when he had arrived here to try Syn-Jern Sorn and it was still a pest hole. The smell, alone, was enough to drive a man insane. Plucking the silk kerchief from the sleeve of his scarlet robe, he held it under his nose, breathing in the scent of jasmine that was his personal favorite.

"Welcome to Virago, Your Worship," the leader of the Tribunal guards said, bowing deeply.

"Have you found him?" Demonicus demanded.

The Tribunal guard shook his head. "I am sorry to report we have not. Prince Tiernan also has…"

"Tiernan McGregor is a fool!" Demonicus stated. "And not to be trusted." He swung his disgusted glower around the wharf. "I was informed the Serenian prince is staying at Holy Dale with Sorn." He turned to the Tribunal guard. "Why are they not here to greet me properly?"

Anson Loure, the leader of the Tribunal guards, felt a shiver of loathing go through his belly as the direct stare of the Brotherhood's highest ranking member settled on him. He could almost feel the cold hands of the man sliding over his flesh and he shuddered.

Demonicus smiled brutally. "Have you a wish for me to lay hands to you, Loure?" he asked.

Anson's heart slammed against his ribcage. "I…I am married, Your Worship," he stammered.

One thick black brow lifted in challenge. "And you believe that would stop me if I wanted you, Loure?" the Arch-Prelate inquired in a silky tone laced with venom. Before the Tribunal guard could reply, Demonicus turned away. "You are not pleasing to my eye so therefore you have nothing to worry about."

A relieved sigh of breath was all Anson could manage. Had the Arch-Prelate ordered Anson to his bed, there was nothing the guard could do about it.

"Where is Sorn?" Demonicus asked.

"I sent word to him you were arriving, Your Worship, but I have heard nothing from him," Anson replied, reaching up to wipe away the cold sweat that had formed on his brow. "Prince Tiernan is still at Holy Dale, laid up with a cold I am told and—"

"And wouldn't come to greet me if his very life depended upon it," Demonicus sneered. "And it just might one day!"

"I have a carriage for you, Your Worship," Anson told the priest. "Whenever you are ready to travel to Holy—"

"I am ready this very moment," Demonicus snapped. "Since neither your men nor McGregor's can lay hands on Syn-Jern Sorn, I have been sent to arrest him, myself!"

"Arrest him?" Anson asked, his forehead creasing. "We were not given orders to arrest him, Your Worship, only to detain him."

"Who do you think is behind the raids of your coffers, fool?" Demonicus demanded.

Anson groaned. It made sense, he supposed, but the thought had never crossed his mind.

"Fool!" Demonicus snapped, easily reading Loure's mind. He shoved the Tribunal guard out of his way. "My valet has come down with fever and will not be able to assist me. Find me a servant to see to my needs else you will find yourself carrying my chamber pot, Loure!"

"There is a priest from the StormWarriors in town and…" Anson got no further before Demonicus snaked out a thin hand and grabbed him by the neck.

"What priest?" the Arch-Prelate hissed. When Anson did not answer immediately, he lifted the hapless guard from the ground, cutting off his air and strangling him. "What priest?"

Anson was choking, but he dared not scratch at the steely hand enclosing his throat. His eyes bulged and his face began to turn blue before he was tossed aside like a child's toy.

"Answer me!" Demonicus thundered.

Anson huddled on the ground, his hand to his bruised throat. "I…do not k…know his n…name, Your G…Grace!" he managed to say.

Demonicus turned to his personal guards. "Find him!"

From the doorway of the tavern, Fiels and Dano watched the Tribunal guards disperse, throwing open the doors to the establishments along the wharf. Saying nothing, the two sauntered toward the swayback horses that had brought them to town and casually mounted.

"You there!" one of the guards shouted at the men. "Have you seen a priest?"

"Ain't needed one in quite some time," Fiels returned.

"No, no, no!" the guard snapped. "A priest here in town. Have you seen one about?"

Anson pushed from the ground, still holding his battered throat, and listened to the two villagers denying having seen a priest. He opened his mouth to call them liars for he had seen the priest sitting with the old man, but he turned to look at the Arch-Prelate who was striding furiously toward the waiting carriage, and managed to shut his thoughts down just in time. He saw the priest glance at him—eyes narrowed into malevolent slits—then continue on his way, no doubt believing the wayward thought he'd partially intercepted was one of dislike.

And it was.

Anson Loure despised the Brotherhood of the Domination, yet he had been forced to serve them many times in his role as Tribunal guard. Keeping his mind carefully blank lest the priest 'hear' his thoughts, he joined his men in searching for the man he hoped they did not find for he was pretty gods-be-damned sure the man they sought was the Outlaw.

And the Outlaw was surely Syn-Jern Sorn.

ꟸ

Lin Su rode ahead of Genny Sorn as they passed beneath the arch of the Carbondale Gate. Once more, the rains had started just as she and her sentinel were about to board the Serenian Star. The morning tide was coming in with such violent surges; the ship's captain had announced a delay in the departure, citing the next day as the probable time for sailing.

"No," Genny had groaned and turned to her companion. "Find us some horses, Lin Su."

Despite the warrior's disagreement and his 'vocal' renunciation of the plan, eventually he had set off in search of mounts.

An hour later, the two were on their way, the rain pelting them unmercifully and both were soaking wet though they wore oilskin slickers.

Miserable, her head aching, her teeth chattering with the cold, Genny managed to speak to the man and woman who passed them. "Miserable day, isn't it?" she called out.

Sara Elizabeth Gill agreed. "Aye, Milady. Good only for ducklings!"

Kerm grunted. He hated going to market, especially in Ciona, though the prices there were cheaper than in Wixenstead. Since he got to pocket the difference in what they paid, he shouldn't complain too much, he thought. Shrugging into the relative comfort of his own slicker, he sighed heavily, wishing himself with his leader in the village.

"Take care, then!" Genny said, waving. She turned to Lin Su. "Pretty lady, isn't she?"

Lin Su gave a noncommittal shrug. To his way of thinking, women of his lady's race could not hold a candle to the delicate beauty of the Chrystallus woman.

Sara twisted in the saddle to take another look at the lady and her escort. "Why would someone of her rank be out and about on a day like this?" she asked her brother.

"Ain't none of our concern, I'm sure," Kerm replied.

Sara frowned. "You don't think…"

Brother and sister stared at one another.

"No," Kerm denied, shaking his head. "Can't be."

"Shouldn't we ask, though?" Sara asked with worry rife in her voice.

Kerm also turned and looked at the couple who were now quite a distance from them by then. "It ain't her, Sara. Why would she be coming this way?"

"What better way?" Sara asked, pulling her mare to a stop. "If'n she didn't want nobody knowing she was here. Wouldn't she be coming in the back way, so to speak." She pointed at the archway of the Carbondale Gate. "And this is the back way!"

"Ain't her," Kerm insisted. The couple they'd been watching could no longer be seen because of the rise of the land. He resolutely turned toward Serenia. "Leave it rest. It weren't her."

Sara kept her mount still even as her brother kicked his into a faster pace, leaving her behind. Gnawing on her lower lip, she glanced once more at the place where she'd last seen the lady. "Maybe Kerm's right," she said and nudged her mare into motion.

ꙮ

One minute Lin Su was seated astride his palfrey, the next he was lying in the middle of the roadway with blood pouring from a wound in his side.

Kicking and screaming, raking her nails into the arms and necks of her attackers, Genny Sorn was on the verge of kicking one bastard in the groin when a fist slammed into the side of her head and knocked her unconscious. She did not feel her limp body being thrown over the back of her own mount nor the vulgar squeeze of her breast Lyle Drake gave her as he tied her body to the horse.

"Hie you back to the cabin and tell His Grace we got the woman," Drake told one of his fellow ambushers.

"He won't know if'n we have a little taste of her," one of the men suggested.

"She'd tell him," Drake snapped. "Now, be off with ye."

"How's she to know if'n she ain't awake to know what we do?" another asked slyly.

"Aye," the third and fourth said in unison.

Drake looked at the unconscious woman. His cock leapt against his britches front and he reached down to rub it.

"Come on, Lyle. Who's ever gonna know?"

Drake hesitated a moment longer then grinned savagely. "Aye," he replied. "Who's ever gonna know?"

## Chapter Fifteen

"WHO THE HELL IS THIS?" TRACE SORN BELLOWED, HIS EYES WERE WIDE and nearly popping from their sockets. "This is a lady, you fool!"

Drake looked from the bruised and battered woman lying on the cot to his master, "You said to take Saur's woman, Milord, and—"

"This is not Saur's woman, you imbecile!" Sorn shouted. "Who is she?"

"You said she'd be coming through the Carbondale Gate at ten of the clock and she was," Drake defended himself. "You said she would be with a hulking fella and she was."

Trace drew his arm over his shoulder and backhanded Drake, staggering the larger man, who crashed to the floor. He bent over Drake. "It was Sara and Kerm Gill I wanted!" he seethed. "Weir Saur is the Outlaw, you ass!"

"How was I to know, Your Grace?" Drake whimpered, fingering his jaw to see if it was broken. "You didn't give me no names."

Sorn swore heatedly then stalked to the cot where the unconscious woman was trying to swim back to reality. He stared at her, taking in the bruises, then slowly turned his head to Drake. "Did you touch her?" he asked, his voice low and deadly.

Drake had killed seven men in his lifetime. He'd done his share of violating women and a few children as well. He considered himself invincible, powerful, and he backed down to no man. But the only man he had ever feared in his life was right there in the cabin with him, glaring at him with murderous rage. Drake swallowed, a sour sweat breaking out on his forehead.

"Did you touch her?" Sorn repeated.

"If'n she ain't the right one, Your Grace, what difference does it matter?" Drake whined.

Trace Sorn's hand went to the dagger at his side. Without another thought, he drew it, flipped it over in his palm, and before Drake could scramble out of harm's way, sent the deadly missile straight into the miscreant's heart.

Drake lowered his head to look at the dagger sticking from his chest. With a hopeless sigh, he looked up at Sorn, then fell to his side, dead.

Sorn hurried to the door, snarling beneath his breath when he found he was alone. The four men who had been hired by Drake were long gone. No doubt they had overheard him questioning Drake and had high-tailed it. Before nightfall, they would be on a ship and out of Virago, never to return if he knew their kind, and he did.

A low groan from the cot drew Trace Sorn's attention and he shut the door. He kicked Drake's lifeless body to its back, stooped down, jerked his dagger from the dead man's chest and with every intention of running the blade across the unknown woman's throat, walked to the cot.

But the woman's eyes were open and she was staring up at him. "Help me," she whispered. "Please help me."

Realizing the woman did not know the identity of her attackers and could not connect him in any way to her kidnapping, Trace relaxed and sat on the cot beside her.

"You are safe, Milady," he said, running his hand over her pale face. "You have nothing to worry about."

"Where am I?' Genny asked. "How did I get here?" She tried to sit up, but gasped, the myriad pains dotting her savaged body bringing instant memory. "Oh, god!" she gasped.

"Hush, Lady," Trace said, a smidgen of chivalry surfacing. He gathered her to him, cradling her against his chest. "You are under my protection now and I shall let no one harm you." He smoothed her hair. "Your attacker is dead and can not harm you again."

Genny could see the body lying on the floor. "You k…killed him?" she asked, shivering.

"I saw them bringing you into the cabin," he replied. "Since I own this land and do not know the men, I hastened to see what they were about. Luckily for me I happened along before they could…" He stopped, a part of him sickened by what had already happened to the woman. She was trembling and that part of him that still held to the teachings of the warrior caste gave rise to an overwhelming desire to make things right for her.

"They…" Genny whispered, her voice breaking. "They—"

"I understand" Trace said, "but no one need know but the two of us."

Tears falling down her cheeks, Genny clung to the man she thought her savior. "Who are you, Milord?" she asked and was totally unprepared for his answer.

"Duke Sorn, Milady," Trace said with pride. "Duke Trace Edward Sorn."

Genny drew back from him, her lips parted in shock.

"At your service, Mam'selle," he said, thinking her stunned look was one of awe.

"Sorn?" she echoed and a shudder of sheer terror running down her body.

"Aye," he replied and smiled. "And what is your name, Sweeting?"

His hand was stroking her hair, his breath warm against her cheek. She could feel the hardness of his chest against her and feel the strength of his arms around her. This man was her husband's mortal enemy: a man who had sent her beloved to a living hell. He was a man capable of murder and deeds even more vile.

"Sweeting?" Sorn pressed. "What is your name?"

Genny swallowed. "Rowena," she said, giving the only name she could think of at that moment. "Rowena…Su." A sob caught in her throat. "Lin Su!" she gasped. "Where is he?"

Sorn surmised she was calling for the man who had been killed on the roadway. "I don't know of whom you speak, but we will find him, Milady."

Memory of the attack washed over Genny. "He's dead," she wailed, covering her face with her hands. "They killed him!"

Trace continued to hold her, never realizing the cause for the sudden stiffness of the woman's body. "I'll take care of you, Mam'selle," he told her. "You have nothing to fear."

Tearing from the loathsome bastard's embrace, Genny buried her head in her arms and cried.

For Lin Su.

For the vile attack on her person.

And for Fate that had dropped her into the lap of Syn-Jern's diabolical brother.

ꕤ

Lin Su sat up, his head throbbing horribly. He put a hand to his side and was not surprised to find it red with his own blood. Though the sword that had skewered him had missed a vital organ, the loss of blood had weakened him greatly. It took most of his energy to gain his feet. Wavering, he looked around him. His horse was gone and so was his lady.

It was his bellow of rage as he dropped to his knees in the dirt that Kerm and Sara heard as they cleared the rise.

"Merciful Alel, what the hell was that?" Sara shrieked.

Kerm pointed. "Look yonder!" He kicked his horse in the ribs. "Geddup!"

Sara was close on her brother's heels for once. Even from the distance at that she was viewing him, she recognized the huge warrior who had been escorting the lady. Fear made her throat close and her heart beat faster than a Chalean drum.

Kerm did not give his mount time to stop before he vaulted from the saddle. He ran to the injured man. "Easy there. Easy!" he insisted.

"I have to find her," Lin Su signed weakly. "I have to find her!"

"What's he waving his hands like that for?" Sara asked breathlessly as she slid from her horse.

"Help me!" Lin Su signed. "What way did they go?"

"I don't know what he wants," Kerm said. "What are you trying to tell us, fella?"

"My lady," Lin Su signed. He grimaced then toppled backward, out cold.

"We gotta get him to a Healer," Sara suggested.

"Where's the lady?" Kerm asked.

"Bandits," Sara replied, shuddering. "They'll be holding her for ransom."

Kerm knew better, but he didn't correct her. He cocked his chin toward her horse. "Get the steed and bring it over. I'll get him up on her somehow and we can take him to Holy Dale. Hurry now!"

ƐOƆƷ

When Syn-Jern arrived back at the cave, he was surprised to see Tiernan waiting for him there.

"Before you ask, there's no one home up there," Tiernan explained. "I have no idea where your brother is, but the woman went into town to meet with her dressmaker."

Syn-Jern's disgust came out in the form of a vulgar word.

"Thanks for the invitation, but not at the moment," Tiernan replied dryly. At Syn-Jern's look, the McGregor grinned.

"I am in no mood, McGregor," Syn-Jern snapped.

"Neither am I, but perhaps later on tonight…" He stopped when Sorn took a step toward him, murder glinting in his pale eyes. "All right! I'm only trying to get your mind off Demonicus."

Syn-Jern's head snapped up. "How did you know he was here?"

"Dano. The priest is on his way here," Tiernan said on a sober note. "That's why I came to warn you. I don't think old Fiels and Dano have ever ridden that fast in their entire lives." He shrugged. "And they weren't all that happy when I sent them away again to get word to Weir and Patrick."

Syn-Jern slumped on his pallet. "At least with that evil son-of-a-bitching cur here, there won't be a chance of him running into Genny."

"I heard about the ship's delay," Tiernan replied. "Would you like me to send someone to be there when she arrives."

"I will be there," Syn-Jern snapped. "She is my responsibility."

Both men tensed as the signal whistle echoed through the corridor to them.

"That's Kerm," Syn-Jern said, relaxing. He intended to rest for an hour or so then head back to Wixenstead.

Sara came running into the cave. "Kerm needs help. We've a wounded man!"

"Who?" Syn-Jern demanded, coming to his feet.

"Don't know him, but he was stabbed," Sara responded.

Between them, the three men were able to drag the big warrior through the corridor and lay him on Syn-Jern's cot.

"We was going to take him to the stables and go after the Healer, but he won't hear of it," Sara said. "He keeps waving his hands around and shaking his head. Seems he don't want nobody but me to sew him up."

"Fugitive," Tiernan commented.

"He was with a lady," Sara stated. She looked at Syn-Jern. "He's from that there country, ain't he, Milord?"

Syn-Jern had already made note of the man's race. He was staring at the semi-conscious warrior with his heart slamming painfully in his chest. "Where is the lady?" he whispered, his breathing coming in short, shallow gasps.

"She weren't with him when we found him," Kerm answered. "Neither was their horses. We figured it was bandits."

"Hasdu, no doubt," Tiernan said with clenched teeth.

"Ain't no Hasdu 'round these parts," Kerm told him.

"That you know of," Tiernan insisted.

"How do you know there was a lady with him?" Syn-Jern asked softly.

"We saw her," Sara said, and she knew. Knew it as sure as the sun rose in the morning. It didn't take the stricken look on the nobleman's face to stamp true to her suspicions.

Lin Su opened his eyes and grunted, tried to get up, but Kerm put a restraining hand on his breastbone and pushed him down gently.

"My sister's gonna sew you so don't be stirring around 'til she can," Kerm warned. "You're with friends."

Syn-Jern locked stares with the shamed eyes of the Chrystallusian.

"I am Sorn," Syn-Jern said. "Her husband."

Lin Su sighed deeply and tears gathered in his chocolate brown eyes. He looked away, his gaze filled with remorse and humiliation.

"How many were there?" Syn-Jern asked.

Lin Su weakly raised his hand and made odd movements that no one could understand. When he realized he was not being understood, he put the fingertips of his right hand together and mimicked writing on a pad.

"Here!" Sara said, fumbling in her pocket for her grocery list. She looked around. "There is no quill!"

Lin Su ran his index finger in his own blood and smeared Sara's grocery list. '5' he wrote.

"Were they Hasdu?" Tiernan inquired, hoping that wasn't the case for those bastards sold the women they took.

Lin Su shook his head. "Lord" he wrote on the paper.

"Lord?" Kerm questioned. "What does that mean?"

"It means he thinks a nobleman took her," Syn-Jern answered.

"Who?" Tiernan queried.

"Who else?" Syn-Jern snarled.

Syn-Jern hunkered down beside the warrior. "Did they hurt her?"

Lin Su's face collapsed and his lips trembled.

At the man's reaction, Syn-Jern sucked in an agonized breath, threw back his head, and howled with sorrow.

"Holy Merciful Alel!" Tiernan gasped, jumping. As Syn-Jern was about to vent his grief once more, Tiernan leapt at him and plastered a firm, restraining hand over his friend's mouth. "Stop that!" he ordered. "Stop it, now!"

Lin Su closed his eyes as the two strangers wrestled his lady's husband to the floor and whispered furiously for him to be still. The grief, the shock on Syn-Jern Sorn's face was too much for the Chrystallusian warrior to bear. He was mortally ashamed of having allowed harm to befall the lady while she was in his care. A low moan of agony pushed from Lin Su's throat.

"I'll sew that wound, now," Sara said gently, interpreting the groan as physical pain. She pushed Lin Su's bloody shirt aside and began to clean his wound.

The warrior welcomed the pain of her astringent and the prick of her needle through his flesh for it helped to blot out the pain of shame in his heart.

## Chapter Sixteen

By the time Demonicus and his escort of Tribunal guards rode into the circular driveway of Holy Dale manor, Tiernan was sitting in the drawing room, staring into the flames. It had taken a bit of doing, but between them, he and Kerm had held Syn-Jern down and Sara had poured tenerse down the man's unwilling throat. At that moment, Sorn was sleeping soundly beside the bulky Chrystallusian warrior.

"They are here," Sara said, her face tight with disgust.

"Aye," Tiernan replied. "I can smell him."

The noise of the Arch-Prelate's arrival wore on Tiernan's nerves, but he made no move to leave the comfort of his chair and the warmth of the fire. If the priest wanted to speak with he, he could gods-be-damned well seek him out. For once, his rank of Prince of the Court of the Winds lent arrogance to Tiernan McGregor. He barely looked up as the door to the drawing room opened and Demonicus Voire strode in.

"Well, young McGregor," the Arch-Prelate sneered, "so this is where you are hiding from me."

Tiernan snorted his reply.

Demonicus walked to the fire and spread his hands over the flames. "I trust your sojourn in this heathenish land has been uneventful." When the young prince did not reply, Demonicus laughed. It was a cold, hateful laugh that frosted the air. "Still as disrespectful as you have always been," Demonicus said. "Well, no matter. Your time with me will come soon enough."

Tiernan turned his head and spat into the flames, leaving no doubt of his feelings. He glared at the Arch-Prelate, then pointedly ignored him.

"Do you think I do not know you have been aiding Syn-Jern Sorn, sweet prince?" Demonicus inquired. He swept the hem of his red robe aside and sat in the chair across from Tiernan. "Do you think I care what you do?"

"Do you know I don't give a damn what you think?" Tiernan shot back.

"Ah, the impetuosity of youth," Demonicus sighed. "Such fire and flame in one so young and so..." He grinned nastily. "Untried."

The threat made Tiernan ill and he looked away from the priest's knowing grin.

"We will catch him, you know," Demonicus said. "And we will hang him this time."

Tiernan remained silent. His hands had clenched into fists on the arms of his chair and his body had grown rigid with anger. Every time he was near one of the sinister Brothers of the Domination, he felt sick to his stomach.

"Be careful, my young friend," Demonicus said, rising, "that you are not hanged alongside him."

"I am not your gods-be-damned friend, priest!" Tiernan threw at the man. "And you can keep your vile threats to yourself. Your kind will never lay hands on a McGregor male. That I can promise you!"

Demonicus' left eyebrow crooked upward. "You think not?" His smile was brutal. "I can promise you there will come a day when father and son from the clan McGregor will lie beneath the weight of the greatest sorcerer to wear the mantle of Arch-Prelate of the Brotherhood of the Domination and be slave to him!"

Tiernan's blood ran cold. "You lie!" he spat, coming to his feet. He ached to ram his fist into the priest's thin, cadaverous face.

"No lie, sweet one," Demonicus replied. "It will come to pass as surely as the Outlaw will hang!"

Sara's eyes were wide in her head as she came into the drawing room, oblivious to the presence of the priest. "Your Grace, Duke Sorn has returned and he has brought a lady with him!"

It was on the tip of Tiernan 's tongue to ask the servant what the hell difference did it make, when he noticed that she was wringing her hands and her face was as pale as the apron she wore.

"I take it the lady in question is not his wife," Demonicus chuckled, turning to the fire. "Will that cause problems this eve?"

Sara glanced at the Arch-Prelate, but did not understand the danger of the man being able to read her thoughts. She started to speak again, but Tiernan cut her off.

"For the love of Alel, woman, why are you bothering me with this shit?" he snapped, storming to her and grabbing her arm in a vicious pinch that made Sara yelp with pain.

"Your Grace, you are hurting me!" Sara cried out, trying to free her arm. With her mind on the pain, she was not thinking of Genny Sorn and that was exactly what Tiernan intended.

He dragged her behind him, his own mind intent on blocking out any thought.

"Your Grace!" Sara whimpered.

"Shut up!" he growled. "Shut the hell up! I am sick to death of your insolence, wench!"

Out into the cold, away from the house, out of sight of Demonicus and anyone else who might see, and into the chill of the barn, he took her. "Scream," he hissed. "Scream as hard as you can."

"What?" Sara asked, his request temporarily obliterating the pain in her arm.

"Scream, damn you!" Tiernan insisted, jerking on her arm. "Scream!"

The cruel twist of her arm made Sara do just that. She shrieked like a banshee riding the Chalean moors.

And brought Kerm running from the cave and Jobe from the kitchen as well as Drae, the Gill's younger brother, from the potting shed.

As the men burst through the stable doors, Sara let out another terrible scream, then managed to jerk her arm from Tiernan's steely grasp.

"What the demon are you doing, Your Grace?" Kerm barked, going to his sister's aid.

"There is a man in that manse who can read minds as easily as you can piss," Tiernan said.

Sara clamped a hand over her mouth, realizing how close she had come to giving Genny Sorn's presence away.

"What has that got to do with you manhandling our sister?" Drae seethed, taking a step toward Tiernan. Prince of the royal house or not, no one mauled his sister and got away with it.

"Think, man!" Tiernan said. "If he can glean Syn-Jern's whereabouts from you, he'll hang our friend and you along with him. Do you not ken?"

Kerm paled. "Sweet Merciful Alel!" he whispered. "Didn't think on that, I reckon."

"'Tis not all," Sara also whispered. "The eel brought the lady here!"

"What lady?" Drae inquired, not having been privy to what had been said in the cave.

"His lady!" Sara said.

"The Outlaw's lady?" Kerm queried, stunned.

"The one and the same," Tiernan agreed. "Now do you know why I had to hurt Sara?" He looked at her. "My apologies, Mam'selle. It was nothing personal."

"What do we do?" Jobe asked, his ancient eyes flitting back and forth.

"Get word to the lady," Tiernan replied. "Let her know her man is safe, but she is not to be thinking of him. Warn her about Demonicus."

"And let her know her escort is alive," Sara said. "She'll believe him dead, I'll wager!"

"Get back to the house and favor that arm," Tiernan advised. "Let them think I punished you for interrupting us. Act like I hurt you worse out here."

"Won't be no playacting on that part," Sara muttered. She'd be favoring her arm for a day or two by her reckoning. She gave the nobleman a look that

Tiernan interpreted as mean and vengeful and he made a mental note to be extra careful what he ate and drank for the next few days.

"Get back to the house, Sara," Tiernan told her, then dismissed her as he turned to her brothers. "Kerm, get down to the cave and make sure Syni is still sleeping. All we need is for him to wake up, hear his wife's voice, and come storming upstairs like an enraged crocodile! Tell her man she's safe for now else he'll be after coming up here, too. Caution him about his thoughts!"

"That's gonna be a hard thing, I'm thinkin'," Jobe said worriedly. "Ain't never had to think a'fore I thought."

"I doubt Demonicus will be delving into the minds of the servants, but we have to be careful. He'll gods-be-damned sure be trying to plumb mine and Trace's," Tiernan told them.

"And the Viper's," Sara reminded him.

"The only thought in that bitch's head is of herself," Kerm sniffed.

"Not lately, it ain't," Jobe put in. "Heard her up there on the balcony a'callin' out the lad's name and carryin' on like she was a widow woman a'missing her old man!"

"Oh, my sweet lord, the magistrate!" Sara gasped. "Weir be bringing him again tonight to listen through the walls!"

"We have to keep Weir from coming here at all," Tiernan said urgently. "Demonicus will find out who Weir is and Weir's connection to Syni's woman and we'll all be hanging from Derry Byrne side by bloody side! I don't know about you folks, but I've of a mind to live to a ripe, stinking old age!"

"I'll ride into town and try to stop 'em," Drae said. "Karl will be at the alehouse this time of the afternoon. The Revenge will be docking around five of the clock. Saur won't be getting off the ship right away so's we got a mite of time."

"Make sure you don't let on to Karl Krueger why he ain't to come out here as planned," Kerm cautioned. "I don't trust that bastard none at all."

"By now he'll know Demonicus Voire is here," Tiernan insisted, "and won't be in a hurry to come here, anyway!"

Sara grabbed Tiernan's arm. "Can we take this priest through the corridors to hear their confessions instead of Karl?"

Tiernan rolled his eyes. "He doesn't give a rat's arse if Syn-Jern's name is cleared or not, woman. Don't you think Demonicus knows who killed Otis Playe?"

Sara released the prince's arm. "I suppose you're right."

"Well it be a moot point now, don't it?" Jobe asked.

"How so?" Kerm replied.

"Seems to me that priest knows it's the lad what's leading the 'Winds. That being the case, the lad is done for I'm thinkin'." Jobe shook his head. "They'll be after catchin' him and bringing' him to justice no matter what. Old murder or not, the boy's done for."

Tiernan had to agree. Demonicus' appearance had changed everything. It was imperative to get Syn-Jern, Weir, Patrick, and Genny out of Virago as quickly as possible.

"Sara!"

Damn," Sara grated. "That's the eel a'callin' me."

"Go!" Tiernan hissed.

Drae and Sara left the stables together. The McGregor watched through a crack in the door as Trace Sorn grabbed Sara's already bruised arm and yanked her up the steps of Holy Dale.

# Chapter Seventeen

GENNY SORN LAY CURLED INTO A FETAL POSITION, HER PILLOW DAMP FROM the tears she'd shed. Trembling, unable to catch a decent breath for the horrid lump lodged in her throat, she stared unseeingly across the room, grieving for Lin Su. The experience of her own defilement had been pushed firmly aside for, to her way of thinking, there were more important matters at hand. With her thoughts on finding Syn-Jern, she paid no heed to the door when it opened; did not acknowledge the servant who came to squat beside the bed.

"Milady, are you up to listening to me?" Sara asked urgently. When the still woman did not reply, Sara's face filled with pity. "Milady, it will be all right."

Very slowly, Genny's eyes shifted to the strange woman kneeling beside her. There was kindness in the plain little face, but there was understanding, as well. Instinctively, Genny knew the woman had endured the same horrific situation she, herself, had, and had found a way to overcome the shame of it.

Sara smiled encouragingly. "Are you listening, Milady?" she repeated.

Genny nodded, but her eyes were wary.

"Then pay close heed to what I've gotta say because it's important," Sara told her quietly. She lowered her voice even more. "There is a man what's come to Holy Dale and he's one of them warlocks from the Temple. He can read minds so we have to be real careful that we don't think nothing he might hear. You understand?"

Genny's eyes focused sharply on the servant. "A sorcerer?" she whispered.

"One of them Brothers from the Abbey in Serenian," Sara informed her, "and he's here looking for your man. He's after arresting him."

Syn-Jern Sorn's wife was a credit to him at that moment for she did not give away by gasp of breath or blink of eye that she knew who the serving woman meant. For all she knew, this could be a trap.

"My husband?" Genny stated in a flat voice. "I have no idea who you mean, Mam'selle."

Sara nodded, understanding. "He's in the cave down under the hidden cellar," she continued, turning her head to look at the closed door before she drew even closer to the bed and her voice lowered to a mere breath of sound. "And so's that monkey man what was traveling with you."

At the vulgar term Viragonians had long ago given Chrystallusians, Genny's jaw clenched, but then she realized what the woman had said and widened her eyes. "My traveling companion?" she queried. "He is alive?"

"He's got himself a mighty dent in his side and lost him a whole heap of blood, but he's alive and sleepin' right about now," Sara explained. "That monkey man wrote down how many varmints attacked you. Soon's The Outlaw heard what had happened to you, he just about busted a gut and we had to seebate him."

Genny blinked. "Sea bait him?" she repeated.

"Knock him out, Milady!" Sara insisted. "Seebate him with tenerse."

"Ah," Genny sighed. "Sedate," she said, understanding. Against her better judgment, she trusted this girl. She sat up. "You're telling me Lin Su is under the manor house and he's been drugged to keep him quiet. Is that it?"

Sara shook her head. "No, Milady. Your husband was the one we had to knock out. The monkey man is sleeping, none the worse for wear, I suppose. He'll be right as rain, although who would really know the way he waves his arms about like the monkeys do!" She mimicked Lin Su's signing. "What is all that, Milady?"

The abyss into which Genny had sunk was falling away behind her as she swung her legs over the side of the bed. Her own misery laid aside, her thoughts at that moment were entirely on Syn-Jern. "Take me to him," she said.

Sara's mouth dropped open. "I can't do that, Milady!" She scrambled to her feet. "I can't take you to him."

"Aye, you can," Genny said. Syn-Jern needed her and she would do what she had to do to keep him safe. "You can take me to Syni and you will, Mam'selle."

Sara shook her head. "Can't or they'll find out and if'n they find out, they'll find him and I ain't gonna allow that to happen," she said, her mouth set in a militant line. "So don't you be thinking you can make me 'cause the McGregor told me what I was to do and that is what I'm gonna do!"

The two women glared at one another for a moment, and then Genny let out a long, aggravated sigh. "I appreciate what you are trying to do, but—"

"Sara Gill!" The strident female voice came from the hallway.

Sara cursed beneath her breath. "That's the viper back early!" she hissed.

"Sara!"

"I'm coming!" Sara yelled back. She turned, heading for the door, but found her sore arm in a brutal grip. "Lords help me, don't tug on me thatta way!"

"Is that her?" Genny asked in a low, insistent voice. "Is that Rosa-Lynn Sorn?"

"Let go!" Sara whimpered, jerking her arm from Genny's grip. "Don't you royals got no other way of getting' a person's attention other than breaking their limbs?" She massaged her arm.

"Is that the bitch?" Genny ground out, her eyes flashing.

"Aye," Sara mumbled. She flexed her arm, wincing at the tenderness.

"Sara!"

"Tell her you're in here," Genny ordered. Her hands were clenched into fists and when Sara hesitated, she took a threatening step toward the servant. "Tell her!"

Sara knew better than to argue. The look on Syn-Jern Sorn's wife's face would have scared the staunchest warrior. "In here, Your Grace!" she called.

The door to the room was flung open and Rosa-Lynn Sorn barged in, her face ugly with displeasure. "When I call you, you have better come, girl!" she spat. "You are one step from being dis…"

Genny found herself staring into the eyes of a woman she would have given her right teat to kill. The bitch who had hurt Syn-Jern so deeply, who was partly responsible for having sent him to prison, was standing only a few feet away, a haughty look on her face.

"Who the hell are you?" Rosa-Lynn demanded, advancing into the room.

"She be a guest of His Grace," Sara explained, casting Genny a warning look. "Thieves set on her and her man outside the Carbondale Gate and—"

"Why is she here?" Rosa-Lynn queried Sara although her full attention was centered on the strikingly beautiful woman standing before her. Her gaze swept over Genny, the expression on her face leaving no doubt she found the other woman lacking in some way.

"His Grace was kind enough to provide me a safe haven until I can be on my way," Genny said, barely feeling her fingernails sticking into the palms of her hands.

Rosa-Lynn lifted her chin in a belligerent way. "And pray tell when will that be, Madame?"

Genny shrugged indifferently. "When I feel strong enough, I suppose."

Despite the fact that Rosa-Lynn had fallen out of love with Trace Edward Sorn and was not in the least enamored of his person—though she still enjoyed their occasional romp in bed—the green eyed monster of jealousy made her lip lift with scorn. "I suggest," she told the stranger, "you start feeling stronger this very moment for I'll not have you intruding in my home!"

Genny arched her left eyebrow. "I'll go when I am feeling up to it, Madame and not a gods-be-damned moment sooner!"

A gasp of outrage exploded from Rosa-Lynn and she would have leapt upon her tormentor had Trace not entered the room to grab her arm to keep her from doing so.

"What are you doing in here?" Trace snapped. When his wife tried to yank her arm from his grip, he pulled her against him. "I asked you what you were doing, Rosa-Lynn?"

"Get that whore out of my home, Sorn!" Rosa-Lynn spat; her eyes were flared in fury. "Get her out before I slit her slutty throat!"

"Be still!" Sorn warned her and when she still struggled to free herself, raking at his hands with her long nails, he backhanded her and sent her reeling across the room. Rosa-Lynn collided heavily with the armoire and slid to the floor.

Despite her hatred of the woman, Genny almost felt sorry for Sorn's wife. Her husband's heavy signet ring had torn open Rosa-Lynn's lip and blood ran from the injury. There would be a livid bruise on the milk-white complexion of the woman's right cheek to attest to her husband's proclivity for violence.

"I am sorry, Milady," Sorn said, his voice filled with contrition, "but oftentimes, that is the only way she can be made to listen."

Sara had witnessed many such attacks on the person of the Duchess and could not have cared any the less what happened to the woman; but she carried a great deal about the safety of The Outlaw's woman and moved closer to Genny Sorn, her own body half-shielding Syn-Jern's wife.

"You'll be sorry you did that, Trace," Rosa-Lynn whispered as she came clumsily to her feet. She wiped the back of her hand across her torn mouth. "I promise you that you will."

"Get the hell to your room, woman," Trace snapped, narrowing his eyes. "And stay there!"

Rosa-Lynn straightened her shoulders. "You will be sorry," she repeated. She gave Genny a murderous look then—head high—she walked regally from the room.

Trace drew in a long, calming breath, then turned to Genny, an apologetic smile on his lean face. "I am sorry you had to witness that, Milady, but my wife often exhibits uncontrollable fits of violence that can only be quelled by the use of force. Please accept my sincerest apologies for my barbaric conduct."

Sara rolled her eyes.

Genny, all too aware of whom this man was and his connection to Syn-Jern dug her nails even deeper into her palms as she forced a smile to her lips. "I quite understand, Milord," she said. She flinched as he hurried toward her, reached for her hand and brought it to his lips.

"You are recovered from your ordeal, I pray?" he asked, placing a soft kiss on Genny's hand.

A wild desire to snatch her hand from his and wipe it on her skirt stiffened Genny's body, but she managed to hold onto her tight smile. "I am…better," she said, lowering her eyes, grinding her teeth to keep from hissing.

"I have sent word to the magistrate and he is on his way here," Trace informed her. "He must be told about the attack and my punishment of your defiler."

Sara's heart began to pound as heavily in her chest as she was sure the heart of The Outlaw's wife was pounding in hers. The two women exchanged a wary look and Sara's head dipped in acknowledgment of the silent request. She curtsied, mumbled something about a cup of strong tea for the lady and left.

"Please, Milady," Trace asked, "rest yourself." He led her to the bed and insisted she sit down. "My servant will bring you refreshment."

"You should not put yourself out for me," Genny told him, easing her hand from his grasp.

"Lady, I would move mountains if it would bring the color back to your lovely cheeks and a smile to your gentle mouth," Trace declared. "Tell me what I can do to help."

Genny put her hands in her lap and entwined the fingers. She stared at them so she would not have to look at Sorn. "I am tired, Milord," she whispered. "It is hard to think."

"Your pardon, Milady!" he was quick to say, coming to his feet. "Where are my manners?" He bowed to her. "Rest and when the magistrate comes, I will handle the situation myself so you will not have to be subjected to his boorish questions."

Before she could stop him, Sorn reached for her hand and caressed it.

"Until then?" he inquired. His handsome face was hopeful.

Not trusting herself to speak, Genny merely nodded.

"Feel free to make use of my servants, Milady," he told her as he walked to the door. "They will be at your command." With that said, he left.

"Son of a bitch!" Genny seethed. Her eyes gleamed hotly with loathing as she scrambled from the bed and hurried to the window. Easing aside the drapery, she surveyed the countryside beyond the oyster-shell driveway. Seeing no one loitering below, she went to the door, cracked it, and poked her head cautiously into the empty corridor. Relieved there was no one in sight, she squeezed through the opening and padded quietly toward the stairs.

ꕤ

Having made a trip to Ciona to look for his sister and not finding her, Weir Saur was as angry as he was afraid. Upon seeing Kerm standing on the pier as the Revenge's lines were being tied to the dock, sour sweat began popping out on Weir's face. Even from the distance that separated them, Saur could see the anxiety puckering the Viragonian's face. Instant unease crept down Weir's back and left a wide band of icy flesh in its wake.

"What's he doing here?" Neevens queried.

"Something's wrong," Weir stated. He shuddered. "Something is bad wrong."

"You reckon the lad's been caught?" Stevens put in.

"By the gods, I hope not," Weir whispered. He swallowed. His imagination put a heavy coil of hemp around his neck and he reached up to stroke his throat.

Thankful Patrick was on the Revenant and that good ship was twenty miles away, Weir ran the back of his hand over his mouth, felt the sweat come away on his flesh, and told his men to stay on board.

"What you planning?" Neevens growled.

"I'm going to talk to Gill and find out what's got him looking like he's got a corncob up his arse," Weir answered.

"You ain't going alone," Neevens snorted.

Weir ignored the remark. "If it looks like there's going to be trouble, cast off those lines and get the hell out of here as fast as the Wind will carry you." He turned to Neevens. "Do you hear me?"

Neevens nodded, turned his head, and spat a stream of tobacco juice over the railing. "I hear you," he said, but had no intention of allowing harm to befall his captain.

Weir appreciated the loyalty he saw gleaming militantly on Neevens' face, but he couldn't allow the man to disobey orders for one very important reason.

"If Syni's been taken and if something happens to me, it will be up to you to find my sister and get her to safety. Do you understand?" His gaze bored into Neevens. "She's all I've got left in this world and I'll see her safe." He put a firm hand on Neevens' shoulder. "Will you see to that for me?"

Put in that light, Neevens nodded. "Consider it done, Cap'n," he replied.

"Good. Now if I'm not back within half an hour, I want you to shove off. Rendezvous with the Revenant and make for Ciona."

Neevens' lips pursed. "I ain't leavin' you here!"

"When you get to Ciona," Weir said as though he hadn't heard Neevens' denial, "disembark and get every manjack you can together. Ride hell bent through the Gate and head straight for Holy Dale. If Syn-Jern's been taken, we'll take the eel and his venomous whore and trade them for Syn-Jern."

"Pardon me for saying my mind, Cap'n," Stevens drawled, "but who'd give a rat's arse about Trace Sorn and that bitch-wife of his'n?"

"Just do it!" Weir barked. "If Syn-Jern hasn't been taken and he's still at Holy Dale, we'll grab him and hightail back into Serenia." He turned to look once more at Kerm's worried face, then shuddered. "Unless it's too late."

"Too late?" Stevens questioned. "Whatcha mean 'too late'?" The old man grabbed Weir's shoulder. "Whatcha mean by that?"

Weir shook off Stevens' restraining hand. "I won't know 'til I talk to Gill, fool. Let me go see what's got him looking so tarnished!"

Before another word of protest could be uttered, Weir was striding heavily across the gangplank, his eyes worried.

Kerm dug his hands into the pockets of his tattered coat, glanced around to see who might be watching, then started walking backwards as Weir advanced on him. As Saur came level with him, Kerm turned. "There's trouble," he stated.

"I gathered as much," Weir snapped. He didn't turn to look at the man, but kept walking toward the horses Kerm had brought from Holy Dale. "Was he taken?"

"No," Kerm responded and heard the sigh of relief coming from the man beside him, but then he heard the immediate intake of harsh breath and was quick to add: "And he's well and safe so's don't be concerned on that side of it."

"Then what?" Weir hissed from between tightly clenched teeth. They had reached the horses and he had one foot already in the stirrup.

Kerm waited until Saur was astride his mount, then put a hesitant hand on the man's leg. "It's your sister."

"Tell me!" Weir ordered.

"She is at Holy Dale," Kerm said, "but you can't go there."

"Watch me!" Weir snarled and would have put his horse to gallop had Weir not grabbed the bridle.

"Demonicus Voire is there," Sara's brother informed Weir. "You are not to go there under no circumstance." His voice hardened. "That is straight from the McGregor's lips, Saur."

Weir's face paled. He understood the implications of Demonicus being at Holy Dale. "Does Syn-Jern know the bastard has Genny?"

Kerm shook his head. "Ain't that way at all," he insisted. "When I rode outta Holy Dale, that warlock didn't know who your sister was and didn't know her relation to the Outlaw. The McGregor wants to keep it that way. He's warned us all to be careful of our thoughts while that priest is there."

"Aye," Weir whispered. "He can read thoughts." He shivered hard. His eyes were haunted as he stared unseeingly at the town. "How did Genny come to be at Holy Dale, then, if Demonicus didn't arrest her?"

Kerm hesitated, then decided if he could get through his own sister's ravaging a few years back, Weir Saur could get over his sister's. The way Saur handled the news would settle a question or two in Kerm Gill's mind. He lifted his chin, waited until Weir was looking his way, then spoke his piece slowly and without inflection.

"The eel must have got a wild hair up his butt and thought you were the Outlaw. He figured if he was to catch you, he'd bait the trap."

"My sister being the bait," Weir concluded. "But how…" Kerm was shaking his head at the misconception. "Then what?"

"We think he sent men to kidnap Sara and hold her 'til you showed yourself to free her," Kerm answered. He looked away. "Men what had brutal notions of their own."

For a moment, Weir said nothing, then the full realization of what could have happened to the woman he had come to love was replaced with the knowledge of the terrible thing that had to have happened to his sister.

"Oh, merciful Alel, no," Weir whimpered. "No!"

"She's all right as far as we know," Kerm was quick to say. "They didn't beat her or nothing like them Diabolusians…" He stopped, knowing he'd said too much. He was sure Sara had not mentioned her rape to Weir; but he was wrong.

"Sara told me," Weir said, his eyes filling with tears. "She wanted no secrets between us. And now my own sister…" A groan of despair burst from the depths of Weir Saur's soul.

"Well, leastways we don't think the eel ordered them to do what the bastards did," Kerm said, his mouth tight. "As best we can figure, once he found out, he killed the man what was in charge though the others of 'em got away."

"How many?" Weir snarled.

"Four, we think. Leastways that's what the monkey man said."

"What monkey man?" Weir demanded. "There was a Chrystallusian involved in Genny's attack?"

"He was protecting her and they stabbed him and left him for dead. He's all right, too, and a'sleepin' aside His Grace." A sheepish smile flitted over Kerm's lips. "We had to pour tenerse down his throat to keep him from getting up and running up them stairs to get his lady."

"So he's safe," Weir said.

"Far as I know he is 'less something's happened since I've been in the village."

Weir caught sight of the magistrate heading toward them and frowned. "I was to take that son-of-a-bitch through the walls again today," he said in a low voice. "We sure as hell don't need him out there now." He lowered his voice. "Get back to Holy Dale and warn the others that we'll be coming after them. Have everyone in the cave and keep watch!"

"Saur!" Karl Krueger called as he came bustling toward Weir. "You have been told the news?"

Weir and Kerm exchanged a look, then Weir nodded, waiting for the magistrate to speak.

"I am on my way out there so this is fortuitous. We can ride together," Krueger suggested.

Weir stiffened. "I have business that can not be postponed. I'll meet you at the manse."

Krueger frowned. "I fail to see anything more important than capturing the Outlaw and hanging his evil ass from the nearest tree," he snapped. "Robbing the warehouses of the Tribunal is one thing; raping a defenseless woman and murdering her escort is another! The people might well cheer on a thief, but they'll not be so enamored once they find out what he's done!"

Kerm opened his mouth to correct the magistrate, but Weir kicked him, catching Gill in the chest to warn him to hold his tongue. "Mind your manners whilst the gentleman speaks, fool!"

Krueger puffed out his chest. "The villagers don't always know their place, Captain Saur," he sniffed, casting Kerm a superior look.

"They'll mind their manners when I'm around, Lord Magistrate," Weir said as he stared into Kerm's angry eyes. "I'll gather some of my men and help you hunt the Outlaw. Gill will accompany you out to Holy Dale, won't you, Gill?"

A tight muscle bunched in Kerm's cheek, but he dipped his head.

"I left something on my ship and once I see to that, I'll be right on your heels," Weir said. He dismounted and hurried back to the gangplank.

From the way his captain was moving and the paleness of the man's face, Neevens knew things were as bad as they could get. "Stevens, have the lines cast off. We're leaving," he said softly.

Even as Weir Saur boarded the Revenge, the ship was preparing to sail.

## Chapter Eighteen

Demonicus looked up from the report he was writing as the woman came into his room without knocking. His hooded gaze flicked insultingly over her, dismissing her.

"You are the Tribunal representative?" Rosa-Lynn asked.

"And you are the ill-mannered concubine of Trace Sorn," Demonicus snapped. He dipped his quill into the inkpot. "I do not wish to converse with you, Madame."

"You're looking for the Outlaw," Rosa-Lynn said.

The Arch-Prelate sighed with displeasure, then turned to look at the woman. "What is it you want, woman?"

Rosa-Lynn sidled closer. "What if I could give him to you?"

Demonicus smiled nastily. "You know where Syn-Jern Sorn is?"

The Duchess answered the priest's smile with one of her own. "Convenient to think it is Syni, isn't it, Your Worship?" she asked slyly.

The priest frowned. "You are saying I have the wrong man?"

Her cheek still throbbed from her husband's slap and the pain put starch in Rosa-Lynn Sorn's spine. "What better way to hide what you are doing than to make it seem someone else is the culprit?" she asked. "Who would suspect a man like Trace Sorn?"

Demonicus' eyes flared. "You can't be serious!" he gasped. "The man is a fool!"

Rosa-Lynn held the priest's stare. "You know he killed Otis Playe," she accused. "I overheard you and him talking after the trial. If the Tribunal hadn't wanted Sorn lands so badly, you would have made sure it was Trace who went to Tyber's Isle, not his brother."

The priest waved a dismissive hand. "That is neither here nor there and counts for very little."

"True, but don't you think it very convenient that the theft of Tribunal gold began only after Trace learned his brother was free?" Rosa-Lynn asked. "If what we have heard is true, Syn-Jern has been free for well over two years yet the robbing began only recently." She cocked her head to one side. "Don't you find it strange that a man no one liked and would have nothing to do with can come back to Virago and marshal a force of men large enough to set upon Tribunal guards on the high seas and across the land?"

That thought had never entered Demonicus' mind. "You know he is the Outlaw?" the priest asked.

"He has bragged to me of it," she responded. "Oft times he has told me of his plans to gather together an army large enough to overthrow Innis Hesar."

"The people hate Trace Sorn," Demonicus snorted. "He could not garner the loyalty of five men, yet you think he could raise five thousand?"

Rosa-Lynn had an answer for that. "No one ever sees the Outlaw, Your Worship. He is always masked. They believe him to be Syn-Jern Sorn, just as you do. They'll follow a man who's suffered at Tribunal hands and is willing to lead them."

Demonicus didn't doubt that for a moment. He had seen the future and knew what was in store for one whom would follow him as Arch-Prelate. Though his talent did not extend to knowing his own future, he feared something similar was entirely possible.

"You will swear the Outlaw is your husband?" Demonicus pressed, his fear overriding his normal wariness.

"In a court of law before the magistrate!" Rosa-Lynn replied.

Demonicus leaned back in his chair. "The magistrate is on his way to Holy Dale even as we speak."

"Why?" Rosa-Lynn asked, suspiciously.

"Something to do with the woman your husband brought here." He could not have cared less. "In regard to her ravishment."

A frown marred the loveliness of Rosa-Lynn's face. "The woman upstairs was raped?" She snorted with unladylike contempt. "She sure as hell didn't act like she'd been defiled!"

The priest closed his eyes and seemed to be falling asleep, yet, in fact, he was probing the ether around them, listening for stray thoughts that might give him a clue to the mischief in the manse. When he opened his eyelids, he smiled hatefully at Rosa-Lynn.

"The woman is the Outlaw's lady," he said. "She is being careful not to let her thoughts stray, but the servant is not as cautious."

Rosa-Lynn knew Trace Sorn couldn't possibly be the Outlaw. Her vindictiveness and revenge would see Trace hanging from the scaffold, but she knew him to be too incompetent and stupid to lead men against the Tribunal. But Syn-Jern on the other hand…

"What's the matter, bitch?" Demonicus grunted as he took in the woman's sudden pallor. "Having second thoughts about having turned your husband in to me?"

"She's his woman," Rosa-Lynn said, the monster of jealousy prodding her.

"I grant you leave to deal with her as you see fit," Demonicus drawled. "The Tribunal cares not for the whores of its enemies."

"His woman," Rosa-Lynn repeated. "Under my own roof!"

Demonicus heard the horses before Rosa-Lynn did and got up from the desk to walk to the window. Looking down into the courtyard, he spied the man he knew must be the magistrate. With him was a small contingent of armed riders.

"I want her hanged," Rosa-Lynn ground out.

Demonicus sighed. "It matters not in the least to me what you do to her." He adjusted the sleeve of his scarlet robe. "Run her through with your own dagger if it pleases you, woman. You'll not be charged with the crime."

Rosa-Lynn did not trust the priest. "You must arrest her when you take Trace," she said. "Let them hang together as a warning to the people who have been aiding him!"

"Ah," Demonicus said, coming back to the desk. "That perhaps is not a bad idea at all." He picked up the arrest warrant he had been writing, wadded it up and tossed it into the flames. He sat down and took a fresh sheet of parchment from the drawer, picked up the quill, dipped it into the inkpot and began to write.

Rosa-Lynn came to stand over the priest's shoulder and when she saw Trace Edward Sorn's name on the arrest warrant, she began to laugh silently.

ꙮ

When Weir Saur, Patrick Kasella, Tarnes, Stevens, Neevens, and the entire crews of both the Revenant and the Revenge rode into Virago, they were met by Kerm Gill.

"They've taken the eel into custody!" Kerm said, barely controlling his prancing mount.

"By the gods, why?" Weir asked.

"They have a sworn statement from his wife that he is the Outlaw!" Kerm answered.

Weir's eyebrows shot up into his sweaty hair. "Why did she do that?"

"Don't know," Kerm replied. He didn't know how to tell Weir the rest and when he looked at the tall blond man sitting astride the roan stallion, he winced.

"What's wrong?" Patrick asked. His sixth sense had been nudging him all day and as they had crossed under the Carbondale Gate, the unease he'd been experiencing had intensified.

"They took her, too, Milord," Kerm said, realizing Patrick must be of a royal house for there was no mistaking the tattoo of the Maze on the man's left wrist.

"The viper?" Weir questioned although his gut instinct had already told him what must have happened.

Kerm shook his head. "They arrested your sister, Saur. The priest signed the warrant for her," Kerm said softly, "naming her the Outlaw's concubine."

"They'll hang Genny, too," Patrick said to no one in particular.

"How long ago?" Weir asked, his jaw set.

"Yesterday afternoon," Kerm answered.

"Does Syni know?" Weir inquired, hoping against hope his brother-in-law was still dead to the world.

When Kerm Gill lowered his head, Patrick Kasella let out a roar of fury. "You let him go after her?" he bellowed.

"What choice did I have, Milord?" Kerm returned. "She is his wife!"

"Where is he now?" Weir demanded.

Kerm shrugged. "I don't rightly know. He took Heil with him and a few others and was gonna try to break her outta jail." He locked gazes with Weir. "That was late last night and we ain't heard nothin' from him or the others since."

Patrick sawed on his mount's reins. "I'm going after him!"

"No!" Weir shouted. "Think before you go tearing off like a Diabolusian bull, man!"

"What is there to think about?" Patrick yelled back.

"There is safety in numbers and we've enough men to overrun Wixenstead, take our people and leave!" Weir declared. "We can make it back through the Gate and be safe in Serenia before the Viragonians can muster a troop to come after us."

"The McGregor has sent word to his father," Kerm said. "He went into town to try to free the woman, but the Viper put the noose right tight around the lady's throat."

"Why would she do that?" Weir barked.

"Pure spite," Patrick told him. "If she's somehow found out Genny is Syn-Jern's wife, she'll think to punish him by having his woman killed."

"Over my dead body," Weir stated.

"Then we'd best be riding," Patrick warned him. "There might be a trial held for Trace Sorn, but the Tribunal has no such laws for a woman. They'll hang Genny outright." He looked to the rising moon. "Come daylight, she'll be swinging from the gibbet if we don't hurry!"

ഊഌ

Syn-Jern Sorn knew the laws of the Tribunal as well as Patrick did. He knew he had to rescue Genny that night.

Lin Su cast a sidelong glance to the steely-eyed man hunkered down beside him and marveled that the irrational fury that had driven Sorn to this spot now seemed to have dissipated. Even as he watched, he could tell the intelligent, methodical part of the man was calming down, honing in on the problem at hand and looking for a way to solve the dilemma.

"They're taking food in to her," Heil whispered.

Syn-Jern nodded. He'd already seen the boy as he came out of the inn down the street. He had momentarily entertained the notion of jumping the teenager and using one of his men to replace him, but the Tribunal guards were being far more attentive than Syn-Jern wished for them to be. The guards were following the boy's progress just as avidly as Syn-Jern was.

As heartsick as it made him to have his lady incarcerated, Syn-Jern knew the only wise thing to do was wait. He refused to believe the gods would not send him a way to free Genny.

Even it meant turning himself in to gain her freedom.

ꕥ

By orders of the McGregor, Sara and Drae Gill and Jobe had been sent under heavy guard to Serenia. Tiernan wanted Weir Saur's lady safe as well as her brother and family friend. Those who had been helping to care for Syn-Jern had also been ordered out of Virago and onto the safety of McGregor land. Alone in the house with the treacherous slut who had turned Syn-Jern's wife into the Tribunal, the Serenian Prince was of a mind to strangle the bitch.

"You have no idea what you've done," Tiernan told her.

Rosa-Lynn did not reply. She refused to so much as look at him.

"He has gone after her."

The woman gave a slight shrug of disdain.

Tiernan's fury leapt up his throat and nearly choked him as he strode to Rosa-Lynn's chair and slapped his palms on the arms. "Look at me, woman!" he shouted.

Very calmly, Rosa-Lynn met his angry glower. "Did he share her with you, McGregor?" she sneered. "Is that why you're so upset?" She tilted her head to one side. "Was she good in bed?"

Tiernan could well understand why Trace Sorn felt the need to hit this woman on occasion. He itched to slap the smug look from her face, himself. "Did you not hurt him enough when you stood in the dock and swore his life away, Rosa-Lynn?" he mocked. "Did you need to do this to him, as well?"

"He probably doesn't even know she's been arrested," Rosa-Lynn mocked. "You did not have time to contact him and—"

"He's been living in the cave under this gods-be-damned manse, woman! He heard them arresting her and broke the jaw of one of my men trying to get to her!" Tiernan threw at her. "It was all we could do to keep him still!"

Rosa-Lynn flinched. Could it be true? Could Syn-Jern have been right under her nose the entire time? From the arrogant, hateful look on the McGregor's face, it would seem that was exactly the case.

"They'll catch him," Tiernan said, "and they'll hang him this time." His lip lifted with contempt. "All because of you."

"Mayhaps not," she said, worried. It had never occurred to her that Syn-Jern would be caught. She had suspected him to be the Outlaw for a good long while and had been silently cheering him on.

"He's ridden into town," Tiernan informed her. "He'll risk his life to free her."

"She's a woman," Rosa-Lynn commented. "We're a dime a dozen or haven't you heard? He'll find another in no time." Her look turned sly. "Maybe he'll come back to me."

"She is his wife!" Tiernan spat, his hands opening and closing in an effort to refrain from beating the woman to a bloody pulp.

"Wife?" Rosa-Lynn repeated and knew from the expression on McGregor's face that it was the truth.

"Aye. Wife," Tiernan snarled with disgust. Before he could attempt what he wanted more than anything to do with Trace Sorn's vindictive whore, he stalked angrily from the room.

Rosa-Lynn sat very still, her eyes filling with tears. She'd lost him again, she told herself. Not only because he had taken a wife—wives could be eliminated in one fashion or another—but because he would know she was the one who had handed the tart over to the Tribunal. He would never forgive her.

She covered her face with her hands and began to sob.

ꙮꙮ

Demonicus lifted his head and sniffed. The smell of lavender was thick in the room. It was a noxious odor that made him ill and brought with it a horrendous headache. He took a kerchief from the sleeve of his robe and held it over his nose to filter the stench of the floral scent.

The woman was sitting on a cot, her arms around her knees. Her bare feet were dirty and her hair in wild disarray. The sleeve of her gown was torn at one shoulder. She had not spoken since being brought to the Tribunal Hall, but the resistance she'd put up as the guards had taken her into custody at Holy Dale, as she tried to hide in the cellar, had left one man with a black eye and another with a decided limp.

"What is your name?" Demonicus demanded.

Genny Sorn ignored the priest. She was concentrating on a childhood memory in order to block her thoughts from being intercepted.

"I only ask so we will know what to carve on your tombstone," the priest said dryly.

A faint contemptuous smile tugged at Genny's lips. She knew enough about Tribunal policy and the fate of a female prisoner condemned to death to know she'd end up in an unmarked grave in the unhallowed portion of the village cemetery.

"You don't have to die, though," Demonicus drawled. The lavender scent was suffocating him and he longed to be outside in the cold, cleansing air. "Tell us where Syn-Jern is and I will set you free."

Genny kept very still. When the Tribunal arrested her, they accused her of being the Outlaw's whore. It was soon apparent that these men thought Trace Sorn to be the man for whom they'd been searching all these months. The thought had almost made her smile.

"You are his wife," Demonicus stated and as the woman slowly turned her head to him, he smiled brutally. "You might have been able to hide your thoughts from me, but the servant woman could not."

Sara, Genny thought with dismay and wondered if the servant had gotten away.

"Oh, we will find her," Demonicus answered the wayward thought. He moved closer to Genny's cell. "I've no particular desire to see you hang. Tell me where he is and I will sign the papers to free you within the hour."

Genny lowered her feet to the cold stone floor, stood, and walked to the bars. She wrapped her hands around the metal and stared hatefully at her tormentor. "Would you like me to tell you where you can go and what you can do with your offer when you get there, priest?" she asked sweetly.

Demonicus stiffened. His eyes narrowed into two thin malevolent slits. "So be it," he said, spinning on his heel.

The door to her cell clanged loudly, shutting out what little light there had been from the interrogation room beyond. For the last two hours, she'd been hearing horrible screams coming from that room and knew without having to be told the screamer was her husband's half-brother. Even as that thought flitted through her mind, another pitiful scream echoed.

Genny walked to the cot and sat. Pulling her knees into the safety of her arms once more, she eyed the rat in the corner of the cell. "Are you one of his minions?' she asked with a snort. The rat lifted a paw and scrubbed at its whiskers, then scuttled through an opening in the stone.

Genny sighed, then rested her head on the damp wall behind her. The screams were reverberating and growing shriller as time passed. Not that she cared one way or the other what Demonicus did to Trace Sorn, or why, but the man had been gentle with her after the attack. A part of her did feel a twinge of pity at his predicament, but not enough to lose sleep over.

If she could sleep.

"Where are you, my love?" she whispered.

By now, he would know her fate and would be beside himself with fear. She hoped and prayed cooler heads would prevail and keep her husband from trying to rescue her.

ജ്ഞ

The bloody mess that had been Trace Sorn was thrown onto the trundle cart. The driver clicked the reins of his dray horse and set the cart into motion. The clip-clop of the hooves caught the attention of a few passersby, but most simply looked the other way as it passed. Traveling the track up to the Bone Yard, as the punishment square was called, the cart rumbled along with one wheel creaking and the other wobbling as though it would fall off the axle.

"What happened, Tully?" someone called out.

"Heart attack," the driver replied in a bored voice. He'd been looking forward to the hanging; had been eagerly anticipating seeing Duke Sorn dangling from the scaffold, gasping for breath. Now, all they had was a crippled body to hoist up as a reminder of the evils of going against the Tribunal.

Sometimes, life just wasn't fair, the driver thought.

From the shadows of the building across from the Tribunal Hall, Syn-Jern Sorn watched the changing of the guards. It was close to dawn and already ribbons of light were showing in the East. He had spied the captain of the guard going into the Hall a few minutes before and wondered how many men were inside the building. He'd counted five outside the Hall, including the two at the entrance. Since there was no back entrance and no windows or doors on any of the three other sides, the only way into and out of the building was through the two black doors flanked by the fresh armed guards.

When the trundle cart had pulled up in front of the Hall, Syn-Jern had known a moment of sheer panic. When he, himself, had been a prisoner in that vile place, a man had died while being interrogated and they had sent for the cart. Outside the triple-thick stone walls lined with sheets of lead to prevent sorcery from either escaping or entering, no one had heard the man's piteous screams. Syn-Jern knew first hand the horrors visited upon those who had been incarcerated in the Tribunal Hall. Though he did think Demonicus would torture Genny, he didn't know that for sure. If the priest thought she had information he could use, the bastard was not above abusing her in any manner he chose.

That, more than anything, tore at Syn-Jern Sorn's heart and set his nerves on end.

"They're bringing a body out," Heil reported from his advantage point a few feet away.

Syn-Jern closed his eyes, praying to whatever Pantheon might be listening that it not be his beloved whose broken body was tossed like so much garbage upon the rickety cart.

"It's Sorn," Heil said, letting out the breath he'd been holding for he knew if the body had been that of a woman, he'd have been hard pressed to keep Syni from shrieking like a madman as he ran pell-mell to the cart.

Syn-Jern opened his eyes and flinched as the cart rolled beneath the flare of the torchlight high on the Hall's entry wall. The gaping mouth and staring eyes of the brother he hadn't seen in over twelve years were hideous to behold.

"Rot in hell, you turd," Heil sneered, then turned, hawked a large wad of phlegm and spat on the ground. He made to leave, but Syn-Jern shook his head.

"My lady is still in there," Syn-Jern said.

The doors to the Tribunal Hall opened again and Syn-Jern was surprised to see Demonicus standing in the opening. Automatically, he shut down his thoughts, tamping them like a smoldering fire. Concentrating on the black dirt at his feet, he slowed his breath and heartbeat.

"I know you are listening, Syn-Jern!" Demonicus called out. "Where else would you be but near your whore?"

Heil jerked and would have fled had Syn-Jern not clamped a staying hand on the man's arm to prevent him from doing so. Though Syn-Jern said nothing to Heil, the other man understood and tried to relaxed, plastering himself against the wall behind them to stay out of any errant beam of light.

"Hear me, Sorn!" Demonicus called out. "At seven of the clock, I will bring your woman to the Bone Yard under ample guard. There, I will have her bound to the stake and burned as the witch she is!"

Syn-Jern bit his lip, dug his nails into his palms, and stopped breathing altogether so his presence would not be 'felt' by the warlock.

"She will die screaming in agony, Sorn, unless you turn yourself in to me!"

Heil turned and looked at Syn-Jern. The man beside him was trembling with the effort of keeping his thoughts hidden.

"Suit yourself!" Demonicus snarled. "Watch her die. It means nothing to me!"

The priest swept through the doors, lifting his hand to indicate they were to be locked behind his passing. As the heavy oak portals slammed shut, Syn-Jern was out of the alley and making his way to the horses.

"Where are we going?" Heil asked. He watched the Outlaw vault onto the back of his horse.

"Where does the Captain of the guard live?" Syn-Jern snarled.

"Loure?" Heil asked. "You mean Anson Loure?"

"Aye!"

Heil scratched his head. "Down at the end of the lane leading out to Veldon. Why?"

"Is he married?" was the growl.

"Aye," Heil said reluctantly. "He's not a bad sort though."

"Children?"

Heil stared into the enraged face of Syn-Jern Sorn and thought he saw death hovering there. He crossed himself then nodded. "Three little ones."

"Mount up," Syn-Jern ordered.

"You're going to take his children?" Heil asked, his disapproval tight on his lean face.

"He took my wife, I'll take his!" Syn-Jern responded. "Mount up!"

"You won't to harm the children?"

A wild streak of fury was pulsing through Syn-Jern and at that moment he would have slain a dozen men to free Genny, but he drew the line at harming children. "I'll harm no one unless I'm forced to, but I will have my lady free. Mount up or get the hell out of my way!"

Heil searched his leader's eyes for the answers he sought and decided he knew Sorn well enough to know he'd not harm an innocent. Without another comment or question, he mounted his steed.

ഊ

Anson Loure read the note.

He read it again, then slowly lowered the parchment roll to his lap. He stared across the room, his heart thudding painfully in his throat. Turning his head to the door behind which lay the interrogation cells, he felt the weight of the world settling on his shoulders.

"What does it say, sir?" one of the guards asked.

Anson had two choices as he saw it: he could turn the note over to Demonicus and allow his wife to be executed by the Outlaw or he could turn the prisoner over to the Outlaw's men and be executed himself for treason. The decision wasn't all that hard to make for Anson Loure adored the mother of his children.

Re-rolling the parchment, Anson shrugged indifferently. "It says we are to escort the prisoner to the Carbondale Gate and exchange her for the Outlaw."

"Lawh!" the other guard whispered. "He really gonna turn himself in for his doxie?"

Anson nodded. "It would seem so." He stood, walked to the fireplace that provided the only warmth in the Interrogation Facility and tossed the parchment into the flames. "Bring her out," he ordered.

The guards left their captain standing at the hearth, his attention on the leaping fire. He was sweating profusely, though his body was as cold as ice. He was peripherally aware of the ticking clock across the room and looked that way, stunned to see it was closing in on five o'clock. He had less than two hours to get the woman out of the facility and into Serenia before his own wife was murdered. They would have to ride as hard as they could to make the deadline and he had to hope Demonicus was not an early riser.

"Here she is, Captain."

Anson had not seen the prisoner and was surprised to see she bore a resemblance to his beloved wife. His heart melted a bit at the sight of the prisoner's bruises and tattered clothing.

"It seems you are to be traded," he informed the woman.

"For whom?" she was quick to ask, her face turning pale.

A part of him wanted to hurt her, to punish her for being the reason his own wife was in dire trouble, but he knew if the tables were turned, he'd be just as uncompromising and vengeful as the Outlaw.

"What does it matter?" Loure snapped. "Shackle her."

"I'll not go if it is Syn-Jern you mean to take!" she told him and struggled with the men trying to slip the heavy manacles into place around her wrists. "Do you hear me?"

Anson had no choice but to have her gagged. One scream from her mouth; one shrill protest could bring Demonicus down on them. But even her scrambling was distracting and would draw attention so he went to her, doubled his fist and slammed it into her chin, rendering her unconscious.

"Lawh," the guard laughed as the prisoner sagged against him. "You know how to handle 'em, don't you, sir?"

"Just get her the hell up and let's get out of here!" Anson growled.

Heil waited until the three horses had cleared the Tribunal grounds before he lifted his fingers to his mouth and whistled softly. From down the street a ways, he heard the answering whistle. He was about to turn to his horse when he saw the door to the inn open and the tall cadaverous priest exiting the establishment.

"Hell!" Heil breathed and started to whistle again. Just as he put his thumb and forefinger into his mouth, he saw Demonicus turn toward him. Dawn was just breaking over the dome of the Tribunal Hall and he knew the priest could see him where he stood. He froze, unable to move, and felt a trickle of urine seeping down his leg. Groaning at the humiliation of pissing his breeches, he felt his face flame.

"Are you afraid of me, little man?"

The thought snaked through Heil's head. The sorcerer's mouth had not opened; he had not spoken. But as surely as the sun was rising higher in the sky, the priest had spoken to Heil and the words brought on an avalanche of piss.

Demonicus threw his head back and laughed. It pleased him to know men feared him and his power so greatly they would do what that one had just done. So filled with his own self-importance, the warlock was still chuckling as he entered the Tribunal Hall. Two minutes later, he was back outside, his face rigid with fury and his hooded eyes seeking the man who had been standing across the square.

"Find him!" Demonicus ordered. "Now!"

# Chapter Nineteen

ANGIE LOURE ACCEPTED THE WATER FROM HER CAPTOR AND DRANK slowly. She watched him as he paced like a weretiger from one side of the clearing to the other. His handsome face was drawn, his eyes haunted, and she felt a great pity well up inside her.

"You love her very much, don't you, Milord?" she asked.

"More than my own life," he answered. He stopped pacing, listened, and his frown grew darker when there was no sound coming from the direction of the village.

"I am not sure my husband will do as you ask," she said quietly, though she knew that was a lie and from the look her captor gave her, she knew he realized it was, as well.

The Carbondale Gate was less than ten feet from where she sat and it would have been easy to get up and run to the other side. Not that his long legs could not easily catch her if she tried such a ploy, she thought as she took another sip of water.

"Do you smell that?" Syn-Jern asked her.

Angie sniffed. "Smells like rotten eggs," she commented. "Mayhaps there is sulfur water nearby."

Syn-Jern put a hand to his forehead. Over the last half-hour, he'd developed a wicked headache and the strong stench of sulfur was making the pain worse. "Where the hell are they?" he asked. "They should be here by now."

Angie yawned and wondered how her mother-in-law was coping with the bantlings. The woman was a selfish sort and had not appreciated being roused from her bed to baby-sit while her son's wife was being kidnapped.

"Where is that smell coming from?" Syn-Jern grated.

His captive started to reply when the sound of thundering hooves shook the ground beneath her feet. She shot up from the log upon which she'd been sitting, and would have thanked the gods for her husband's arrival had the racing horses not been coming from behind her on the Serenian side of the border instead of in front of her from Virago.

Syn-Jern drew his sword and ran to the woman, grabbed her arm and pulled her with him into the safety of the trees. He had no idea who was in such a gods-be-damned big hurry but a lone man and woman against so many weren't the kind of odds that were in his favor. He yanked her down beside him so that they were hidden in the undergrowth beneath a gnarled cypress tree. Too late, he realized her mount and his were tied right out in the open. The passersby had no chance of missing them. He groaned, slapping a hand to his forehead.

"Milord!" Angie whispered. "They're stopping!"

Syn-Jern's grip tightened around the hilt of his sword and he looked at her. "Run," he told her. "Get as far from me as you can!"

Angie opened her mouth to protest, not wanting to be separated from him, but he was already up, moving away from her. She looked around her, saw a pathway through the trees, and scrambled to her feet, moving as quickly as her long skirt would allow.

"Syn-Jern!"

Angie stopped, looked behind her, and saw Kerm Gill dismounting. With a sigh of relief and a hand to her wildly beating heart, she stayed where she was, watching the men—there were close to a hundred of them—filling the clearing beneath the Gate.

Relieved the horsemen were his own men, Syn-Jern sheathed his sword and pushed his way out of the thick growth into which he'd hidden himself. "By the gods, but it took you long enough to catch up with me," he grumbled. He wasn't surprised to see Weir and Tiernan with the men, but didn't see Patrick among them.

"What the hell are you doing out here?" Weir barked, flinging a leg over his horse's head. "Where is Genny?"

The sound of riders coming from the Viragonian side of the border put the sword hand of every man there on the hilt of his weapon. The skirl of blades being drawn from their sheaths rang on the morning air.

Angie backed into the darkening shadows of the forest. She was of the opinion that she would not make her presence known to even her husband until the matter of the Outlaw's woman was settled. With all her heart, she wanted the tall blond man to gain his lady, cross over into the sanctuary of Serenia, and flee to some distant shore where they could live happily ever after.

"Tribunal guards!" Neevens called out. He was standing in the stirrups, peering down the road. "Three horses, two guards, one…" He stopped, then smiled broadly. "One awfully mad-looking woman!"

Syn-Jern was standing directly beneath the arch of the Carbondale Gate. He wasn't listening to Neevens. His full attention was on the cloud of dust being thrown by the hooves of the advancing steeds. The sun had gone behind a cloud and the air was chillier than it had been a few moments before. That vile stench of sulfur was even more pronounced and made his eyes water so badly he had to rub away the moisture.

"Anson," Angie whispered as she recognized her husband when he rode into the clearing. With him was his second in command, Rynen. She braced her hand against the bole of a huge white oak tree and peered from behind it.

"I've your woman," she heard Anson shout when he was a hundred yards away. "Where's mine?"

Syn-Jern glanced toward the spot where he'd last seen the Tribunal captain's wife. He was not surprised to see her making her way toward him. He'd not abused her in any way so she had no reason to fear him.

"She's here," Syn-Jern replied. "Bring my wife to me!"

Anson saw Angie coming from the trees and breathed a sigh of relief. The sky was lowering, the light fading. He looked up, stunned to see the sky boiling black as midnight in places. If it was going to storm, he wanted to get his lady home to safety before the vicious Viragonian weather started zinging and popping all about them.

"I'll bring her to the Gate," Anson answered. "Angie, are you all right?"

"I am fine, husband," Angie replied. "I am happy to see you, though." She came to stand beside Syn-Jern, smiling shyly at him.

"Thank you, lady," he whispered for he knew she could have made matters much worse if she had been of a mind to.

Behind him, Weir and Tiernan, who had dismounted as well, flanked Syn-Jern. Their weapons were lowered, but it would not take much for either of them to bring those deadly blades into play. Weir was looking at Genny, half-amused at the gag clenched between his sister's teeth. Tiernan was looking at the sky, his forehead creased with concern as lightning began crawling across the firmament.

"Syn-Jern," Tiernan said uneasily. "Have him hurry up. I don't like the looks of the sky."

"I've no great desire to be toasted, either," Anson said, having heard the Serenian nobleman. He stopped his horse a few feet from Syn-Jern, dismounted, then walked to Genny's horse. With great care, he helped her down, fished in his pocket for the key to her shackles, unlocked them, them stepped back as his prisoner jerked the gag from her mouth. "Lady, I am sorry I hit you," he said earnestly, "but it was a necessity."

Genny did not reply to his apology. She ran to her husband, grateful to feel his arms enclose her.

Grice Rynen was as loyal to the Tribunal as a man could be, but he made no move to stop the prisoner from running across the border and throwing herself into the arms of the Outlaw. He was not a stupid man and realized what the situation was.

He also knew what the stench wafting around them meant. He turned the head of his mount, put heels to the steed's ribs and galloped away, never looking behind him.

"He'll protect his arse, I'm thinking," Angie remarked as she went to her husband.

"Aye," Anson allowed. "He'll tell them he didn't know what I was about." He shrugged. "That is true." He enfolded his lady within the protection of his strong arms and looked over her head, straight into the eyes of the Outlaw.

"He only did it to get her back, Anson," Angie said quietly.

"I know why he did it, Angie, but that doesn't matter. I'm the one who'll have to pay for it."

Syn-Jern heard the remark. He eased Genny from him and pushed her toward Weir. "Come with us, then," he said. "Unless you're so enamored of the Tribunal you can see no other way of life."

Anson shook his head. "My life is in Virago, Sorn. I'll stand my punishment for allowing her to escape."

"They could well hang you," Syn-Jern warned.

Angie tightened her grip around her husband's waist. She looked up into his worried eyes. "He is an honorable man, husband. We could do no better than to go with him."

"You trust him?" Anson asked. At her nod, he demanded to know what of their children.

"I can send word to have them brought to us," Syn-Jern told him. He shielded his eyes from the harsh wind that had suddenly sprung to life around them.

"And have them be fugitives all their lives?" Anson queried. "What life is that for a child?"

"What life is it where a woman can be discarded like so much trash?" Genny asked.

Angie dug her hands into her husband's shirt. "She's right, Anson. We've two daughters to think of. What if a nobleman wanted them as concubines? We would not be able to stop them."

"There is no such dishonor in Chrystallus," Genny called out. "Come with us! Find a better way to live."

The wind began to roar so loudly, it was impossible to hear Anson Loure's reply. Around them, the leaves were being whipped into frenzy and the tree branches overhead clicked together with a vengeance.

Genny was shivering with the chill that had swept down from the Serenian Alps and was grateful for the cloak her brother laid over her shoulders. She turned to thank him and as she did, her attention went to the Western horizon.

She screamed and those gathered turned to see what had frightened her.

It was eel-like, Its elongated neck plated with ebon scales. Two glowing red eyes filled the sky as the demon squirted across the heavens toward them.

"Raphian," someone named the demon slithering out of the clouds.

The horses screamed with terror and began to twist and buck beneath their riders until all but a few of the men had been thrown to the ground. The frightened animals bolted, turning tail and running back the way they had come, the remaining riders hanging on for dear life.

"Syn-Jern!" Genny screamed, trying to walk against the wind to get to her husband. She put out her hand; he put out his; and just as their fingertips touched, the sky split open with a vicious stab of lightning.

The wind pushed against Syn-Jern and he stumbled to the ground as a vortex swept past him, caught Genny within its grip, and swirled her to the other side of the Gate.

Anson Loure was thrown against a tree and knocked unconscious, unaware that his wife was hovering over him, shielding him from the flying debris being pitched about in the gale force winds.

"Genny!" Syn-Jern bellowed. He scrambled to his feet only to be tossed aside like a child's toy. He rolled along the ground, barely missing the stampeding hooves of the fleeing horses of his men.

Weir and Tiernan had been forced to the ground; their arms over their eyes as stinging missiles of tree limb and sand spiraled about them. The overpowering odor of sulfur and the punishing sand made it difficult to breathe. Neither man was able to move in the crush of the devastating wind.

Lin Su, buffeted by a solid sheet of sand, was trying to reach his mistress, but the wind kept him back, pushing him farther and farther from her with every step he tried to take.

Kerm Gill and his little brother had managed to bury their faces in the protection of their coats, but the lashing wind whipped about their unprotected hands and left savage cuts on the flesh.

On the Viragonian side of the Gate, Genny was swept up into the funnel of the wind. Her hair was whipping about her face, cutting her. She screamed with terror as the wind took her higher and higher.

Syn-Jern shielded his eyes from the stinging intrusion of the sand, but could not see his wife. He was on the Serenian side of the border. "Genny!" he called.

"Sorn!"

With the calling of the name, the wind died completely. The sand fell from the air and pooled at the feet of the men. Leaves and branches fell into heaps at the side of the road, and the air—though still saturated with the stench of sulfur—grew still.

Weir was the first to notice the priest. He grabbed Tiernan's arm. "Demonicus!" he gasped.

Syn-Jern got to his feet, turning, searching for Genny. He yelled her name and would have crossed the border into Virago had Tiernan not reached out to keep him from doing so. He glared at the priest. "Where is my woman?" he shouted.

"Look!" the priest shouted and pointed toward the heavens.

Syn-Jern groaned with fear and fell to his knees, his head back as he stared at the sight above him.

Genny was suspended in mid-air as though she lay in the arms of an invisible giant. Hovering over her was Raphian, the demon Destroyer of Men's Souls. The vile beast's maw was open, Its glistening teeth sharp and dripping venom.

"You want her to die such a death, Sorn?" Demonicus asked.

"Genny," Syn-Jern whispered as though his heart would break.

"Cross over," Demonicus ordered and as he spoke a dozen or more horsemen rode into the clearing. The priest had no need to turn to the Tribunal guards who had come to do his bidding.

"Syn-Jern, don't," Tiernan warned. "He'll kill her anyway."

Weir was as white as the snow atop Mount Serenia. He stared at his sister's inert body and wondered if she still lived.

"Aye, she lives," Demonicus intoned and waved his hand. Genny lifted her head, realized where she was and screamed again.

"Don't hurt her," Syn-Jern pleaded.

"Cross over into Virago," Demonicus told him.

Syn-Jern looked away from his wife, turning his full attention to Demonicus. "Don't hurt her."

"She is of no use to me and Raphian does not particularly care for the taste of female flesh," Demonicus answered, laughing at the stricken look on Syn-Jern's face. "Cross over, allow my men to bind you, and I will place that whore as gently in her brother's arms as a feather falling to ground from a duckling's molt." He shrugged hatefully. "I'll even allow your men to go their own way. I want you, Sorn, not them."

"No, Syn-Jern," Tiernan told him. "The bastard can't be trusted."

"What choice does he have?" Demonicus asked. "Either he surrenders to me or his precious wife will be Raphian's next meal and I'll order the lot of you hunted down like the dogs you are!" He pointed to the demon. "You can escape the Tribunal, but you will not be able to escape the retribution of the Destroyer!"

Above them, the demon roared in anticipation of such a treat, its vile breath bringing instant nausea to those gathered. Even the Arch-Prelate turned his head in disgust.

There was no choice, Syn-Jern knew. Genny, as well as his men, would be cast to the demon if he did not obey Demonicus' wishes. What was one life compared to all the others? Without giving himself time to think of the agony in store for him, he stepped over the invisible line that separated Serenia—and safety—from Virago. As soon as he was out of reach of his men, the Tribunal guards rushed toward him, intent on subduing him, but neither they, nor the priest, counted on the awesome power Sorn could wield. Before the first guard reached him, all six were flung backwards with the wave of the Outlaw's arm.

"Bring her down!" Syn-Jern shouted. When Demonicus did not move quickly enough for him, Syn-Jern waved his arm again, and the Tribunal guards still mounted flew from their horses.

"Stop!" Demonicus ordered. In his haste to arrest the Outlaw, he had completely forgotten the man's own magical abilities.

"Bring her down and I will allow your men to bind me. Until then…" Syn-Jern pointed a rigid arm at the priest and Demonicus rose into the air and hung there, four feet from the ground.

The priest's thin mouth twisted with outrage and he turned his attention to Genny. With a sweep of his red-clad arm, Syn-Jern's wife plummeted from the sky like a rock.

Lin Su gasped, his eyes popping from his head as he rushed forward. He caught his mistress, staggering beneath her weight as she landed heavily in his arms, and went to one knee in the sand to keep from dropping her.

"Take him!" Demonicus snarled.

With his men safely on the Serenian side of the board, his wife unharmed in the arms of her protector, Syn-Jern made no attempt to escape as the Tribunal guards rushed him once more. He flinched as his arms were dragged behind his back and the heavy manacles were clamped savagely around his wrists. The weight of the chains pulled his shoulders back and the discomfort was immediate.

"Use your power, Syni," Weir called out. "Use your power!"

"Aye," Demonicus laughed. "Use your power, my sweet thief, and break free!"

Syn-Jern knew he could not. He hung his head as the guards put rough hands on his upper arms to lead him to the horses.

"Syn-Jern, use your power!" Weir shouted. "Genny's safe. Use your power!"

"He can't," Tiernan said quietly.

"Why not?" Weir demanded.

"The shackles are made of lead," Demonicus answered for the McGregor. "No sorcerer can defeat that element!"

Weir would have rushed across the border, some of his men with him, but Tiernan stepped directly into Saur's path. "No," he said. "Don't. You'll only end up as fodder for the demon."

Saur turned his attention skyward and groaned with frustration. Raphian was still lurking in the black boiling sky, its forked tongue lapping hapless birds into its giant maw. Its crimson eyes glowed with anticipation; the wicked fangs glinted with promise.

"We've lost him," Tiernan said and his voice was filled with grief. "We can't fight a creature such as this one."

"I will not accept that!" Weir hissed. He looked about them, searching for the only other man he knew would risk life and limb to gain Syn-Jern's freedom. "Where is Patrick?"

No one knew. Kasella had not been with them when they had ridden from Ciona.

"Has no one seen him this morn?" Weir demanded, realizing that he had not seen Patrick since around midnight.

The men shook their heads. Kasella's whereabouts were a mystery.

A moan from Genny as she began to regain consciousness brought her brother's immediate concern to her. He ran to her and took her forcibly from Lin Su's arms. Cradling her against his chest, he smoothed her hair and cooed to her.

"Syn-Jern?" she questioned.

Weir glanced at his brother-in-law as Syn-Jern's was placed astride one of the Tribunal horses. "We'll get him back, Dearling. I promise you we will," he told his sister.

Genny gasped, realizing what must have happened and began to struggle to break free of her brother's hold. "Syn-Jern!" she yelled, scrambling to her feet. When she saw the predicament into which her husband had fallen, she ran toward the Gate, intending to join him.

"Tiernan, stop her!" Syn-Jern shouted.

The McGregor leapt after the running woman and managed to grab her wrist just as she reached the archway of the Gate. He jerked her backward and spun her into the hard imprisonment of his arms. Although she fought him, twisting, and turning to break free of his grasp, he held her even tighter, refusing to allow her to do so. She cursed him, scratched his arms, and kicked his shins with her bare feet, but her struggles were in vain. Tiernan McGregor had no intention of allowing Syn-Jern's wife to join him in his fate.

"Syn-Jern!" Genny cried, her heart breaking. She managed to free one arm and extended it toward her husband in pleading. "Syn-Jern!"

Demonicus swung into the saddle of his own mount and sawed on the reins. Without looking behind him to make sure the Tribunal guards followed, he kicked the palfrey into motion.

"Your Worship, what of the captain?" the guard holding the reins to Syn-Jern's horse asked. He glanced at Anson Loure and met the pleading eyes of the captain's wife.

The priest did not hear the question. His mind was on the torture he planned for Syn-Jern Sorn.

"He was trying to save his lady," Syn-Jern told the guard. "You would have done the same."

"Shut your mouth, thief!" the guard growled.

"Leave him be, Halton," another guard suggested. "The captain will resign. Mark my words. He's a Tribunalist to the core."

"Aye, but he'll hang alongside the Outlaw for letting the woman escape," Halton predicted. Without another glance at the captain's wife, the guard urged his mount to forward.

Syn-Jern jerked in the saddle as his horse leapt forward. He twisted, wanting, needing one last look at his wife. Tears came into his eyes when he saw her stricken face and trembling lips. "I love you," he called to her and was rewarded by Genny's cry of uncontrollable anguish.

Angie Loure tried to rouse her husband, but the man lay like a rock on the hard ground. "Anson, wake up!" she begged. "We have to leave this place." She looked up at the demon still hovering overhead and would swear every day of her life the evil thing winked at her. "Anson!"

"Help her," Tiernan told Kerm and the big man hurried to the Loure's aid.

Angie glanced at the McGregor. When the man nodded in reply to her silent question, she relaxed. Someone would go after her children and bring them to her and Anson. Only death and dishonor awaited her husband in Virago and she would have none of that. She smiled at Kerm as he bent over to scoop Anson from the ground.

"Sure knocked him out cold," Kerm stated.

"He's got a right hard noggin'," Angie said.

"And will have a right brutal headache I'm thinkin'," Kerm replied.

Genny pulled loose of Tiernan's hold and sank to the ground. She covered her face with her hands and began to keen. She rocked in her torment, her knees digging into the hard ground, but she did not feel the pain. Her world had ceased at the moment her husband had been taken from her; what was a physical pain?

"Syn-Jern," she whispered over and over again. "Syn-Jern."

Her tears flowed like molten silver down her cheeks and she reached up to swipe at the moisture.

"Syn-Jern, I love you. *I love you!*"

It was a pitiful moan of anguish: the voice of a breaking heart.

"Syn-Jern!"

The Outlaw's woman threw back her head and howled her pain to the heavens.

"Lords alive," Neevens whispered. "She sounds like a Chalean banshee, she does."

Lin Su went to his mistress and hunkered down beside her. Though he did not touch her, his support was there and those who came near her were warned off with a scowl.

"It's leaving," Weir said, and all eyes went to the heavens.

The sky was boiling, the clouds swirling counterclockwise like an inverted cyclone. Raphian opened its grotesque maw, bellowed, then was sucked through the bruised sky. Almost immediately, the stench of sulfur dissipated.

"Mount up!" Weir ordered. "We'll go af—"

"No," Tiernan told him. "We stay where we are."

"The hell we will!" Weir shouted. "I am going after my friend! Do you actually think we'd leave him to the Tribunal's tender care?"

"Aye!" the men shouted. Kerm's voice was the loudest.

"We'll go back to Ciona and foment a plan, Saur," Tiernan stressed. "One that won't get the lot of us killed or jailed alongside him. Demonicus will sign arrest warrants for every man he can put a name to who was here today. There's not a one of us—myself included—who'll be safe from Tribunal justice."

"Then what do you suggest, Prince Tiernan?" Kerm asked.

"We'll have to leave our countries," Tiernan said sadly. "Head for Chrystallus or Ionary. Anywhere the Tribunal does not hold sway."

"Our families, too?" someone asked.

"Aye," Tiernan sighed. "Your families, too." He hung his head, knowing he could never go back to the Court of the Winds at Boreas Keep. He would not endanger his brothers or his father, the King. He, too, was an outlaw, now.

"Didn't think on this happening," Kerm said, voicing the thoughts of the other men. "Didn't think we'd have to leave Virago."

"Until we have Syn-Jern with us," Weir vowed, "we ain't going nowhere!"

## Chapter Twenty

PATRICK HAD DREAMED OF HOLY DALE MANOR MANY TIMES OVER THE years. Long before he ever met Syn-Jern Sorn, he'd had dreams of the country estate and the cave beneath the cellar. He knew of the hidden excavation in the mountain beyond where horses and men could be housed and had been the one to tell Weir of its existence.

It would have been easy for the Ionarian to find his way through the cave to the trapdoor that led into the false cellar, but he did not enter Holy Dale that way. He walked boldly through the front door, climbed the stairs to the upper floor, and entered the bedroom of Rosa-Lynn Sorn.

"Come to slit my throat, McGregor?" the woman asked. She was seated at the window, her back to the door.

"I would like nothing better, but I've other plans for you," Patrick told her.

Rosa-Lynn turned her head to look at the man whose voice she did not recognize and was stunned. At first, she thought it was Syn-Jern standing in the doorway, but the eyes were wrong. "Who are you?" she whispered.

"Does it matter?" he asked.

She stared at the stranger for a long moment, then shrugged indifferently. "I suppose not." She turned back to the window.

"Feeling sorry for yourself, Duchess?" Patrick sneered.

"No," she replied and was surprised to realize she had spoken the truth. What she felt was a numbness that had turned her cold. "For the man I've betrayed thrice now." She hung her head and buried her face in her hands. "Whose life is forfeit because of my selfish ego."

"Do you want to help him?"

"It's too late."

"There is a way."

Rosa-Lynn sighed. "There is no way. He is deep within the bowels of the Tribunal Hall, my friend. No one can get to him."

"His priest can."

She slowly lifted her head and turned her bleak gaze to him. "For what purpose?"

Patrick stuck his hand into the pocket of his jacket. He withdrew a small vial made of ruby glass. "This is Maiden's Briar," he said. "It is the most potent poison in the world."

"You would kill him?" she asked incredulously.

Patrick Kasella raised his chin. "I would rather see him die a painless death than suffer the tortures that await him come morning." He went to her and stood looking down, the pain evident in his eyes. "They will brutalize him, Rosa-Lynn. They will hurt him in ways you can not begin to understand." His voice broke and he had to stop. Squeezing his eyes shut, he paid no heed to the tears falling down his cheeks.

"We can not allow that," she said softly, recognizing love when it confronted her.

"No," Patrick replied, "we can not."

"How do we stop it?"

"According to Tribunal law, he can have one visitor on the night before he is executed. It can only be a family member," Patrick explained. "You are his only living family save Genny and it would be folly to allow her to visit him."

The fate of Syn-Jern's wife meant nothing to Rosa-Lynn. "You want me to go to him and give him…" She pointed at the vial lying in Patrick's palm. "That?"

He shook his head. "I would not ask it of you, Lady. I will do it."

"How?" she asked incredulously.

"Take me with you as your spiritual advisor."

"Me?" she snorted. "I have no spiritual advisor."

"Does the Tribunal know that?" Patrick challenged.

Rosa-Lynn thought on it for a moment, then shook her head. "I see no reason why they should, but the priests who visit here are known by the guards, I'm sure. They would ask questions you may not be able to answer."

"They'll ask me no questions, Lady," he replied. "I guarantee it."

"And just how will you do that, Milord?" she asked.

"I will dress as one of the Brethren of the Mists. No guard would dare come close enough to question me."

Rosa-Lynn shivered, thinking of the leprous clerics from the Isle of Dayle. She stared at him, her appreciative gaze wandered over his handsome face, then she shook her head. "It will not work. Even were we to rub floured water over your face, your male beauty would shine like a new copper coin." She shook her head again. "No, it would not work."

Patrick laid the vial in her lap then reached once more inside his jacket. This time he withdrew one of the many masks he'd carved over the years and slipped it over his face. "Even if I looked like this?" he asked.

Rosa-Lynn recoiled, her hand flying to her mouth. Her eyes wide, her throat clogged with bile, she pushed his hand from his face. "Put that away!" she hissed, the mask far too real for her peace of mind.

"It will work," he told her. "The guards will take one look at this gruesome thing and not come within a mile of me."

She swallowed the bitter vetch in her mouth and looked down at the mask dangling from his fingertips. She studied it for a long while, then turned to him. "It might work," she said.

"It has to work," Patrick insisted.

Rosa-Lynn cocked her head to one side. "You love him that much?" she asked.

Patrick did not hesitate. "With all my heart and all my soul for as long as I draw breath and even when I do not." He smiled sadly. "Even into the next world and beyond," he whispered.

"Yet you would do this to him?" she asked, touching the vial.

"I can not bear the thought of him suffering in any way," Patrick answered. "If I can prevent it, I will move heaven and earth to do so."

She lifted her hand and laid it gently against Patrick's cheek. "Would that I could find a love so pure and so selfless." She sighed. "I have a feeling such is the love he bears this woman Genny."

"You would be right in assuming so," he replied. He reached up to cover her hands with his. "Will you help me, Lady?' he asked.

"Aye," she answered. "It is the least I can do for him."

ꕥ

Syn-Jern lay on his side in the cell, his knees drawn up to help ward off the cold and the pain from the repeated blows that had broken at least two of his ribs. His breathing was ragged and the musty smell of the hay on that he lay made it even more difficult for him to draw air into his bruised lungs.

They had beaten him so severely, he was disoriented, his thinking clouded. The dank cell spun each time he tried to lift his head. Although they had pummeled his body and kicked him twice in the head, his face was untouched.

Deliberately so.

"Do not hit him in the face," Demonicus had ordered as he sat watching the beating. "I want no visible proof that he has been misused."

Why that was, Syn-Jern could not guess. Surely the priest did not think the people of Wixenstead stupid. Each of them knew what went on behind the thick doors of the Tribunal Hall's interrogation facility. Hadn't Trace Sorn's battered and broken body been hoisted up the scaffolding at the Bone Yard for everyone to see?

"Not his face!" Demonicus had bellowed when Rynen's fist plowed into the side of Syn-Jern's head.

The blow had brought the stars down from the heavens and Syn-Jern had passed out.

He shifted on the straw, gasping as pain broke over every portion of his ill-used body. The floor beneath him was wet with his own urine and the cloying feel of it on his britches was almost more than he could bear. When he heard the door open down the corridor, he groaned, thinking his tormentors were returning to beat him again.

There was a strange scraping sound, then the clink of keys against the iron door.

"You've visitors, Outlaw!" a guard said nervously as he unlocked the cell door.

With the room shifting around him, Syn-Jern could not make out the faces of the two people who entered his cell. The faces kept swirling out of focus and he finally closed his eyes to keep the nausea the motion brought from getting the better of him.

"Would you like to stay with us, sergeant?" one of the visitors asked.

The guard backed away from the priest. "No offense, Your Grace, but I've got things to see to!"

Syn-Jern opened his eyes and tried desperately to focus for he'd recognized Patrick's voice. "Pat…" he began, only to have something coarse cover his mouth.

"Be still, you poor misguided creature," Patrick said.

"Argh!" the guard whined when he saw the leper put his vile hand—covered with burlap though it was—over the prisoner's mouth. Shuffling away as fast as he could, he shuddered at the thought of touching Sorn now that one of the Brethren had laid hands to him.

"He's gone," Rosa-Lynn whispered just as the door to the interrogation room clanged shut.

"You know what to do," Patrick told her.

Rosa-Lynn nodded. She left the cell and hurried to the locked door through which the guard had exited. "Open up!" she demanded, banging on the door. "Don't leave me in here with that foul beast!" She banged twice more before the door opened.

As soon as the door closed behind Rosa-Lynn, Patrick took his hand from Syn-Jern's mouth. "Listen to me very carefully, Syn-Jern," he said, wasting no time. "There's no way in hell I can get you out of here, but I can make damned sure you will suffer no more abuse at the hands of these bastards." He fished a hand into the sleeve of his robe and drew out the red vial. "This is Maiden Briar's. Do you understand?"

Although the room was spinning, Syn-Jern's thought processes were returning to normal. He understood very well what Patrick Kasella was offering him. His vision jumped to the vial, skidded off, and returned.

"It is painless, Syn-Jern," Patrick assured him. "You will feel nothing."

The room tilted crazily then straightened and as it did, Syn-Jern's vision cleared somewhat and he was able to see Patrick's face. He sucked in a gulp of air that almost sent him back into unconsciousness with the pain of it.

"You recognize my friend Brother Yul?" Patrick said, his voice filled with a touch of humor.

"Patrick?" Syn-Jern questioned and was rewarded with his friend lifting the mask just long enough for Syn-Jern to be sure it was Patrick beneath the horrid apparition.

"Good disguise, eh?" Patrick asked.

"Aye," Syn-Jern agreed. "I can see how you were able to get in here."

"We have Rosa-Lynn Sorn to thank for that." At Syn-Jern's look of disbelief, Patrick shrugged. "The woman is beside herself with guilt and was more than willing to help me."

"Don't trust her," Syn-Jern warned.

"I don't," Patrick answered.

Syn-Jern's gaze went to the ruby red vial. "No pain?" he asked.

Patrick bit his lip, then answered, his voice breaking. "I promise you, on my love for you, there will be no pain."

Despite the agony in his battered ribs, Syn-Jern lifted a hand and touched Patrick's cheek. He smiled sadly as Patrick turned his lips into the palm and kissed the dirty flesh.

"I never meant to hurt you, Patrick," he said.

Patrick took Syn-Jern's hand in his own. "You did not." Tears cascaded down Kasella's face. "I knew you could never love me. I—"

"I do love you, Patrick," Syn-Jern said. "As the brother I never really had."

Patrick drew in a strangled breath and his grip tightened on Syn-Jern's hand.

"Give me the vial, Patrick," Syn-Jern asked. "Before I change my mind."

Patrick was trembling so violently he almost dropped the vial as he uncorked it. With infinite care, he lifted Syn-Jern's head and placed the rim of the vial against his friend's lips. As Syn-Jern's eyes met his, Patrick whimpered with grief and had to look away as the dark blue liquid flowed into the mouth of the man he loved.

The taste was sweet, but it burned Syn-Jern's mouth and made his eyes water. Almost immediately, his world began to shut down. The room grew fuzzy; the floor beneath him seemed to melt away. "Hold me," he asked.

Patrick sat down beside Syn-Jern and drew the limp man into his arms. He cradled him against his chest, rocking him, crooning softly. He stroked the damp hair from Syn-Jern's dirty face then lowered his head to place a gentle kiss on the other man's brow.

"Patrick?" Syn-Jern said, the word slurred. He found the strength to touch Patrick's forearm.

"Aye, my beloved?" Patrick answered.

"Take…care…of…her…for…me."

"I will."

The hand on his arm fell away and Patrick threw back his head and sobbed.

ꕥ

"I ain't touching that diseased beastie!" the guard gasped. He pointed at the priest lying on the floor of the Outlaw's cell. "I ain't doing it! Ain't my fault he keeled over dead!" He looked at the prisoner sitting so still in the corner of the cell and wondered how the man could sleep through all the noise the Duchess was making.

Rosa-Lynn snorted with contempt. "Then go out and find someone who will!" she demanded. "You can't leave him there!"

"Who you gonna get to touch one of them things?" the guard demanded.

The Duchess pushed past the man and stomped down the hall. "Open the gods-be-damned door, fool!" she yelled to the man on the other side.

The door opened, but the man who had admitted her stepped well back from the woman, afraid she might be carrying the vile disease on her clothing.

Rosa-Lynn did not stop until she was at the double entry doors of the Tribunal Hall. She flung them open herself, went out into the courtyard, and looked about her. "Five gold pieces for the one of you who will help me!" she said to the raggedy-dressed men loitering there.

"What we'uns gots to do to earn it, Your Grace?" a stooped beggar asked slyly.

"Carry my priest from the cell of the Outlaw!" she snapped.

The beggar sidled closed. "What's wrong wid 'em?"

Rosa-Lynn ground her teeth together. "He is one of the Brethren and—"

"The hell you say!" the beggar snarled. "I ain't touching none of that!"

"Six gold pieces!" she called out as the man moved away. When he kept walking, she upped the price to eight.

"Nah," the beggar spat.

"The man is dead. He can't harm you!" Rosa-Lynn ground out. "Nine!"

The beggar turned, his grimy face pocked with acne. He walked back to her, scratching at the stained crotch of his breeches. "Make it twenty and I'll do it," he countered.

Rosa-Lynn curled her lip, but she knew if Demonicus found Patrick Kasella in Syn-Jern's cell come morning, the priest would be after her. "Done," she said, knowing she had no other choice. "Follow me."

The beggar ambled slowly behind her, twice telling the uppity woman to hold her water when she bade him hurry. Once inside the Tribunal Hall, he grinned at the guards. "Gonna have me plenty of the drink tonight, boys!" he chortled.

"You better drink your fill, then, fool," the sergeant warned, "for you'll catch what that one has sure as shit!"

A maniacal laugh erupted from the filthy man as he sidled down the corridor after the Duchess.

"By the gods, will you make haste!" Rosa-Lynn threw at him.

"You want me help or not, woman?" the beggar asked her.

"He's in there," Rosa-Lynn said, pointing.

The beggar found the priest lying on the floor. He looked at the body, turned to look at the prisoner who was sitting slumped in the corner, then stooped down to heft the priest into his arms. "By the gods, but this'n stinks," he said.

The guards who had followed at a safe distance moved back into the interrogation room. They wanted no contact with the woman, the beggar, or the priest.

"Lock that door behind you, Your Grace," the sergeant called out.

Rosa-Lynn glared at the man, barely able to see him he was so far away from her down the torch-lit corridor. Leaving the cell behind the beggar, she turned and pulled the cell door shut. Muttering a filthy word beneath her breath she reached for the key and turned it in the lock. She turned away from the door, took a step or two down the corridor, then stopped. She stood there for a moment, then her proud shoulders slumped.

Behind her was the only man who had ever really loved her. Though she had betrayed him and been the cause of his death, she found she could not simply walk away without asking for his forgiveness. He would not hear her in this world, but she had to believe he would hear her from the next. She could not live with herself otherwise.

Squaring her shoulders, she walked back to the cell door. Through the dim glow of the torchlight, she stared at him for a long moment, then very quietly, she asked his pardon for the sins she had committed against him and his.

"Your Grace!" the sergeant called. "You're time is up with the prisoner. Come away now!"

Rosa-Lynn knew she would hold the image of Syn-Jern Sorn sitting in the darkened corner of his cell for the rest of her life. She would see his splayed legs, his hands lying curled—palms up—in his lap. Her dreams would be filled with the tousled blond hair that covered his lowered head, shielding the face she so longed to see, even in death.

"Your Grace!"

"All right!" Rosa-Lynn yelled back, turning to send an angry glower to the beastly man. "I'm coming!"

With the intention of taking one last look at the man she had helped destroy, Rosa-Lynn directed her attention into the cell once more and found herself looking into the amused eyes of Patrick Kasella.

## Chapter Twenty-One

THE HARD-FACED MEN POSITIONED ABOUT THE BONE YARD WERE HEAVILY armed, their steely eyes glued to the crowd gathering for the hanging. No weapons were allowed beyond the wrought iron gates of the punishment yard for fear the peasants would revolt and try to free the Outlaw as he was brought to meet his fate. No ships were being allowed into the harbor for that same reason. Ships loaded with primed cannons blocked the entrance to the harbor and the guns on the battlement of the Tribunal Hall were pointed out to sea.

The roads into town were manned with checkpoints and identity papers were checked thoroughly. Those who could not be vouched for, were not allowed into the village and were turned away at sword point.

"A fine day for a hanging, eh, Your Worship?" the magistrate, Karl Krueger, commented. "The people will learn a lesson here this day!"

A muscle in Demonicus' jaw tightened. No one but he, himself, knew the prisoner being hanged this day was not the Outlaw, Syn-Jern Sorn. It would have been disastrous to let the townspeople know their hero had managed to escape the noose. Infuriated beyond endurance, upon finding a stranger in Sorn's cell, the Arch-Prelate had ordered the guards who had allowed this perfidy to occur, executed on the spot.

"But why, Your Worship?" the magistrate had asked, horrified when he'd heard the news.

"They allowed him visitors without consulting me!" Demonicus had roared. "That is unacceptable!"

Though the Duchess had managed to escape his net, the priest had no doubt he would eventually find her and she would die screaming in agony for her part in the deception.

What enraged Demonicus more than the escape of Sorn, was the calm way in which the man being hanged this day had stood the tortures inflicted upon him. Not once did he scream during even the most excruciating torments and he had not revealed his identity. Even the graduated rods could not spur him to reveal his secrets.

"Do you think they'll try to rescue him?" Krueger inquired, casting a sidelong glance at the angry Arch-Prelate.

"No," Demonicus sneered. "They'll not try."

Why should they? The priest thought viciously. They had their hero and the sacrificial lamb that had taken his place was going to his death without remorse.

The bell on the steeple of the temple rang once.

The magistrate rubbed his hands together. "It's starting!"

The bell tolled again with a ten seconds pause before the next peel.

The drums could be heard as the procession from the Tribunal Hall commenced. Heads turned in that direction and fingers pointed as the double black doors opened.

Two guards marched from the Tribunal Hall, their pikes at the ready. Behind them came the prisoner, shuffling along in the heavy manacles that bound him hand and foot. More guards followed the procession.

"He don't look none the worse for wear considering," the magistrate remarked. He couldn't help wincing at the terrible bruises and cuts on the prisoner's face.

"There is nothing I hate more than a brave man!" Demonicus spat. He narrowed his eyes. "Unless it is a man who would give his own life for another out of a misguided notion of justice!"

"True," Krueger sighed. "So very true, Your Worship."

Patrick Kasella was so detached from the goings on around him, it was all he could do not to giggle. The Maiden's Briar he had ingested the night before had numbed him to the world and enveloped him in cottony warmth. His nerve endings having been destroyed by the potent drug, pain was not something he could even feel. A sip or two more would have killed him, but that would have defeated the purpose.

"The Wind be at your back, Your Grace!" someone called to him from the crowd.

Patrick smiled. If there were any of these people gathered who realized he was not Syn-Jern Sorn, they would never admit to it. Here and there, he saw shocked expressions as he passed, but he wasn't sure if that was because his face had been mutilated by Demonicus' wrath or if those people knew he wasn't Syni.

Ah, Syni, he thought as he stumbled against the weight of the heavy lead chains dragging his shoulders down. Syni, my love. My heart. Are you safe, my beloved?

He lifted his head and looked about him, searching for that one face, that one friend whose presence he needed to see.

"Get up there!"

The crowd hissed as the lash was laid to the prisoner's back. Angry voices pulsed through the gathering.

Patrick climbed the stairs of the scaffold clumsily, the heavy weight of his shackles threatening to topple him from the structure. Had the black-masked executioner not put out a hard hand to keep him from doing just that, Patrick knew he would have fallen into the ranks of the guards flanking the apparatus.

There was no need to read the charges against him for there had been no trial.

There would be no last words allowed for it was no longer possible for Patrick Kasella to speak; the Maiden's Briar had paralyzed his vocal chords.

There would be no priest to give him absolution.

There would be no hood to block out the sight of the crowd as his neck snapped.

The rope was draped over his head and the noose tightened.

Patrick surveyed the crowd one last time and finally found the one face he'd been looking for.

On the balcony of the tax house, Lin Su lifted his hands and spoke to Patrick Kasella.

Patrick smiled.

What he had wanted to know, needed to 'hear', had been said.

He could die happy.

And he did as the trapdoor sprang and his body dropped through the opening.

# EPILOGUE

HE STOOD WITH HIS HANDS ON THE RAILING OF THE SHIP HE CALLED HIS own and stared out to sea. His midnight blue eyes were glazed with an inner pain that kept all but the companion at his side from disturbing him. The brisk sea wind tousled his long blond hair, whipping it around his face, but he did not seem to notice. His entire being was concentrated on the landmass falling away behind them. He barely noticed the other ship trailing in the wake of the Revenant.

Genny Sorn kept the silence with her husband. She did not reach out to touch him nor did she impose in any way upon the grief that had engulfed him. Though she did not intrude on his self-imposed solitude, she knew he did not wish for her to leave his side. The one time she had tried, he had reached out a gentle hand to stay her. So she kept vigil with him as the last faint smudge of Virago's coastline disappeared beneath the rim of the horizon.

"We will return, Patrick," Syn-Jern whispered. "On my honor, I swear we will return and bury you properly." He reached for his wife's hand, needing the comfort only she could give.

Genny threaded her fingers through Syn-Jern's and leaned against his arm, sensing he was ready to acknowledge her presence.

"I will bring you home, Patrick," she heard her husband say. "Home to Holy Dale."

He turned from the rail and looked up into the clear blue of the heavens, then hung his head and began to cry.

At the helm of the Revenge, Weir looked away from the sight of his sister comforting her husband. He, too, was feeling the awful grief of having lost his best friend. Many on board the Revenge were going about with reddened eyes this day.

Save for the lone woman at the rail who was as silent as the Chrystallusian aboard the Revenant.

"She ain't gonna have an easy time of it, is she, Weir?" Sara asked as she huddled beneath the warmth of her new husband's great cape.

Weir cast another look at Rosa-Lynn Sorn and shrugged. "She'll make the most of whatever's sent her way. Her kind always do."

Tiernan nodded his agreement. "But I think just narrowly escaping with her head intact has put the fear of the gods in that one," he said, begrudgingly admiring the beauty of Rosa-Lynn.

"She helped him, though," Kerm put in. "Weren't for her, that plan of Kasella's wouldn't have worked."

"Lucky for Syni you went back to Holy Dale to make sure Sara and Drae was gone," Bryce Heil quipped.

Kerm nodded. "Aye, well she ain't paid me my twenty gold pieces yet!"

Heil grinned. "Since she come onboard the Revenge with nothin' but the clothes on her back, don't hold your breath in getting them twenty gold pieces, Gill!"

Angie Loure smiled at her husband and wiggled closer against him as the brisk wind churned the sea around them. "Best go check on the bantlings," she told him and Anson gave her a gentle kiss on the nose.

"Everybody's got a woman, but me," Tiernan complained and his eyes went once more to Rosa-Lynn Sorn.

Kerm started laughing and the others turned to look at him. He shook his head. "I was just remembering what the lad says to me when he comes awake on the Revenant."

Anson was the only one not privy to the remark and when the others laughed, he asked to be let in on the joke.

"Well, he was right comical, really," Kerm chuckled. "At first he was all groggy and didn't know where he was. When he realized what Kasella had done, he got all miffed and said he was getting tired of people drugging him all the time."

The others laughed, then sobered as Kerm's face lost its smile.

"But then he understood just what Kasella had done and he was real upset."

"Took four of us to hold him down," Weir said quietly.

"And drug him," Sara put in, her remark bringing uneasy laughter.

"It was a touching thing Patrick did," Tiernan said. "And I hope one day Syni will understand why Patrick had to do it."

"He knows," Rosa-Lynn said, turning to face the others. She pulled her wrapper closer around her shoulders. "Patrick could not have lived if they had hanged Syn-Jern. He would not have wanted to and would have taken his own life." She shuddered with the chill and with the emotions running rampant through her. "I believe that as surely as I believe Syn-Jern Sorn will return to Holy Dale one day as her master. I'll sign the papers over to his firstborn and on the day Demonicus dies, that child can inherit what is rightfully his." She shivered again, her lips trembling.

"Are you cold, Milady?" Tiernan asked and flung the great cape from his shoulders. He went to her and draped the heavy wool around Rosa-Lynn.

Sara Saur frowned. "Damn me if I don't believe he ain't gonna get him a woman 'fore this trip is out!"

Weir sighed. "The gods help him," he replied.

ಐ೧ಆ

The elderly couple walked hand in hand to the glade beside the pond and stood there in silence for a long while. Just as the sun began to set, the old woman laid a blood red rose atop a grassy mound marked with a single stone. Together, they said the prayers for the dead, then sat down on a fallen tree trunk to watch their grandchildren splashing in the pond.

The old man lowered his head and began to mumble. To his grandchildren, it was a sign of his advancing senility, but the old woman sitting beside him knew the truth of it. He was talking to an old friend, telling news of mutual acquaintances and asking for a forgiveness she knew wasn't necessary.

To the casual passersby who might be on their way to Wixenstead Village, the family who lived at Holy Dale manor was an enigma.

The wealthy old couple had purchased the manse ten years before, but no one knew from whence they'd come. They kept to themselves, yet never turned a needy person from their door. It was common knowledge in the village that if you needed help, Patrick Kasella and his wife Genevieve were the ones to ask.

Only a very select few knew the old man was really the Outlaw, Syn-Jern Sorn, and the old woman was Genny, the love of his life.

## Charlotte Boyett-Compo

Charlee is the author of thirty-five books, the first ten of which are the WindLegend Saga. She is a member of the Romance Writers of America, the HTML Writer's Guild, and Beta Sigma Phi Sorority.

Married thirty-six years to her high school sweetheart, Tom, she is the mother of two grown sons, Pete and Mike, and the proud grandmother of Preston Alexander and Victoria Ashlee.

A native of Sarasota, Florida, she grew up in Colquitt and Albany, Georgia and now lives in the Midwest. Currently, she is at work on a new book.

Visit Charlee's web site: http://www.windlegends.com/

Don't miss any of these
other exciting novels

- ➢ Death to the Centurion
(1-931201-26-9, $16.95 US)

- ➢ Jerome and the Seraph
(1-931201-54-4, $15.50 US)

- ➢ Unraveled
(1-931201-11-0, $15.50 US)

- ➢ WindFall
(1-931201-51-X, $18.50 US)

**Order Form**

If not available from your local bookstore or favorite online bookstore, send this coupon and a check or money order for the retail price plus $3.50 s&h to Twilight Times Books, Dept. FD405 POB 3340 Kingsport TN 37664. Delivery may take up to four weeks.

Name: ______________________________

Address: ____________________________

____________________________________________________________

Email: ______________________________

I have enclosed a check or money order in the amount

of $__________

for ______________________________________ .

If you enjoyed this book, please post a review
at your favorite online bookstore.

Twilight Times Books
P O Box 3340
Kingsport, TN 37664
Phone/Fax: 423-323-0183
www.twilighttimesbooks.com/